All royalties from this book have been kindly donated by the authors and will be paid half-yearly to the following animal charities The Blue Cross, Redwings and Yorkshire Wildlife Rescue Centre.

ACKNOWLEDGEMENTS

Special thanks to the contributors for their kindness and generosity of spirit.

Many thanks to Clive Barker, Anthony Barker of Tanjen, John Gullidge publisher of *Samhain*, Richard Dalby, Steve Midwinter at Dark Carnival, Allan Bryce editor of *The Darkside*, Andy Cox publisher of *Zene*, Simon Wady publisher of *Squane's Journal*, Susan Ford at Harper Collins, David Bell publisher of *Peeping Tom*, Robert Parkinson and The British Fantasy Society for encouragement, advice and publicity.

Heartfelt thanks to all the staff and volunteers at The Blue Cross, Redwings Horse Sanctuary, Yorkshire Wildlife Rescue Centre and charitable animal welfare organisations everywhere.

Thanks also to my family and friends for their unwavering support for this project, right from its earliest stages.

Finally and most importantly, a big thank you to *you*, the reader, for having the good sense and decency to part with your cash.

SCAREMONGERS

ISBN 1 901530 07 8

Printed and bound in Great Britain by
Redwood Books, Trowbridge, Wiltshire

British Library Cataloguing in Publication Data.
A catalogue record for this book is available
from the British Library.

Tanjen Ltd
52 Denman Lane
Huncote
Leicester
LE9 3BS

for Ben, and animals like him ...

COPYRIGHTS

CONTENTS

INTRODUCTION

In April 1995 Clive Barker gave a talk at the Leeds branch of booksellers Waterstones. During the course of this interesting and highly entertaining discourse, Clive told the assembled audience about an American news story concerning a litter of Alsatian puppies. These puppies, unwanted by their owner, weren't sold to the local pet store, given to friends, or even put to sleep at the vets. No, their "respectable" middle class US businessman owner thought it better for all concerned if he simply buried them . . . *alive.*

When interviewed by the relevant authorities the guy couldn't understand what the problem was; after all, they were only animals.

Such was Clive's sense of outrage at this display of savagery that he remarked that the events would probably manifest themselves in one of his future projects. Well, maybe they already have. As I write this introduction I have on my desk a copy of Clive's latest paperback best seller *Sacrament*, a novel with the animal kingdom very much central to its plot.

In part, the act of cruelty described by Clive, proved the catalyst for the book you have now (hopefully) purchased. For many years I have been concerned with the way in which animals are often neglected. Some through ignorance — as in the case of all too many household pets. Others through greed — witness the conditions livestock endure on the modern farm. Possibly worst of all though, is the pleasure that certain individuals derive from the barbaric slaughter of animals under the guise of blood sports. A half correct title for these extremely sick pastimes, insomuch as there is blood in abundance, but nothing any right-minded person could term sportsmanship involved in them.

My own financial status (penniless writer) didn't allow me to do a great deal to help the plight of any suffering creatures, but I did have plenty of time, notepaper and stamps. All of which were put to good use badgering (sorry, couldn't resist the opportunity to slip in a cheap animal pun) well known and respected authors of the fantastic for their contribution to a proposed anthology of horror fiction, that would, through its sale generate much needed cash, to be donated to charities or organisations who specialised in the field of animal welfare.

Because these writers had faith enough in the project to send me their work I had what I felt sure was a strong enough package of talented and original writing to show to a prospective publishing house.

Where some larger publishers dithered and told me that the book needed a theme, Anthony Barker, owner of Tanjen Ltd, accepted it for what it was, a collection of good, strong horror stories all very different to each other in terms of style and approach. It is thanks to Anthony's enthusiasm that my hopes became a reality and *Scaremongers* actually made it into print.

So now, whenever a copy of *Scaremongers* is sold, 10% of the cover price will go to the charities involved, all of whom, I'm happy to tell you, expressed no qualms about or reservations at being associated with a book of horror fiction. Which is extremely heartening, when all too often the horror genre as a whole is looked down upon by certain sections of society. Usually by the same people who think it is fine to eat eggs produced by chickens kept in the appalling conditions of the battery farm method, and will tell you that a fox actually enjoys being chased by a pack of baying hounds intent on ripping out its innards.

These charities are:

Yorkshire Wildlife Rescue Centre, 252 Park Lodge Lane, East Moor, Wakefield, W. Yorkshire, WF1 4HX — Tel: (01924) 201288
An organisation that specialise in caring for wildlife casualties and returning them to their natural habitat.

Redwings Horse Sanctuary, Hill Top Farm, Hall Lane, Frettenham, Nr Norwich, NR12 7RW — Tel: (01603) 737432 Fax: (01603) 738286
A sanctuary that cares for badly treated and unwanted horses and donkeys, allowing them to live out their remaining years in comfort.

Blue Cross, Shilton Road, Burford, Oxfordshire, OX13 4PF — Tel: (01993) 822651 Fax: (01993) 823083
This year the charity celebrates 100 years of helping animals and

their owners, via the network of adoption centres, hospitals and clinics. Throughout its history the Blue Cross has found thousands of new homes for unwanted and abandoned animals, whilst simultaneously providing veterinary care for pets belonging to people unable to afford private veterinary fees.

By purchasing *Scaremongers* you have already contributed to these excellent animal welfare charities. Should you have a desire to help them further please contact them directly. Every penny helps them to continue their good work.

Well, I've almost detained you long enough with my ramblings, it's nearly time to let you get at the horrific happenings that await you in the ensuing pages. But before I allow you to leave, I would briefly like to draw your attention to the part our furry and feathered friends have played in horror fiction over the years.

Many horror novels, short stories and poems have used animals as their central theme; James Herbert's *The Rats*, Stephen King's *Cujo* and *Pet Sematary*, Peter Benchley's *Jaws*, Edgar Allan Poe's *The Black Cat* and *The Raven*, H.P. Lovecraft's *The Rats in the Walls*, Sir Arthur Conan Doyle's *The Hound of the Baskervilles* being only a small selection of better known examples from the thousands that have found their way into print. Neither should we forget the contributions made by the countless wolves, black cats and bats to the general atmosphere of eeriness pervading many a classic ghostly tale.

The animal kingdom has also enriched the English language with a multitude of phrases and descriptive terms; *dogged* determination, stubborn as a *mule* and *bird*-brained are all terms that could be attributed to a person. The latter being particularly apt for the literary agent I encountered whilst trying to get *Scaremongers* into print, who said that Ray Bradbury wasn't well known.

Free as a *bird*, sick as a *parrot*, the *cat* is out of the bag, raining *cats* and *dogs* and having a *whale* of a time, are just a few of the phrases that have insinuated themselves into everyday usage. Indeed rather amusingly, *Scaremongers* and its charitable aims were described by a Jehovah's Witness acquaintance of mine as "a wolf in lamb's clothing".

Therefore, I feel I must warn you, kind reader, that by association you are now damned to eternal Hell. Of course you could always return *Scaremongers* to your bookshop, repent your sins, forsake horror fiction for ever and purchase the latest Barbara Cartland instead. Any takers? Thought not.

So, turn the page and prepare yourself for a taste of life's darker side, and if the assembled scaremongers have done their job correctly, by the end of the book you will no doubt agree with me that animals are infinitely more civilised than human beings.

Andrew Haigh
Batley, W. Yorkshire
September 26th, 1997

"I think the cause of your anthology is tremendous" — Clive Barker.

RAY BRADBURY

DOGS THINK THAT EVERY DAY IS CHRISTMAS

Dogs think that every day is Christmas
They lap it with their necktie tongues
Devour it with wide bright eyes
That say 'Look at the weather!
Try it on! Just my size!'
They lean out car windows
Like drunks at bars, snuffing gin
While drivers in those self-same cars running, lose
They win!
They mark each tree in passing
Just to let the world know
'I was here. Do you see? I was here!'
From the start of a glorious season
To the end of a marvellous year.
All smiles, with a guidon-staff tailwag
They silently shout-bark 'Gee whiz!'
Because dogs wake each morning to Christmas
And, damn, stop and think now:
It is!

MARK CHADBOURN

ABOVE, BEHIND, BENEATH, BESIDE

It was fifteen hours since they discovered the body and he had finally put away the option of suicide. He didn't know how he had managed to negotiate the crowded motorway or by what chance he had located the village when for much of the time he could barely remember his own name. But now his identity was back — Dale Kingsley — and with it the agonisingly raw emotions he couldn't bring himself to examine.

Dale pulled the car over to look down on Croxton baking in the Leicestershire countryside beneath a blazing sun suspended in a colourless sky. The view was picture-postcard perfect, a church, thatched roofs, an unspoiled pub, in a sea of green fields where indolent cows flicked their tails irritatedly at clouds of flies. Paul should have hated it, he thought obliquely. For too long he had wondered what Paul was thinking when he moved there from London's nightlife and excitement and all the things he loved. After so many years of friendship, it had almost seemed like a love affair ending, emphasised by the dwindling letters and then the long silence from someone he had spoken to almost every day since he was a boy. At the time, none of it seemed to make sense.

Unconsciously, he felt the bump in his jacket on the seat beside him where the stuffed envelope lay morbidly. Then he fired up the engine and pulled slowly down the hill into the village. He would rather be anywhere than there, even back in London making the funeral arrangements, but it was his once chance to find the freedom he had only just realised he needed to survive. His freedom and his absolution.

Dale had a sudden urge to put his foot down when he passed the sign *Croxton Welcomes Careful Drivers* but his attention was distracted by a faint sound rustling out from the empty back seat. A whisper.

His heart pounding, Dale jerked his head round while simultaneously bringing the car to a sharp halt. He didn't know what he expected — no one could have been there — but the whisper had seemed so real. He almost imagined he understood the words.

In the morning, glory cries.

Grief does strange things to people, he thought sourly, but guilt does much worse.

Although Dale drove round the village for fifteen minutes, Paul's house remained elusive. Finally, with irritation exacerbated by the heat, he screeched into the pub car park and marched into the bar.

It reminded him of a Wild West saloon in a dusty, no-hope Arizonan town. Two men lolled at the bar like dogs in the sun while the landlord hopelessly attempted some tabloid crossword. In the corner, two old men sat hunched over a game of draughts, their half-drunk pints growing warm in the stupefying heat.

'Can you help me out with some directions?' Dale ventured as amicably as he could manage.

The landlord raised his eyebrows hopefully, but his stare was implacable, pig-stupid. He was country stock, with a broad frame that balanced his beer belly and cheeks that glowed like the sun.

'I've been driving round trying to find this place, but it doesn't seem to exist.' He showed the address at the top of one of Paul's letters.

As he took the letter in his chubby fingers, the landlord let his gaze wander over Dale's fashionable clothes with the kind of surveillance reserved for another species. The pause before he spoke was a little too long. 'Burnt down.'

The words were clipped, dismissive, but for an instant Dale had seen some odd emotion flicker across the landlord's face that suggested he was not as detached as he made out.

'When?' Dale suddenly felt everything was slipping away from him. 'What happened to the bloke who lived there?' He became aware of the other drinkers watching him intently.

'Couple of months ago. The owner just upped and went, so I hear. Packed up what was left of his stuff and cleared out.'

'This is a small village — didn't you know his name? Where he might have gone?'

'Kept himself to himself.' The landlord shrugged. 'Never used to come in here,' he added as if that explained everything.

For a moment, Dale was lost. To buy himself time, he asked, 'Can

I get a room here for the night?'

The landlord seemed to weigh the prospect for an inordinate amount of time. 'If you come back in half an hour, I'll have one made up.'

Dale retreated into the heat where the desolation overwhelmed him.

It was hardly surprising he had missed the site of Paul's house. From the road it looked like a vacant lot, just a jumble of bricks and blackened wood in front of an overgrown garden that resembled a wasteland. The place hadn't simply burnt down, it had been razed to the ground. Dale wandered around the site in astonishment; everything remaining had been carted away: most of the masonry, roof tiles, the fire-damaged contents. It was as if someone had attempted to eradicate its existence.

'Terrible, isn't it?'

Dale turned to see a woman of about twenty leaning on the gate post. He felt relief to see some trappings of sophistication in her clothes and hair style; at least she wouldn't make him feel like an outsider.

'Do you know what happened?'

'Not exactly. I live in London. I'm just back to see my parents in the next village for a few days.' She looked around the scarred plot. 'I came over to see the damage — must have been quite a blaze.' Then a warm smile: 'There's not much to talk about round here.'

Suddenly a spasm rippled through Dale's right arm, jerking it upwards as the fingers curled into claws. He yelped as a bolt of pain shot up to his shoulder.

'Are you okay?' The woman ran to his side, watching worriedly as he clutched feebly at his wrist. His arm seemed to have a life of its own.

Just as quickly, the attack stopped. The woman helped him down on to a pile of blackened bricks as he massaged his arm back to life.

'What was that? An epileptic fit?' she asked, concerned.

Dale stared at his errant limb anxiously. 'I don't know,' he replied. 'I've never had anything like that before.'

'Look, I'm Melanie,' she said with a smile. 'If you want me to call a doctor —?'

He shook his head. 'It's probably nothing.'

After he had introduced himself, she asked, 'Did you know the

19

man who lived here?'

'He's my best friend. I've known Paul since we were kids.'

'My mother says he disappeared the night of the fire. Everyone thinks he did it to get the insurance, then ran off when his plot went wrong.' She tried to read his expression. 'Gossip is like quicksilver in this part of the world.'

'That sounds like Paul.'

'Any idea where he's gone?'

Dale shrugged. 'Knowing Paul, he could be anywhere. I haven't spoken to him in a while. Not since he moved here. He wasn't on the phone.'

'What possessed him to come to Croxton?'

Dale shrugged, nursing the lie he had kept for so long. 'Peace and quiet. One day he just announced he was moving out to the country.'

She followed Dale's gaze to the overgrown garden. 'He wasn't much of a gardener, I see.'

'Paul wasn't really one for responsibilities.'

It wasn't quite how he had described it. One event separated the old Paul from his decision to make a clean start. Just one night that carried a lifetime of repercussions. Even now he didn't know exactly what *had* happened; there were just impressions, like lung shadows, warning of impending doom. If only he had seen the signs.

'What made you suddenly decide to visit him?' she asked.

Dale chewed over the question, then plumped for total honesty; he had little left to lose. 'I wanted to show him some pictures. Then I was going to kill him.'

Where did it all go so badly wrong? He had always known Paul had flaws. At school they were known as the Mirror Boys because to the casual eye they seemed reflections of each other, both physically and intellectually; the same lustrous black hair and dark eyes, the same wild edge that kept them permanently on the fringes of what both parents and teachers deemed acceptable. The differences were much more subtle, but to Dale they clearly came down to one thing: Paul was always prepared to go one step further, with no regard for other people's safety, or even his own. He seemed bereft of the internal checks and balances that kept others within society's rules. It was that air of danger which drew Dale closer to Paul, while his head was telling him to stay well away.

One incident from their childhood summed up their whole sorry relationship. There was an old house on the outskirts of the village which all the other kids thought was haunted; Paul was drawn to anything with a whiff of the extraordinary. Empty for years, the house was on the verge of collapsing in on itself, but on the corners of the roof were a collection of gothic carvings which Paul had decided were gargoyles. After talking about them for several weeks, he decided he had to have one; he was going to climb on to the roof and prise one loose. Dale did everything he could to stop him — the beams were rotten, half the slates were missing — but Paul's mind was made up. And so, as best friend, Dale had to accompany him. Paul also convinced the easily-led Carl Summers without much difficulty and none of Dale's protestations would keep Carl away. Paul's thinking was transparent and that irritated Dale; he could have made the effort to hide it. Carl was unpopular, fat, geekish, but he hero-worshipped Paul with a passion that was embarrassing. And Paul thought he might need some extra muscle to get the gargoyles down to the ground.

High above the village with the stars twinkling in the big sky above them, even Dale had to admit the expedition was exhilarating; it was one of the reasons he hung around with Paul. That is, until the roof gave way and he and Carl plunged down into the yawning dark. As the scream burst from his lips, one of the broken beams snagged in his shirt and brought him to a jarring halt. A second later he heard the sickening thud as Carl's body crashed through the gaping floor beneath to the hallway far below.

Dale recalled looking up through tears of fear to see Paul's face framed in the jagged hole in the roof. He screamed for help until his throat was raw, but Paul simply smiled and returned to prising free the sculpture. The fear he felt hanging there was terrible, thinking of Carl and the sound of the fall, and it didn't diminish until long after the whole sickening episode was over.

That set the pattern for the rest of their lives: he had numerous chances to break away, but Paul's light was too bright; Dale was dazzled. The attraction, he knew in his quiet moments, was that he secretly wished he was Paul, but he didn't have the guts, or the madness. Like a drug, he knew the risks, but he kept going back for the thrill until in the end Paul's influence enveloped him; there was no escape. And now they would all have to pay the price for his weakness.

'I don't know why I'm sitting here with a confessed killer,' Melanie said with mock-haughtiness. She was lounging in the broad window of the pub's sole guest room, watching Dale splash water in his face at the chipped wash basin.

'Potential killer.'

'How can you make a statement like that and then not tell me the story behind it?'

'It's none of your business.'

'You said he was your best friend,' she continued as if she hadn't heard him.

'He was.' Dale dried himself off before removing the envelope from the pocket of his jacket which lay on the bed. He carefully selected a creased photograph, examined it for a second or two, then offered it to her hesitantly. As she reached out to take it, his arm spasmed once more and the picture fell to the floor. He looked away before she could ask him if he was okay.

'You make a good-looking couple,' she said, examining the snap. 'Very alike.'

'So people say.'

The photo had been taken at some warehouse club in North London three years earlier, before everything fell apart. They had their arms around each other's shoulders, mugging for the camera, off their faces on E.

Melanie stared at it intently, then said, 'There had to be a woman involved. That's the only thing that could split up such good friends.'

'Very perceptive.' Dale eyed her cautiously, but gave nothing else away.

'Boy, you're a closed book. How were you going to kill him?'

He nodded to his jacket. She picked it up and shook it, feeling the weight. In the pocket opposite the one in which he kept the envelope was a gun. Melanie fished it out with two fingers and wrinkled her nose as if there was a bad smell.

'Big-time gangsta,' she said contemptuously.

'Never fired a gun in my life.' He lay back on the bed with his hands behind his head and closed his eyes. 'I had to trawl around the East End for most of the night before I could convince someone to sell it to me.'

'And you'd use it on your best friend?' From the faint tremor in her voice, Dale could tell it had finally dawned on her that it was no joke. 'What the hell did he do to you?'

He swallowed, losing himself in the darkness behind his eyelids. After a long beat, he said quietly, 'He damned me.'

A crescent moon was shining through the window when Dale awoke to the distant murmur of voices in the bar below. Disorientation washed over him as he discovered he was naked under a single sheet. As he began to clamber out of bed, his elbow brushed sleek hair and he realised with a start that Melanie was in bed with him. His confusion became a tidal wave. She was naked, breathing regularly. The scent of sex perfumed the air. Roughly, he shook her shoulder.

'Jesus, what is it?' she grumbled sleepily.

In the moonlight, with her eyes half-lidded and her hair falling across her face, he had the sudden, aching impression that she was Caitlin, back with him again. The image unleashed a flood of conflicting emotions that forced him to look away.

Melanie reached out and stroked his cheek. 'You can be quite the charmer when you want to be. It usually takes flowers, dinner and the obligatory three dates to get me into bed.'

'I don't remember any of it.' He swung his legs out of bed and searched around for his clothes to hide his growing panic.

Melanie snatched her hand back. 'Charming,' she said sulkily.

'I mean it. The last thing I remember is lying down on the bed, talking to you.'

'You dozed off for a second, then woke with a start.' She stared at him incredulously. 'What's wrong with you? Have you got some illness you're not telling me about?'

'Not that I know. It's probably just stress. Come on, let's get a drink.'

The bar was half-full with a clientele which looked almost exclusively local, their eyes marking the outsiders the moment they set foot in the room. There was something in their stares which made Dale uncomfortable; it went beyond suspicion, encompassing threat and the icy glint of fear.

They took their drinks to a table in the corner and tried to start up a conversation, but the atmosphere stifled any warmth.

'Friendly place,' Dale said under his breath.

Melanie glanced around uncomfortably. 'They're not usually like this.'

'Then it must be me.'

Before they could continue, a burly man with a barrel chest and the red skin of an outdoorsman marched over, repressed rage darkening his eyes. He rested two ham-like fists on the table and hissed: 'He's cleared off so why don't you do the same?'

Dale looked him in the eye unflinchingly, but before he could speak a paper-thin whisper rustled behind his head.

Kill him.

His back was to the wall; there was no one nearby who could have spoken. Melanie seemed oblivious, her fearful expression fixed on the local.

'Do you hear what I'm saying?' the man growled, drawing his face closer to Dale's.

'I hear.'

His head was swimming. He felt detached, like he was on drugs.

Kill him, the voice came again.

Against his will, his hand began to creep towards the inside pocket of his jacket. Desperately he tried to stop it progressing to the gun, but it was as if there were hooks in his flesh pulling it closer. The skin of his back grew cold with sweat.

The local's eyes were bugging with fury, but Dale could no longer hear him. As his fingers closed on the cold metal of the gun, Melanie's hand clasped on to his arm, pinning it against his chest.

'Don't,' she said quietly.

The monstrous urge passed as quickly as it came and his hand dropped into his lap.

Before the local could do anything else, two other men grabbed him by the arms and led him gently away. They stood at the bar, plotting and flashing menacing stares.

'You wouldn't have really done it?' Melanie hissed in disbelief.

'No,' he lied.

'I think we need to get some air,' she said, hauling him outside.

Paul had killed three times, as far as Dale knew. There may well have been more. He claimed the first two were accidents and Dale didn't push the matter any further, but in his heart he knew the truth. Paul never told him about the third.

The deaths were the logical culmination of Paul's voracious hunger for all that life had to offer. Insatiable in his desires, he was always seeking more, and to his warped way of thinking the occult seemed an easy way to achieve it. The first time he mentioned he was exploring ritual magic, Dale laughed and bought him a wizard's hat from a costume shop which Paul accepted with his usual good grace. But then Dale glimpsed the new circles Paul was moving in, the men and women with staring eyes and unstable personalities who matched Paul's appetites and had, if anything, an even looser grip on morals; without any restraining influences, he knew Paul would be unstoppable.

The first death was a young woman Paul picked up outside a club one Saturday night. Still tripping, she had been searching for a cab and Paul had charmed her into coming home with him. She never saw the dawn.

Dale remembered Paul's call, the tears, the recriminations, the vows that he would never do it again. Just a little game of ritual sex using ligatures to heighten arousal, he said. But he had blacked out and when he awoke she was blue and growing cold. 'Don't turn me in, Dale,' he pleaded.

Dale didn't even ask him what he did with the body.

The second victim was a gay man enticed back with the false promise of sex. He fell down the stairs and split his head open. Paul said.

And the third . . .

'I think they killed him.' Dale's voice sounded uncommonly loud in the still of the warm night.

Melanie jumped, then collected herself. 'Who?'

'The villagers. Some of them. All of them.'

She laughed with faint mockery. 'This isn't the backwoods of Arkansas, Dale.'

After a while she glanced at him, but the rural dark obscured his features with shadows. Somewhere nearby a dog began to bark with a terrifying ferocity until it was suddenly and disturbingly cut off.

'What makes you think that?' The humour had drained away from Melanie's voice.

'A gut feeling. Instinct. Paul and I were close, like brothers. I often knew what was going through his head before he said it. And now I feel he's dead.'

'Why would anyone want to kill him?'

This time it was Dale who laughed. 'Paul was a danger to everyone. He followed his own agenda and he didn't care who got trampled underfoot.'

'Lots of people are like that. But to anger someone enough to commit murder . . . What could he possibly have done?' She waited for an answer that never came.

They smelled the stink of charred wood long before they arrived at the site of the house. Dale held open the incongruous garden gate for Melanie to pass and then they walked together over the rubble into the overgrown garden.

'Paul was into the occult,' Dale said flatly. 'He believed all that mumbo-jumbo. He was obsessed about it. The people he mixed with convinced him there was a way to gain power.'

'What kind of power?'

Dale shrugged. 'Power to make you rich. Power over other people. Power to survive death. But even in that crazy world, nothing's free.' His words hung uncomfortably in the air and for a second Melanie thought he wasn't going to continue. Then he said quietly, 'A ritual killing, that was the price.'

'You're joking! He wouldn't —'

'He'd killed before. More than once. It didn't work so he did it again.'

Melanie grabbed him by the shoulders and spun him round. 'Are you serious?'

'Yes.'

'And you didn't turn him in?'

Dale suddenly bobbed down and picked something from among the long, yellow grass. In the moonlight, she saw it was a desiccated bouquet. Around her feet, other shrivelled blooms lay; a tribute to an innocent who had passed.

'Paul always covered his tracks well. They wouldn't have been able to do him for murder. But in a tiny community like this, someone would have known. The villagers got justice in the end.'

Melanie lurched several paces away from him, the horror creeping through her with a relentless pace.

Dale smiled at her sadly. 'You're right, I'm as guilty as Paul. I could have shopped him long ago. But he was . . . a good laugh.' He paused at the sick irony. 'Charming, charismatic, good fun to be with. I liked him. We were mates. I suppose when you come down to it, he gave me something that was missing in myself so I turned a blind eye —'

'To murder?' Her voice rose sharply.

'The real world isn't like a comic book,' he said sharply. 'You don't have heroes and villains. You have good and bad in the same person. And sometimes you have very good and very bad — you can't throw one out without the other. Paul was a true friend and you can forgive friends any crime. Except one.'

'Which is?' Her disgust for him was almost tangible.

'Betrayal.'

Slowly he pulled the thick brown envelope from his inside pocket and offered it to her. Inside she found snapshots of a pleasantly attractive young woman; long, dark hair, a face untroubled by worry; at the seaside, in the pub, in the garden, on Dale's arm.

'We were going to be married.' His voice was almost too faint to hear. 'The last time I saw her, Paul, Caitlin and me had been smoking some hash in my flat, having a laugh. I had to go off to work. When I came back, Paul told me Caitlin had broken down soon after I'd gone. He said she claimed she'd had an affair with someone else and she was going abroad with him. The marriage was off. At first I thought he was winding me up, but when she didn't come back I started to get worried. Over the next few months, I called all her relatives — no one had heard from her. Everyone who knew her was in a right state. That was around the time that Paul left London.'

He watched the shadows underline her changing expression.

'There was a derelict house next to our place. It was just left to rot during the property slump, but last week the builders moved in to renovate it. And yesterday they found Caitlin's body.'

Melanie hugged him tightly. He seemed like wood beneath her arms.

'I might as well have killed her myself.' His voice broke and he swallowed. 'In my weakness, I allowed Paul to take over my life,' he added emptily, 'You can never see the repercussions of your actions, but you still have to pay the price.'

Melanie tried to read his expression, but it was like looking into the face of an alien.

'The only hope I had was to make a clean break from Paul and his influence,' he continued. 'To punish him for what he had done because no one else would be able to, and then try to find some absolution from that act. To get my freedom back, that was the only way I could live with myself. And now he's dead and I'll never be able to escape from the memory.'

'But at least he won't be around.'

'"In the morning, glory cries, Tears of blood for the lost ones. Carry them through to another life. Take this soul to light the night."'

'What's that?'

'The final prayer of the ritual Paul had been working on. His masterpiece. The reason Caitlin died.'

Melanie felt a shiver run through Dale. She hugged him tighter, but the shiver turned into the ebb and flow of a heavy tide, and then he was thrashing madly in her arms. She yelped as he slumped to the ground in wild convulsions.

Before she could help him, there was a cracking in the undergrowth, and a second later the burly man from the pub and his two friends emerged from the shadows.

'Help him!' Melanie said, dropping to her knees, but the men simply gathered round and watched Dale's contortions.

'If you're friends of that bastard you don't deserve any help.' He snorted and Melanie smelled the stink of beer on his breath. 'You don't deserve to live.'

'You killed him,' she blurted, then instantly regretted it.

'No one will be able to prove anything. We burnt him up like a rat in his filthy lair, then we smashed up what was left of him and dumped him in the sewers.'

Melanie stifled a sob.

'After what he'd done . . . my niece . . . she was only three . . .' His voice trailed away, but then returned with force. 'Even at the end, when he knew he was going to die, there was no fucking remorse! I watched the flames eating him up and he just stood there, spouting some gibberish, then saying we could never kill him.' He glanced at his friends, then nodded at Dale. 'Let's sort him out.'

Melanie screamed and tried to force them off, but the burly man caught her with the back of his hand and she flew backwards on to the ground.

When the stars cleared, she realised the men were stock still. Dale's convulsions had ended and he sat upright, brandishing the gun. But the most disturbing thing was his expression; it kept switching from a mocking grin to one of confusion and fear as if he couldn't decide what to feel.

'I can't help it,' he whined. Then he raised the gun and blew away the burly man's face. The other two fled before the body hit the ground.

Melanie was paralysed, her thoughts bursting like fireworks in the night.

'He's here!' Dale sobbed. 'I can feel him inside me, all around me, in the air that I breathe! Now I'll never be rid of him!'

'The ritual worked?' she muttered.

'Oh God, save me!' he pleaded. His hand moved the gun up to his forehead, teased the skin, and then twirled away in a flourish; Melanie watched his eyes fearfully follow its course. 'He's like a fog swallowing me up. I can barely see you!' Another sob. 'There's no escape now! He's going to be with me for the rest of my life!'

Then she froze as the grin she had seen during sex sprang back to Dale's lips, and he slowly raised the gun to her head.

SIMON CLARK

THE BURNING DOORWAY

'I told you I saw them moving.'

The night-time attendant at the crematorium had almost shouted the words into the phone. This thing had frightened him, his hands were shaking and he wanted to blast loose a mouthful at his supervisor who obviously didn't give a toss. The lazy bastard was probably sitting at home, can of beer in his greasy hand, watching television. What did he care that his tuppenny ha'penny assistant was alone in the crematorium with them moving about in there, making those noises that made him sick in his stomach.

'I've looked in there, Mr Winters, I can see them moving about.'

He heard his boss over the phone give a tired sigh. 'Danny. When you were offered this post, you were told it wouldn't be very pleasant. To be bloody blunt, our job is to burn dead people to ash. Specifically, your duties are to watch over the equipment at night. If it malfunctions, if someone tries to break into the place then phone me. Otherwise, just leave me to a bit of peace and quiet, okay?'

'But they're moving around in there, Mr Winters. And they're making these horrible sounds. You can hear them above the gas jets; I bet you can hear them over the phone. They're going —'

'Danny, Dan — just listen to me, Danny. If I come down there now, I'll have to file a call out report. When my gaffer sees why I've had to come out at midnight you'll be out faster than shit off the end of a shovel. Now, do you still want the job?'

'Course I do. It's the first one I've had in a year.'

'Didn't any of the blokes down there tell you what to expect?'

'They said I'd got the cushiest job going. Just sit here all night and keep checking the burners are working all right.'

'Bugger,' said his boss stoically. 'Look, Danny. As I said it's not a pretty job. We burn people right? Burning people isn't like burning old cardboard boxes. They're complicated mechanisms made up of skin, muscle, bone. Inside they've got organs, bags of fluid and gas. You with me?'

'Aye.'

'Also they've got mouths and arseholes. So if you heat them up fast, fluids boil, and I'm talking about blood and piss now, gasses expand and they've got to come out somewhere. So what you're hearing is basically belching and farting. Sometimes it works the vocal chords so you can actually stand outside the crematorium oven and it sounds like someone is groaning their head off. I've heard it. It is nasty and takes some bloody getting used to. Believe me, Danny, I've heard a burning corpse actually sound as if it's singing; it nearly turned my bastard hair white.'

'But how can they move?'

'Well, you must have good eyes, Danny. When I look through the spy-hole into the ovens all I can see is flames. How do they move? It's the muscle. When it burns it shrinks. I've heard stories of burning corpses suddenly sitting up. There's other things too. You might hear bangs. And I mean really loud bangs like a cannon going off. Fluids boil in the stomach making it inflate like a balloon. Eventually the pressure's so great — bang; it explodes.'

'I didn't know that. They never told me.'

'Alright Danny. They should have warned you. You all right now?'

'Yes, Mr Winters. Sorry to disturb you. It gave me a bit of a scare that's all.'

'Don't worry, Danny. As the blokes at the Crem said, you've landed a good job. All we're asking is you keep an eye on the place. Apart from that the time's your own. Is that radio still down there?'

'Yes, over on the fridge.'

'Switch it on, it'll drown out the sounds.'

'Thank you, Mr Winters.'

'Good night, Danny.'

The phone clicked and purred softly into Danny's ear. He replaced the phone and switched on the radio. Country and Western music. He wasn't fond of it, but it hid the sounds coming from the oven doors.

He did feel better now that he'd talked to his supervisor. So, it'd all been natural what he'd seen and heard. It had given him a bloody fright though. He made himself a cup of tea and sat on a chair with his back to the wall, facing the oven doors. The room consisted of bare white washed walls and a concrete floor that was still damp and reeked of industrial strength disinfectant where it'd been sluiced down earlier. This was basically the loading bay for the crematorium oven, he'd been told. In the crematorium chapel they held the funeral services. The coffin rolled along the conveyor belt and through the curtained hatchway into here, where it was stored with the other coffins until evening. Then the evening shift stacked the day's crop of coffins, and their contents into the oven, removing lids and brass handles as they did so. When all the coffins were inside, the doors were shut, the controls set, gas ignited and they'd burn through the night until all that was left was white ash.

This was the easy job. Just sit and watch and wait. Then clock off as the morning shift came on at six to clear out the ovens. Even so, Danny, like most, was frightened of dead people. Even in butchers' shops it's rare to find a recognisable dead animal. All you get is nicely processed meat. No pig's heads with ears and eyes, no cow's legs covered in fur.

This job frightened him. But it was the only job he was likely to have again. For thirty years he'd been a skilled craftsman in an engineering firm, cutting differentials for tractors. He'd been proud of his work. So, what if he did wear a boiler suit? He was a professional with skills that took years to acquire. Then, in his early forties, he'd been struck by crippling Osteo Arthritis. The back pain could be so bad he had to move around on all fours at times. Then just a week after his fiftieth birthday they'd sacked him because he'd been forced to take so much sick leave. If you're short term sick you get cards and sympathy. If you're long term sick you're treated to contempt and cruelty. Like wild dogs that turn on one of their own kind that's diseased, society turns nasty on you.

But he'd got this job, thank the Lord. He was determined to keep it.

Keep busy he told himself. Don't let it prey on your imagination. But it isn't easy when you know that just behind that steel and asbestos door twenty men and women, even children are being burnt up to fertiliser.

Danny went to the employees' rest room. It was a cluttered place with girlie pin-ups mixed up with work rotas and union circulars on the walls. Scattered on the sink work-top, pieces of pastry and bacon rind, bits of foil that had wrapped sandwiches, tea stain rings, used tea bags in the sink. On the radio some part-time cowboy was yodelling about his best friend being killed in a bar fight. It drove him back to the loading bay.

For a while he stood and stared at the oven doors. The thing might as well have been a magnet; he found himself putting one foot forward. Then another. Before he even knew it, he stood at the doors. The spy-hole covered in inch thick glass glowed white from the fires inside.

It had been a shock. He'd looked in expecting to see nothing but vague oblong shapes being gobbled by the inferno. What he saw had been very different.

He swallowed at the bitter taste in his mouth. He felt queasy again, his ears rang, and his neck ached where the muscle tensed.

'Never mind, Danny boy — only ten more years of this, then you can retire.'

The first time he looked through the spy-hole he saw nothing. It was pretty much like looking through one of those viewing windows at swimming pools. You know the sort — you look out under water; it's a bluey colour and every so often a body appears as someone jumps in, in a mess of bubbles and arms and legs. Here, instead of water you see fire filling the space between the walls; it fills it completely like it's a molten liquid.

Then as his eyes adjusted to the glare he made out the oblong shapes of coffins on fire. Then suddenly, as if someone had rung a bell he'd seen bodies just sit bolt upright in their coffins. His eyes bulged; he couldn't move his head. All he could do was watch twenty dead men and women sit bolt upright in this yellow fog of gas flame.

Mow-wurr . . . Mow-wow-wurr-harrr . . .

When they had begun to groan out loud, Danny moved back so quickly it brought pain jabbing through his back.

He limped away holding his back. The bloody thing seemed to ring like a bell with jabbing pains.

Mow-wow . . . uck-uck-uck-urrr . . .

Now he knew it was just expanding gas forcing its way outward through the anus or vocal chords. But the sound was still bad, so bloody, bloody bad. It sounded as if they were crying to be let out. As if the fire hurt them.

'Christ, bury me when I die. Please bury me.'

He put his eye to the spy-hole. 'Don't put me in there with . . . *Jesus!*

Inside the oven, within all that fire and light, he saw the twenty burning men and women. They were working.

'How did it go, Danny boy?'

It was one of the morning shift, grinning and walking in swinging a plastic bag full of sandwiches.

'Fine . . . Not much happens does it?'

'Dead quiet.' The man laughed. 'See y'later, I'm going for a dump.'

Danny's mouth didn't have so much as a pin head of spit in it. Dry as the ash the morning shift would soon be raking. He didn't know how he managed to say the words, or drive to the supermarket to buy the bottle of whisky he'd drink at home while his wife worked. He drank so much he couldn't walk, but the words kept coming out of his mouth: 'I looked in. I saw them. They're dead. But they're working.'

Two emotions worked powerfully in Danny. He was frightened sick by it all. But also curious. The next night he clocked on early. Was it some kind of miracle he was meant to see? Or was it some kind of nightmare he wasn't?

Soon he was alone in the crematorium loading bay; the concrete floor still wet; the stink of disinfectant roughening the back of his throat.

The gas jets had been burning for half an hour now. Already it would be hot enough to melt metal in there.

He stood ten feet from the spy-hole, building himself up to look in. The muscles in his neck were so tight they curved his arthritic spine like a long bow. Pains sparkled up and down his back, the slightest movement made him wince. But he had to see what happened in there. If it happened again. Last night, he'd looked in to see the burning corpses moving around. The heat was so tremendous it had ignited the fatty tissues so they moved round crackling with flame, spitting out gobs of fat like burning chip pans. Thankfully, you couldn't see their faces; only that they were incandescent people shapes.

Danny held his breath, then put his eye to the glass. His eyes adjusted to the brilliant glare. Now! It was happening now!

He let out a stuttering blast of air from his lungs through sheer shock. One, two . . . three, four, five . . . six. One after another they sat up in their burning coffins.

What now? What did they intend to do? What drove them? Was this proof there was a God? Did He make them do this?

Jesus . . . Jesus . . . My back . . . Christ. He didn't scream with his mouth; his back did all the screaming for him. The muscles spasmed and clutched around his spine as if a sharp toothed animal was trying to bite its way out.

He held his breath again, leaning forward against the oven doors;

his open palms taking some of his weight. He must keep watching. Only his back wanted to force him from the oven. He clenched his jaws together, screwed his eyes against the intense glare and watched.

They were out of the coffins now; moving with speed and agility; even the geriatrics. Now he could see funeral clothes flash into flame to drift off in layers like burning tissue. The flames ate the skin, peeling it off in feathery pieces of ash.

But the flame had no effect on their purpose. Danny watched them work.

They picked up the coffins and quickly stacked them into two pillars side by side with perhaps a yard between them. It reminded Danny of his days at the tractor factory watching the old skilled workers. These people, even though they burned like fireworks, spitting jets of flame from mouth and ears, they worked like craftsmen, knowing exactly where each component went. When the coffin pillars were complete they laid the lids across from one pillar to the other until they had formed something like an archway.

Even in that raging inferno they took their time, making careful adjustments to the archway as if it needed aligning perfectly with some invisible line.

By now, even once fat corpses were thin as soft, fatty tissues boiled off into vapour, ribs began to show naked, fingers dropped away. Arms and legs became jerking sticks. Movements became clumsier.

But the work was nearly complete.

Danny whispered in wonder: 'What are they making? For God's sake, what are they making?'

His eyes watered so much from staring into the brilliant flames, he had to look away and blink until they were clear.

When he looked back, the shock of what he saw forced him to recoil so violently he fell flat on his back.

Because, there on the other side of the glass, a face looked back at him. The face burned furiously. The picture burned into Danny's mind was of a beautiful girl with hair blowing around her face; only the hair was aflame. Skin burned away in layer after shrivelling layer. The teeth were chips jutting from bubbling gums. The tongue a charcoal stick sliding from side to side. The eyes alone seemed untouched; they stared back at him, coolly, with such a shocking intensity he couldn't breathe. He saw them scrutinising his face, assessing from his expression why he was there and what he was thinking. Maybe the burning girl wondered if he would interfere with their work. When she seemed satisfied he would not, she returned to her labours.

After the furious pains in his back had at least eased sufficiently, he pulled himself back to the oven doors and looked in through the spy-hole.

Through the roaring gas jets, so bright he had to screw his eyes almost shut, he saw what the burning corpses had built. It was a doorway, made from coffins and coffin lids. The wood blazed furiously. In that intense heat the construction would last more than a few minutes.

Then, as Danny watched, the burning corpses began to slowly file through the doorway. They never came out the other side. One by one, the burning corpses simply vanished.

'Ahh-ah!' The pains in Danny's back grew so intense that he had to hobble through to the restroom. He dissolved three solpadol in a mug then swallowed the fizzing liquid down in one. Then he dragged himself back to the crematorium oven and the spy-hole.

With a huge effort of will he forced himself to see through the inferno. The gateway was little more than a white flare; the outline skeletal now that it had been burnt almost to ash. It couldn't hold together much longer. But still the dead men, women and children walked through.

Through into what? Into where?

The painkiller oozed through his body dampening down the back pains, lightening his head. He wasn't afraid, no, only curious. In the name of God, what lay beyond that incandescent doorway?

Then for a second, he saw.

Going, going . . . gone. The doorway collapsed into ash. Those that hadn't made it through the doorway, stood and stared vacantly at the pile of burning embers. Then they began working in an unhurried way on a second doorway. Only it was far too late now. Bone burnt to cinder manoeuvred coffins that were little more than shells of ash. Futile. Within moments, the gas jets had devoured them; one by one the corpses that had been left behind sank to the floor where they stopped moving, to lay in this bath of roaring fire. In the morning they would be shovelled into urns.

Danny staggered panting and red-faced to the rest room; there he sat on the floor, back to the fridge. It had only lasted a second but he'd seen beyond the doorway. He'd seen cool green meadows, a stream lined with willows; in the distance a great mountain of grey rock. Only this mountain had a human face. He'd seen the dead leave the inferno and walk into paradise — because he was certain it must be paradise — and he'd seen the burnt dead instantly grow young again. The expressions on their faces stayed nailed inside of him. Happy. Happier than he'd ever seen anyone before.

He closed his eyes; before his brain shut down, the word HAPPY circled round and around inside his head like a new moon caught by the gravity of a cold and lonely planet.

'Danny boy, the pipes, the pipes are calling,' he sang as he waited for it to happen the next night. He knew that it would. Inside, something new orbited the centre of his mind. Revelation. He knew, without the tiniest, most insignificant scrap of doubt that he witnessed a miracle take place every night. Would he tell anyone?

Would he hell! *Share your cake at school, Danny*, said his teacher. He'd been left bleeding crumbs. Danny had learnt the tough way that sharing really meant let others take your possessions. No one's taking this. This is mine!

He'd lost his job; lost his health; lost his self-esteem. Now, he'd found the burning path to happiness.

Eye to the spy-hole, he watched that day's crop of corpses work in their life-giving atmosphere of flame. He rehearsed mentally what he'd do. As soon as the doorway was complete and they had begun their exodus to paradise, then he would follow them there.

The exodus began. Danny spun the gas valves shut, killing the flames. The heat would still be enormous, but he'd be in through the doors, across the floor and into the doorway in less than three seconds.

Danny gripped the brass valve wheel and spun it shut, then he swung open the oven doors.

Disaster. The hot air scalded his face; he gasped; eyes watered; roast meat smells filled his nose; post mortem grunts filled his ears. Without the flames the corpses simply collapsed to the floor. Danny stepped over them as they lay vomiting boiling blood. From mouths and anuses jetted fierce blue flames like Bunsen burner jets as expanding gases stuttered outwards.

The doorway of still burning coffins was closed. All that lay beyond was the asbestos block wall. Choking, his skin scorching painfully, Danny stumbled back out into the loading bay, where he limped back to the rest room, dissolved more solpadol into a mug and gulped it down.

Yes, it was a setback, he told himself as he glared at his scorched face in the mirror, but he'd find a way through. All it needed was effort and commitment, then he would pass through to the other side, where pain, loneliness and misery could not survive.

Danny was ready the next night. The burning corpses had finished the doorway and were filing through into the cool meadows.

Without fire, that incandescent life fled from the corpses, and killed the doorway. Tonight, Danny must leave the gas jets blazing.

He would simply open the doors, dash into the oven and through the doorway. To give him some protection from the inferno he'd made a suit of kitchen foil and sacking; on his head, a helmet of wire netting covered in layers of foil. Two tiny eyes punched by needles served as eye holes. For a whole five minutes he'd sluiced himself from the hosepipe; that and five solpadol to deaden the pain from the fire should get him through the burning doorway. He sang to himself as his gloved hands pulled back the oven doors. Anyway, he promised himself, any burns he suffered would be supernaturally healed the second he passed through the doorway. He'd rest for a while then he would enjoy a pleasant stroll to the mountain with a human face.

The heat from the oven hit him like a concrete slab. Winded, he wanted to gasp for air but he knew he must hold his breath or the heat would reduce his lungs to paste. Through the eye holes he saw his goal. He waded through the sea of flame, pushing aside corpses that waited patiently in line to file through the doorway.

He could see nothing but blazing yellow. Adrenaline and solpadol quashed the pain but he knew he was burning; he could feel the itch of bubbling skin on his back and arms; his hair singed into a molten cap inside his helmet.

He fought his way through the line of burning corpses. Now faces lunged into view, flames jetting out of mouths and ears, eyeballs popped with a puff of steam; faces peeled away like they were plastic masks. He felt hands grip his arms. *They're attacking me*, he thought panic struck. But then he realised they were helping him. The burning dead supported and guided him towards the doorway; they knew his need was greater than theirs.

There it was. He was six feet from the doorway of burning coffins. Beyond — lush meadows, sprinkled with a million golden dandelions like stars, willows swayed in a light breeze; and in the distance the mountain with the human face. It was smiling.

The flames were eating into his hands now, fingernails went black and spalled from the fingers; the skin bubbled red and brown like pizza in an oven, but:

'I'm there! I'm going through! Oh, thank God! Thank God!'

A six year old child, grossly humped with tumours, stood in his way; eagerly he pushed it away where it burst against a wall like fried egg yolk.

Nearly there!

But clumsy in his suit, Danny's flailing arm brushed the burning doorway. He hardly touched it but it toppled. It hit the floor in a cascade of sparks that streamed up into his masked face like a machine gun tracer.

Howling now, more from frustration than pain, he swung round at the burning corpses who stood placidly watching him.

'Work, you bastards . . . Work!'

They had to build another doorway. They had to do it quickly. Wood coffins were becoming ash. Gaping holes appeared in his suit letting the flames lick his skin. Through his eyeholes, he saw his hands trailing skin, grab at coffins and begin to stack them.

Inside his head his mind detonated into splinters; one screamed with burning agony; one, insanely optimistic, believed he could build another doorway in time and slip through into cool, cool paradise; the other realistic, knew time was running out. He'd blown his one and only chance of heaven; that soon the fist size chunk of muscle that beat in his chest would, like a worn out engine, begin to judder.

And finally stop.

DENNIS ETCHISON

THE SCAR

This time they were walking a divided highway, the toes of their shoes powdered white with gravel dust. The little girl ran ahead, skipping eagerly along the shoulder, while her mother lagged back to keep pace with the man.

'Mind the trucks,' called the woman, barely raising her voice. Soon the girl would be able to take care of herself; that was her hope. She turned to him, showing the good side of her face. 'Do you see one yet?'

He lifted his chin and squinted.

She followed his gaze to the other side of the highway. There, squatting in the haze beyond the overpass, was a Weenie Wigwam Fast Food Restaurant.

'Thank God,' she said. She thought of the Chinese Smorgasbord, the Beef Bowl, the Thai Take-Out and the many others they had seen already. She added, 'This one will be all right, won't it?'

It was the edge of town, RV dealerships and fleet sales on one side of the road, family diners and budget motels on the other. Overloaded station wagons and moving vans laden with freight hammered the asphalt, bringing thunder to the gray twilight. Without breaking stride the man leaned down to scoop up a handful of gravel, then skimmed stones between the little girl's thin legs and into the ditch; he held onto one last piece, a sharp quartz chip, and deposited it in his jacket pocket.

'Maybe,' he said.

'Aren't you sure?'

He did not answer.

'Well,' she said, 'let's try it. Laura will be hungry, I know.'

She hurried to catch the little girl at the crossing. When she turned back, the man was handling an empty beer bottle from the roadside.

She looked away. As he moved to join them, zippering the front of his service jacket, the woman forced a smile, as if she had not seen.

In the parking lot, the man took their hands. A heavy tanker geared down and pounded the curve, bucking and hissing away behind them. As it passed, the driver sounded his horn at the traffic. The sudden blast, so near that it rattled her spine, seemed to release her from a bad dream. She laced her fingers more securely with his and swung her arm out and back again, hardly feeling the weight of his hand between them.

'This is a nice place,' she said, already reading a banner for the all-day breakfast special. 'I'm glad we waited. Aren't you glad, Laura?'

'Can I ride the horse?' asked the little girl.

The woman looked down at the sculpted gray-and-white Indian pinto, its blanket saddle worn down to the fibreglass. There were no other children waiting at the machine. She let go of his hand and dug in her purse for a coin.

'I don't see why not,' she said.

The little girl broke away.

He came to a stop, his empty hands opening and closing.

'Just one ride,' the woman said quickly. 'And then you come right inside, hear?'

On the other side of the glass, couples moved between tables. A few had children, some Laura's age. Families, she thought. She wished that the three of them could go inside together.

Laura's pony began to wobble and pitch. But the man was not watching. He stood there with his chin up, his nostrils flared, like an animal waiting for a sign. His hands continued to flex.

'I'll see about a table,' she said when he did not move to open the door.

A moment later she glanced outside and saw him examining a piece of brick that had come loose from the front of the restaurant. He turned it over and over.

The menus came. They sat reading them in a corner booth, under crossed tomahawks. The food items were named in keeping with the native American motif, suggesting that the burgers and the several varieties of hot dogs had been invented by hunters and gatherers. Bleary travellers hunched over creased roadmaps, gulping coffee and estimating mileage, their eyes stark in the chill fluorescent lighting.

'What would you like, Laura?' asked the woman.

'Peanut butter and jelly sandwich.'

'Do they have that?'

'And a vanilla milkshake.'

The woman sighed.

'And Wampum Pancakes, Papoose-size.'

She opened her purse and counted the money. She blinked and looked at the man.

He got up and went over to the silverware station.

'What's he doing?' said the little girl.

'Never mind,' said the woman. 'His knife and fork must be dirty.'

He came back and sat down.

'And Buffalo Fries,' said the little girl.

The woman studied him. 'Is it still okay?' she asked

'What?' he said.

She waited, but now he was busy observing the customers. She gave up and returned to the menu. It was difficult for her to choose, now knowing what he would order. 'I'll just have a small dinner salad,' she said at last.

The others in the restaurant kept to themselves. A man with a sample case ate a piece of pecan pie and scanned the local newspaper. A young couple fed their baby apple juice from a bottle. A take-away order was picked up at the counter, then carried out to a Winnebago. Soft, vaguely familiar music lilted from wall speakers designed to look like tom-toms, muffling the clink of cups and the murmur of private conversations.

'Want to go the bathroom,' said the little girl.

'In a minute, baby,' the woman told her. A waitress in an imitation buckskin mini-dress was coming this way.

The little girl squirmed. 'Mom-*my!*'

The waitress was almost here, carrying a pitcher and glasses of water on a tray.

The woman looked at the man.

Finally he leaned back and opened his hands on the table.

'Could you order for us?' she asked carefully.

He nodded.

In the rest room, she reapplied make-up to one side of her face, then added another layer to be sure. At a certain angle the deformity did not show at all, she told herself. Besides, he had not looked at her, really looked at her in a long time; perhaps he had forgotten. She practised a smile in the mirror until it was almost natural. She waited for her daughter to finish, then led her back to the dining room.

'Where is he?' said the little girl.

The woman tensed, the smile freezing on her lips. He was not at the table. The food on the placemats was untouched.

'Go sit down,' she told the little girl. 'Now.'

Then she saw him, his jacket with the embroidered patches and the narrow map like a dragon on the back. He was on the far side of the room, under a framed bow and arrow display.

She touched his arm. He turned too swiftly, bending his legs, his feet apart. Then he saw who it was.

'Hi,' she said. Her throat was so dry that her voice cracked. 'Come on, before your food gets cold.'

As she walked him to the table, she was aware of eyes on them.

'I had a bow and arrow,' he said. 'I could pick a sentry out of a tree at a hundred yards. Just like that. No sound.'

She did not know what to say. She never did. She gave him plenty of room before sitting down between him and the little girl. That put her on his other side, so that he would be able to see the bad part of her face. She tried not to think about it.

He had only coffee and a small sandwich. It took him a while to start on it. Always travel light, he had told her once. She picked at her salad. The people at the other tables stopped looking and resumed their meals.

'Where's my food?' asked the little girl.

'In front of you,' said the woman. 'Now eat and keep quiet.'

'Where's my pancakes?'

'You don't need pancakes.'

'I do, too!'

'Hush. You've got enough.' Without turning her face the woman said to the man, ' How's your sandwich?'

Out of the corner of her eye she noticed that he was hesitating between bites, listening to the sounds of the room. She paused, trying to hear what he heard. There was the music, the undercurrent of voices, the occasional ratcheting of the cash register. The swelling traffic outside. The chink of dishes in the kitchen, as faint as rain on a tin roof. Nothing else.

'Mommy, I didn't get my Buffalo Fries.'

'I know, Laura. Next time.'

'When?'

Tomorrow? she thought. 'All right,' she said. 'I'll get them to go. You can take them with you.'

'Where?'

She realised she did not know the answer. She felt a tightening in her face and a dull ache in her throat so that she could not eat. Don't let me cry, she thought. I don't want her to see. This is the best we can do . . . can't she understand?

Now his head turned toward the kitchen.

From behind the door came distant clatter as plates were stacked, the squeak of wet glasses, the metallic clicking of flatware, the high good humour of unseen cooks and dishwashers. The steel door vibrated on its hinges.

He stopped chewing.

She saw him check the room one more time: the sharply-angled tables, the crisp bills left for tips, the half-eaten dinners hardening into waste, the full bellies and taut belts and bright new clothing, too bright under the harsh fixtures as night fell, shuttering the windows with leaden darkness. Somewhere outside headlights gathered as vehicles jammed the turnoff, stabbing the glass like approaching searchlights.

He put down his sandwich.

The steel door trembled, then swung wide.

A shiny cart rolled into the dining room, pushed by a busboy in a clean white uniform. He said something over his shoulder to the kitchen crew, rapid-fire words in a language she did not understand. The cooks and dishwashers roared back at his joke. She saw the tone of their skin, the stocky, muscular bodies behind the aprons. The door flapped shut. The cart was coming this way.

He spat out a mouthful of food as though afraid that he had been poisoned.

'It's okay,' she said. 'See? They're Mexicans, that's all . . .'

He ignored her and reached inside his jacket. She saw the emblems from his Asian tour of duty. But there were also patches from Tegucigalpa and Managua and the fighting that had gone on there. She had never noticed these before. Her eyes went wide.

The busboy came to their booth.

Under the table, the man took something from his pant's pocket and set it beside him on the seat. Then he took something else from the other side. Then his fists closed against his knees.

'Can I have a bite?' said the little girl. She started to reach for the uneaten part of the sandwich.

'Laura!' said the woman.

'Well, he doesn't want it, does he?'

The man looked at her. His face was utterly without expression. The woman held her breath.

'Excuse,' said the busboy.

The man turned his head back. It seemed to take a very long time. She watched, unable to stop any of this from happening.

When the man did not say anything, the busboy tried to take his plate away.

A fork came up from below, glinted, then arced down in a blur, pinning the brown hand to the table.

The boy cried out and swung wildly with his other hand.

The man reached under his jacket again and brought a beer bottle down on the boy's head. The boy folded, his scalp splitting under the lank black hair and pumping blood. Then the cart and chairs went flying as the man stood and grabbed for the tomahawks on the wall. But they were only plastic. He tossed them aside and went over the table.

A waitress stepped into his path, holding her palms out. The salesman stood up, long enough to take half a brick in the face. Then the manager and the man with the baby got in the way. A sharp stone came out, and a lock-back knife, and then a water pitcher shattered, the fragments carrying gouts of flesh to the floor.

The woman covered her little girl as more bodies fell and the room became red.

He was going for the bow and arrow, she realised.

Sirens screamed, cutting through the clot of traffic. There was not much time. She crossed the parking lot, carrying the little girl toward the Winnebago. A retired couple peered through the windshield, trying to see. The child kicked until the woman had to put her down.

'Go. Get in right now and go with them before . . .'

'Are you going, too?'

'Baby, I can't. I can't take care of you anymore. It isn't safe. Don't you understand?'

'Want to stay with you!'

'Can we be of assistance?' said the elderly man, rolling down his window.

She knelt and gripped the little girl's arms. 'I don't know where to go,' she said. 'I can't figure it out by myself.' She lifted her hair away from the side of her face. 'Look at me! I was born this way. No one else would want to help us. But it's not too late for you.'

The little girl's eyes overflowed.

The woman pressed the child to her. 'Please,' she said, 'it's not that I want to leave you . . .'

'We heard noises,' said the elderly woman. 'What happened?'

Tall legs stepped in front of the camper, blocking the way.

'Nothing,' said the man. His jacket was torn and spattered. He pulled the woman and the little girl to their feet. 'Come on.'

He took them around to the back of the lot, then through a break in the fence and into a dark field, as red lights converged on the restaurants. They did not look back. They came to the other side of the field and then they were crossing the frontage road to a maze of residential streets. They turned in a different direction at every corner, a random route that no one would be able to follow. After a mile or so they were out again and back to the divided highway, walking rapidly along in the ditch.

'This isn't the way,' said the little girl.

The woman took the little girl's hand and drew her close. They would have to leave their things at the motel and move on again, she knew. Maybe they would catch a ride with one of the truckers on the interstate, though it was hard to get anyone to stop for three. She did not know where they would sleep this time; there wasn't enough left in her purse for another room.

'Hush, now.' She kissed the top of her daughter's head and put an arm around her. 'Want me to carry you?'

'I'm not a baby,' said the little girl.

'No,' said the woman, 'you're not . . .'

They walked on. The night lengthened. After a while the stars came out, cold and impossibly distant.

STEPHEN LAWS

DEEP BLUE

If I think back about it, the whole thing really began with Charlie Otis and his drunken talk about what music can do to you, depending on what kind of mood you're in.

He felt like talking that night, so I let him. That's the thing about The Portland. It's a kind of haven for people who feel the need to get seriously drunk or talk, or get seriously drunk and listen. It's a pub that's managed to survive the plague of brass and chrome that's infected so many of the city-centre drinking places since the late seventies. Just your old-fashioned, no-nonsense, peeling wallpaper kind of place with a scarred bar top and fast service for the professional drinker. It's the kind of bar where a draughtsman, a Chief Executive, a shipyard welder and a solicitor can get drunk and talk about their problems with whoever's there, without resorting to talk of work, influence or profession. Anybody who breaks the unspoken rule gets the cold shoulder. Anyway, I digress, and you may as well know from the beginning . . . I'm no bloody good at telling stories. But bear with me.

So anyway, Charlie Otis worked at the Breweries, something in the Orders Section I think (not that it matters, like I say). I'd already got a couple under my belt when he walked in, but he was onto his fourth before I'd ordered my third, and he was pissed off. He didn't want to talk about his problem, whatever it was . . . just around it. There's a time for talking and a time for listening. In The Portland, you've got to be intuitive. So I in-tooted, and listened.

'That's the thing with some music,' he said. 'If you're in a good mood, you can listen to a real bluesey piece, about some fella who's lost everything, you know? And you can enjoy it, get into the feeling of it, without feeling too bad. Know what I mean? But if you're already blue . . . well, it can make you suicidal. You must know what I mean

47

— you play that sort of stuff for a living.'

Time for another digression. He's right, I'm a professional musician. I played Working Men's Clubs for years with a group — if you can call our rag tag bunch that — by the name of "The Hellbenders". Yeah I know it's a corny title. But we'd seen a Spaghetti western back in the sixties with that title, and it sort of stuck with us. We were what you call "soft-rock", I suppose. My ambitions for super-stardom vanished a long time ago, and I don't play the clubs anymore. I'm a session man, but strictly small-time stuff. You ever listen to the music that backs those kids' commercials? You know the sort of thing — the heavy rock stuff behind *Super Auto Man* or *Lightning Raiders*. I'm proud of some of it, actually. Even cut a single of the *Raiders* theme, but it didn't go anywhere. Anyway, whereas the work pays the bills and the maintenance money for my ex and two kids, it doesn't have any sort of street cred, so I don't talk about it too much.

So I said: 'It's just a job to me, Otis.'

'Come on, don't give me that,' he says. 'You're a musician. You've got to feel what you're playing.'

'If I felt everything I played I'd be burned out.'

'But that's the point, see?' He was on his fifth, and I was starting to tune out. 'I mean, if you really felt some kinds of songs, I mean really *felt* them it would depress he hell out of you, wouldn't it? I mean . . . take "Run for Home", that Alan Hull song. I can't bear to listen to it, 'cause that's the day Alice walked out on me . . .'

And so on and so forth.

Okay, so we're skipping ahead now. This is about a month later. I was in the same bar, and the same seat, getting on the outside of some happy hour Canadian Gold whisky, when Gerry walked in.

Now I'd known Gerry for a long time. He had his faults, but he was basically okay. Actually, I owed him, because it was thanks to Gerry that I got started in the commercials work. He was involved with Implosions Studios in town, and that's where I recorded most of my stuff with the other session men that Gerry used to pull together for these kids' adverts. We were good and we were cheap, and the stuff we thrashed out for those London firms was bloody good, if I say so myself. But the thing with Gerry was . . . well, he was an entrepreneur. He thought he was Big Time, but he wasn't. And you had to ignore the way he went on sometimes about wanting to make the *Big* Big Time. For a while, I was dragged along in the enthusiasm of Gerry's dreams, but experience taught me that most of those dreams would stay that way. Gerry wasn't involved with commercials anymore at that time, he had moved off in search of his Big Dreams. Despite that, despite the fact that I've probably turned into some aged rock and roll cynic, we still had a beer occasionally in the Portland and I let him prattle on about the big deals he was always going to pull off.

Now, this was the second conversation, so I'll try and get it right. Just how the hell we got around to talking about Buddy Holly, I don't know. But we did.

'Ask anybody,' said Gerry. 'Anybody . . .' (and he belched loud enough to draw the attention of the barman) 'anybody who knows. And they'll tell you that Buddy Holly was the greatest, the most influential . . . the greatest . . .'

So I wasn't really going to argue with him. You know, it had been a really hard day and all I was really looking forward to was to wind down a bit, not wind up. So I took another mouthful of Canadian Gold and started picking idly at one of the rough scratches on the battered bar counter, remembering the time Stanley Usher had his teeth knocked out on it by some pissed-off long distance lorry driver.

'Who's arguing?' I said. 'I think he was great, too.'

And Gerry swigged down some more of his Newcastle Brown and said: 'But . . . I mean . . . he was the *greatest*.'

And round about then I started to think he'd already been drinking tonight before he came into the pub. And maybe one too many snorts of the happy-baccy. I wasn't in the mood that night for meaningless, meaningful discussions, know what I mean?

'Know how he died?' asked Gerry.

'Plane crash,' I replied. 'Him and the Big Bopper.'

'September 7th 1936 to February 3rd 1959,' said Gerry. 'And here's a quote: "One day soon the reservoir of Holly's songs will be drained. I give the cult five years. Adrian Mitchell, London Daily Mail 13th July 1962." Gerry ordered another Brown Ale and a whisky for me. So who was arguing?'

'The Day The Music Died,' I said in return. 'Don McLean's "American Pie". And he was singing about the day that Buddy Holly died.'

'But it's not dead,' Gerry said. And here was something about the way he spoke that made me wonder if he was as stoned as I thought he was. 'Not anymore.' There was an eagerness about the way that he spoke; the keenness cutting momentarily through his drunken blur.

And then he fumbled in his inside pocket and took out a brown manila envelope, swatting it with dramatic emphasis on the bar. He sipped his drink again and sat back, leaving the envelope there, staring at me with that intense expression on his face — like I was supposed to say or do something. Instead I shrugged, inviting him to carry on.

'Know what's in there?' he asked.

'A contract for me to play with Bruce Springsteen on a world tour.'

'You wish. But in fact, it's better than that. More than better. This is a bloody goldmine.'

There was a pause then, and Gerry seemed to be savouring the moment. Then he nodded at the envelope, inviting me to open it. With a sour smile at his dramatics, I swept it from the bar and did just that. Inside were two sheets of yellowed paper. When I opened out the heavily creased and folded pages, I could see that it was old music paper with two staves on it. It was a song. Handwritten, with the blue ink faded to grey. The scrawl at the top of the first sheet was hard to decipher, not helped by the Canadian Gold blur in my head.

'Deep . . . deep . . .'

'Deep Blue,' finished Gerry, swigging back his drink and ordering another for both of us. 'It's a blues number. Read the signature.'

I squinted at the scrawl again, holding the page up to the light for a better view.

'Buddy . . .'

'Holly,' finished Gerry again.

I looked back at him for a long time.

'You're telling me that this is an original manuscript for a song by Buddy Holly.'

'Not only that. But it's the last song he ever wrote.'

I finished my drink, still looking hard at Gerry. When our two refreshers came, I sipped at it for a little while, and then said: 'Bullshit.'

'I'm telling you. It's Buddy Holly's last song. Never been played, never been recorded. It's a goldmine.'

'It's a forgery.'

Gerry seemed impatient now. I'd obviously not reacted according to plan.

'No it's not. It's the real thing. I guarantee it.'

'There's one big reason why it can't be a Buddy Holly song.'

'Why?'

'Because Buddy couldn't read music, much less write it. He was self taught.'

'You think I don't know that.'

'And you still say it's genuine.'

'I've had the handwriting for the lyrics tested by experts. Not only that, but every crotchet and quaver matches the handwriting style.

They were written by the same hand, by the same man. Buddy Holly.'

'I still say, bullshit.'

'I've got the evidence. Look, you're not telling me anything I don't already know. But — maybe he'd started to learn. The simple fact is — it's his song. And it's his last.'

'Where did you get it?'

'Indirectly — from the site where his plane crashed.'

'You mean someone just picked it up off the ground, and it's never been heard of for more than thirty years.'

'That's right.'

'That bull is still straining in the ditch, Gerry.'

'Some hillbilly farmer picked it out of a tree. Didn't know what he'd got, but his daughter did. Just like a lot of kids back then, she thought Buddy was Number One. Devastated by what had happened, she just kept those two pages locked in her trunk. A last personal reminder. Never let on about it. Just took it out of that trunk every once in a while and looked at it.'

'And never thought about selling it? Maybe make a fortune out of it a few years later?'

'She died. Suicide or something. Someone else found it in that trunk.'

'So how come *you're* the first to get your hands on it?'

Gerry tapped his nose. 'I'm not the first. I'm number ten, to be accurate.'

'Nine people have had this song — and it's never been recorded?'

'All nine owners died.'

'They all died,' I said, kind of flat, to get a reaction out of Gerry.

'They died. Tell you what, that song was *destined* for me.'

'Sounds like you're spinning me a tale. What is this — a song with a curse?'

'A song that's never been recorded. This is the one that's going to make the big money.'

'You sure this song wasn't composed by Tutankhamun?'

'What?'

'You know. A curse or something.'

'Don't be bloody stupid.'

'I still think it's bollocks.'

'Yeah? Well, bollocks to you, an'all. I was going to cut you in on a piece of the action. I've got something really Big lined up. Special feature on a prime-time television special. And you could have been playing lead guitar on this one.'

'Here, let me see.'

'Hands off! You think it's all bollocks, remember? You may be able to sight read, and I might not know a crotchet from a jockstrap — but this is *mine*. And you just blew your chance to be part of Rock and Roll history.'

Maybe it was the booze making him more touchy than normal, or maybe he was just so hyped up about the whole thing that he wouldn't take anything except wonder and amazement and envy from anyone hearing his crazy Buddy Holly story. But that was when Gerry stamped out of the bar, jamming that envelope back in his pocket. No one looked up as he made his angry way to the door — melodramatic exits were rather a feature of The Portland — and this only served to make him more angry. I could hear him cursing all the way out into the street. I could remember laughing quietly then as I turned back to my drink, wondering just how much Big Money Gerry had coughed up for the rights to this forgery.

I haven't laughed since.

All the way home that night, in my blurred state of senses, I had this peculiar feeling. You know the sort of thing I mean? As if you've forgotten to do something, something important. And it nags away at the back of your mind. Even when I let myself through the front door of my rented apartment, I paused on the threshold and tried to remember just what it could be. Nothing would come. Inside, I decided against coffee and took the whisky bottle out of the cupboard. Had it got something to do with Angela, my ex-wife? Had I forgotten to send this month's maintenance money for the kids? Maybe it was the kids themselves. Jamie and Paula. No, their birthdays were four and eight months away. Pouring myself a house-measure of the old anaesthetic, I pulled my acoustic guitar out of the cupboard, flopped on the sofa and began to strum a few chords.

After a few minutes, I realised what had been chewing at the back of my mind.

It was the so-called Buddy Holly song.

Just as Gerry had said, I'm a pretty good sight reader from sheet music, and I also have a pretty good memory. I've only got to play a new number through once, and I can generally log it up in the old beanbox and remember it for the future. And although I'd only had a brief glance at the forgery, I could still see an image of it imprinted on my retina. It was a standard 4/4 signature, but there was something about the chord combination that seemed curious. I closed my eyes, and tried to strum out the brief snatch of what I'd seen. There was a chord change here from E major to A minor which was easy enough. Sorry, maybe you don't know what the hell I'm talking about. Now what can I liken that chord change to? Well, it's used a lot by that film composer, John Barry. It's the opening two chord-stabs from *Goldfinger*, and he uses it a lot in his other stuff. Unusual to start a Blues number with a dramatic "stab" like that. But, anyway, I kept on, swigging on the whisky bottle and trying to remember how it went on from there.

Yeah. A minor to A, then G — then . . .

Then I don't remember a lot after that.

What I do remember isn't very pleasant at all.

I remember the sounds of screaming, a feeling as if the whole world was tilting. When I try to think back about it, I only see "flashes": like I'm seeing some kind of psychedelic film that makes no sense. I remember something made of glass breaking. Later, they found that my front window was broken and there was blood on the panes, so I suppose it must have been that. They found the guitar out there too, on the street. I seem to remember running through rain (although it wasn't raining that night), and with the sounds of that hideous screaming all around me. I seem to see faces swimming out of mist, leering at me. But in retrospect those faces must have been passers-by on the street shrinking back in fear as I hurtled past them in the night.

Then I remember the car, swerving around the corner with its headlights stabbing the night. I remember a shrieking of brakes that matched the terrifying shrieking all around me. Then the impact. A horrible black gulf of pain that killed the screaming dead. A feeling of flying, and the knowledge that the screaming was not coming from all around me, but was actually coming *from* me.

Then it was like I was a kid again, at the dentists. Back then, when I had gas for an extraction, I would suffer the most terrible hallucinations. I reckon it must have been some reaction to the gas, because the experiences were always hideously painful. Jumbling black-white-and-red shapes. Magnified sounds, like the crashing echoes of someone dropping a tray of cutlery. And the twisting and turning of those shapes, and the sounds of that crashing cutlery were all, in themselves causing the must hideous, gouging pain. Distorted voices moaning obscenities. Waves of nausea creeping and swelling through the pain . . .

And then I was awake again, fully expecting to be leaning forward to the unconvincing voice of a dentist telling me that everything was alright and would I please spit into the bowl. I tried to struggle up, but that hideous pain had transferred to my leg. I slumped back. I wasn't ten years old, I was forty.

I was in a hospital bed.

Sweat soaked my face, and I could feel it in the small of my back. And oh God, had I pissed myself as I lay there?

I lay there a while, breathing deep and trying to orientate myself.

There had been an accident. I remembered the car with its blaring horn and its shrieking tyres. My leg seemed to be in some sort of splint under the covers. Yes, that was it — I'd been hit by a car. But what about all that other stuff? The screaming and the breaking of glass and the running through the streets — and something to do with music? No, that must all be part of the shock of the accident. If I just lay still for a while and took it easy, everything would come back to me gradually. Maybe I'd just left Gerry in the pub, and walked outside, full of whisky — straight in front of a car. That made much more sense.

Gerry.

Somehow, I could hear his voice. I rubbed my face, screwed my fist into my eye sockets, shook my head. I could still hear his voice, then I could hear the shrill Liverpudlian voice of a famous TV star — and the sounds of an audience laughing.

I looked up.

There was a television set high up on a shelf, just off to my left.

And there was Gerry — on the screen. Chatting to the TV star.

My senses were still a little blurry. I tried to rise again and felt the pain, thought about ringing the bell at the side of the bed for assistance.

'So tonight's the night,' said the woman in the bright red hair. 'After all these years. You must be feeling very excited.'

'More than excited,' said Gerry's familiar voice. 'I'm proud. Just proud that I'm part of such a big moment in Rock and Roll history.'

'So no one's heard the song, none of the band back there have rehearsed it?'

'That's right. This is the first time that his last song will have been played to an audience. Just like the band back there, the viewers will be hearing *Deep Blue* just as Buddy composed it — for the very first time.'

'I can't wait, chuck. Believe me. So viewers, tune in for tonight's Big Event — just after the regional news . . .'

And that's when I tore the IV wires out of my arm and shoved the stand aside. The wires sprayed liquid over the bedspread. I knew that the pain was going to be bad, but hadn't appreciated just *how* bad as I pulled myself out of bed and my strapped-up leg swung down to bang against the mattress. The pain almost made me throw up. I gritted my teeth, felt the enamel scraping — and hobbled to the cupboard. I was right, my clothes were in there. I dragged them out as the loud and brassy television theme music filled the room. My head was still swimming as I dragged the clothes on. There was a walking stick beside a chair in the corner. I grabbed it and hobbled to the door. So far, no one had noticed that I'd come around. I staggered, putting too much weight on my splinted broken leg. This time, I did throw up; reeling to one side as it came out of me.

In the next moment, I was out of the ward and hobbling down the corridor head down. I hoped to God that no one would stop me. Each step of the way, I gritted my teeth or chewed at my lips with the pain. By the time I'd reached the end of the corridor, there was a salt taste of blood in my mouth.

Outside, it had begun to rain. I stood aside as an ambulance pulled up at the entrance, kept my head down and tried to pretend that I was just a patient having a breath of fresh air as the back doors of the ambulance banged open and two of the crew loaded out some poor old guy on a stretcher with an oxygen mask on his face. As soon as they passed me, I hobbled out into the night.

How long had I been lying in that hospital bed? Days, weeks, months?

Prime time television special, Gerry had said. How long would it have taken him to fix up a deal like that?

I stared out into the darkness. I'd never make it to the main road with this leg, and there was no guarantee that I would be able to flag down a taxi. I had to go back inside the hospital, find a telephone, hope that I wasn't spotted. How the hell could I convince anyone at the studio?

Then I saw the driver's keys, still in the ignition of the ambulance. Now or never.

I yanked open the door, threw the walking stick inside, drew a deep breath and began to clamber in. My leg bumped against the door as I climbed in — and I'm sure that I passed out then. In a kind of dream I saw myself being hauled out of the ambulance, put onto a stretcher and taken back inside. But then the dream dissipated, and there I was, half-in half-out, lying across the seat. My leg was on fire. I struggled up and pulled the door shut. The walking stick was going to have to serve the purpose of my damaged leg on the accelerator.

I gunned the engine into life — and the ambulance screeched off down the hospital ramp. I expected to see the two crew members gal-loping out after me, yelling and screaming. Expected to hear the sounds of police sirens at any minute. But there was no one to stop me as I came off that ramp into the hospital forecourt, and the ambulance screeched out on to the main road. If anything had been coming, there would have been no way I could have stopped. There would have been a pile-up, and that would have been the end of it. But, thank God, nothing came.

Where the hell was the siren on this thing? If I could find it, then I could get where I was headed with no problems of being snarled up by traffic. The other bastards would have to stop.

Nine previous owners of that song.

I found it — just before I went through that first set of red lights. A Volvo swerved up onto the pavement out of my way, juddering to a halt. Now I knew — I'd never get to that studio on time, would never get past the security guards in this condition. I rammed the gears into reverse and screeched down a side road. There was one other place I had to get to — and it was near.

Nine previous owners, all of them dead. Suicide, Gerry had said. That first girl who found it committed suicide. What about the others?

How long had I got? How long did the local news last for God's sake?

There were roadworks at the corner of the street I was headed for.

Buddy Holly composed it. Somehow. On that plane.

I swerved the ambulance in hard, tried to avoid the hole that the British Gas workmen had been working in. The left side wheel jud-dered on the edge as the ambulance slewed across the street, slamming into the red and white wooden barriers, splintering them and sending traffic cones whirling and clattering in the night.

He plays it for the first time. On that night, 3rd February 1959. He plays it on the plane.

Somehow, I didn't go sideways into the hole as I tugged at the wheel. The ambulance righted and roared down the street.

Those on board the plane hear the song. And something happens then. The plane pitches out of the sky, slams into the earth killing everyone on board.

I jammed down hard on the brakes, pitching myself forward; the juddering agony in my leg making me yell out loud. But I couldn't stop now; not now, when I'd managed to get this far. I dragged open the door, leaving the siren wailing. Already, the curtains in the windows of this small side-street were twitching as those inside came to find out what the hell the noise was about. That was good. Let them come. Let them get away.

And out of that carnage, a sheet of writing paper flutters in the wind, coming to rest in the branches of a tree. There to be found, eventually, by a young girl. Taken away — and kept. A love song to her. From Buddy — or perhaps — from Something Else.

There was no way I could clamber down from this height, it was going to take too long. There was only one way. I gripped my leg hard, and rolled out of the seat, head down, hunching my shoulders to take the impact as I hit the ground. All the way down to the ground, I gripped hard on my leg trying to make sure it didn't bang against anything. The impact seemed to judder very bone in my body. Something ripped in my shoulder and now I couldn't see straight. Had I concussed myself?

And then the realisation. As I'd run screaming down the street, having played that song. That horrible realisation as the car swerved and its horn blared. The car was swerving to avoid me — but I'd heard, and now — I WANTED to die. I had thrown myself under that car deliberately.

No time to think, no time to lose. I dragged myself up, pulled the walking stick out of the cab and hobbled furiously towards that familiar front door.

It began to open as I approached.

It was Angela.

In her dressing gown, hair wet and looking as if she had just got out of the bath.

'Oh my God,' she began. 'It's you . . .' It was an automatic response of weary disgust, but her words shrivelled in her mouth when she saw my face, saw what kind of state I was in. Her mouth opened wide, and she had no time to react as I hit that half-opened door hard with my free hand. In shock, she staggered back against the wall and I blundered straight in past her.

'The kids!' I yelled. 'Where are the kids?'

'They're watching the telly — what the *hell* do you think you're doing, busting into my house like that? There's a restraining order against you coming here. You know that? And what the *hell* is that ambulance doing . . .?'

I shouldered the living room door open. James and Paula were already looking my way as I came in, eyes wide and fearful.

On the television, the red haired woman said: 'And without further ado — not that there's been any ado going on anyway (laughter) — Gerry Cainton's band, *Surefire*, are here to play — for the very first time — Buddy Holly's *Deep Blue*.'

As the audience applause filled the room, I limped towards the television set, forcing myself not to care about the agony in my leg.

The band played those first two chords. Major to minor. The intro.

God in Heaven, I couldn't bend to switch the damn thing off, or even pull the plug out of its socket. The pain was too great. If I was to fall, I'd never get up again with this leg.

From the corner of my eye, I saw the kids shrinking back on the sofa, away from me.

The drums began, the bass started a riff. The lead guitarist strutted forward to his microphone.

And I seized the top of the television, yanking it from its table and screaming like a wild animal at the pain as the weight of it forced me to stand firm on both legs. Then I lunged forward as that first lead guitar phrase filled the room — and stumbled towards the window.

The set's lead jerked free from the socket just as I hit the window. It shattered with a juddering crash, and the set went straight out into the street in a glittering wave like broken ice. I fell over the jagged edge, feeling the glass slice through my clothes and across my stomach and chest. I saw the television hit the gleaming pavement; saw the screen explode with a hollow cough, spitting out blue sparks, glass and shattered filaments in its last buzzing, spluttering death rattle.

I couldn't get my breath.

As I tried to suck in lungfuls of night air, as the rain spattered through that shattered window and the sounds of that ambulance siren wailed in the living room, I was racked by a keening, sobbing convulsion deep in my chest. It had something to do with the pain, the agony — but it was more to do with relief, with the fact that I never thought deep down that I was going to get there in time.

Now, there were hands on my shoulders. Small hands, gentle but strong.

That sobbing seemed to be convulsing my whole body as I was lifted out of the broken window. It was Jamey and Paula, their faces no longer terrified, their eyes no longer wide with fear.

'Here,' said Jamey. 'Here, Dad.' And they were both trying to guide me to the sofa.

In the doorway, I could see Angela in her dressing gown. Face white and set in a mask of fury. She was on the telephone. I knew from that expression that she had just dialled 999.

'Police!' she snapped firmly at the 'phone, her eyes still fixed on me.

'Oh God, Dad . . .' said Paula, her voice filled with a kind of soft horror. 'What's that?'

I struggled to control that sobbing, and turned to see her looking past me, back out of the window.

'Listen,' she said.

And I heard what she had heard, even above the sound of the ambulance siren.

Someone, somewhere out there in the night, was screaming.

And even as we listened, we heard the sounds of other voices joining in. The sounds of someone in mortal pain, or in an agony of distress. Another voice, and another . . . and another. Then the sound of breaking glass, another clattering smash out there somewhere on the streets. A shriek of tyres, another juddering crash. More voices were joining that swelling chorus. Now it sounded like the caterwauling of night animals; a hideous and insane shrieking. Like the sounds of souls in Hell, souls in torment, filling the night air.

It was growing louder and nearer.

Now, people were screaming behind the doors of houses on this street.

An insane, heart-rending cacophony. The sounds of desolation and despair.

Those sounds had drowned the ambulance siren, as the kids clung close to me, staring out wild-eyed and frightened into the night.

When I turned back to Angela, she had dropped the telephone. It swung at the end of its flex from the table in the hall. Her face was still white, but this time not with fury as she stood silently watching and listening.

'Wha . . .?' she began.

And I could give her no more answers than I can give you now.

D.F. LEWIS

BETWEEN THE FLOORS

The house was two rooms up, two rooms down — and none, needless to say, between.

Yet, of course, there was at least *some* need to say it — if only because, when I was trying to get to sleep upstairs, I heard things moving around beneath me and, upon pottering about with daytime chores downstairs, I heard the same things from up above.

I describe them as "things" for the simple reason that people (or, even, animals, come to that) do not move around in such jolts, shuffles, hops and dragging of weights. It was a real sound-shambles, a potpourri of false manoeuvres — purely gratuitous shifts from space to space which no creatures with feet or paws (not even those who slither on their backs or fronts) could possibly summon in such apparent combinations of false-starts, slip-sliding, head-to-toeing together with a relentless progress from wall to wall and back again.

When I told Grace, she said I must be hearing things.

'Yes, yes, Grace, that's exactly it!'

She looked quizzical. She had long since learned to take anything I said with a pinch of salt. A nice girl at heart, a homely lady, with cosy breasts, and a roaring open hearth. We had been courting for at least five years without any sign of marriage in the wings. I think she must have found it hard to make the big jump from casual affair to one that demanded a little more commitment. I often sensed her teetering on the brink of making overtures along these lines. But, no, she always pulled back at the last minute. As for me, I couldn't do it for her, could I? She had to come up with the idea quite independently of me or, otherwise, there would be no substance nor consistency behind any such proposal for formal union between what were after all two autonomous entities.

'Well, why is it I can't hear them now, then?' She looked towards the ceiling. Needless to say, we were in the lounge, not upstairs in my bedroom. Couches were seemly vehicles for unrubberstamped love. But, as for beds, well, need I continue?

'They know when there's someone else in the house.' I spoke in all seriousness.

'And so they don't move about? Are they afraid of people other than you, then? And, by the way, Jeremy, how *many* other someone-elses *do* you have visiting you here? I thought I was the only one.' She had donned her stern air, tailed off with a cold smile.

'Only Mother. She comes on Wednesdays.' I knew I lied or, at least, was economical with the truth.

'You told me she was dead yonks ago!'

'Well, she is — sort of.' Now I was more confident of the facts of the case. Mother *was* dead, but she visited me on Thursdays.

'Now I know you're completely barmy. How can I believe anything you say, when you make cock-eyed statements? You live in a dream world, Jeremy. It's about time you snapped out of it. We've got no future if you carry on like this.'

'Future? We have a future, then? After five years, this is the very first time you've spoken of a future.'

'Yes . . . well, it's about time one of us spoke of the future. We can't go on like this forever.'

'Why not, Grace?'

'Because . . . because . . . well, just *because*.'

'Because?'

'All this talk of your dead mother visiting you and hearing things upstairs when you're down here and things downstairs when you're up there, it's crazy talk, Jeremy. And I can't see any future with a man like that.'

'There you go again. You've mentioned the future again. We're alive now. We see each other only in the present. Not in the future. The future can very well take care of itself. Like the past. It's either gone or will never be.' I knew what I meant but seeing Grace's bemused look, it was obvious that she was not only adrift but sinking fast. Her bemusement soon turned to pleading. She needed to reschedule our relationship's agenda. Not in those words, exactly. But I could see her meaning in her eyes better than she could.

'I always wanted us to be together.' Her words belied anything she really wanted to say.

'Well, here we are — together.' How many more cue lines did she need? Surely, today was the day we'd become engaged. If only . . .

Then, things were on the move.

She looked startled, flagrante delicto. She had already taken off her nylons, with the tantalising twin pop of each leg's suspender-belt catches. This was the furthest we had ever got in five years of conscientious courting and her hesitation was tantamount to coitus interruptus as far as I was concerned.

'Shhh, what's that noise upstairs?'

'It's nothing, Grace. Your imagination.' I had lied again: I simply knew it was my imagination that was the culprit.

'No, I definitely heard something . . . there it goes again!'

This time I had heard it for real. To put no finer point on it, I was shit-scared. All my talk of hearing things had set my nerves a-twanging. Wish-fulfilment. No, dread-fulfilment, rather. All my worse dreams were fast in the process of becoming true.

'They sound so HORRIBLE!' Her voice quavered on the edge of something that neither of us could put our finger on. And, of course, the sounds were just as I had described them. Stuttering. Slop-slapping. Muck-raking. Loofahing. And so forth.

One even seemed to be spilling downwards in short sharp jolts from tread to tread, scattering stair-rods in its wake. Its screeching hid Grace's own mouthful of terror. I was not exactly as quiet as a mouseful of pins, either. I suffered my own breakdown with a queer sort of mewing plaints from each bodily innard in turn. Or so it seemed at the time.

Yet, in hindsight, everything was quite natural. Only an instantaneous diary entry could possibly have got it *so* wrong. Now, in a relatively quiet interlude, Grace and I cuddle each other, listening for further encroachments of our privacy. The thing that actually ventured down the stairs still snuffles on the other side of the lounge door, no doubt bemused at the various sounds of our fitful grappling in front of the roaring fire. More fun than on the couch.

Perhaps I'll ask Mother tomorrow how she and Father did it.

PETER TENNANT

THE GIVING OF NAMES

'What's in a name?' asked the poet, and answered that, 'A rose would still smell as sweet.' It is a conclusion with which I cannot agree. Rather, like the thinkers of the modern school, I am of the persuasion that name dictates destiny. When we bestow a name on a man we also confer an identity to which he must conform, whether he will or not. It is a bitter lesson, but one I have come to learn well, and for the tuition I must thank Mr. Charles Dickens, a writer many now foolishly regard as the fair Swan of Avon's peer.

Every year, on the anniversary of my birth, I go to Westminster Abbey and stand before Dickens's tomb in the Poet's Corner, not to pay homage to the writer's memory, as the *hoi polloi* are want to do, but to console myself with the concrete fact of that old monster's death. This year I shall bring him a present, my own small tribute to the great writer's powers of creativity, of which I have been a major beneficiary. I do not believe Mr. Dickens will care for that which I shall bring, wrapped in string and pages torn from one of his own volumes. If so then justice will have been done at last, for I did not greatly care for that which he bequeathed to me.

Of my childhood, the so called formative years, I have few happy memories. Born with a club foot, I was always a sickly child, one not expected to be long for this world as the saying goes, though I have outlasted many of my contemporaries. My father was the junior clerk at a firm of solicitors, thankless labour that he performed for a mere pittance until the day he died, and I never heard him complain even the once. We were a poor family and did not live well, but there was always food on the table of an evening and pennies to be had when I needed medicine.

I do not know how my father came to meet Charles Dickens, but for a few weeks in the summer of 1842 the two men were acquainted, and the writer was often a guest at our humble lodgings in Cheapside. Already he was lauded as a doyen of the London literary circle, a respected novelist and social commentator of note, though his reputation would in later years attain to heights that were then unimaginable. No doubt my father was flattered by the attentions of such a personage. As for me, I cared nothing for Mr. Dickens's accomplishments. To me he was simply a kind man who always had the time to sit a little boy on his knee and tell him stories.

At some point my father and Mr. Dickens argued. To this day I still hold vivid memories of lying in bed one night with my brothers and sisters, all of us shivering with cold as the wind whistled round the house and snow beat against our window, the sound of voices raised in anger coming from the next room, those of the two men and my mother. After that night Dickens never set foot in our house again and my father would not permit the writer's name to be spoken in his hearing. I was never to discover what had caused this rift, though many years later I heard a rumour, which I was unable to substantiate, that the writer had made an improper advance towards my mother.

People have praised Dickens as a great man, but like many who are public figures he was capable of mean, spiteful acts in private. It was in 1843 with the publication of "A Christmas Carol" that the full weight of the author's ire descended on our poor family's head. I cannot say for certain that Dickens intended the slight; he may simply, as so many writers do, have used his own experiences for fictional ends without any thought of the consequences for those he unfeelingly lampooned. It does not matter; for our family the results were the same regardless of the writer's culpability. "A Christmas Carol" enjoyed unparalleled success. It was read in every corner of the land but only in our own squalid backwater of London was the truth known, that my father and those under his protection had been gifted immortality of a kind as the wretched Cratchit family.

My father remained aloof, while my mother and siblings soon came to terms with their new found celebrity. It was I, and I alone, portrayed as a pitiful cripple, who bore the brunt of this disaster. Timothy Heringay was gone as if he had never been, and in his place stood the pathetic Tiny Tim, ridiculed and jeered at by boys who had previously been my friends. I had only to put a foot outside the door for that mocking cry of 'God bless us all!' to ring out on the street. The adults, who I looked to for respite from this unending torment, regarded it all as a great game, just the harmless teasing of which children are so fond, and, not wishing to become an object of pity as well as ridicule, I allowed them to believe so, never revealing how I felt inside. Nobody realised the pain that I suffered; they did not guess that my good humoured smile was simply a mask to keep the tears at bay. I began to dread leaving the sanctuary of my room. My physical shortcomings, which previously I'd done my best to ignore, were brought home to me with an undeniable force. Whereas before I'd always been happy and cheerful in spite of my illness, I now became a morose and sullen child, constantly brooding on the great injustice nature had done me. And this transformation in my character was down to the unthinking malice of a writer's pen. Charles Dickens had given me a name and made me into his creature, my own identity subsumed and lost until now.

As I grew older my health improved. I was never to be any taller than five foot two and the club foot always remained to remind me of the flesh's infirmity, but I developed a robust constitution and the illnesses that had constantly beset me became a thing of the past. Doctors had attended me since birth, and I could imagine no higher calling than to be one of their number. With my family's blessing I determined to train to become a physician. As a healer of the sick I hoped to win the respect that would always elude me as the earthly incarnation of that pitiful wretch whose name was Tiny Tim.

Somehow money was procured to send me to medical school, in whose august corridors I foolishly imagined that I would find a future and leave my past behind. It was not to be. The glamour of names is not so easily thwarted. Names follow you wherever you go and twist the events of your life to fit their pattern. No sooner had I assumed my new life of study than that dreadful name returned to haunt me. There was nothing overt, nothing said openly, but I knew what was happening. I recognised the signs. Whispered asides whenever I passed by, conversations that broke off at my approach, barely disguised laughter as I left a room. I knew what was going on. The whole student body had conjoined in private to mock that pitiful cripple boy of Dickens's devising, who was none other than my own self. Even the patients given in to my care would smile slyly when I examined them. I tried to ignore all that was happening, to pretend that it didn't matter to me. I formed no close friendships and threw myself wholeheartedly into my studies, but it was all to no avail. I graduated at the top of my class, but in spite of that achievement I felt that in some indefinable way the respect I hungered for had eluded me and would remain forever out of reach.

With the timely gift of an inheritance from a maiden aunt who had lived in the West Country, I set up consulting rooms in a cul-de-sac off Whitechapel. For more than thirty years I healed the sick and prospered, and all that time the canker in my soul festered and grew until it threatened to consume me. I became a pillar of society, a society from which, in my heart of hearts, though I knew all the rules of etiquette and could converse with the finest gentleman as an equal, I felt myself to be truly excluded. All doors were open to me as a physician, yes, but no sooner had I taken my leave than I knew that mocking cry of "Tiny Tim" would sound and the laughter would begin. I knew that I was not truly accepted into the houses of the rich people who were my patients, that my presence was merely tolerated in the way that a fool or a court jester is tolerated. I was a source of amusement to these people, the butt of their jokes and nothing more. I knew of the ridicule that lurked behind all of their polite words and calculated smiles. I knew, and how I hated the hypocrisy of it all.

The women were the worst, beautiful but shallow creatures who made a great show of finding my company agreeable while in private they whispered slanders against my name. How I loathed their duplicity, the sweet words that they spoke so full of subtle venom, the laughter in their eyes, the way in which they watched me when they thought I didn't see. I never took a wife, though such was expected of a man in my position. I could not long endure the company of any woman. When sore beset by those base cravings of the flesh that only a woman's ministrations can ease, like so many of my class I sought out the doxies of Whitechapel. No need for lying words and polite manners in the company of such honest working women, so long as there is coin of the realm to hand.

I was with such a woman when the moment of revelation occurred, like a lightning flash on a winter's night, laying bare every tawdry detail of the life I had been forced to accept as my destiny. She told me her name was Polly. She tapped my chest with a dirt caked finger and said , 'Tim.' Then she reached into my breeches and took out my swollen member. She held it in her hand, laughed once and whispered, 'Tiny Tim.' What happened next I can only remember in fits and starts. There was red and the glint of steel honed to razor sharpness, a blinding light inside my head and at my groin a sensation more intense than any I had ever felt while in the throes of passion. For a few moments I passed out. When I regained my senses the woman lay dead on the cobblestones at my feet. There was blood on my sleeve and my surgical scalpel was clutched in my hand, its blade wet with scarlet. I gathered up my things and fled from that place as fast as my feet would carry me.

Poor dumb Polly. She was the first, but she was not to be the last. It was several days before the fear of discovery loosened its grip on my reason and I was able to come to an understanding of what had occurred on that fateful night of bloodshed. In cutting that woman's flesh I had also in some way cut loose my own past. More than forty years of ridicule and mockery had been expunged forever in that moment of mad abandon, as if by killing that woman I had also struck a fatal blow at all those who had tormented me. If name confers identity then I was now free to bestow a new name on myself, to assume a new identity. It would be a name of power, a name to strike terror at the heart of the world that had so cruelly laughed at and scorned that pitiful child Tiny Tim.

Spread out on the table in front of me are a kidney and ovaries. I wrap them carefully in sheets of paper to present as a blood offering at my true father's tomb. And as I work I croon quietly to myself. Jack. My name is Jack.

'And God bless us all, Mr. Dickens! God bless us all!'

STEVE HARRIS

MINIMUM VISIBILITY

According to his watch, Gary West unlocked the door of the white Ford Transit at twenty to nine. That made him ten minutes late already, but these days it was still pretty good going. He hadn't got to work on time in three months now, and, not so strangely, he supposed, he was on his last warning.

Gary shrugged and smiled wearily. He didn't really care either way, and it wasn't going to be much of a problem today anyway since he didn't have to go straight in. Last night he'd loaded the van with cable to be delivered first thing this morning. Well, it *was* roughly first thing, wasn't it?

And I've got to get petrol, he reminded himself. The chances were he wasn't going to arrive at his destination by nine, as promised, but it was the rush hour, wasn't it? And the traffic round here in the morning was phenomenal. Then there was the fog to take into account. The weather this morning didn't look good.

Who's going to worry about ten minutes? he asked himself. *Not me, that's who!*

He climbed in and sat down in the cold, damp-feeling seat wriggling his back into a comfortable position, sighing. These days, just *looking* at the Transit made his back ache.

I wasn't cut out for this, he told himself as he pulled out the choke and thrust the key into the ignition. *Especially in this weather. I was born in the wrong country.*

The engine burst into life at the first turn of the key and Gary let it run at a fast tick-over while he got out again to mop the mist from the windows and wing mirrors.

Gary didn't exactly hate October, but it wasn't a month he dearly cared for, either. It meant mornings like this one, for one thing: chilly and foggy. And from October onwards it just got colder, wetter and darker. If there was ever a candidate for S.A.D., Seasonally Affected Disorder, it was *this* guy mopping the windows of *this* Transit.

Maybe I should fly south for the winter, he thought. *Or at least buy a sun-bed.*

From where the van was parked outside his flat, Gary could see the main road about a hundred yards away. The cars that passed were little more than vague outlines, pencil beam headlights reflecting off the fog like lasers.

Gary wished he'd stayed in bed. His throat was sore and his head was stuffy which was a sure sign of an oncoming cold. He'd thought about calling in sick earlier, when the alarm woke him and after five minutes of indecision, his guilty conscience got the better of him. He'd had so much time off sick already this year he could probably get into the *Guinness Book of World Records*.

Guilt, Gary decided as he climbed back inside the Transit and wriggled himself comfortable again. *Whose bright idea was that one? Nice one God! Here I am doing a job I hate when I could be tucked up warm in bed and all because I feel guilty.*

The sad fact was, though, where work was concerned Gary had plenty to feel guilty about. He was not a model employee and knew it. Add to that the fact that yet another *absence through illness* would probably find him down the dole office tomorrow and you had one artist who was almost miserable enough to give Van Gogh a run for his money.

I need a rich patron, that's what I need, he told himself as he snapped the light switch to the on position.

He drove to the bottom of the road and turned left onto the main drag, heading toward the firm's filling station, a garage which held a General Motors sales and repair franchise and which still advertised its petrol prices on orange and yellow signs in gallons although the pumps only showed litres.

Well, there's always the inheritance, his mind whispered. *You already have that rich patron, don't you?* Scowling, Gary cut off the thought. He wasn't going to sponge off Sandy, however much she said she loved him. For one thing, she was just a kid and might change her mind about him in a month or two. And where would *that* leave him? In debt to an ex-lover with no hope of paying her back, that was where.

And for another thing, that black part of his mind added, *you can't get your greasy little paws on it for another three years, can you?*

'Bollocks!' he said aloud, wondering where these snidey little thoughts had started to pop up from. It was almost as if Gertie herself was making him think them. *I wouldn't take Sandy's money even if she did have it to spend at this very moment. Even if she wanted me to take it.*

The traffic was heavy and slow along the half mile to the garage, and, Gary noted, sandwiched too tightly together to take evasive action if there was an accident. He left a big gap between his van and the car in front — just in case. In ten years of driving for a living he'd seen far too many ruined cars and mangled bodies to take any chances.

The heater had just come alive and was threatening to take the chill out of the van when Gary pulled up at the filling station. He drove to the nearest vacant pump, got out and filled the tank, feeling the cold now, and wishing he'd put a shirt on under his sweater.

I should be in Thailand right now, he told himself, *painting paddy fields in that special dawn light they have. Or Greece, wrapped up warm because the temperature's down in the fifties. Anywhere the light's good would do.*

Sauntering into the office to sign the account sheet, he was slightly cheered by the sight of an old lady who couldn't get the locking petrol cap off her brand new Saab Turbo. If she was still there when he came out he would give her a hand.

'Good morning, Damon Hill,' the woman behind the counter sang as he came inside. She didn't look up as she filled the transaction details on the form.

'What's so good about it then, Sophia Loren?' Gary asked lightly. 'It's freezing cold and foggy as . . . er . . . foggy as a foggy kind of morning out there.'

Italy, he thought, the moment he said Sophia Loren, *the light is good in Tuscany this time of year, I'll bet!*

'Huh! You should have seen it earlier on,' she replied, still scribbling. 'When I came to work you couldn't see your hand in front of your face. Ten miles an hour all the way here.'

Gary feigned disbelief. 'Your pogo stick goes *that* fast?' he asked.

She looked up and slid the form to him so he could sign it. 'I'll thank you not to refer to my lovely Harry Honda as a pogo stick. Moped is the word you're searching for, you illiterate. Anyway it could beat your old rust bucket through the town in rush hour any day.'

'Yeah, but can your Harry Honda carry a ton of cable on his back?' Gary said, signing the form Harry Honda just for a change. Yesterday he'd been Turner. The day before, Matisse.

She shrugged and grinned. 'He can manage me. Enough said.'

'I'm sure you don't weigh a *whole* ton,' Gary said, sliding the form back.

She pulled a face. 'I'm on a sea food diet,' she said, taking the form from him and placing it back in the file. 'See food and eat it. Anyway, I noticed the rust-bucket was limping a bit when you came in. Where you going with your ton of cable, hotlips?'

'Dan Air. Lasham. First drop today.'

'Last of the long distance lorry drivers!' the woman taunted. 'Lasham is all of, what, six miles?'

'It's a tough job, but somebody's got to do it,' he said, then stopped smiling as he remembered the mountain of cable deliveries waiting for him back at the works. It was going to be another hard day at the orifice. And he was going to be late home, too, if this fog didn't lift.

'What's the time?' he asked. 'I'm supposed to be there by nine.'

'You're going to drive fast, Mister Schumaker, it's ten to already.'

Gary sighed. 'Oh well, time to apply nose firmly to the grindstone. See you later!'

As he went through the door, she called out, 'Mind you don't get lost in this fog!'

And Gary experienced one of those frozen moments he sometimes had. It was something to do with being artistic, they said. Many artists, so they said, suffered from a form of mild epilepsy; a kind of *petit mal* during which they had moments of extreme clarity. This particular moment frightened him. He had no idea why.

'Yeah,' he replied, as everything swam back to normal with a sickening lurch. 'I'll be okay, I've got a compass.'

He shivered as he went out into the cold air. The Saab woman now had the petrol cap off her car and was spilling four star all down the bodywork as she tried to fill the tank. The van still stood where he'd left it, tilting slightly to the right under the uneven weight inside it, the forecourt and pumps all still looked the same . . . and yet something seemed to have changed.

Gary shrugged off the strange feeling and climbed back into the van. Perhaps he really *should* have stayed in bed this morning.

He drove away, wondering if Sandy was up yet. Sandy who was just nineteen and twelve years his junior. Sandy who had moved into his flat last week against the wishes and in spite of the prophesies of doom of her mother (who had called him — without a great deal of originality in Gary's opinion — a *no-good cradle snatcher*).

Gary had nothing against Sandy's mother except the fact that she had hated him on sight. Her name was Gertrude, and he didn't even hold that against her; after all, she hadn't chosen it for herself. But living with it seemed to have soured her outlook on life — and men especially. Maybe her father had been called Gary.

With a blissful ignorance of the psychology you had to use on teenagers, Gertrude Amies had forbidden her daughter to see Gary. Naturally, this had strengthened Sandy's resolve and she'd rebelled. Gertie had tried to poison her daughter's mind against Gary in all sorts of ways, none of which, to her undying disappointment, had done her the slightest bit of good. Not for her, anyway. If there was anyone in Gary's life who was a money grabber, it was Gertie herself.

In spite of what had happened between Sandy and her mother, Gary was still a little stunned at suddenly finding himself with a live-in love. He was delighted, of course, but still a little dizzy at the speed with which it had happened.

Sandy had simply turned up last week, tears rolling down her face and a battered red suitcase in her hand.

'Here I am,' she'd said. 'I hope you want me.'

Gary *did* want her, of course. He wanted her very much. But he hadn't expected her to have made up her mind about him as quickly as this. After all, they'd only known one another three and half weeks. More stunning than *that* was what followed the tearful hugs and the tender lovemaking. They'd lain entwined in one another's arms and Sandy had finally begun to explain.

'We had a big row about you,' she said. 'Mum accused you of being a gold digger.'

Gary could clearly recall the way the expression of puzzlement had felt on his face. 'Gold digger?' he'd asked, mystified. Sandy was middle class, not rich. Her mother's home was a semi-detached in an ordinary part of town. You didn't dig gold around people like this.

'She said you only wanted me for my inheritance,' Sandy said. 'She said you were a liar and a thief and that you were far too old and too common for me. I told her I loved you and you loved me and that we were made for one another.'

'Inheritance? *What* inheritance?' Gary asked.

'She said you'd taken my virginity and corrupted me. Brainwashed me into thinking that I want to be with you.'

Gary tried to remain calm and clear-headed. It was difficult. He wasn't so much confused as totally astounded. 'Virginity?' he gasped.

Sandy kissed the tip of his nose. 'I was saving myself for the right person.'

'You were . . .?'

She grinned. '*Were* is the right word. Anyway, it just got worse and worse. She said you were a no-hoper. I reminded her about your exhibition in London last month. How you sold two and half thousand pounds' worth or paintings. How the critics had loved your work. I even tried to show her the clippings from the papers but she wouldn't read them. "Art critics are all queers" she said. And she said she thought you were one, too. None of it made any sense. She's just angry about the inheritance.'

'I don't want to know about the money,' Gary had said. 'And I don't want it. If I'm going to be successful and wealthy, I'll do it by being good at what I do. What I do want is Sandy Amies. Forever and ever.'

And he meant it.

And when a little more money starts to come in, he thought, turning right on to the ring-road, *it'll be goodbye to Grayford's Cables. Maybe even goodbye to Basingstoke and hello Paris or Florence . . . on my money.*

He put thoughts of his future out of his mind as he caught up with a slow moving Bedford van which had an oversized Luton box body. He pulled into the fast lane and overtook, catching a glimpse of the driver from the corner of his eye. The man was wearing a black overcoat and a green scarf and he looked half asleep. Their eyes met and the driver pulled a face at Gary and poked out his tongue. For some reason this action sent a thrill of fear through Gary and he hit the accelerator and sailed by the Bedford, thinking that this wasn't going to be his day.

People had been driven off the road in this town, or even stopped and beaten up for no reason whatsoever, and in spite of the visibility being less than a hundred yards in this fog, Gary kept his foot down until the Bedford was lost in the mist behind him. The knowing look that had been on the driver's face as he overtook made him feel extremely uncomfortable.

As he drove up the ring road towards Hackwood road roundabout, he reviewed all his Basingstoke drops, trying to remember if he knew the driver. He couldn't place him at all.

Gary turned right at the Hackwood road roundabout, thankful there wasn't the usual queue which would have meant the Bedford catching him up.

As he left Basingstoke at the next roundabout, he began to relax a little. The guy in the Bedford wasn't a psycho, hell-bent on catching up and killing him after all. He glanced over at the Crest Hotel which was only a vast shape looming in the fog, changed up to fourth and drove slowly up the Alton road.

The fog became thinner about a mile outside of town, putting the visibility up to about three hundred yards. The traffic was light and Gary knew every curve and pot-hole in the road by heart and kept the van at a steady forty five, hoping to make up at least a little time.

The road dipped and he slowed the van for the lazy curve to the left which could have you on the wrong side in the oncoming traffic if you were careless and driving too fast. The van was warm now, the Transit's heater blasting it out. Ford's were famous for their hefty heaters. Gary wound down his window a little, allowing a hint of cool air in, and groped in his pocket for his cigarettes, fighting with the inertia reel seat belt as he did so. The belt always managed to seal up the tops of his jacket pockets.

He lit up as the road started to climb and curve to the right. There was a large lay-by at the start of the hill but this morning it was empty except for a pale and battered workman's caravan which seemed deserted.

It was on the long straight which went past Herriard crossroads about half a mile away from Lasham airfield that Gary noticed the approaching headlights in his rear view mirrors. The vehicle was shrouded by the mist, but with a chill of fear, Gary realised what the vehicle was. It was drawing closer now; not close enough for him to see its colour, but close enough for him to discern its shape. The large square bulk could only belong to the Bedford he had overtaken back in Basingstoke.

His heart began to hammer. Gary butted his cigarette and floored the accelerator, realising that he wasn't going to leave the Bedford behind this time. It was going far too fast, and there was a tight bend ahead which he wouldn't be able to take at more than thirty at the most. The boys from the blackstuff were building a new stretch of tarmac to cut out this sharp bend but they hadn't finished it yet. His pulse sounding in his ears, Gary flew round the right-handed curve, the van leaning precariously under the cable's weight.

He glanced from the road to the rear view mirror and back again several times as the big shadowy Bedford took the bend. The maniac behind the wheel wanted the van to go round the bend faster than Gary had. Too fast for it not to roll, in fact. In spite of this, the Bedford didn't lose contact with the tarmac. It didn't tip up on its side, it didn't skid and slide into the hedge and it didn't do any of the other things Gary had so fondly hoped it would. In fact, the van didn't seem to even notice the sharp bend.

What the fuck is he doing? Gary thought, his blood-pressure rising another notch. *Why is he chasing me?* It was a pointless question. As Gary was well aware, you didn't have to *do* anything at all to upset one of these crazies. Just being in the right place at the wrong time was enough to set them off.

The Ford's engine peaked in third and he slammed the gearstick back into fourth again and stood on the accelerator.

You know what this is, don't you? that snide voice asked him. *If you don't then give it a little thought. You'll soon understand.*

Gary knew exactly what that part of his mind meant. It meant that good old Gertie just might have hired someone to run him off the road. There were two things that stood between her and her daughter's inheritance. Gary West and Sandy Amies.

She wouldn't! Gary told himself, but Gertie was poison on legs. It was quite within the realms of possibility that she *would*.

As he drew level with the junction where the old road met the new, unfinished one, a yellow dumper truck pulled out in front of him, chugging puffs of black diesel smoke into the cool mist. The driver, wrapped up against the cold morning air in a lumberjack jacket and a green and yellow woolly hat, didn't even look down the road before he pulled out.

Oblivious of any cars that might be hurtling round the next bend toward him, Gary threw the van back into third, almost jammed his right foot through the floor with the force as he hit the throttle. He wrenched the wheel to the right, and nearly flew the screaming van around the dumper, his left hand punching the horn button.

In his rear view mirror he saw the navvy give him the finger. The Bedford van was close up behind it. The dumper driver, clearly pissed off with the lunatics in vans that God was presenting him with this cold and foggy morning, pulled the truck out into the middle of the road in a defiant *everyone else stays behind me from now on* gesture.

Well done that man. And thanks, Gary thought shakily as he pulled away from the queue that was rapidly forming behind the dumper.

Several hundred yards further on, Gary turned left and then right onto the little tarmac track that led on to Lasham airfield.

The airfield was about three quarters of a mile long and half a mile wide. The perimeter road ran in a big, easy-cornered rectangle. The main runway bisected the field and ran the full distance, end to end. At the left side of the perimeter road Gary was approaching was Lasham flying club's buildings and bar. Dan Air's hangers and workshops were situated on the far side of the main runway on the right hand side of the rectangle. A half a mile behind the hangars, on a tarmac road of its own, stood the Space Technology satellite tracking station, a small installation of Nissen huts and radar dishes of various shapes and sizes. Gary sometimes delivered there too and although the place was ostensibly a weather satellite tracking station, he fancied that several of the dishes were pointed low over Eastern Europe.

Lasham airfield wasn't an airport and there was no commercial traffic in and out; just gliders from the flying club and the Dan Air planes which flew in to be serviced.

Gary reached the perimeter road where he would have to turn right to go to Dan Air and stopped to light another cigarette. If anyone ever needed a smoke more than he did now, he wanted to know who that person was. He lit up, peering out at the white nothingness that lay before him.

And behind and to either side, too, he added.

The fog on the airfield was thicker than it had been on the road. Much thicker.

You could probably take a pair of scissors and cut slices off it, he thought.

The Transit's headlights reflected back off it, blinding him. Sighing, Gary put the van in gear, crawled forwards and turned right, drawing to a halt when he was on his own side of the road and facing the right direction. Visibility was at an absolute minimum now; he could only just make out the tarmac directly in front of the van and about two feet of the grass on his left. He could see nothing of the bordering fields that surrounded the outside of the airstrip; couldn't even see the other side of the road.

He was about to drive on, following the line where grass met tarmac to guide him when he heard the muffled sound of another vehicle enter the airfield. He looked around and felt the colour drain from his face as the big blue Bedford pulled up alongside of him and stopped.

The driver got out and walked round to him. The guy was tall and had mad hair. He was frowning and grimacing in a way that could be construed as dangerous. Gary didn't like the look of him one little bit. He looked like the kind of guy who would trash you for a single wrong word and not even work up a sweat. And like Michael Jackson had squeaked years ago, Gary was: *a lover, not a fighter.* In a fight — especially with a guy who was several sizes larger than him, just like Mr. Big Blue Bedford was — there could be only one outcome.

Gary was certain all the way down to the marrow in his bones that he was going to be assaulted, either for some sin he didn't even know he'd committed, or because he'd fallen in love with Sandy. He was also painfully aware that in this fog no one would be able to see the attack and that his shouts for help would be hopelessly muffled.

Shit, he thought and did what seemed like the only sensible thing given the circumstances. He rolled up his window, pushed down the button to lock the door and put the van in first gear. This was not something Jean Claude Van-Damme or Arnie would have done, but he didn't get paid as much as they did.

Gary's legs seemed to have turned to jelly. His right foot found the accelerator, but the leg attached to the foot on the clutch was shuddering hopelessly. This didn't bode well for a controlled getaway.

Gary didn't know who'd coined the term *kangaroo petrol* but in the seconds that followed he discovered exactly how apt the description was. The van surged forward, leapt, slowed, surged and stopped when the engine stalled.

Frantically, Gary tried to twist the ignition key, forgetting in his panic that he had to turn it all the way back before starting from scratch again. The net result was that nothing happened.

In his mind, a picture lit: when Mr. Big Blue Bedford reached the window, he was going to pull out a old-time Thompson sub-machine gun from beneath his long coat. He was going to tap on the window with the barrel and say, 'Here's a present from Gertrude Amies to you,' then walk back a few paces and pepper Gary and the van with bullets.

Still fighting with the key — which now didn't seem to want to turn in *any* direction, Gary stared resolutely out of the windscreen. He didn't even look when Mr. Big Blue tapped on the side window — with something that sounded metallic.

Then the fight went out of him. It was too late to get away. Gary drew a deep, shuddering breath and turned his head.

He was surprised by two things, neither of which seemed possible. The first was that Mr. Big Blue hadn't tapped on the window with a gun-barrel at all. Or a crowbar. Or anything resembling a weapon. He'd tapped with the gold signet ring on the middle finger of his left hand — the one that was raised ready to tap again. The second surprising thing was that he had a big, friendly grin fixed on his long face.

'Bloody foggy over here, isn't it?' Mr. Big Blue yelled through the closed window.

Still in shock, Gary rolled his window down and said, 'Can't see shit, can you?' Then he simply ran out of words and stared at the man, open mouthed.

'You got trouble?' the Bedford driver asked.

Only if you start it, Gary thought, and said, 'No, I'm all right.'

'Just wondered. When you went by me in Basingstoke you looked as if you were burning a lot of oil. Left a vapour trail of blue smoke. Thought maybe you'd conked out. Thought I'd stop, y'know, see if I could be of any assistance. Well, if you're okay . . .' He started to walk away.

Ask him who's put him up to this, Gary thought, still believing that the driver was trying to put the frighteners on him, and at the same time telling himself he was being stupid. *Okay then, ask him why he poked his tongue out at you earlier on. Go on, why don't you?*

Because I'm too bloody scared, he answered himself, *that if I do, the terrible truth will be revealed. This guy will suddenly turn into the maniac I thought he was, if I do.*

Halfway back to his big blue Bedford, the driver turned and looked at Gary. The fog shrouded the expression on his face and when he spoke, his voice sounded flat and dead as the fog tried to swallow his words whole. Gary heard them though, before they vanished into the mist. Oh yes, he heard them all right, and over the next few hours they would come back to him time and time again, first in the driver's voice and then in the woman at the filling station's voice.

'Mind you don't get lost in this fog,' the driver called as he walked away.

How did he know? Gary asked himself as the Bedford roared away round the perimeter road. The speed with which the van moved suggested the driver was equipped with his own personal radar vision.

Coincidence, he decided; there was nothing more to it than that; no tie up with the woman at the pumps, no connection with the terrible Gertie. He started the van again (easily this time), eased the gear lever into first and pulled away at something less than a walking pace, his eyes glued to the small area of grass/tarmac border which would lead him to the main runway.

All he would have to do after that was drive in a straight line until the grass reappeared and he would be almost there. He hoped that no one was coming the other way on his side of the road, because the visibility was so bad they would have no chance of seeing each other until it was too late, even with the lights on. He hoped that the Bedford driver would leave at the southern exit; if he came back this way at the speed he'd been doing just now, there was no telling what might happen.

As he crawled along, he found himself thinking of Sandy once more. In the three weeks since he'd met her (and it seemed *much* longer really) and fallen in love with her (at first sight, as incredible and sappy as it might sound) he'd decided that here was the girl he would marry. *Marry*, for God's sake! The word marriage hadn't even been in his vocabulary until Sandy had come along.

But in every good tale of romance there's a fly in the ointment, isn't there? Gary thought. *In this case Gertrudefly.*

Gary didn't really blame Gertie for wanting to keep her daughter to herself. In another three years, Sandy (and Gertie too, if it remained just mother and daughter together) was going to be rich. And who knew: something might *happen* to Sandy and then the money would all be Gertie's. It might have been fantasy, but on several occasions Gary had considered the possibility that Gertie might really do her daughter harm. He'd even dreamed that Gertie had killed Sandy and hidden the body, and like artists the world over, Gary took notice of his dreams.

In spite of his protestations that he didn't want to know about the inheritance, Sandy had told him. It was important that he knew what he was taking on, she'd said. So Gary had given in. The story of the money being made wasn't impressive, really. Not unless your world revolved around finance.

The short version was that Granddad (Gertie's father) had been a whiz kid on the Stock Exchange and had made himself a cool five million from a tiny investment way back in the between war years. Back then, five million was a *lot* of loot. A king's ransom several times over. Serious money indeed. And from then to his death, the money had been wisely invested. The money he'd left when he died — almost twenty five and a half million now — was currently in a trust fund awaiting Sandy's twenty first birthday.

People would kill for a lot less than that.

What was more interesting than the *making of the money* as Sandy called it, were the circumstances surrounding the old boy's death and his will.

According to Sandy, Gertrude had profoundly upset her father in some mysterious way, years before. The result of this was that she'd been cut out of his will. The money, which was rightfully hers, she maintained to this day, went to Granddad Amies' first grandchild. Of course, Gertie hadn't know that her father had changed the will until after the old boy's death. It was a neat trick in Gary's opinion, and one that Dirty Gertie deserved.

As yet, Gary hadn't discovered exactly what Gertrude had done to put her father's nose out of joint in such a big way. It must have been something pretty awful, but Sandy wouldn't tell him what it was. At first she'd denied all knowledge of it, then she'd said that she couldn't tell him what it was. Not now, and possibly, not ever.

All good romances had a fly in the ointment, and all good mysteries contained a letter. There was a letter present in this mystery, too. Sandy's grandfather had written it and lodged it with his lawyers to be hand-delivered to her after his death. The letter, so Sandy said, explained everything.

By this time, Gary had been almost crawling up the walls with curiosity, but Sandy wouldn't tell. The words "all in good time" had been bandied about and when Gary had begun to sulk, Sandy had dropped several enigmatic hints.

All Gary could work out from these was that the old boy had caught Gertie *doing* something. What that thing actually *was* was anyone's guess.

He had asked if Gertie had been caught making a cuckold of her husband (who, he learned later, had vanished off the face of the earth one fine day in June nineteen seventy four) and grinning, Sandy had assured him that it was nothing like that. 'Worse,' she'd said. 'Try harder!'

Gary suspected that the old boy thought Gertie had had something to do with her husband's disappearance, but from the things that Sandy had said, this didn't seem to be all there was to it. It seemed as though everyone was sure Gertie had vanished her husband, but not by murdering him. Perhaps Grandfather Amies thought Gertie had used a much more terrible and arcane method of disposing of her spouse. This was Gary's favourite theory anyway; especially as Gertie fitted the role of The Wicked Witch of the West so well.

Sandy evidently hadn't been convinced by whatever it was her granddad had told her, and until Gary had walked into her life, had been content to stay at home with her mother. So the chances were that Gertie hadn't killed her husband or done anything else awful to him. Gary could easily understand how a man might simply vanish from her life. If he'd been her husband, he would have done likewise.

The curve of the perimeter road was almost finished now, as far as Gary could make out; it seemed to become less and start to straighten. *Another fifty yards*, he estimated, *and I should see the right hand end of the runway appear*. He continued at about a mile an hour for over a minute and although the road had now completely lost its curvature, there was no sign of the landing strip.

Must be going slower than I thought I was, Gary decided. He eased the throttle pedal down just enough to make the speedo needle quiver and move off its stop to between nought and five miles per hour.

Still no runway.

He was having difficulty seeing as far as six feet ahead now and with a start he realised that the windscreen was fogged with condensation. He switched the wipers on, wondering why he hadn't noticed until now. The patch of cracked tarmac he *could* make out, rolled slowly towards him, sliding out from beneath the fog and disappearing under the van.

For a few moments, he entertained the stupid notion that the van was standing still and the road was moving. The fog, lit with the twin glaring beams of his headlights, swirled and billowed as if it was the same patch all the time. It didn't seem to move toward the van at all; just laid there, six feet away and stationary, a heavy woollen blanket that had cut him off from reality.

Must have missed the runway, he thought. *I must have passed it without seeing it. This mist is thicker than I imagined.* He wondered what had become of the Bedford and its driver with the protruding tongue and suffered an involuntary shudder when he remembered the driver's final remark: *Mind you don't get lost in this fog!*

Gary peered out at the weirdest weather he'd encountered in more than quarter of a million miles of driving and wished again that he'd called in sick this morning and had stayed snuggled up to Sandy's warmth.

Soon see the hangars, he assured himself. *Must be nearly there by now.*

The Transit rolled slowly forward.

Five minutes had passed. An entire five minutes. Three hundred seconds. On a stretch of road that should have lasted little more than two minutes, if his estimation of his position was correct.

Obviously it wasn't correct.

Frowning, Gary checked his watch again. Five minutes ago the watch had said five past nine and now it said ten past. That, he *was* sure of. He was also sure the watch was still working properly: he could see the seconds passing by at what seemed to be the right rate. Except that it wasn't *possible* to have spent this long getting from the curve of the perimeter road to the hangars. Even at less than one mile per hour he should have reached the buildings by now.

But I haven't, he pointed out.

Then he realised *why* he hadn't and began to grin at his total stupidity.

You fuckwit! You've turned on to the main runway! You're rolling right down the landing strip! He groped in his pocket for his cigarettes and lit one, smiling and ignoring the rebelling voice in his head that was saying: *Not possible!*

The obvious thing to do was turn around and go back.

Not possible because . . .

He didn't let himself finish, just turned hard right and swung the van round to face the other direction, panicking for a moment when he couldn't find the grass verge on the other side of the runway. He relaxed when it appeared and his mind took advantage of the moment to finish its unwanted statement.

Not possible because to turn onto the runway would have meant a ninety degree left turn, and you didn't make one of those, did you?

'No, I don't think I did,' he agreed, feeling the panic start to rise again. After a few seconds he turned hard right again, found the verge and drove in the direction he'd first been headed in, telling himself that it didn't matter if he *was* going down the runway, nobody was going to land a plane in this weather, were they?

The runway was only a mile long at the most, and when he came to the end he could turn left back on to the perimeter road, couldn't he?

A mile long. That was one minute at sixty, two at thirty, four at fifteen and eight at seven and a half miles an hour. He accelerated slightly, bringing his speed up to ten miles an hour. Now he would know more or less when to expect the end of the runway. He checked his watch which was now nine eighteen and decided that the end of the runway should come up at around nine twenty-five (depending of course on how far down it he had already come).

The tarmac continued to roll out from under the fog and vanish beneath the van, and the reflection of the headlights still dazzled him. He turned them off once, and was left with only the dull whiteness of the swirling fog to look at. And the fog seemed to close in on him, heavy and oppressive. He had to turn them back on when his claustrophobia threatened to make him scream.

Time seemed to have slowed down now. Each digital second that appeared on his watch seemed to take an entire minute to pass by.

Still the road rolled on, its cracked black surface filled with pitch, turning it into a huge scale crazy-paving, the slice of grass at its side, dark green and featureless. Crazy theories started to form in Gary's mind in spite of his attempts to concentrate only on the driving and the time passing.

Nine twenty-five crawled on to the face of his watch and there was *still* no sign of the curve where the runway met the perimeter road. Neither was there at half past. At nine thirty-seven, Gary took the speed up to fifteen miles an hour and started to see things looming up out of the mist at him. He had experienced this phenomenon before when driving in fog and realised that it was only his eyes getting tired and playing tricks on him.

When his Timemaster Quartz (the most reliable timepiece in the world, the blurb had claimed) read nine forty-five and still nothing had appeared except more blacktop and more blacktop, more grass and more grass, Gary began to wonder if he could possibly have reached the end of the runway and negotiated the sharp turn back on to the perimeter road without noticing he'd done it. He was sure that he hadn't turned the steering wheel more than a few degrees either way, so . . .

You couldn't have, could you?

The answer to *that* question, as Groucho Marx would have told him, was, *a duck.*

Gary tried to count back the minutes and review them one by one to see if he could find one in which he'd made that turn. The trouble with driving was that you were apt to abandon conscious thought and drive without thinking; a sort of sub-conscious automatic pilot took over. On plenty of occasions he'd arrived at the Swindon depot, fifty miles away and had no memory whatsoever of the journey. The trip round this airfield had turned out to be pretty much like one of those Swindon trips. Gary couldn't remember making that turn at all.

But the upside is you can't remember not *making it, either,* he thought and tried to summon a smile that wouldn't come. *You'll just have to assume you* did *make it. Anything else is impossible. Either you drove all this way and all this time along a one mile long strip (and that's a liberal estimate if you don't mind my saying so) or you made the turn. If you didn't make the turn, you've gone bananas or . . .*

Gary shut off the internal voice before it had finished. He *had* turned. He checked his watch. It now read nine fifty-five, which was ten minutes steady driving at

Mind you don't get lost in this fog!

fifteen miles an hour and thirty minutes since the end of the runway should have reappeared in his narrow field of vision as a sharp falling away to the left of the grass verge. The verge in question had been running arrow straight ever since the perimeter road's first bend. Logically this was impossible; he remembered turning on to the perimeter road and he remembered the first bend to the left. After that the road straightened, went past the hangars, did another lazy ninety degree turn, them narrowed where it became the property of Space Technology. There was a metal barrier there with all sorts of warnings against trespassing attached, and he would have to have taken the van to the centre of the road to pass through the gap in the middle of it, so he hadn't got down there; he would have remembered losing the grass that guided him. It would have been impossible to have seen the verge from the gap in the barrier, so he wasn't on Space Tech's property.

So where the hell am I? he asked himself.

The tarmac continued to slip beneath the van and Gary began to do mental arithmetic which he hoped would stave off the empty despair rising in him and give him some idea of what had happened.

Thirty minutes at fifteen miles an hour meant seven and a half miles — a child would have had no problem with that one. *What the child* would *have had trouble with though*, Gary thought, *was relating that distance to the size of the airfield*. Even if the field was square (which he was sure it wasn't) and a mile long on each side, he would have had to have driven around it at least twice to travel this far. And that meant eight fairly obvious

Mind you don't . . .

left hand turns

. . . get lost in this fog!

which he certainly hadn't made.

He took a deep breath. 'Okay then, starting from now, I'll time myself and watch the clock. I must have made some sort of a mistake in my calculations. Maybe my watch has gone silly. What's happened is, I've gone down the runway and back up the perimeter road, and now I'm going down the runway again. This time I'll make sure I steer in a straight line for a least a mile. Two if I have to. Sooner or later I'll have to run either off the end of the runway, or off the end of the perimeter road. All I have to do is drive in a dead straight line . . .'

He clamped the wheel firmly and looked away from the grass, peering into the impenetrable mist instead. Ahead of him, fog-phantoms swirled, flew at the van and vanished. Gary tried to keep his mind empty, his speed steady and his hands on the wheel.

Five slow miles later he was still driving in a straight line, and now he was grinding his teeth, trying to stop himself remembering a ridiculous article he'd once read in *Mayfair* magazine.

Except that it didn't seem quite so ridiculous now, did it?

The article had been about a supposed machine called a

Psychotronic Generator which could amplify the power of people who were psychic. If a man could move a dried pea by the power of thought alone, this machine could enable him to move a housebrick. Or maybe something larger. Apparently, the Russians had one and everyone else wanted one too.

It was obvious now to Gary that there was a Psychotronic Generator residing in one of the buildings at Space Technology and while they were testing it out this morning it had gone badly wrong.

'Shut up, you idiot,' he told himself aloud. 'You just got lost in the fog and your watch has gone wrong.'

This theory (especially spoken in a very shaky voice) held even less weight than the science fiction one had. The truth was, Gary didn't have a clue what was happening. The truth was he thought he'd gone stark staring mad.

Because of the odometer on the speedo, he thought. *If you merely got lost in the fog, that must have gone wrong too. And that seems terribly unlikely, doesn't it? The answer isn't a duck at all, it's our old friend insanity. Better painters than you have stepped on to that slippery slope and skidded all the way to the bottom.*

Gary spent the next five minutes wrestling with the panic which had seemingly replaced his blood and was now coursing around his veins, chilling his flesh and trying to paralyse him, making his limbs weigh a ton apiece and slipping steel bands around his chest and throat.

He wanted to stop the van and turn the engine off, stretch out across the seats and go to sleep so that when he woke up he wouldn't be lost on Lasham airfield at all, but snug in his king-sized double bed with Sandy's measured breathing comforting him.

Perhaps he *was* asleep. A tiny ray of hope lit in his frozen heart. Then died when he slapped his face with his right hand. It stung and then died to a warm glow. *That* didn't happen when you were asleep.

Gary laughed then, a little hysterically. It wasn't a pleasant sound and it went on for far too long.

The van rumbled slowly down the endless tarmac.

It was ten past ten by the time Gary got himself under control again. A distant part of his mind wondered what was happening in the *real* world. The real world where there were trees and cars and people and houses and airplane hangars four hundred yards from the airfield entrance.

'This *is* the real world,' he assured himself and that snide part of his mind whispered, *yeah, and I'm a Chinaman!*

And there it was!

Gary gave out a screaming whoop of triumph and punched the air when he saw the Coke can on the edge of the runway. It was just a crushed, empty can, but for Gary it was salvation. It was *proof* that he was somewhere different, that he had indeed travelled some miles and hadn't just been rolling on the spot. One moment its misty red shape was there in front of him, the next, it had vanished under the wheels.

But he hadn't seen it before, so it was *proof!*

In celebration at actually getting somewhere, Gary put his foot down and took the van up to thirty miles and hour, ignoring the excruciating feeling of impending impact.

Three minutes later, and in spite of the fact that Gary was still driving in a dead straight line, the Coke can went by again. This time he thought he saw something dripping from the triangular hole at the top of the can. He was still wondering what it was when he passed the can yet again.

Or another can, he told himself. *What's so unusual about seeing three empty Coke cans?*

At half past ten, Gary did the very thing that all professional drivers dread the most. He dropped off to sleep. It was warm in the cab and the white monotony of the fog and dull rumble of the Transit had half hypnotised him. The adrenaline overdose and the ever-present fear had weakened him. One moment his eyes were heavy and he was thinking about opening the window for some fresh air and the next he was waking up again with a vicious start.

This fresh shock caused a deep ache in the side of his chest. Gary cursed himself, grabbing the left side of his chest with his right hand. It wasn't a heart-attack. He was fit and healthy and relatively young and he'd never suffered shortness of breath . . .

Liar!

. . . or had any kind of chest pain at all, except the odd muscle strain.

I'll have to cut down on the fags, he told himself, glancing at the verge as the Coke can flitted past again.

It's an hallucination, he decided, forcefully, *and so is the stuff you think you can see running from it.*

He busied himself with little tasks as he drove; things he could do that would keep his mind from rebelling. He found an old J cloth in the glove box and cleaned the dust that had accumulated around the speedo dial (thirty miles an hour all right, but the odometer was still telling lies) and the dashboard. Then cleaned the side window and the screen, using physical energy to keep his mind in its place. But like they said, the mind was a monkey, and today, Gary's mind was a monkey on speed. The harder he pinned it down, the more it tried to cartwheel, making his sense of balance desert him. And while he fought to stay the right way up, it whispered obscene things to him about what Gertie had done to her late husband.

It was eleven now by Gary's watch. At some point during the last ten minutes his mind, like a prisoner who has tired of banging against his cell door and finally realises he isn't going to get out, had quietened. Gary was absolutely exhausted. His eyes were heavy again and his body felt like a drained battery.

Gary summoned up a smile and thought, *Okay, there's a good way to get round that particular problem, isn't there?*

He would sleep and drive at the same time.

Well it isn't as if you're gonna hit anything, is it now?

Still the tarmac rolled.

Still the wheels hummed.

The Coke can passed.

Gary took his foot from the accelerator and let go of the steering wheel. The van slowed to a tick-over; in fourth gear this meant a rolling speed of about four or five m.p.h. The van ran true. That was Ford engineering for you. Ninety-five thousand miles on this old dog and it still ran in a straight line when you let the wheel go.

Gary clambered out of the driver's seat and laid down across the double passenger seat. Within thirty seconds he was asleep. Within sixty, he was dreaming.

He was with Sandy in his flat, laughing at some joke she'd told him, probably an obscene one. Gary gathered her up in his arms, crushed her to him and spun her round, enjoying the sensation of her body against his, the touch of her soft cheek against his neck, the way her ribcage moved as she giggled. Then they were kissing and for what must have been the thousandth time Gary was marvelling at the moist warmth of her welcoming mouth, at its special taste. When she broke off the kiss, she smiled at him and said, 'Don't you worry about *her.*'

And then it was night and Sandy was gone and Gary was hiding behind a bush in a large, dark garden watching Gertie, about whom he didn't have to worry. The fact that he could still hear Sandy's words in his head didn't stop his heart hammering, or the fear rising in him. *Get me out of here,* he thought, but he was locked in place and the better part of him wanted to *see* anyway.

Rain was falling. Gary couldn't feel it, but he could see it. Dark clouds roiled in the sky, racing east. Ahead of him, Gertrude Amies was kneeling in the centre of the lawn, facing him but not looking towards him. She was wearing a dark winter coat that was clearly several sizes too large for her and she was busy arranging something on the lawn. Gary couldn't see what it was, but he knew it was something terrible. Something of which Gary was already very frightened.

Gertrude made a final adjustment and gave a nod. She struggled to her feet and peered down at her handiwork, her gnarled old fingers plucking at the buttons on the overcoat while her lips moved as if she were speaking.

A moment later she shucked off the overcoat. Beneath it, she was naked. Wattles of grey flesh hung from her ribs. Her slack breasts reached almost all the way down to her navel. From her navel to her ankles, Gertrude was covered in thick black hair. Gertrude didn't have feet now, she had huge cloven hooves that looked like sawn-off boots. Her hooves were sinking into the lawn under her weight and when she moved, she left cow-sized imprints in the lawn.

And suddenly Gertrude was holding a live chicken in her left hand. She had hold of its neck and was keeping its struggling feet well away from her body. In her other hand she held what looked like a butcher's meat cleaver. On the lawn was a porcelain milk jug and a small red item that Gary couldn't quite make out.

Gary knew what she was then and wasn't surprised. All the veiled hints Sandy had given him, and all the things her Granddad had suspected, fell into place for Gary. Gertie really *was* a witch. Or a demoness, a she-devil.

In a low, powerful voice, Gertrude slowly began to chant. Gary didn't recognise the language, but he didn't need to. The words possessed an intense energy and once spoken, they didn't fade, but hung heavily in the air like living things. And a part of Gary understood them. As Gertrude spoke, the garden seemed to fill with motion that couldn't be seen. It seemed as if the air had suddenly filled with invisible sharks that were circling, waiting for a meal. Waiting for the first drop of blood to be spilled and the feeding frenzy to begin.

Gary looked at the struggling chicken in Gertrude's left hand and then at the darkly gleaming cleaver in her right and he knew that this wasn't the first time she'd done this. Gertrude had done it before. Shortly before her husband had vanished off the face of the earth.

Gary knew he had to stop the blood being spilled if he was to have any chance at all, but like all the best nightmares, this one wouldn't let him move. It would let his fear build to a crescendo that felt as though it would kill him and it would let his aching need for action burn him like a branding iron, but it wasn't going to let him do anything else but watch.

Gertrude raised the cleaver.

Gary tried to look away and failed. But it wasn't going to be so bad, he assured himself, knowing he was lying. A single swipe would cut off the chicken's head and then it would all be over.

But it wasn't going to be. Gary knew this. The circling shark-words in the air communicated that much to him. They didn't want a clean kill, they wanted agony. They wanted to feel life running away slowly, painfully.

Gertrude held out the chicken and slashed the cleaver down the length of its body, splitting it in two from its neck to its legs. The chicken screamed and kicked and beat its wings as its entrails unravelled and swung in the thick air, glistening red and grey.

The movement in the air increased, speeding until it reached a fever-pitch.

Still chanting and summoning up yet more demons, Gertrude held the fluttering chicken over the milk jug, collecting its blood. The liquid that missed the jug and fell on the grass vanished in puffs of white smoke and around Gary, the air thrummed with power.

When the still-kicking bird was drained, Gertie tore off a strip of its innards, fed it into her mouth, chewed and swallowed. Then she held the chicken over her head and began to speak again, offering it up. A moment later, she threw it into the air above her head.

The chicken exploded.

Whatever hit it, hit it hard and from several directions at once. But not a scrap of meat, or a single feather reached the ground. The chicken was consumed as it fell.

And then the shark-words and the things they'd brought had gone and there was only Gertrude, standing on the lawn looking up, her arms raised to heaven. A few moments later she dropped her arms, looked directly towards the spot where Gary stood behind the bush and grinned. Then she picked up the milk jug and the small red thing. As if she knew *exactly* where Gary stood *and* that he hadn't been able to make out what the red thing was, she held it out towards him.

The red thing was an empty Coke can.

As Gary tried to scream, Gertrude poured the blood into the can.

He woke up screaming and clawing at the air, his heart hammering so hard he half expected it to burst out of his chest. Gary sat bolt upright on the passenger seat of the Transit and was just in time to see the coke can flash by again.

It took a long time for him to calm down.

It was midday by Gary's watch and the odometer read 209 miles since he'd started counting. That wasn't possible if he had been rolling at five miles an hour, but there it was on the clock. The fuel gauge showed that there was just under a quarter of a tank of petrol left. The fog remained thick and silent.

Gary's mind seemed to have come loose in his head. He was unable to think logically anymore. None of this could be happening. None of it was possible. And yet here he was, living it all. He'd used most of the petrol covering over two hundred miles on a stretch of tarmac only a mile long at the most.

It doesn't make sense.

But it did make sense. It did if the dream was true. If Gertie had arranged his disappearance.

But that was only a dream! he protested.

'And so is this . . . I hope,' he muttered.

Gary stopped the van, took it out of gear and yanked up the handbrake. He would walk to the hangars. He got out of the Transit, leaving the engine running and the lights on; maybe if he couldn't find the hangars the sound of the engine and the lights would help him find his way back here.

Outside, the fog swept over him, hugging him with its moist, chilling arms; pressing itself to him as if it wanted to become part of him. He fought off the feeling of constriction, the screaming claustrophobia, and took a few paces away from the van across the tarmac.

When he reached the point where the runway (or perimeter road, or whatever it was) met the grass on the other side, Gary could barely make out the shape of the van, or see the lights. The engine was muffled by the clammy blanket and hardly audible. He walked on to the grass and his feet were immediately soaked by the cold moisture. He took five more paces and turned. The van had been swallowed up. There was no sign of it at all now.

Gary emptied his mind and set off at a steady pace toward where he thought the Dan Air buildings were.

He walked for half an hour across cold, wet grass. Then for an hour, the fog pressing down on him. Still there was no sign of the hangars. After another ten minutes he turned back, knowing he would never find the van now, and asking himself how he could have been so stupid. He hadn't even left tracks he could follow back.

When he heard the dull thrumming of the Ford's engine it was six in the evening by his watch. He was cold, wet, hungry, thirsty and emotionally drained. He sat in the van and sounded the horn until he thought his head would split open. Then he smoked a cigarette and sounded it again, one long, painful tone that made his ears ring and his brain threaten to go insane right now if he didn't stop. Then he wept. Then he screamed himself hoarse.

When all that had failed, he prayed.

Some time later he found himself calling out for his Sandy. A while after that, he realised he had bitten his tongue badly while cursing Gertie.

The petrol gauge was on the red low-tank-contents warning now. Gary drove away, full throttle, the engine screaming as he worked up through the gears.

Sixty. Seventy. Then eighty, eighty-five.

The tarmac flashed out of the fog in a blur of black and criss-crossed lines of pitch. The green verge remained flat and featureless.

The Timemaster read seven thirty-three when the Ford ran out of petrol.

Gary put his foot on the clutch and knocked the van out of gear, letting it roll until it stopped.

He remained motionless in the cab for three hours, his mind reeling.

It should have been dark then; at half past ten in October it should have been dark.

But it wasn't.

Gary got out of the van and stood in the damp fog in the dimming beam of the headlights, smoking a cigarette and wondering if the ex Mr. Amies was here in this phantom zone with him somewhere, and if Sandy would believe what was in her granddad's letter now.

'You won, Gertie,' he muttered bitterly as he began to walk down the foggy runway, away from the lifeless van. 'You got your own way again, you bitch!'

At midnight it was still light; if you could call this light. It was more twilight. Gary had smoked all his cigarettes and still he walked.

At one fifty the following morning

Mind you don't get lost in this fog!

Gary sat down on the wet tarmac. He was exhausted. He listened but there was no sound. He strained his eyes, trying to see through the minimum visibility mist, but there was nothing to see.

It was still light at three a.m. when Gary wandered off the runway on to the grass, his leg muscles hardly holding him upright. His feet had blistered from the walking and the blisters had burst and rubbed until they bled, so he pulled off his socks and shoes and let the damp grass cool his feet. At four a.m. he could walk no more and sank to his knees, utterly defeated. He sprawled forward and let the grass chill his face.

Then he saw something red from the corner of his eye.

A Coke can, crumpled and dripping.

He crawled over to it and picked it up, inverted it. Cold and half congealed blood ran from the opening.

He looked at the can for a long time. Then he got up again and walked.

MICHAEL MARSHALL SMITH

DIFFERENT NOW

She was out of the door before Chris had time to grasp what was going on. What had started as a run of the mill argument had suddenly escalated out of control, bored misery giving way to alarm. Then the flat seemed very empty, and she was gone.

Until moments before it had just been the usual depressing bickering, the holding up of past hurts for inspection, and he'd been wondering how much longer he was going to defend his corner. There had been a time when he'd been prepared to stay up all night, had felt genuinely bound to hang on in there until the swapping of grievances could be steered towards a new compromise. A time when he could not have contemplated sleeping next to her unless they did so as friends.

But *so many nights*. For a few months or weeks things would be alright, and then suddenly the familiar slow spiral towards confrontation would start. And she would shout, and he would mutter: both completely in the right, and both utterly in the wrong. These days he didn't have the energy to argue until dawn when he knew any truce was only temporary; or the stomach to put up with melodrama when what they needed was discussion. When the point of diminishing returns had clearly been reached he usually went to bed, to be joined an hour later by Jo, vicious and sniffling. The next day would be very unpleasant, the day after less so. Sooner or later both would apologise so they could start living their lie for a little longer, go on inhabiting the same fragile world.

Chris grabbed his keys and ran for the door. He tripped over the pile of newspapers left in the middle of the floor by leave-it-where-it-drops Jo and almost fell, but his beat of irritation was perfunctory. This was very bad. He'd looked at her and for the first time seen that he didn't know her any more, that he was in the room with an utter stranger. Suddenly it hadn't been just another row, a chance for both to be flamboyantly hurt: the cord which had always somehow remained between them had lain there, exposed, waiting for the axe.

Fumbling to lock the door Chris dropped his keys and swore. He didn't like the note of slight hysteria in his voice. It wasn't like him. However loud the shouting, he always stayed distant enough to watch, even when he was centre stage. Stuffing the keys in his jeans he leapt down the steps to the hall four at a time.

The outside door was open, swaying slightly from the strong wind outside. Rain spattered the familiar black plastic bags habitually left in the hall by the tenants of the downstairs flat, who he suspected were also responsible for the grey camper van which had sat outside on four flat tires since before he'd moved in.

He shouted at their door with all his strength, throat rasping: 'Oh what a surprise: someone's left some fucking rubbish in the hall!'

Frightened by his fury he bolted out of the door and ran to the end of the short path, wildly looking up and down the street. All he could see was waving branches and wet moonlit patches. He'd hoped that she would grind to a halt just outside the house, but clearly she'd got further. Swearing desperately he trotted back and pulled the door shut before heading out onto the pavement.

She couldn't have had much more than two minutes' start on him, which made it very likely that she'd gone right. Though it was theoretically possible she could have covered the two hundred yards or so to the end of the road on the left side, it seemed unlikely.

Chris jogged to the nearer corner and stood at the insignificant cross-roads, straining his ears for the sound of footsteps. All he heard was the sound of distant traffic on the Seven Sisters Road: the featureless cramped streets of terraced houses facing him were silent apart from the sound of rain on swaying leaves. He called her name and heard nothing more than the thin sound of his own voice. Head down and shoulders hunched against the wind-whipped rain he trotted out of Cornwall Road, across the small junction and into the road that began the most direct route to the station.

After a couple of minutes he stopped, panting slightly. There was still no sign of Jo, and there were now a couple of choices as to which way she might have gone. Assuming she would have been walking towards the station to head for home, she should have taken the left fork — but she had only walked the route a couple of times, and always with him. Chances were that she wouldn't have had any clear idea of the way, and the alternative road was actually slightly wider than the one which led to the station. Chris had a sneaking suspicion that faced with the choice she might have assumed that was the best way to go. Not that there was any real way of telling: he didn't know if she had headed for the station at all.

Shivering, simultaneously wishing he'd thought to bring a coat and realising that going back for one would lose him any chance of catching up, Chris headed for the wider road, walking quickly.

It was impossible to see very far down the road, as it curved quite sharply round to the left, presenting a blank face of wall broken by occasional squares of light. From his level all Chris could see was patches of ceiling and snatches of curtain. It seemed very easy to believe there was no-one on any of the rooms, that they were empty and always had been. In one ground floor room a black and white television flickered by itself, somehow making the sight even less hospitable than the windows that were dark and reflective black. Disturbed, Chris turned his attention back to the pavement. Somewhere, a long way off, a car horn sounded.

Suddenly he saw a movement some way ahead, and hurried forwards. It was difficult to see very clearly in the steadily falling rain, and hard to see what might be there against the pocks and puddles in the pavement. A shape moved out from behind a car, but it was only a small dog, white and shivering. Wiping rain from his face Chris trotted up to the next junction.

The streets all looked the same. All bent slightly, all had pavements torn apart through years of patching, and all looked orange and shiny black with water, the patterns of light changing as branches of grey leaves slashed in front of the streetlights. There was still no sign of Jo, no sign of anyone. Chris picked a road at random and headed down it.

He was far from sure what would happen when he found her. Nothing like this had ever happened before. If she'd headed for home, which would involve a tube to a mainline station and then an hour on a train, that was bad. If she'd not even been thinking as clearly as that, but had just set off, that was even worse, given her paranoia about walking any streets late at night. Either way it seemed possible that things might finally have broken down, and he realised suddenly that he didn't want them to. However bad things might be between them, she was the only person who really knew him. And more than that, he loved her.

Another turning, another road. Chris felt increasingly desperate, felt an already bad situation getting away from him, and he was now far from sure where he was. Not having a car meant that he didn't know the area very well, his movements restricted to walking to the station and the nearest shops. He thought that the station was probably still over to the left, but when he started to choose left turns the roads bent and doglegged, bringing him back or taking him in the wrong direction, through rows and rows of three storey brick punctuated by sheets of dark glass.

Finally he stopped and rested, hands on his knees and chest aching. After a few moments the pain felt at once less urgent and more deep-seated, like the feeling he remembered from after horrific cross-country runs at school. Then, too, the rain had sheeted down, looking as if it had settled in for ever. Still leaning on his knees Chris raised his head, squinting into the lines of water.

Someone was standing at the top of the street. Chris straightened, and took a pace forward. About fifty yards away, motionless and grey behind the rain stood a woman of Jo's size and shape. It had to be Jo. Feeling a lurch of compassion, Chris walked quickly towards her, and then started to trot.

As he neared her he slowed to a walk. She was facing away from him, shoulders slumped, heedless of the rain which coursed down her soaking hair and clothes. She made no movement as he approached and Chris felt tears welling up: Jo hated the rain, and there are always things about someone which, however trivial, make them more them than anyone else.

He stood at her side for a moment, and then gently touched her shoulder. For a moment there was no response, and then she looked up slowly, timidly.

It wasn't Jo.

Chris took a step backwards, confused. The woman continued to look at him as rain ran down her face, not staring, just including him in her gaze.

'I'm sorry, I thought . . .' Chris stopped, unable to finish the obvious sentence, transfixed by her face. It wasn't Jo, but it so nearly was. The face was so similar, so *equal* to Jo's face, and yet something was different. He took a few more steps backwards, shrugging to show his harmlessness, and started to turn away.

As he did so the woman turned too, and he caught a glimpse of her face in three-quarter view. The woman began slowly to step through the puddles, heading up a road he'd already tried. Chris stared after her, and knew what it was about her face.

It was the face of someone he didn't know. The face of someone you catch sight of across a room, the face of a stranger you don't know yet, a face before you've seen it thousands of times, loved and kissed every inch of it, seen its every smile and frown. It was the face that Jo would always have had had he not plucked up his courage on a night four years ago, and walked across the room to timidly make her acquaintance.

Had he not met her and loved her, had she not become his world, she would always have had that face. The woman's face was Jo's in a world where they'd never met.

Chris started up the road after her, just as she turned the corner. Anxious to keep sight of her he slipped on a patch of lurid moss glistening blackly on the pavement. Narrowly avoiding a sprawling fall he awkwardly maintained his balance, twisting his knee. Slowing to a fast lurch he painfully rounded the corner in time to see the flap of a coat disappearing from sight. He rubbed his knee for a moment and then set off in pursuit.

He hadn't tried this particular road, and didn't recognise it or the turning. Wiping water from his face he trotted into the sheets of rain, feeling the silence behind the hissing patter of drops. He slipped again navigating the turn at speed but kept his balance. At the end he stopped, chest heaving again. She had disappeared.

There was no obvious way she could have gone. The other three roads all stretched straight for many yards before curving, and it should have been possible to see her whichever way she'd taken. Chris glanced about wildly, peering into the rain. Then he noticed something. The road opposite was Cornwall Road.

Bewildered, he took a few steps forward, into the middle of the road. He turned and looked the way he'd come. The road was unfamiliar, curving a wholly different way to the road he walked down to the station. The road that cut across was different too: it was narrower and had more trees. The whole junction was different, and yet . . .

He walked slowly into Cornwall Road. There, about ten yards up on the left, was the familiar white gateway, the entrance to Number 7, and light fell weakly down from the upper window. Proceeding forwards like a nervous gunfighter, casting frequent glances behind, Chris tried to marry the two views in his mind. But they wouldn't gel, couldn't.

Cornwall Road now joined with different roads, and the grey camper van was gone.

He pushed open the dark green gate and stepped up to the door. Through misted glass he saw that the hallway was clear. He turned and looked at the entryphone. The label by the topmost buzzer said "Price", which was not his name. He wondered briefly where Jo was now, but already the name seemed unfamiliar, ordinary, like that of someone he'd met once at a party, some years ago. His key did not turn the lock, was made for a different door.

Chris took a last look at the house and then turned and faced the rain, pausing for a moment before stepping out into it. He had no idea where he lived, who he loved, where he should go.

Things were different now.

RHYS H. HUGHES

THE PURLOINED LIVER

'Purloin My Liver,' said Edgar.

'I beg your pardon?' Annabel frowned and steered around the carcass of a sheep. Flies rose in a dark cloud.

'The village.' Edgar folded the map and gestured at the collection of thatched cottages. 'Purloin My Liver. An old market town. Stop in that pub and I'll buy you a drink.'

Annabel assented and parked off the road. As she stepped out into bright sunshine, she gazed at the signpost that hung from the side of the building. 'Odd name for a pub!'

Edgar shook his head. 'We're in the sticks now. This is rural heritage.' He followed her gaze upwards. 'The Plucked Eyeball? Sounds rather quaint to me. I like it.'

Annabel shrugged and followed him inside. The bar was deserted and gloomy. The warped beams of the low ceiling forced them to crouch down to avoid striking their heads. 'Anyone home?' Edgar cried.

The barman appeared from the cellar. 'What'll it be?' He was a grotesque figure, obese and hunched, a meerschaum pipe in the shape of a screaming skull protruding from his mouth. His dirty moustache drooped like dying vines. A single, bulging, working eye rolled endlessly in its socket; the other dangled loose on his cheek.

'What do you have on cask?' Edgar inquired mildly.

The barman rested his gnarled hands on the unlabelled pump-handles. 'Leprous Pustule, Purple Haemorrhage, Garrotted Baby, Witch Burn, Eat My Cousin and Twisted Ear.' He turned to another part of the bar. 'This is Severed Torso, a sour cider. Bloodless Zombie is a pale ale.'

'A pint of Twisted Ear please,' said Edgar.

'Half a Severed Torso for me,' added Annabel.

The barman drew the pints. 'Travellers eh? Off to the Fair at Grind My Bones? Should be good this year. A wicker man stuffed with virgins. Reverend Cleaver grew them himself: real virgins!'

Edgar remained nonchalant. 'Sounds fine.' He knocked back his pint. 'We'll give it a try.' He seized Annabel's glass, drained that one as well and handed money over the counter. 'Have one yourself.'

'Very kind of you sir, don't mind if I do!' The barman poured a foul green mixture. 'Crucified Toad. I brew this one myself.' Instead of placing the glass to his lips, he held it under his cheek and lowered his prolapsed orbit into the murky depths. Once immersed, the eyeball took on a life of its own; it rose and fell in slow circles, refracted to hideous dimensions by the viscous fluid.

Outside again, Annabel smirked. 'What an odd fellow!'

'Not at all; we're in Shropshire now,' Edgar reminded her. 'Look, sorry for hurrying you on. But I'd hate to miss that wicker man. These are real country ways! Cream teas and brutal prejudices!'

Annabel started the engine and pulled out onto the road. 'What's so special about burning virgins? Why not teetotallers or bank-managers or poets? Why not travellers for that matter?'

Edgar chuckled softly. 'It's just that virgins are flammable. Most other people aren't. It's like pebbles and coal.' He consulted the map. 'Grind My Bones is the next village along. Left at the fork.'

'I see.' Annabel turned a sharp left and followed the road between towering hedge-rows. Conditions grew steadily worse; the car began to bounce and shudder. She cleared her throat. 'What did your pint taste like? Mine tasted like squeezed abdomen.'

'I know.' Edgar nodded to himself. 'Mine was sort of waxy. Real ale, you see. None of that fizzy rubbish we get in the city.' He leaned out of the window. 'I can't see any wicker man. I can't hear any virgins screaming either. They do scream, don't they?'

'Perhaps they just whimper.' Annabel cursed as the road became a mud track. They reached a dilapidated farm-house and saw it was a dead-end. 'We must have come the wrong way.'

'That's impossible. Stop the car and I'll ask directions.' Edgar waited for Annabel to pull up and then jumped out of his seat. The front door of the farmhouse was covered in human hands nailed to the rotting wood. Edgar prised one of these hands loose and rapped on the door with it. Bolts slid back and a thin man peered out.

'Yes?' The man blinked at Edgar. His eyelids worked upwards; his eyes had obviously been put on upside-down.

'Is this Grind My Bones, or anywhere near it?' Edgar asked. 'We're off to see virgins burn and smoulder.'

The man sighed sympathetically. 'This is Applaud My Death. You must have taken the wrong turning on the road.' He squinted at the map Edgar offered him. 'Oh no, you don't want to be trusting them old things. The men who draw them are liars.'

'Really?' Edgar rubbed his jaw.

'Besides,' the thin man continued, 'you'll be lucky to see anything roast today. The wicker man's been cancelled. Reverend Cleaver's virgins all caught the pox and died. He hasn't been able to rustle up any more. Why do you think I'm at home?'

A sudden idea struck Edgar. He whispered something to the thin man. The emaciated fellow chuckled and rubbed his palms together. 'In that case you'd better come in and have a bite to eat. I've got some Minced Grandmother in the pantry, or you can have Basted Forehead.'

'What's the traditional local dish?' Edgar asked.

'Shepherd's Pie with vegetables. Real shepherds: crook, smock and dog. Watch the splinters. The vegetables are brain-dead poachers. Or you can have Poacher's Pie with brain-dead shepherds.'

Edgar walked to the car and returned with Annabel. They followed the thin man into the interior of the farm-house. They sat down at a table in the kitchen while their host rattled pots and pans over the stove. 'This is real living!' Edgar enthused. 'Honest food and honest folk. They really know how to force agricultural labours between pastry here! No corners cut; the whole labourer, with a cheese topping!'

'Sounds grand.' Annabel licked her lips. She picked up the knife and fork before her. The knife was fully twelve inches long, a vicious blade encrusted with blood. The fork had a tongue impaled on each of its cruel tines. She tentatively licked one; it was a male tongue. Edgar glared at her and she blushed bright red.

'Hussy!'

The meal was astonishingly filling. It was washed down with glasses of Adam's-Apple Cider. The thin man disappeared for some minutes to make a phone-call. Edgar and Annabel could hear him mumbling something in the hallway. Edgar covered his smile with a grimace picked from the pie. Annabel shook hands with her meal. 'Stop playing with your food!' Edgar roared. He belched a red belch. 'Yum!'

Eventually, the fellow rejoined them. 'Well that's settled then. Are you ready for desert?'

Annabel shook her head. 'We'd better be off, really. We're just passing through, you see; on our way to Stafford to visit relatives. We thought it would be nice to make a detour through Shropshire, rather than taking the motorway.'

'Nice?' The thin man seemed confused. He pulled at his forelock, the one strand of hair that remained on his head. 'Is that a foreign word?' He brightened. 'The road between Impale My Dog and Heretic On Pyre is blocked. You won't reach the border by nightfall.'

Edgar reached out and placed a hand on her arm. 'We don't want to cause offence. Let's just stay a little longer.'

Annabel shrugged and assented to desert. It turned out to be a type of Spotted Dick — though the thin man insisted it was called Diseased Tom. As she ate, she could not fail to notice the way Edgar and her host kept glancing anxiously at the clock on the mantelpiece.

Edgar make a small cough. 'Have some more, my dear.'

'No thank you,' she replied, but the thin man had already ladled more of the crusty pudding onto her plate. He held up a jug within which something quite foul stirred sluggishly.

'Clotted?' he inquired.

She shook her head. After she had devoured this second helping, they sat in silence for a while. She rapped her fingers impatiently on the table. Edgar and her host cleared their throats and kept looking at the time. The thin man stood over by the window and peered through the grimy glass. 'He should be here by now.'

'Who?' Annabel demanded. She frowned at Edgar, who affected not to notice and pretended to be suddenly interested in the condition of his fingernails. 'What's going on?'

'Perhaps he's had an accident. Reverend Cleaver is a poor driver at the best of times. I told him not to fit those scythes on the wheels of his tractor. Won't fit down the lanes, I said. Would he listen? Not on your life! I bet he's mangled a cow.'

'What's going on?' Annabel repeated in a firm voice. She rose from her chair and moved towards the door. Without thinking, she kept the long blood-encrusted knife in her hand.

'Sit down.' There was desperation in Edgar's voice. 'Please don't spoil things! We may never get another chance like this one. This sort of life is dying out. Heritage!'

Annabel snorted. 'Well you can stay if you want. I'm off.' She reached into her pocket for her car-keys and dangled them in front of him. His eyes grew wide with a sudden panic.

'Wait for me!' he cried.

As they left, the thin man turned his face towards them and nodded courteously. But there was bitter disappointment in his strange eyes. 'Pleased to meet you. Come again some time. Visitors are always welcome at Applaud My Death. Well farewell! Unsafe journey!'

Annabel climbed into her car, watched in mordant amusement as Edgar scurried in beside her, and roared off. She placed the long knife on the dashboard. They bounced back down the lanes they had driven up. 'What's going on?' she asked.

'Nothing!' Edgar squirmed uneasily on the seat. Before long, they came across a tractor lying on its side in a ditch. A broad man dressed in a black cassock, with a dog-collar, was kicking the exposed engine. Blades and bovine flesh lay tangled together.

Annabel slowed the car and wound the window down. 'Can we help you reverend?' She was astonished when the huge figure turned round with a mouth full of highly imaginative oaths.

'I was off to Applaud My Death,' he said, when he had recovered his composure, 'but ran into this ridiculous creature. Harry Spleen rang me earlier to tell me that a travelling couple were sitting in his kitchen. The woman is a virgin, apparently.'

'I see. Well we can't help you there, I'm afraid. We don't know any virgins.' She stepped on the accelerator and screeched away. Back on the main road, she pulled into a lay-by and turned to face Edgar. 'You told that thin man I was a virgin! How could you?'

Edgar was apologetic. 'I'm sorry. It's just that I've never seen a wicker-man before. The chance was too good to miss.'

'But it's a lie; I'm not a virgin!' Annabel shook her fist at him. 'I might not even have burned properly. What would you have done then? Siphoned some petrol from my car?'

Edgar laughed. 'They wouldn't really have set you on fire. All that is just a metaphor. Country-speak. You don't really believe that they burn virgins round here? You'll be telling me next that you think all these place names actually mean what they say.'

'Don't they?'

'Of course not!' Edgar wiped tears of mirth from his cheeks. 'What? Purloin My Liver and Grind My Bones and Applaud My Death? They're just colourful similes. Like the names of the drinks and the food. It's all an elaborate act. Tradition, you see.'

'Well the landlord of the Plucked Eyeball had obviously had his eyeball plucked. And that Shepherd's Pie really did taste of smock and crook. How do you account for that?'

'Coincidence. Anyway what about Purloin My Liver and Applaud My Death? Nothing happened in any of those places that could possibly be linked to their names.'

'Well your liver was stolen for a start.' Annabel blinked and clucked her tongue. 'I saw it happen.'

'What?' The shadow of a doubt crossed Edgar's face. His fingers prodded his side. A sudden horror enveloped his features. He gazed at Annabel with terrified eyes. 'Where?'

'In the pub. A dwarf stole it. I thought you knew.' She picked up the knife from the dashboard, held it up to the sunlight for a moment, and then thrust it deep into Edgar's side. She worked it backwards and forwards and then pulled it out. No blood followed. She pointed at the gaping wound and the empty space beyond. 'See?'

'It's true!' Edgar was incredulous. He pulled the wound open and thrust his fingers in. After some minutes of groping around within, he gulped and clutched at Annabel. 'But without a liver I'll die!'

'Of course.' Annabel returned the knife to the dashboard and once again started the ignition. 'Perhaps I can sell your body to a local brewery.' This time she made no attempt to avoid the carcass of a sheep that lay in the path of her car.

Edgar went into convulsions and began moaning. A little while later he fell silent. Reaching over, Annabel checked his pulse and smiled. Then she took both hands off the steering-wheel for an instant and burst into spontaneous applause.

STEVE SAVILE

MEEK

A blackboard.
Chalk and dust resting in the gutter beneath.
You reach out, experimenting with a basic pincer-grip. Clasping.
Relaxing. Clasping.
The chalk feels odd.
They are all talking behind your back.
They can't know how much you hate them.
Your lips twitch into a tight grin as you write: "HOW TO DI" in block
capitals, and stop. Spelling is not your forte.
You turn to face the class . . .

Meek sat in the old rocker, feet up on the seat, knees tucked under his chin, arms wrapped around his shins. The dead lay in pools of faded print on the bare floorboards of his council flat. Seventeen lives stripped to memories and celluloid, his own sweet Jenny somewhere among them. He had cried his tears for her and them, and now he rocked. The motion was strangely therapeutic. He could understand how idiots drew comfort from clutching their legs to their chest and just rocking, rocking, rocking.

A cutthroat razor was sheathed in the split grain of the chair's leg — a curious way to protect the blade, but an effective one nevertheless.

The flat was a mess. After Jenny's death Meek had let the place run to seed, and the backlash, fuelled wholly by his anger, had been suffi-cient to see the carpets ripped up from the floor and entire sheets of wallpaper torn down from the walls. Only a few stubborn deadman's curls clung to the plasterwork where he had grown subdued, washed out, dissatisfied with aggression as anger and its pollutants drained out of his system. Now the walls were a patchwork of newspaper articles and paint splashes, a feast of unwholesomeness; grotesqueries lovingly recreated or selected from glossy magazines and journals, cut out and pasted over the cracks in his life.

Oh, Jenny . . . Sweet, loving Jenny . . .

The music from the compact disc had shuffled into silence, yet to begin again in its ceaseless round of repeats. So, for a moment at least there was no sound but the steady, shallow rise and fall of Meek's breathing. No intrusion from the outside world. He listened to that instinctive rhythm, painfully aware of its fragility. Meek remembered Jenny, how easily, how very, very easily the fire of her life had been extinguished.

The centrepiece above the coaldust fire was a crucifix rising from the ashes into flames, the crosspiece holding scales piled high with gold coins on one side and a litter of bodies on the other. The body of the crucifix was an elaborate intermeshing of carvings. No simple paint here, the artist had taken a chisel to the stonework and engraved as much suffering as any one man could hope to understand into a collage of faces and bodies writhing around the stump of a religion he had no more use for. The result was both repulsive and compelling. It craved the eye's attention whilst demanding the stomach's rebellion.

The world outside the window was dour and gloomy. The peculiar passage of streetlight and moonlight through the glass transformed the dead limbs of the sycamore in the garden into a man dying in the moonlight on the hardwood floor.

And Meek had chosen to make his home in this strange shrine. Somehow, home had become an elusive intangible. The man on the floor died countless deaths within the phases of the moon and the sun. New faces joined those already doomed to Meek's disturbing gallery. Only the streetlight remained constant, and the more things changed around it, the more things trapped within it stayed the same.

With the exception of the rocker, the room was empty of any furnishings; a television and video recorder stood on bare floorboards in the corner, the coaxial aerial cable looping its way back up to the window like some bleached umbilicus. Likewise, the stereo rested on the floor beneath the window, its own serpentine cord trailing back to the same powerpoint. Three brass door knobs lay on the mantelpiece beside a grass stained trainer. The other shoe was propped up against the gas fire, drying out redly around the man-made upper.

Inside his head Meek saw a girl's face drying out too, a ribbon cut down one cheek by a Stanley knife, a peg of matchstick spliced between the two slicing blades to make the gash unstitchable. Days-old blood the colour and consistency of rust congealed around the cut. Meek imagined the knife, cutting, cutting . . . It set the ghost of a shiver chasing up the ladder of his vertebrae. Cutting, cutting . . . There was more than just a face's worth of blood inside his head though, more that one track of bloody tears. The blades had carved and sliced marking their passage across the flat surface of her belly, down to the vee between her legs, across her lips and around the moons of her buttocks. The blades had carved their own faces into her back before they disappeared inside to lay her open.

You stare them down, all of their hungry faces.

They look to you for something you can't give them because it isn't there inside you to give.

They look to you for guidance.

They look to you as an example.

You hate them. All of them. You hate them almost as vehemently as you pity them.

Your class.

Your chosen, lucky few.

Such delights you have to show them.

Such sweet lessons for them to learn . . .

From nothing the singer's voice started up again. He had lost count of how many times he had heard her say she wanted to spit in their faces but she was afraid of what that might bring . . . No, that wasn't true. He had never started counting, not even when he set the repeats going, two days after Jenny. Jenny had been gone six months now. Six months against the thirteen years since she had first smiled her "butter-wouldn't-melt-in-here-lover' smile. They had knocked on his door at three o'clock that Saturday morning to say her body had been found in the Dene. They didn't tell him, not at first, but he knew she had been interfered with. Violated. Chewed up and spat out. Meek had identified her and come home to be by himself. His balance was precarious. For weeks he had haunted the streets around the Dene, grabbing complete strangers out from the crowd to demand an answer to his: 'Why?'

They looked at him, each and every one of them, as if he were a lunatic. There was *real* fear in their tiny eyes. A skitter to the movements directed by their tiny minds. Now that was something to behold.

From there, the first cutting and the first picture on the wall were a logical progression for a mind teetering on the verge of self destructive oblivion. Meek owned seventeen dead so far. They were his. Their eyes stared out from the montage of cuttings strewn across the floor. Eyes glazed over by the wintry bleakness that so well described death. Letters and names had been carved into the wall of remembrance, landmarks to the most hateful kind of cruelty. He knew all of their names. Knew the contours and texture maps behind all their features. Meek talked to them sometimes, assuring them that they weren't forgotten. Not by this man. They were his to carry next to his heart. He talked to them. Loved them so they could never be lonely.

After Jenny, Meek had walked into the newsagent's beneath the viaduct spanning the furthest corner of the Dene and seen the covers of the tabloids. Jenny's smiling face. Their words. WOMAN BRUTALLY MURDERED. He had reached down and taken one from the top of each pile, collecting her reduced form. Celluloid and later, memory. At the corner he had paid with a damp five pound note, the secret inside him burning to shock the old man out of his closeted, comfortable respectability: 'I did this. This was me.' He felt compelled to say.

But there was no ownership for this. No recognition for a murderer's sick artistry. Though his name was on everyone's lips the name that lingered there was not his own. The name they whispered behind the backs of their hands was not Meek. Hushed voices venerated another, the one they knew only as the Salvation Savage in deference to the first in a series of headlines run by the local newspaper: VICTIM OF SAVAGE MURDER FOUND IN SALVATION ALLEY! Sweet Bethany, his first victim. Nine. Innocent and painfully trusting. Soft and beautiful. She held his hand as he guided her out of the lights. He stole her eyes so he might once again see the world as an innocent. He took all of their eyes, hungry for their perspectives. They were in a mason jar on the floor beside his sleeping bag. Eyes of every hue, staring wildly out of the glass jar, thirty-four orbs floating in saline.

A month later, and despite the protestations of his principal, Meek had resigned his position as English Teacher at the local comprehensive. Everyone had been so supportive it had made him sick. They all sincerely believed they understood how he felt, but how on earth could they? They offered him trite words of sympathy: How could something so ghastly happen to such a nice — *normal* — person? Meek wanted to yell at them until they understood that even normal people were capable of the worst sorts of atrocity. He hated them for not being capable of understanding. Sarah Byrne, the maths relief even went so far as to offer him sex as if it might somehow ease the pain. Meek took it. Used her like the meat she offered herself as. Chewed her up and spat her out the moment she threatened to become addictive.

You hold your audience rapt, captivated by your insights.

You lay the unfortunate creature on the polythene, ready to unmake it before your class.

It is kicking, screaming. You pull its hind legs apart. Press down on its neck to pin it to the table.

It knows.

There is pity in your eyes, though there is no humanity in your lesson. No flavoured sugar for the poor rabbit.

You hypnotise yourself with your own lesson, desensitised to the sickness of the scene by its familiarity, suturing the wounds as you dice. Your scalpel paints a bloody mosaic on the polythene for as long as the slow dissection progresses . . .

He was a curious reflection of his surroundings, running to seed as his interest in the outside world waned. Listening to Crucify, that painfully strange song by the American girl, Meek pushed himself out of the rocker and grabbed a still glowing coal from the fire. He dragged it across the wall as if he were somehow chalking a representation of the abyss line with it. Meek knew which side of the line his kind of monster fell.

Into the darkness.

The coal seared it creases into his palm until he couldn't stand to hold it any longer. The scar was like a mouth in the flat of his hand. Meek looked helplessly at it as if expecting some words of wisdom or chastisement to issue from the wound. Some words of magic. He hovered, anticipating Ascension. The wound was silent, it had to be. It wasn't a sign or a Messiah, it was a burn. Nothing more.

Meek wandered through to the bedroom. The decor in the room was a menagerie of reds and blacks. There was no more furniture in this room than in the lounge; a clear polythene sheet spread out over the bare floorboards to catch the splashes as he cut, cut, cut; his sleeping bag laid out on top of the polythene, around it a bundle of clothes, his own and the unfortunates'; the mason jar full of blind eyes beside the bag; two video cameras on tripods, one set to capture a hundred and eighty degree arc of cutting space, the other angled to capture the remainder with the minimum of overlap. A third video was fixed to a meccano construct built into the ceiling above the door. The third eye in the sky was set up to take in the whole scene from overhead so he missed nothing, no expression of glimmer or fear, no nuance before, during or after the dissection.

He pulled on a pair of black denims and red hiking socks, rolling them up over the cuffs. Rooting through the bundle Meek found his white LAST TEMPTATION OF CHRIST tee-shirt, with Willem Defoe wearing a crown of thorns across the chest. He laced a pair of Caterpillar boots and shucked into a petrol coloured nubuck reefer jacket. He looked at himself in the mirror, ran a hand through his unruly blonde hair. The corners of his lips twitched into a smile. The man in the mirror was distressingly normal. One of the crowd. There was nothing exceptional or strange about him to make him stand out from anyone else in that gathering, not when he was out amongst them.

And when he was out there, haunting the streets, no one steered their children around him. No one gave him a wide berth or whispered behind their hand: 'Look at him, he's the Salvation Savage.' They accepted him amongst them, accepted him as one of them because he was one of them. With all of his sickness he was still one of them, indistinguishable because there was no sign that could hang around his neck long enough to say leper. No black halo to denounce his wickedness. He had bones beneath his skin the same as they did. Wore skin over an intricate motorway of veins the same as they did. Sprouted hairs the same as they did. The sickness that made him different was under the skin, and as long as it remained there it was wholly invisible to the world at large.

Only when the knifes came out, only then was he different.

When the sun went down Meek plucked up enough of the courage he needed to open the door on that real world and walk out into it.

As you pass the opening where the old movie theatre used to be, Sweet Bethany steps out of the shadows to join you.

She trails in your wake, her injuries slowing her.

As you pass the steel cage of the supermarket, Little Ellen steps out of the shadows to join you and Sweet Bethany.

She labours behind you, her injuries slowing her.

As you cross the turgid depths of the river, Smiling Kelly steps out of the shadows to join you, Sweet Bethany and Little Ellen.

And so it goes on, the dead stepping from the shadows to join you on his road to Ascension . . .

In six months Meek had learned a routine of backstreet to alley and back to backstreet that took him through the worst parts of the city. His route was so ingrained, that he could walk it without second thought to direction or destination. He passed landmarks that weren't on any tourist map. Sites where he had found his cast of unfortunates.

He maintained a laboriously slow pace, no looking back allowed, and at each little landmark he slowed to offer up a token. Something of his. Something personal. For one, he left a tie-pin. For another, a rose. The pockets of his reefer offered up boiled sweets and other treats. He left what he had and continued on his grizzly pilgrimage.

You walk the streets now, the dead flocking together to trail in your wake.

A rag-tag army. They make a grotesque sight. You look for nothing out of life, no quest for thrills, for pleasures, but what do you find? Only dirty old alleys and bodies that scream and bleed and bleed and scream.

But no one looks. No one sees you and your ragamuffin following.

So you shuffle through the streets, reading the billboards and the graffiti, thinking to yourself that the world around you has gone insane . . .

Meek knows better than that. He understands the fundamental difference between his and our universes. He does — he acts — while we think. While we harbour that tense secret, covet the glimmer of *difference* that it brings into our lives. How it makes us feel.

We think: *But for the grace of God . . .*

Meek thinks: *I am the grace of God.*

The difference is subtle, its repercussions shocking.

He walked through the graffiti-laden warren of his town looking for an unfortunate to practice his art on. The perfection, he knew, was in the cutting. The gateway to Ascension. The faces he made from the moonskin, expressions so lovingly rendered across taut bellys, mouths summoned from smooth pubis. But truly he suffered for his art. He made *sacrifices.*

The thought conjured the glimmer of a smile on his dour lips.

115

Meek walked in the rain. Tasted the faintest tang of acid on his tongue. Knew that one day his town would be so badly corroded by the gunk infiltrating the rain, the people so hideously deformed, he would be needed for a different kind of cleansing. Maybe there, in that moment, lay the secret of Ascension. That was a day both he and the knives awaited eagerly. A day of cutting when he no longer suffered the restrictions of care or conviction.

Then he saw his unfortunate, picked it out from the crowd because unlike Meek it had its halo, its crown of thorns that set it apart form the sheep. It shines bright on some of them, an attractor that cries out to Meek and his kind.

You are walking still, uncomfortably now.

These dead, they cling to you with all the determination of limpets. Their slime leaves marks of passage along the street, marks there for those who can see to follow.

Their expressions, long dead in many cases have ceased to be beatific. Lips form and reform the same shapes over and over, words: Ascension. Salvation Savage. Ascension. Salvation Savage. Ascension. Salvation Savage. He did this. This is his art all around you.

But you cannot see. You have no idea. You harbour your petty hates; your work; your clothes; your hair; but against him, well, you are nothing.

His victims reach out to you, claw at your skin and clothes — the ones that you hate so much — they shriek and scream in your face like the rabbit you so wilfully dissected.

And what are they trying so desperately to tell you, dear heart?

He's here, the Salvation Savage. He sees you — your petty hates — for what you are.

Unfortunate.

You can hear his footsteps, the brush of his boots on the floor behind you if you listen hard. He's done this before. Seventeen times, man, woman and child. Seventeen.

When you see his face, in that instant before he takes your eyes, you'll know. You'll see it there.

He's not meek at all . . .

PETER CROWTHER

CONSTANT COMPANION

There's something about the Gulf Coast in the summer.

I think the word is "heat".

I've always been a sucker for the white sands of the "American Riviera" so long as I don't have to sit out there and bake. I love the food — the seemingly endless supply of shrimps and oysters — and I enjoy the simple, sun-slowed conversation that drifts languidly around and across the impossibly blue water of the Gulf Stream.

It's a far cry from New York and its sticky humidity, the dopplered cry of lonesome police cruisers searching the streets and the crazy-eyed stares of the down and outs sheltering in the relative cool of the subway stations. Just being a few miles from all that was all the tonic I needed. And here I was several hundred miles away.

But I was working.

I had gone down to Sanford, about 50 miles inland from Florida's Daytona Beach, to spend some time with Jeff Sandusky. It had been booked since early spring and the arrangement was I just go down and turn up at the door, obligatory case of beer firmly packed with the shorts that got tighter each year I pulled them out of the dresser. There was no need to phone or write, Jeff had told me repeatedly. Just come.

I came.

But when I got there, things were not so casual. In fact, they were downright tense. You can recognise it most any time, but when you're geared up for sun and fun and days filled with the promise of shooting the breeze and pulling up ring-tabs, you notice it more than ever. Jeff had even forgotten I was coming. He didn't say so, but I could see it in his face.

People wear worries like ill-fitting clothes. You notice them straight away. Three beers in — and two of those mine — he told me about it.

It was his sister. She had gone missing.

Jeff's sister, Irma, had married some guy over in Mobile and they'd gone to live in a little Mississippi backwater name of Greenville, situated just inland — but still only a good spit from the sea — between Bay St Louis and Picayune and close enough to Lake Pontchartrain not to wear shoes if you went walking.

It sounded good to me, I told him. He brightened up and we cracked a few more cans and hit the sack before the alcohol made the walls creep. We were on the road before sun-up next morning.

We came off US31 at Gulfport at around eight pm, having ridden the late afternoon blacktop through Escambia and Baldwin Counties, taking in some of the finest examples of blue-highway, smalltown Americana you could find, our bellies filled with catfish nuggets, taco salad and Lone Star beer and eyelids reaching for our jawbones with a strength and a determination you just wouldn't credit.

Irma's house was modest.

The mailbox displayed one scrawled word — Wilberton — and defied gravity reaching for a clump of nettles and crab grass littered with potato chip packets and beer cans. The earthen path led to a two-step walk-up. Standing in the shadow of the swing door was a man who could make a couch potato seem anorexic. I heard Jeff mutter 'Son-of-a-bitch!' as I pulled the car off the road and switched off the engine.

I leaned back in the seat and stretched, more to give Jeff the opportunity to get out first and start the introductions. These introductions were like Central Park in January — bone-numbing cold and overcast with the constant threat of bad weather.

Jeff stood out of the car and nodded. 'Beauregarde,' he said.

The man returned the nod. 'Sandusky.'

I got out into the cool of the conversation. It was too stuffy in the car.

Jeff pointed to me. 'Koko Tate, a friend of mine.' He turned to me. 'Koko, this is Beauregarde Wilberton. The man Irma married.'

'Bo,' said the man. 'B-O, Bo.'

'Bo,' I said, holding out my hand. 'Good to see you.'

He grunted. 'You want to wash up?'

The hand was like baking dough, the vaguest hint of warmth amidst a clammy coolness. Like something that was alive a while back but wasn't any more. I turned to Jeff.

'Where is she?' Jeff said.

'She's gone, Sandusky,' Bo Wilberton relied coolly. Was that a hint of pleasure in his face or just the sun pulling facial shadows into a rictus grin?

'Gone where?'

'If I knew that, now, would I be here?'

Jeff didn't answer.

'You coming in to wash up or are you going to stand out there all night. Gets cold when the sun goes down.'

'Come on, Jeff. Help me get the things.'

We went around to the trunk and pulled out a couple of overnights. Just fresh shirts, clean denims, couple pairs of socks and shorts and my trusty .38. Grizzly Adams backed into the house and let the screen door slam, the small flap cut into the mesh squeaking to a stop. For a second I thought I'd been shot.

We ate in silence.

Wienies and stale rolls. But there were lots of them and, after the endless road, they tasted like haute cuisine.

Washing down my fourth dog with the first slug out of my third Bud, I felt almost human. It helped looking across at Bo Wilberton. He'd make grazing cattle feel like aristocracy.

'So?' Jeff wiped his mouth and reached for another can.

'So, she's gone. What's to say?' Wilberton tucked his collection of chins into what passed for a neck — or badly squeezed-up belly — and let out a loud belch.

'She leave a note?' I said, joining in the after-dinner repartee.

Wilberton shook his head. He reached into his pants pocket, fumbled for a few seconds and pulled out a ring. 'This is all she wrote,' he said, holding the ring high for us to see. 'Left it on a dinner plate over there on the table and split for parts unknown.' He lifted his beer to just in front of his mouth and added, 'and good riddance is what I say.'

I ignored the crackling electricity coming from Jeff Sandusky and leaned over the table, frowning like I was thinking. I wasn't. I was trying to avoid a brawl. 'You and her have a fight?'

Wilberton laughed and shook his head. It was a forced laugh. 'Hell, no. Nobody in his right mind would take on Irma. She makes me look slim!' He patted his gut for effect.

It was hard to believe. Only a scale model of the State of Texas could have made Bo Wilberton look slim. I let it ride.

But Jeff didn't. Hell, he couldn't. 'And you made her that way, Beauregarde,' he said. 'It was you drove her to eating.'

Wilberton sniggered again. 'Ain't a truck big enough to drive Irma anywhere,' he said.

'She take anything with her?' I asked him, swigging beer and watching Jeff out of the corner of my eye. 'Like clothes and things?'

'Few things.' Wilberton nodded. *All* of him nodded. 'And that fucking cat. Took that, too.'

'She took her cat?'

Wilberton looked suddenly defensive. 'Fucking cat,' he said again while he thought of what to say next. 'Fucking constant companion . . . crawling 'round the place, scratching and mewling, smelling the place out shitting and farting all the time. Bringing in those damned carcasses.'

'Carcasses?'

He looked over at Jeff through piggy eyes encased in thick folds of face. 'Yeah, carcasses. Birds and mice and things, all chewed up and stiff-legged.' He was starting to motor on this one, enjoying himself. 'Wandered in through the goddamn door and dropped the things right down on the carpet in front of Irma like they was fucking trophies,' he said, misting the air in front of his mouth with spittle-spray.

Jeff stood up. 'I'm getting some air,' he said and he stalked to the door and left us there, watching each other and measuring up what we saw.

I spoke first. I'd run out of measure. 'Did the cat have a lead?'

'A lead?' His face folded in on the question.

'Yeah, you know . . . a lead for Irma to keep it by her while she travelled.'

Wilberton shrugged.

I sipped my beer. Looking through the window I could see Jeff throwing stones across the road at the bushes.

'You can sleep on the sofa and the floor,' Bo Wilberton said around a glassy emission. He crunched his empty can and tossed it towards the trash container over beside the oven. In a cleanliness competition the trash container would have won hands down.

I walked outside to catch the end of the day.

'He's an asshole,' Jeff said when he saw it was me.

'He's an asshole but maybe that's all,' I said.

Jeff stared at the thin line of orange squeezed down onto the tree-tops over on the horizon. The clouds bunched together slickly, like dirty taffeta, and promised a storm. 'Maybe,' he said.

I didn't believe it either.

The storm was up before us.

Bo Wilberton's living room smelled like a bunkhouse on Sunday-morning. Which was pretty much the way it smelled when we came in.

Outside, rain swirled and wind buffeted the wooden walls and set the cat flap to squeaking in the screen door. That was all there was between us and the elements — if there had ever been an inside door, there wasn't one now. It was like we were lost at the end of the earth. Lost and very much alone.

Wilberton hadn't shown up by the time we'd washed up and dressed so we just left to get some decent breakfast.

If Greenville was a one-horse town, then it was lame.

The road that Wilberton's house sat upon continued about half a mile and wound up at a filling station, a general store and a truck-stop café. Beyond that, the bushes started again and the road wound on to US 51 and Jackson. It might not be Louisiana officially — though it was only a tired man's spit away — but it was beyond bayou country nevertheless.

As we'd walked through the stinging rain we'd been able to hear the slopping of the waters in the wetlands behind the trees and the undergrowth. It wasn't a place to take a late night walk after a few beers. At least not in this weather.

Inside the truck-stop the smell of cigarette smoke, frying bacon and fresh coffee seemed like the purest country air. We sat at the counter on a couple of riveted stools that may have been there since Huey Long's days and ordered. I looked around for a Wurlitzer but the only entertainment was a high-mounted television showing a heady mix-ture of Hanna-Barbera cartoons and static. Pity about the cartoons.

Jeff spoke to the waitress, a woman in her mid-thirties who looked twice that age — Rosie, her name was — and asked if she knew Irma. Yes she did, Rosie told him. Did she have any idea where she'd gone? No she didn't. He said he'd thought she might have come in here the day she left looking to catch a ride someplace. No, not that either, she said, and did we want more coffee.

I spoke to a fat man in a plaid shirt and a Dodgers baseball cap — he obviously worshipped them from afar — about Irma. He looked at me suspiciously. Kept himself to himself, he said. The underlying mes-sage was *I don't want no trouble, mister*. A couple of other guys finished their coffee and went which left only a single truck driver sitting at a window table thumbing through the *Enquirer* and nodding vacantly to something on a personal stereo. Rosie was the only female representative.

After a large helping of scrambled eggs and bacon, plus a side order of flapjacks and maple syrup, we were just about ready to hit downtown Greenville to ask a few more questions when the screen door blew inwards with a flurry of rain and movement. I looked around from the Dodgers fan at the same time as Jeff turned around on his bar stool.

'Jesus H. Christ, what a day,' a voice boomed over the canned laughter of *The Jetsons*. 'Rosie, pot of coffee and a double chocolate when you're ready.'

'Coming right up, Ted,' Rosie answered with a smile and wandered off through the waist-high saloon doors into the cooking area.

Ted was in his early forties, a tall man dressed in full length oil-skin britches and wading boots. He sported a thick beard, a thick head of hair tied back in a pony tail and slicked down with rain, and a wild, disarming smile. He nodded to everyone who was paying him any attention, set down a large bag of fishing tackle and proceeded to unzip his waterproof jacket.

'Great weather for fishing,' I shouted over to him.

He opened the door and lifted in three rods and a holding net, all bound together with twine, and stood them against the comic book stand just inside the door. 'If the fish can stand it then I guess we should be able to,' he replied. 'A day's about as much as I can take in a sitting though,' he added. 'Weather report says it's set in for more than that.'

Ted walked over to the bar, sat on a stool next to Jeff. I wandered over with my coffee and sat on Jeff's other side. 'You do this for a living?' I asked him, leaning over.

'I do it,' he said with a laugh, 'and I live . . . barely. I doubt I'll ever make a million though.' He looked over our faces, took in Jeff's expression and held out his hand. 'Ted Chambers,' he announced.

We took the hand in turn, returned the firm shake and gave our names.

'Where you guys from?'

'Daytona,' Jeff said, picking up the lead. 'He's a New Yorker.' He indicated me with his thumb. 'So you can't tell him nothing about weather.'

'Guess not,' Ted said. 'What you doing in these parts?'

Jeff told him as Rosie placed a cup of fresh, steaming coffee on the counter alongside a plate containing the biggest and gooiest chocolate doughnut I've ever seen. Ted became suddenly animated.

'Yeah, Irma. I know her,' he said spraying crumbs on Jeff. 'Nice lady. Nice lady. She married to that dork B-O Wilberton?'

Jeff nodded and motioned for Rosie to fill up his mug.

'Yeah. Now that's an aptly named man if ever there was one,' Ted said with a shake of his head. 'B-O.' He laughed. 'I seen skunks that smelled a sight sweeter than that feller. Got a temperament to match, too. Don't blame Irma for finally getting the courage to leave him to it.'

'You didn't realise she'd left?' I said.

Ted shook his head and took a drink of coffee. 'Nope. I don't see her all that regular, mind. Just now and again. She was a sad lady though, I could see that. Sad in spite of all that eating — if you'll pardon me for saying.'

'No offence taken,' Jeff said. 'She ate for comfort.'

'That's a fact,' Ted agreed. 'Seemed she didn't get any other kind at home. She had put on the pounds though.'

'At least she had her cat,' I said.

Ted threw back his head and laughed loudly. 'Yeah, that cat! Jesus H. Christ but that damned cat followed her everywhere. It was a real hard-eyed feller, too. Could catch a rat or a bird quick as that.' He snapped his fingers in the air. I watched him enviously — it was something I'd always wanted to do but had never been able to perfect. What good's a private investigator who can't snap his fingers?

We took up the next half hour or so talking about the fishing scene, wondering how long the rain would stay set in this way and about what it was like to live in New York. He listened like a small boy while I told him about Central Park and the subways, about the Empire State and Radio City. Then he zipped himself up, picked up his belongings and made set to hit the weather.

'You could ask around the houses down the road, see if anybody's seen your sister. Most folks'll know who you're talking about. You get up a mile or so further and you're about ready to hit Route 11, up there to Hattiesburg, and 51 which goes all the way to Jackson. Could be somebody saw her trying to hitch a ride.' He shrugged as if to say he didn't expect we'd have much luck and walked off into the storm.

Jeff paid up and we followed him a few minutes later. We weren't optimistic.

The day wore on the way it had started out. Wet.

We ran back to Wilberton's house and got a couple of zippered jackets out of my trunk. Jeff went inside the house to tell Wilberton where we were but he still wasn't out of bed. It was a little after 11 by that time. Then we set out for the intersection with Route 11 and a house-to-house search for anyone who might have seen Irma Wilberton on the day she left her husband.

It was hopeless.

Wet and hopeless.

The weather reflected our feelings of despair. But, as we checked house after ramshackle wooden house, it somehow strengthened Jeff's resolve. He didn't believe Irma had wandered up the road to stand with a case and her cat trying to hitch a ride with some sticky-fingered truck driver bound for God knows where. I didn't believe it either.

But, though most of the folks we asked knew Irma at least by sight, not a single person recalled seeing her on the day she left.

It was with empty bellies and soaked to the skin that we finally decided to head back. Dusk had fallen early with the rain and, though it was only a little after eight o'clock, night-time lay heavy on the land. I knew it lay heavier on Jeff's heart. We had made up our minds to leave Greenville, drive back to Gulfport and make some enquiries there. Jeff figured that, if she *had* left, Irma would head back towards him and not in the opposite direction. The first town of any real size was Gulfport.

Walking back, dodging puddles on the uneven road, we spoke little, preferring to listen to the sound of the night wind blowing squalls of rain through the trees. The first crack of thunder sounded from over New Orleans way just as Beauregarde Wilberton's well-lit house came into view.

He was watching a *Honeymooners* re-run, sat with his feet propped against the table, swigging Miller from a can and working his way through a pack of bagel chips.

We stood just inside the door and dripped on his floor. He didn't look away from the television when he said, 'Had a good day?'

Another crack of thunder sounded — nearer this time — and a flash of lightning lit up the outside letting us see the rain for a brief moment. Jeff walked over to the sofa and shuffled his clothes into his bag.

'You changing?' I said.

He shook his head.

'What you fellas been doing anyway?' said Bo Wilberton. *The*

Honeymooners had finished and he sat up and turned off the set.

'Looking for Irma,' Jeff said.

Thunder rattled the house and set the cat-flap to swinging. I could hear it squeaking and catching the mesh of the screen door. I was looking at Jeff and trying to decide whether to change clothes but it was Wilberton's face that made me turn to look at the door.

It was a cat

Irma's cat.

It had come home.

It stood there, soaked and muddy — dirty, filthy, muddy . . . the stuff was caked onto its fur — and its eyes were gleaming like they were on fire. Just for a second it stood there, with me and Bo Wilberton staring at it, and then it walked slowly and stealthily past me and past Jeff over to Wilberton's chair where it stopped. It sat down right next to him, leaned forward and dropped what looked like a thick piece of twig onto the carpet.

Wilberton's eyes were open wide, wide like they were going to fall right out of his head and land next to the piece of twig. Only it wasn't a piece of twig at all. It was a finger. A very fat finger . . . with a very large knuckle.

Jeff looked at the ragged fray of skin and then stared at Wilberton. He looked up at Jeff and seemed to gulp. Then he looked at me. And then he looked past me. That's when I realised his eyes hadn't been open wide at all. *Now* they were wide. And his face was white. His eyes rolled up and he slumped back into his chair.

I turned around and looked at the door just in time to see another flash of lightning illuminate the path to the door. To see the figure walking stiffly up towards the house, straining through the rain and the wind. To hear the laboured sound of feet schlepping through the water and the mud.

The thunder rolled like someone banging a tyre iron on a metal bath. The screen door opened slowly.

'Jesus Christ,' I said quietly.

Jeff shook his head.

'Been out in the creek,' Ted Chambers announced proudly, shifting the dripping, canvas-wrapped bundle in his arms. A hint of skin could be seen through a rip around the middle . . . a rip just about big enough for a small animal to get through.

'You wanna see what the cat dragged in?' he said.

RAMSEY CAMPBELL

CAT AND MOUSE

You couldn't say that the house crouched. Yet as we came off the roundabout on whose edge the house stood, and stooped beneath the trees which hung glistening over the garden, I had an impression of stealth. It couldn't be related to anything; not the summer glare nor the white house within the garden. But silence settled on us, and the circling cars hushed. And although the sunlight glittered on the last raindrops dripping from the leaves, a waiting shadow touched us and the quiet in the garden seemed poised to leap.

I had to struggle with the key in the unfamiliar lock; my wife Hazel laughed, annoying me a little. I'd wanted to throw the door wide and carry her in, enjoying my triumph; God knows I'd gone through enough to buy the house. But at least I enjoyed her delight once I managed to open the door.

We'd seen the house before, of course, when we were furnishing the rooms, but now we both felt a shock of unfamiliarity. The white telephone amazed us; so did the stairs, a construction of treads like the tail of a kite which was the major addition we owed to the previous tenants. Hazel's was the reaction I could have predicted; she rushed through the downstairs rooms and then clattered upstairs, eager to own the rest of the house. As I watched her run up the open stairs I felt a dull surge of desire. But when I made my own tour of the pale green living-room, the white kitchen cold as a hospital, the bathroom with its abstract blocks of colour and its pink pedestal, I felt imprisoned. The air smelled slightly dank, like fur. Of course Hazel had been wearing her sheepskin coat, but it seemed odd that the entire ground floor should smell of wet fur, a smell that trailed with me like a cloak. I began to open windows. Perhaps, since we'd lived on a third floor for years, I simply needed time to adjust to entering a house whose windows weren't open.

I found Hazel within a maze of double-jointed lights and drawing-board and cartons of books, in the room we'd decided to use as an attic. The smell was stronger here.

'Come down and I'll make some tea,' she said.

'Just let me tidy up a little.'

'You've done enough for a while, love.'

'You mean selling myself?' I said, thinking of my ideas and my art which I'd battered against the advertising agency where I worked until they had been battered half out of shape.

'No, I mean selling your talent,' Hazel said, then with an edge of doubt: 'You do like our house, don't you?'

'Of course I do. That's why I worked to buy it,' I said and stopped, peering down at the windowsill. We had liked the rough wood of that sill, and had left it unpainted. But now, trying to peer closer without appearing to do so, I saw that the sill looked chewed. Or clawed. The former owners must have had a cat or a dog. That was the explanation, yet I was disturbed to think that they had locked it in here, for nothing else could have driven it to such a frenzy that it would have left its claw-marks on the sill and even in the putty around the window-pane.

'I'm sure you'll sleep now that we're here,' Hazel said, and I started. 'What are you looking so worried about?' she said.

I was thinking how, when I'd stripped the attic to paint it, I had noticed claw-marks tearing through the wallpaper without realising until now what they were, but I didn't want to upset her; besides, I wished she wouldn't probe me so often, even though it was out of love, she did so. 'I'm wondering where the stereo is,' I said.

'It must be on its way,' she said. 'They'll take care of it. They can see how expensive it is.'

'Yes, well,' I told her, faintly annoyed that I should feel bound to explain this point again, 'it's the most sensitive. You have to pay for sensitivity.'

'I know you do,' she said smiling, and I realised she'd found another meaning, a personal meaning which she wanted to share with me. Sometimes her insistence on puns infuriated me; often it made me love her more. I coaxed my gaze away from the patch on the wall where the paper had been clawed. 'I wouldn't mind dinner,' I said.

The stereo arrived after dinner, halfway through my third cup of coffee. The workmen were clearly annoyed that I should supervise them, as if I were showing them how to do their job. But it was only a job to them; to me it was perfection in jeopardy. When they'd left I played *Ein Heldenleben* at full volume, caring nothing for the neighbours, since they were beyond the garden. Hazel listened quietly, more in order not to disturb me than out of a genuine response to the music. Somehow I felt trapped; the Strauss surged against Hazel's tranquil uncommunicative face, against the padded silence of the room, and never broke. I crossed to the windows and flung them high, and the feeling streamed out into the dark garden, where its remnants clung to the trees.

That night I could neither make love nor sleep. Outside the bedroom window cars whirred lingeringly by, like a sound by Stockhausen passing across speakers. My wife slept buried in the pillow, frowning, her thumb in her mouth. The tip of my cigarette glowed and reddened the landing; it opened in the gloss of the doors like a crimson eye, watching from the attic and from the other bedroom whose purpose was beginning to seem increasingly futile. I had meant to go downstairs, but down there or in my ears lay a faint ominous hiss, quite unlike the threshing of the leaves above the garden. I listened for a few minutes, then I scraped my cigarette on the ashtray by the bed and pulled the covers up.

Hazel woke me at noon. I gathered she'd awoken only recently herself. I unstuck myself from sleep and followed her downstairs. I must have looked disgruntled, judging by Hazel's glances at me. When we reached the living-room she said: 'Darling, listen.'

I heard only the words, which were the formula she used when she wasn't sure that I would agree. Of course her tone implied another meaning, but I wasn't awake enough to notice. 'What is it?' I demanded.

'No, *listen*.'

That was the second half of the formula. I often spent an hour before sleep juggling ideas and an hour after breakfast waking up; nothing angers me more than to be called upon to make a decision before I'm awake. 'Look,' I said, 'for Christ's sake, now that you've dragged me out of bed —'

Then I saw that she had been gazing at the stereo. From its speakers came a sound like the hiss of a hostile audience.

'You see, it moves back and forth,' Hazel said. 'The stereo must have been on all night. Will it have gone wrong?'

'I take it you've left it on to make sure it will?' I couldn't tell her that I wasn't shouting at her but at something else, because I didn't dare admit it to myself. But as I pulled out *Ein Heldenleben* and almost ripped it with the stylus I felt the movement of the hiss, felt it loom like a lurking predator, an actual dark physical presence, as it crept from one speaker to another. Then the Strauss rushed richly out. It sounded perfect, but aside from that it meant nothing. I took it off, scowled at Hazel and stumped back to bed.

I was running upstairs, and the stairs tilted steeply like a ladder. Suddenly sliding gates clanged shut at both ends of the staircase, and something groped hugely through the wall and felt around the trap for me. I awoke struggling. The blanket lay heavy and fluid on my body like a cat, and my skin prickled with what felt like the memory of claws. I threw off the blanket and sat up.

For a moment I was lost; I stared at the blue walls, the grey wall, the impossible silence. I struggled to my feet and listened. It was five o'clock, and there should have been more sound; Hazel should have been audible; the silence seemed charged, alert, on tiptoe. I made my way downstairs, padding carefully. I didn't know what I might find.

Hazel was sitting in a living-room, a book in her hand. I couldn't tell whether she'd been crying; her face looked scrubbed as it would have if she had wept, but I was confused by the thought that this might be the impression she had contrived for me. More disturbingly I felt that something had happened to change the silence while I had been asleep.

She came to the end of a chapter and inserted a bookmark. 'I like to sleep too, you know,' she said.

'No doubt,' I said, and that was that. Through dinner we didn't speak, we hardly looked at each other. It was less that each of us was waiting for the other to speak than as if the silence itself was poised to pounce on the first to succumb.

Several times I was almost frightened enough to speak, so that at least my fears might be defined; but each time I determined that it was up to Hazel to begin.

I don't know what music I played after dinner; I recall only visualising fists of sound crudely battling the blankets of silence. I looked at Hazel, who was trying to read against the barrage of noise which for the moment had lost all meaning. I felt grief for what I might be beginning to destroy. 'I'm sorry,' I said. 'Maybe I'm starting to crack up.'

Sometimes Hazel would dodge around the bedroom and I, having pinned her to the bed, would rape her; we seemed to need this more and more often. But tonight we waltzed gently over each other, exploring delicately, until I was too deep in her to need ornamentations. 'You're a deep one,' I said.

'What, love?' she gasped, laughing.

But I could never offer her puns more than once, and now less than ever, for my body had stiffened and chilled. Perhaps, despite her reassurances, I was cracking up. I knew that at that moment I was being watched. I peered down into Hazel's eyes and tried to gaze through them, and as I felt her nails move on my back I remembered the sensations of claws at the end of my dream.

The next day, Monday, I came home tired by a lunch which one of our clients had bought me; my constant smile had felt more like a death-grin, and certainly had expressed as little emotion. Returning to the agency I'd walked though shafts of envy which had penetrated even my six whiskies. Our house should have offered peace, but all I felt as I opened the front door was the taut snap of tension. I felt awaited, and not only by Hazel.

In the early evening cars passed with a muffled undulating hum, but soon faded. I remembered that back at our flat we could always hear the plop of a tap like a dropper or the echoing cries of children in the baths across the road. Here in the house the silence seemed worse than ever, threatening to drown us, and our speech was waterlogged. Yet it wasn't the silence I found most disturbing. Over dinner and afterwards, as we sat reading, I glimpsed an odd expression several times on Hazel's face. It wasn't fear, exactly; I should have described it as closer to doubt. What upset me most was that each time she caught me watching her, she quickly smiled.

I couldn't stop thinking that something had happened while I had been at work. 'How was our house today?' I asked.

'It was fine,' she said. 'Oh, while I was out shopping . . .'

But I wouldn't let her escape. 'Do you like our house, then?' I asked.

'What do you think?'

I was certain now that she was hiding something from me, but I didn't know how to find out. She could elude my questions by any number of wiles, by weeping if necessary. Frowning, I desisted and put Britten's *Curlew River* on the stereo. Of all Britten's work I love the church parables more than any; their sureness and astringency can make me forget my crumpled colleagues at the agency and their clumsy machinations. I thought *Curlew River* might help me define my thoughts. But I didn't get as far as the second side, with its angelic resolution. Peter Pears' eerie vocal glissandi in the part of a madwoman chilled me like the howls of a sad cat; the church which the stereo recreated seemed longer and more hollow, like a tunnel gaping invisibly before me in the air. And the calm silences with which Britten punctuates his parables seemed no longer calm. They seemed to pounce closer and to grow as they approached. Determined to respond to the music, I closed my eyes. At once I felt a dark stealthy shape leap at me between the music. My eyes started open, and I glanced at Hazel for some kind of support. The room was empty.

And it was dark. On the wall opposite me the wallpaper hung clawed into strips. It was not the living-room. Perhaps I cried out, for I heard Hazel call, 'Don't worry, you're all right,' and something else inaudible. I saw that the wallpaper was after all not clawed, that it was merely shadows that had made it seem so. Then Hazel came in with a tray.

'What did you say?' I demanded.

'Nothing,' she said. 'I crept out to make some coffee.'

'Just now, I mean. When you called out.'

'I haven't said a word for ten minutes,' she said.

After Hazel had gone to bed I stayed downstairs for an hour of last cigarettes and fragments of slogans. The month looked slack at the agency, but I couldn't stop thinking, and I preferred not to think about the house. Eventually, of course, the house overtook my thoughts. All right, I argued in mute fury, if I were moved by Britten's melodious angels then I might as well admit to a lurking belief in the supernatural. So the house was haunted by the presence of a dog or, as I sensed intuitively, a cat: so what? It didn't worry me, and Hazel hadn't even noticed. But if my grudging belief was the latest fashion in enlightenment, the retreat from scepticism, it didn't seem to be helping me. Spectral cats could have nothing to do with my hearing Hazel's voice when she hadn't spoken. I felt that my mind was beginning to fray.

A paroxysm of dry coughs persuaded me to stub out my cigarette. I threw the scribbled scraps of paper into the fireplace and came out into the hall. As I turned out the light in the living-room, a shadow leapt from the hall to the landing with a single bound.

Of course I wasn't sure, and I tried to be less so. I crept upstairs, feeling my heels hang over the open treads of the staircase. For a moment my nightmare returned, and I was heaving myself up a tilted ladder which grew steeper as the gaps between the treads widened. Halfway up I could hear myself panting with exhaustion, perhaps from lack of sleep. On tiptoe, I opened the bedroom door. I had drawn it back only inches when a fluid shadow rippled through the crack into the room.

I threw the door open, and Hazel jumped. I was certain she had, although it might have been the bedroom light jarring her blanketed shape into focus. As I undressed I watched her, and after a minute or two she shifted a little. Now I was convinced that she hadn't been asleep when I entered, and was still only pretending. I didn't try to make sure, but it took me some time to turn out the light and slip into bed. For minutes I stood staring at Hazel's obscure body, wondering where the shadow had gone.

I awoke feeling lightened. The room gave out its colours brilliantly; beyond the window waves of leaves sprang up glowing in the sun. It was only as sleep began to peel back a little that I wondered whether Hazel's absence had lightened me.

Once downstairs I didn't go to her. Instead I walked dully into the dark living-room and slumped on the settee. I began to wonder whether I was afraid of Hazel. Certainly I couldn't talk to her about last night. My eyes began to close, and the living-room darkened further. Shadows striped the wall again; in a moment the wallpaper might peel. Or a claw might tear through . . . The door gushed light and Hazel came in, carrying plates of breakfast. She smiled when I leapt to my feet, but I wasn't greeting her. The living-room was bright, as it had been since I entered. I had realised whom I might see. After all, the house was his responsibility.

'How do you feel?' I said, staring into my coffee then glancing up at her.

'All right, love. Don't start worrying about me. I should try and have a rest today if I were you.'

I didn't know whether the shadow was speaking; in any case, I resented the implication that I looked incapable. 'I'm going to take a couple of hours off this morning,' I said. 'If you want to come . . . I mean, if you want to get away from the house for a while . . .'

'Silly,' she said. 'You'd be upset if dinner wasn't ready.'

My suspicions were confirmed. I couldn't believe that she wouldn't take the chance to escape the house unless it had infected her somehow. I was glad that I hadn't told her where I was going. I managed to kiss her, forgetting to notice whether the feel of her had changed, and hurried round the corner to the car. Muffled thunder hung in the air. For a moment I regretted leaving Hazel alone, but I was afraid to return to the house. Besides, perhaps she was past rescuing. I drove blindly around the roundabout, not looking at the house, and was at the estate agent's within half an hour.

I had forgotten that the office wouldn't be open. I had a cup of coffee and a few cigarettes in a café across the road, and by the time the estate agent arrived I had perfected my smile and my story. A faint astringent scent clung to him, and he pulled at his silver moustache more often than when first I'd met him. I convinced him that I had merely been passing, but still he drew his rings nervously from his fingers and paced behind his desk. At last I fastened on the shrill garrulous couple who had been leaving as I entered, and guided the conversation to them.

'Yes, abominable,' he agreed. 'I suppose I dislike people, I decided to live with cats a long time ago. People and dogs can be led, where cats can't. You'd never train a cat to salivate at your whim.'

'Were there cats in our house?' I said.

'Have you been dreaming?' he demanded.

'Just a feeling.'

'You're right of course,' he said. 'To me, you know, the most frightful act is to kill or maim a cat. Don't offer me Auschwitz. People aren't beautiful. Auschwitz was unforgivable, but there's nothing worse than a man who destroys beauty.'

'What happened?' I said, trying to be casual.

'I shan't go into detail,' he said. 'Briefly, your predecessors were obsessed with pests. One mouse and they were convinced the house was overrun. There are none there now, of course. People and cats have one thing in common: they can lose themselves in their own internal drives to the exclusion of morality, or reality for that matter.'

'Go on,' I said.

'Well, these people left five cats in the house without food while they went away on holiday. Starve a cat to kill a mouse, you see — as stupid and vile as that. Somehow the attic door was closed and trapped the cats. When our friends returned they opened the front door and one cat ran out, never to be seen again. The others were in pieces in the attic. Cannibalism.'

'And no doubt,' I said, 'if someone exceptionally sensitive were to take the house —'

'Yourself, you mean?'

'Yes, perhaps so,' I said defensively. 'Or for that matter, if one left some piece of sensitive electrical equipment running —'

'I don't pretend to know,' he said, but there was despair around his eyes. 'Ghosts of cats? I'll tell you this. People underrate the intelligence of cats simply because they refuse to be taught tricks. I think the ghosts of cats would play with their victims for a while, as revenge. Sometimes I wonder what I'm doing in this job,' he said. 'You can see I don't care.'

When I left I drove slowly through the city, thinking. The lunchtime crowds eddied about me; eventually the thickening sky above the roofs was split by lightning, and gray rain leapt from the pavements, washing away the crowds. I drove on as the rain smashed at the windscreen. 'Playing with their victims' — there was something to which that was the key. If I were to believe in ghosts, however absurd it seemed beneath the tic of traffic lights, I might as well accept the idea of possession. Was the house playing us as hunter and victim? But I couldn't altogether believe that one's personality could be ousted; I could imagine a framework within which this might sound logical, but I wasn't sure that I felt it ought to be real. Yet I noticed that here, caged in by hopes of rain, I still felt more free than recently: free of the house's influence.

Suddenly I wanted to be with Hazel. If I had to I would drag her out, whatever was within her, however dangerous she might be. I could telephone my agency when I arrived at the house. I turned my car and it coursed through the pools of the city.

Along the carriageways out of the city the trees looked bedraggled and broken. Occasionally I passed torn cars, steaming where they'd skidded in mud. I was hardly surprised, when I reached the house, to see that the telephone wire had snapped and was sagging between the roof and the trees in the garden. As I drove past the roundabout it occurred to me that if Hazel were a victim she was trapped now. She would have to admit that she was as vulnerable as me. No longer would I have to suffer the entire burden of disquiet.

I think it was not until I got out of the car that I perceived what I had been thinking. I felt a chill of horror at myself. I loved her hands on my back, yet for a while I had turned them into claws. All along Hazel had been frightened but had tried to hide her fear from me. That was the doubt I'd seen in her eyes. At once I knew that what had blinded me, what had sought to destroy her. The rain dwindled and the sun blazed out; a rainbow lifted above the carriageway. I rushed through the garden, lashed by wet leaves, and dragged open the door to the house.

The house was dark — darker than it should have been now that the sun had returned. It was dim with stealth and silence. There was no sound of Hazel. I hurried through the ground floor, stumbled upstairs and searched the bedrooms, but the house seemed empty. I gazed down from the landing and saw that the front door was still open. I was ready to run out and wait for Hazel outside, yet I couldn't rid myself of the impression that the staircase was far longer and steeper than I remembered. Trying to control my fears I started down. I was halfway down when a shadow crept across the carpet in the living-room.

For a moment I thought it was Hazel's. But not only did its shape relate to something else entirely — it was far too large. I stood on the edge of the stairs. If I ran now, whatever it was moving in the dim room might misjudge its leap. I wavered, fell down two stairs and jumped clumsily to the hall. At that moment the telephone rang.

In my terror I could see it only as an ally. I backed up the stairs, reached down and caught up the receiver. I muttered incoherently, then I heard Hazel's voice.

'I've got out,' she said. 'I hoped I might catch you before you came home. Is the door open?'

'Yes,' I said. 'Listen, love — don't come back in. I'm sorry. I didn't understand what was going on. I blamed you.'

'If the door's open you can make it,' she said. 'Just run as fast as you can' — and then I remembered that the telephone wire was down, remembered the voice that had called to me from the other room.

As I dropped the receiver the air came alive with hissing. It was the sound that the stereo had trapped, but worse now, overpowering. I launched myself from the stairs and came down in the middle of the hall. One more leap and I would be outside. But before I regained my balance I had seen that the front door was closed.

I might have wasted my strength in trying to wrench it open. But although I didn't understand the rules of what was happening, I felt that if the house had tried to convince me that Hazel was safe that meant she was still inside somewhere. Behind me the hall spat. I clutched at the front door. I told myself that I was only using it for support, and turned.

It took me sometime to determine where I was. In the dimness the hall seemed green, and a good deal smaller. I might have been in the living-room. But I wasn't, for I could see the stairs; the walls weren't closing like a trap; the shadows hadn't massed into a poised shape, ready to sink its claws into my back. My mind began to scream and scrabble at itself, and I concentrated on the stairs. Eventually, after some hours, the hall imperceptibly altered and seemed stretched to dim infinity. The stairs were miles away. It wasn't worth making for them. There was an acre of open space to be crossed, and I knew I had no chance.

I cried out for Hazel, and from somewhere above she answered my cry.

That cry I knew wasn't faked. It was scarcely coherent, pulled out of shape by terror; it was scarcely Hazel, and in some way I knew that guaranteed its truth. I ran to the stairs, counting my footsteps. Two, and I was on the stairs. I had control of the situation for a moment. I should have kept going blindly; I shouldn't have looked around. But I couldn't help glancing into the living-room.

The doorway was dark, and in the darkness a face appeared, flashed and was gone, like the momentary luminous spectres in a ghost train. I glimpsed an enormous black head, glowing green eyes, a red mouth bared with white teeth. Then I tore my gaze away and looked up to the landing, and I saw that the stairs had become a towering ladder, a succession of great treads separated by yawning gaps which I could never cross. The air hissed behind me, and I could go neither up nor down.

Then Hazel cried out again. There was only one way to conquer myself, and my mind was so numbed that I managed it. I shut my eyes tight and crawled upwards, grasping each higher stair and dragging myself painfully over space. Beneath me I felt the stairs tremble. I wondered whether they would throw me off, until I realised that something was climbing up behind me. I tightened every muscle of my face to keep my brain from bursting out, and heaved myself upward. I felt a purring breath on my neck, and then I was on the landing.

I stumbled to my feet and opened my eyes. Unless the house was able to blot Hazel from my gaze, she could only be in the one room I hadn't searched, the attic. As I ran across the landing, a huge face flashed at the top of the stairs. Its eyes gleamed with bottomless hatred, and for a second it seemed to fill with teeth. Then I had reached the attic and slammed the door.

I slumped. The attic was so crowded with lamps and cartons that nobody could have hidden there. The objects massed, suffocated and strung together by cords of dust; I didn't see how I could even make my way between them. I might be trapped in the maze and cut off from Hazel, if indeed she were in the room. I knocked one of the looming cartons to the floor in an attempt to clear the view, and on the thud of the carton I heard breath hiss in muffled terror.

At once the room rearranged itself, and I saw Hazel. She was crouched in a corner, her knees drawn up to her chin, her arms pressed tight over her face. She was sobbing. I moved gently towards her, loving her, bullying the fear from my mind. My feet tangled in wire. I looked down and saw the cord for the lamps. I knew where the socket was; I plugged in the lamps and let them blind the door. Then I went to Hazel.

'Come on, love,' I said. 'Come on, Hazel. We're going now. Come on, love.'

Her arms drew back from her face. She looked up at me; then she shrank into the corner and her eyes gaped in horror. I fell back. But her lips moved. She was trying to speak to me. She wasn't frightened of me. I looked behind me, towards the door.

The door had opened, and the doorway was half-filled by an enormous face. Its mouth yawned wide and a tongue sprang dripping across its teeth. I grabbed the lamps and shone them into its eyes, but they didn't blink. Its face began to bulge in through the doorway, and behind it others leapt across the landing to hover grinning above the first. With a surge of pure energy and terror I hurled the lamps at the faces.

What happened I don't know. I never heard the lamps strike the floor. But the surge of energy carried me across the room to heave the window open. I ran to Hazel and pulled her to her feet, although she shrank sobbing into the corner. I threw her across my shoulder and staggered with her to the window. I glanced back into the room, where faces with gleaming eyes capered in the air and flew at us in a single toothed mass. Then I jumped.

I think the house must have overlooked that. Mice might fall from a window, but they aren't supposed to jump. So I spent time in hospital with a broken leg, while Hazel was furious enough by the end of the week to visit the estate agent's. Once she had made him admit that he wouldn't spend a night in the house, the rest was easy. 'I have no time for horror,' he told her. My leg soon improved. Not so Hazel's insomnia; and yet when we lie awake together talking through the uneasy hours, I think there are times when we're grateful. Somehow we could never talk that way before.

POPPY Z. BRITE

SELF-MADE MAN

Justin had read *Dandelion Wine* seventeen times now, but he still hated to see it end. He always hated endings.

He turned the last page of the book and sat for several minutes in the shadows of his bedroom, cradling the old thumbed paperback, marvelling at the world he held in his hands. The hot sprawl of the city was forgotten; he was still lost in the cool green Byzantium of 1928.

Within these tattered covers, dawning realisation of his own mortality might turn a boy into a poet, not a dark machine of destruction. People only died after saying to each other all the things that needed to be said, and the summer never truly ended so long as those bottles gleamed down cellar, full of the distillate of memory.

For Justin, the distillate of memory was a bitter vintage. The summer of 1928 seemed impossibly long ago, beyond imagining, forty years before blasted sperm met cursed egg to make him. When he put the book aside and looked at the dried blood under his fingernails, it seemed even longer.

An artist who doesn't read is no artist at all, he had scribbled in a notebook he had once tried to keep, but abandoned after a few weeks, sick of his own thoughts. *Books are the key to other minds, sure as bodies are the key to other souls. Reading a good book is a lot like sinking your fingers up to the second knuckle in someone's brain.*

In the world of the story, no one left before it was time. Characters in a book never went away; all you had to do was open the book again and there they'd be, right where you left them. He wished live people were so easy to hold onto.

You could hold onto *parts* of them, of course; you could even make them part of yourself. That was easy. But to keep a whole person with you forever, to stop just one person from leaving or gradually disintegrating as they always did . . . to just hold someone. *All* of someone.

There might be ways. There had to be ways.

Even in Byzantium, a Lonely One stalked and preyed.

Justin was curled up against the headboard of his bed, a blood-stained comforter bunched around his bare legs. This was his favourite reading spot. He glanced at the nightstand, which held a Black & Decker electric drill, a pair of scissors, a roll of paper towels, and a syringe full of chlorine bleach. The drill wasn't plugged in yet. He closed his eyes and allowed a small slow shudder to run through his body, part dread, part desire.

There were screams carved on the air of his room, vital fluids dried deep within his mattress, whole lives sewn into the lining of his pillow, to be taken out and savoured later. There was always time, so long as you didn't let your memories get away. He had kept most of his. In fact, he'd kept seventeen; all but the first two, and those he didn't want.

Justin's father had barely seen him out of the womb before disappearing into the seamy nightside of Los Angeles. His mother raised him on the continent's faulty rim, in an edging-toward-poor neighbourhood of a city that considered its poor a kind of toxic waste: ceaselessly and unavoidably churned out by progress, hard to store or dispose of, foul-smelling and ugly and dangerous. Their little stucco house was at the edge of a vast slum, and Justin's dreams were peppered with gunfire, his play permeated with the smell of piss and garbage. He was often beaten bloody just for being a scrawny white boy carrying a book. His mother never noticed his hands scraped raw on concrete, or the thin crust of blood that often formed between his oozing nose and mouth by the time he got home.

She had married again and moved to Reno as soon as Justin turned eighteen, as soon as she could turn her painfully awkward son out of the house. *You could be a nice-looking young man if you cleaned yourself up. You're smart, you could get a good job and make money. You could have girlfriends*, as if looks and money and girlfriends were the sweetest things he could ever dream of.

Her new husband had been a career Army man who looked at Justin the way he looked at their ragged old sofa, as leftover trash from her former life. Now they were both ten years dead, their bones mummified or scattered by animals somewhere in the Nevada desert, in those beautiful blasted lands. Only Justin knew where.

He'd shot his stepfather first, once in the back of the head with his own Army service pistol, just to see the surprise on his mother's face as brain and bone exploded across the glass top of her brand new dinner table, as her husband's blood dripped into the mashed potatoes and the meat loaf, rained into her sweating glass of tea. He thought briefly that this surprise was the strongest emotion he had ever seen there. The sweetest, too. Then he pointed the gun at it and watched it blossom into chaos.

Justin remembered clearing the table, noticing that one of his mother's eyes had landed in her plate, afloat on a thin patina of blood and grease. He tilted the plate a little and the glistening orb rolled onto the floor. It made a small satisfying squelch beneath the heel of his shoe, a sound he felt more than heard.

No one ever knew he had been out of California. He drove their gas-guzzling luxury sedan into the desert, dumped them and the gun. He returned to L.A. by night, by Greyhound bus, drinking bitter coffee and reading at rest stops, watching the country unspool past his window, the starlit desert and highway and small sleeping towns, the whole wide-open landscape folding around him like an envelope or a concealing hand. He was safe among other human flotsam. No one ever remembered his face. No one considered him capable of anything at all, let alone murder.

After that he worked and read and drank compulsively, did little else for a whole year. He never forgot that he was capable of murder, but he thought he had buried the urge. Then one morning he woke up with a boy strewn across his bed, face and chest battered in, abdomen torn wide open. Justin's hands were still tangled in the glistening purple stew of intestines. From the stains on his skin he could see that he had rubbed them all over his body, maybe rolled in them.

He didn't remember meeting the boy, didn't know how he had killed him or opened his body like a big wet Christmas present, or why. But he kept the body until it started to smell, and then he cut off the head, boiled it until the flesh was gone, and kept the skull. After that it never stopped again. They had all been boys, all young, thin, and pretty: everything the way Justin liked it. Weapons were too easy, too impersonal, so he drugged them and strangled them. Like Willy Wonka in the technicolour bowels of his chocolate factory, he was the music maker, and he was the dreamer of dreams.

It was a dark and lonely revelry, to be sure. But so was writing; so was painting or learning music. So, he supposed, was all art when you penetrated to its molten core. He didn't know if killing was art, but it was the only creative thing he had ever done.

He got up, slid *Dandelion Wine* back into its place on his crowded bookshelf, and left the bedroom. He put his favourite CD on shuffle and crossed his small apartment to the kitchenette. A window beside the refrigerator looked out on a brick wall. Frank Sinatra was singing "I've got you under my skin."

Justin opened the refrigerator and took out a package wrapped in foil. Inside was a ragged cut of meat as large as a dinner plate, deep red, tough and fibrous. He selected a knife from the jumble of filthy dishes in the sink and sliced off a piece of meat the size of his palm. He wasn't very hungry, but he needed something in his stomach to soak up the liquor he'd be drinking soon.

Justin heated oil in a skillet, sprinkled the meat with salt, laid it in the sizzling fat and cooked it until both sides were brown and the bottom of the pan was awash with fragrant juices. He slid the meat onto a saucer, found a clean fork in the silverware drawer, and began to eat his dinner standing at the counter.

The meat was rather tough, but it tasted wonderful, oily and salty with a slight undertone of musk. He felt it breaking down in the acids of his saliva and his stomach, felt its proteins joining with his cells and becoming part of him. That was fine.

But after tonight he would have something better. A person who lived and stayed with him, whose mind belonged to him. A homemade zombie. Justin knew it was possible, if only he could destroy the right parts of the brain. If a drill and a syringeful of bleach didn't work, he would try something else next time.

The night drew like a curtain across the window, stealing his wall brick by brick. Sinatra's voice was as smooth and sweet as cream. *Got you . . . deep in the heart of me . . .* Justin nodded reflectively. The meat left a delicately metallic flavour on his tongue, one of the myriad tastes of love. Soon it would be time to go out.

Apart from the trip to Reno and the delicious wallow in the desert, Justin had never left Los Angeles. He longed to drive out into the desert, to find again the ghost towns and nuclear moonscapes he had so loved in Nevada. But he never had. You needed a car to get out there. If you didn't have a car in L.A., you might as well curl up and die. Los Angeles was a city with an enormous central nervous system, but no brain.

Since being fired from his job at an orange juice plant for chronic absenteeism — too many bodies demanding his time, requiring that he cut them up, preserve them, consume them — Justin wasn't even sure how much longer he would be able to afford the apartment. But he didn't see how he could move out with things the way they were in here. The place was a terrible mess. His neighbours has started complaining about the smell.

Justin decided not to think about all that now. He still had a little money saved, and a city bus would get him from his Silver Lake apartment to the garish carnival of West Hollywood; that much he knew. It had done so countless times.

If he was lucky, he'd be bringing home company.

Suko ran fingers the colour of sandalwood through haphazardly cut black hair, painted his eyes with stolen drugstore kohl, and grinned at himself in the cracked mirror over the sink. He fastened a string of thrift-shop Mardi Gras beads round his neck, studied the effect of the purple plastic against torn black cotton and smooth brown skin, then added a clay amulet of the Buddha and a tiny wooden penis, both strung on leather thongs.

These he had purchased among the dim stalls at Wat Rajanada, the amulet market near Klong Saensaep in Bangkok. The amulet was to protect him against accidents and malevolent ghosts. The penis was to increase his potency, to make sure whoever he met up with tonight would have a good time. It was supposed to be worn on a string around his waist, but the first few times he'd done that, his American lovers gave him strange looks.

The amulets were the last thing Suko bought with Thai money before boarding a California-bound jet and bidding farewell to his sodden homeland, most likely forever. He'd had to travel a long way from Patpong Road to get them, but he didn't know whether one could buy magical amulets in America. Apparently one could: attached to his Mardi Gras beads had once been a round medallion stamped with an exaggerated Negro face and the word ZULU. He'd lost the medallion on a night of drunken revelry, which was as it should be. *Mai pen rai. No problem*.

Suko was nineteen. His full name was unpronounceable by American tongues, but he didn't care. American tongues could do all sorts of other things for him. This he had learned at fourteen, after hitching a midnight ride out of his home village, a place so small and so poor that it appeared on no map foreign eyes would ever see.

His family had always referred to the city by its true name, Krung Thep, the Great City of Angels. Suko had never known it by any other name until he arrived there. Krung Thep was only an abbreviation for the true name, which was more than thirty syllables long. For some reason, *farangs* had never gotten used to this. They all called it Bangkok, a name like two sharp handclaps.

In the streets, the harsh reek of exhaust fumes was tinged with a million subtler perfumes: jasmine, raw sewage, grasshoppers frying in peppered oil, the odour of ripe durian fruit that was like rotting flesh steeped in thick sweet cream. The very air seemed spritzed with alcohol, soaked with neon and the juices of sex.

He found his calling on Patpong 3, a block-long string of gay bars and nightclubs in Bangkok's famous sleaze district. In the village, Suko and his seven brothers and sisters had gutted fish for a few *baht* a day. Here he was paid thirty times as much to drink and dance with *farangs* who told him fascinating stories, to make his face prettier with make-up, to be fondled and flattered, to have his cock sucked as often as he could stand it. If he had to suck a few in return, how bad could that be? It was far from the worst thing he had ever put in his mouth. He rather liked the taste of sperm, if not the odd little tickle it left in the back of his throat.

He enjoyed the feel of male flesh against his own and the feel of strong arms enfolding him, loved never knowing what the night would bring. He marvelled at the range of body types among Americans and English, Germans and Australians. Some had skin as soft and pale as rice-flour dough; some were covered with thick hair like wool matting their chests and arms. They might be fat or emaciated, squat or ponderously tall, ugly, handsome, or forgettable. All the Thai boys he knew were lean, light brown, small-boned and smooth-skinned, with sweet androgynous faces. So was he. So was Noy.

From the cheap boom box in the corner of the room, Robert Smith sang that Suko made him feel young again. Suko scowled at the box. Noy had given him that tape, a poor-quality Bangkok bootleg of the Cure, right after Suko first spoke of leaving the country. Last year. The year Suko decided to get on with his life.

The rest of them, these other slim raven-haired heartbreakers, they thought they would be able to live like this forever. They were seventeen, fifteen, younger. They were in love with their own faces in the mirror, jet-coloured eyes glittering with drink and praise, lips bruised from too many rough kisses, too much expert use. They could not see themselves at thirty, could not imagine the roughening of their skin or the lines that bar life would etch into their faces. Some would end up hustling over on Soi Cowboy, Patpong's shabby cousin where the beer was cheaper and the tinsel tarnished, where the neon flickered fitfully or not at all. Some would move to the streets.

And some would simply disappear. Suko intended to be one of those.

Noy was just his age, and smart. Suko met him on-stage at the Hi-Way Bar. They were performing the biker act, in which two boys sat facing each other astride the saddle of a Harley-Davidson, wearing only leather biker caps, tongue-kissing with sloppy abandon and masturbating each other while a ring of sweaty *farang* faces gathered around them.

Immediately afterward, while the come was still oozing between the thrumming saddle and the backs of their skinny thighs, Noy murmured into Suko's mouth, 'Wouldn't they be surprised if we just put this thing in gear and drove it into the crowd?'

Suko pulled back and stared at him. Noy's left arm was draped lazily around Suko's neck; Noy's right hand cupped Suko's cock, now tugging gently, now relaxing. Noy smiled and lifted one perfect eyebrow, and Suko found himself getting hard again for someone who wasn't even paying him.

Noy gave him a final squeeze and let go. 'Don't make a date when you get done working,' he told Suko. 'Take me home with you.'

Suko did, and even after a night on Patpong, they puzzled out one another's bodies like the streets of an unfamiliar city. Soon they were the undisputed stars of the Hi-Way's live sex shows; they knew how to love each other in private and how to make it look good in public. They made twice as much money as the other boys. Suko started saving up for a plane ticket.

But Noy spent his money on trinkets: T-shirts printed with obscene slogans, little bags of pot and pills, even a green glow-in-the-dark dildo to use in their stage show. In the end, Noy was just smart enough to make his stupidity utterly infuriating.

I'm really leaving, Suko would tell him as they lay entwined on a straw pallet in the room they rented above a cheap restaurant, as the odours of *nam pla* and chilli oil wafted through the open window to mingle with the scent of their lovemaking. *When I save up enough, I'm going to do it. You can come, but I won't wait for you once I have the money, not knowing how many ways I could lose this chance.*

But Noy never believed him, not until the night Suko showed him the one-way ticket. And how Noy cried then, real tears such as Suko had never thought to see from him, great childish tears that reddened his smooth skin and made his eyes swell to slits. He clutched at Suko's hands and slobbered on them and begged him not to go until Suko wanted to shove him face-first into the Patpong mud.

This is all you want? Suko demanded, waving a hand at the tawdry neon, the ramshackle bars, the Thai boys and girls putting everything on display with a clearly marked price tag: their flesh, their hunger, and if they stayed long enough, their souls.

This is enough for you? Well, it isn't enough for me.

Noy had made his choices, had worked hard for them. But Suko had made his choices too, and no one could ever take them away. The city where he lived now, Los Angeles, was one of his choices. Another city of angels.

He had left Noy sobbing in the middle of Patpong 3, unable or unwilling to say goodbye. Now half of a world lay between them, and with time, Suko's memories of Noy soured into anger. He had been nothing but a jaded, fiercely erotic, selfish boy, expecting Suko to give up his dreams of a lifetime for a few more years of mindless pleasure. *Asshole*, Suko thought, righteous anger flaring in his heart. *Jerk. Geek.*

Now Robert Smith wanted Suko to fly him to the moon. As reasonable a demand, really, as any Noy had handed him. Suko favoured the boom box with his sweetest smile and carefully shaped his mouth round a phrase:

'Get a life, Robert!'

'I will always love you,' Robert moaned.

Suko kept grinning at the box. But now an evil gleam came into his black eyes, and he spat out a single word.

'*NOT!*'

Justin hit the bars hard and fast, pounding back martinis, which he couldn't help thinking of as martians ever since he'd read *The Shining*. Soon his brain felt pleasantly lubricated, half-numb.

He had managed to find five or six bars he liked within walking distance of each other, no mean feet in L.A. Just now he was leaning against the matte-gray wall of the Wounded Stag, an expensive club eerily lit with blue bulbs and black lights. He let his eyes sweep over the crowd, then drift back to the sparkling drink in his hand. The gin shattered the light, turned it silver and razor-edged. The olive bobbed like a tiny severed head in a bath of caustic chemicals.

Something weird was happening on TV. Justin had walked out of Club 312, a cosy bar with Sinatra on the jukebox that was normally his favourite place to relax with a drink before starting the search for company. Tonight 312 was empty save for a small crowd of regulars gathered around the flickering set in the corner. He couldn't tell what was going on, since none of the regulars ever talked to him, or he to them.

But from the scraps of conversation — *eaten alive, night of the living dead* — and edgy laughter he caught, Justin assumed some channel was showing a Halloween horror retrospective. The holiday fell next week and he'd been meaning to get some candy. You ought to have something to offer trick-or-treaters if you were going to invite them in.

He heard a newscaster's voice saying, 'This has been a special report. We'll keep you informed throughout the evening as more information becomes available . . .' Could that be part of a horror filmfest? A fake, maybe, like that radio broadcast in the thirties that had driven people to slit their wrists. They'd been afraid of the Martians, Justin remembered. He downed the last of his own martian and left the bar. He didn't care about the news. He would be making his own living dead tonight.

The Wounded Stag had no TV. Pictures were passé here, best left to that stillborn golden calf that was the *other* Hollywood. Sound was the thing, pounds and pounds of it pushing against the eardrums, saturating the brain, making the very skin feel tender and bruised if you withstood it long enough. Beyond headache lay transcendence.

The music at the Stag was mostly psycho-industrial, Skinny Puppy and Einstürzende Neubaten and Ministry, the Butthole Surfers and Nine Inch Nails and My Bloody Valentine. Justin liked the names of the bands better than he liked the music. The only time they played Sinatra here was at closing hour, when they wanted to drive people out.

But the Stag was where the truly beautiful boys came, the drop-dead boys who could get away with shaving half their hair and dyeing the other half dead black or lurid violet, or wearing it long and stringy and filthy, or piercing their faces twenty times. They swept through the door wrapped in their leather, their skimpy fishnet, their jangling rings and chains as if they were precious jewels and ermine. They allowed themselves one contemptuous glance around the bar, then looked at no one. If you wanted their attention, you had to make a bid for it: an overpriced drink, a compliment that was just ambiguous enough to be cool. Never, ever a smile.

Like as not, you would be rejected summarily and without delay. But even if a spark of interest flared in those coldly beautiful black-rimmed eyes, what sordid fantasy! What exotic passion! What delicious viscera!

He had taken four boys home from the Stag on separate nights.

They were still in his apartment, their organs wrapped neatly in plastic film inside his freezer, their hands tucked within easy reach under his mattress, their skulls nestled in a box in the closet. Justin smiled at them all he wanted to now, and they grinned right back at him. They had to. He had boiled them down to the bone, and all skulls grinned because they were so happy to be free of imprisoning flesh.

But skulls and mummified hands and salty slices of meat weren't enough any more. He wanted to keep the face, the thrilling pulse in the chest and guts, the sweet slick inside of the mouth and anus. He wanted to wrap his mouth around a cock that would grow hard without his having to shove a finger up inside it like some desiccated puppet. He wanted to keep a boy, not a motley collection of bits. And he wanted that boy to smile at him, *for* him, for *only* him.

Justin dragged his gaze away from the swirling depths of his martian and glanced at the door. The most beautiful boy he had ever seen was just coming in. And he was smiling: a big, sunny, unaffected and utterly guileless smile.

Suko leaned his head against the tall blond man's shoulder and stared out the window of the taxi. The candy panorama of West Hollywood spread out before them, neon smeared across hot asphalt, marabou cowboys and rhinestone drag queens posing in the headlights. The cab edged forward, parting the throng like a river, carrying Suko to whatever strange shores of pleasure still lay ahead of him this night.

'Where did you say you were from?' the man asked. As Suko answered, gentle fingers did something exciting to the inside of his thigh, through the ripped black jeans. The blond man's voice was without accent, almost without inflection.

Of course, no one in L.A. had an accent. Everyone was from somewhere else, but they all strove to hide it, as if they slid from the womb craving flavoured mineral water and sushi on Melrose. But Suko had met no one else who spoke like this man. His voice was soft and low, nearly a monotone. To Suko it was soothing; any kind of quiet aimed at him was soothing after the circuses of Patpong and Sunset Boulevard, half a world apart but cut from the same bright cacophonous cloth. Cities of angels: *yeah, right*. Fallen angels.

They pulled up in front of a shabby apartment building that looked as if it had been modelled after a cardboard box sometime in the 1950s. The man — *Justin*, Suko remembered, his name was *Justin* — paid the cabdriver but didn't tip. The cab gunned away from the curb, tires squealing rudely on the cracked asphalt. Justin stumbled backward and bumped into Suko. 'Sorry.'

'Hey, no problem.' That was still a mouthful — his tongue just naturally wanted to rattle off a *mai pen rai* — but Suko got all the syllables out. Justin smiled, the first time he'd done so since introducing himself. His long skinny fingers closed around Suko's wrist.

'Come on,' he said. 'It's safer if we go in the back way.'

They walked around the corner of the building, under an iron stairwell and past some garbage cans that fairly shimmered with the odour of decay. Suko's foot hit something soft. He looked down, stopped, and backed into Justin. A young black man lay among the stinking cans, his head propped at a painful angle against the wall, his legs sprawled wide.

'Is he dead?' Suko clutched for his Buddha amulet. The man's ghost might still be trapped in this mean alley, looking for humans to plague. If it wanted to, it could suck out their life essences through their spinal columns like a child sipping soda from a straw.

But Justin shook his head. 'Just drunk. See, there's an empty bottle by his leg.'

'He looks dead.'

Justin prodded the black man's thigh with the toes of his loafer. After a moment, the man stirred. His eyes never opened, but his hands twitched and his mouth gaped wide, chewing at the air.

'See?' Justin tugged at Suko's arm. 'Come on.'

They climbed the metal stairs and entered the building through a fire door wedged open with a flattened Old Milwaukee can. Justin led the way down a hall coloured only by shadow and grime, stopped in front of a door identical to all the others but for the number *21* stamped on a metal plate small as an egg, and undid a complicated series of locks. He opened the door a crack and ushered Suko inside, then followed and turned to do up all the locks again.

At once Suko noticed the smell. First there was only the most delicate tendril, like à pale brown finger tickling the back of his throat; then a wave hit him, powerful and nauseating. It was the smell of the garbage cans downstairs, increased a hundredfold and overlaid with other smells: cooking oil, air freshener, some caustic chemical odour that stung his nostrils. It was the smell of rot. And it filled the apartment.

Justin saw Suko wrinkling his nose. 'My refrigerator broke,' he said. 'Damn landlord says he can't replace it till next week. I just bought a bunch of meat on sale and it all went bad. Don't look in the fridge, whatever you do.'

'Why you don't —' Suko caught himself. 'Why *don't you* throw it out?'

'Oh . . .' Justin looked vaguely surprised for a moment. Then he shrugged. 'I'll get around to it, I guess. It doesn't bother me much.'

He pulled a bottle of rum from somewhere, poured a few inches into a glass already sitting on the countertop and stirred in a spoonful of sugar. Justin had been impressed by Suko's taste for a straight sugared rum back at the Stag, and said he had some expensive Bacardi he wanted Suko to try. Their fingertips kissed as the glass changed hands, and a tiny thrill ran down Suko's spine. Justin was a little weird, but Suko could handle that, no problem. And there was a definite sexual charge between them. Suko felt sure the rest of the night would swarm with flavours and sensations, fireworks and roses.

Justin watched Suko sip the rum. His eyes were an odd, deep lilac-blue, a colour Suko had never seen before in the endless spectrum of American eyes. The liquor tasted faintly bitter beneath the sugar, as if the glass wasn't quite clean. Again, Suko could deal; a clean glass at the Hi-Way Bar on Patpong 3 was a rare find.

'Do you want to smoke some weed?' Justin asked when Suko had polished off an inch of the Bacardi.

'Sure.'

'It's in the bedroom.' Suko was ready to follow him there, but Justin said, 'I'll get it,' and hurried out of the kitchen. Suko heard him banging about in the other room, opening and shutting a great many drawers.

Suko drank more rum. He glanced sideways at the refrigerator, a modern monolith of shining harvest gold, without the cosy clutter he had seen decorating the fridges of others: memo boards, shopping lists, food-shaped magnets trapping snapshots or newspaper cartoons. It gave off a nearly imperceptible hum, the sound of a motor running smoothly. And the smell of decay seemed to emanate from all around the apartment, not just the fridge. Could it really be broken?

He grabbed the door handle and tugged. The seal sucked softly back for a second; then the door swung wide and the refrigerator light clicked on.

A fresh wave of rot washed over him. Maybe Justin hadn't been lying about meat gone bad. The contents of the fridge were meagre and depressing: a decimated twelvepack of cheap beer, a crusted jar of Golden's Spicy Brown mustard, several lumpy packages wrapped in foil. A residue of rusty red on the bottom shelf, like the juice that might leak out of a meat tray. And pushed far to the back, a large Tupperware cake server, incongruous among the slim bachelor pickings.

Suko touched one of the beer cans. It was icy cold.

Something inside the cake server was moving. He could just make out its faint shadowy convulsions through the opaque plastic.

Suko slammed the door and stumbled away. Justin was just coming back in. He gripped Suko's arms, stared into his face. 'What's wrong?'

'Nothing — I —'

'Did you open the fridge?'

'No!'

Justin shook him. The strange lilac eyes had gone muddy, the handsome features twisted into a mean mask. '*Did you open the fucking fridge?*' Suko felt droplets of spit land on his face, his lips. He wished miserably that they could have gotten there some other way, any way but this. He had wanted to make love with this man.

'DID YOU —'

'NO!!'

Suko thought he might cry. At the same time he had begun to feel remote, far away from the ugly scene, as if he were floating in a corner watching it but not caring much what happened. It must be the rum. But it wasn't like being drunk; that was a familiar feeling. This was more like the time Noy had convinced him to take two Valiums. An hour after swallowing the little yellow wafers, Suko had watched Noy suck him off from a million miles away, wondering why anyone ever got excited about this, why anyone ever got excited about anything.

He had hated the feeling then. He hated it more now, because it was pulling him down.

He was afraid it might be the last thing he ever felt.

He was afraid it might not be.

Justin half-dragged, half-carried Suko into the bedroom and dumped him on the mattress. He felt the boy's delicate ivory bones shifting under his hands, the boy's exquisite mass of organs pressing against his groin. He wanted to unzip that sweet sack of skin right now, sink his teeth into that beating, bleeding heart . . . but no. He had other plans for this one.

He'd closed the door to the adjacent bathroom in case he brought the boy in here still conscious. Most of a body was soaking in a tub full of icewater and Clorox. Suko wouldn't have needed to see that. Justin almost opened the door for the extra light, but decided not to. He didn't want to leave the bedside even for a second.

His supplies were ready on the nightstand. Justin plugged the drill's power cord into the socket behind the bed, gently thumbed up one of Suko's makeup-smudged eyelids and examined the silvery sclera. The sleeping pills had worked fine, as always. He ground them up and put them in a glass before he left. That way, when he brought home company, Justin could simply pour him a drink in the special glass.

He used the scissors to slice off Suko's shirt, which was so artfully ripped up that Justin hardly had to damage it further to remove it. He cut away the beads and amulets, saving the tiny wooden penis, which had caught his eye back at the Stag. His own penis ached and burned. He pressed his ear against the narrow chest, heard the lungs pull in a deep slow breath, then release it just as easily. He heard blood moving unhurried through arteries and veins, heard a secret stomach sound from down below. Justin could listen to a boy's chest and stomach all night, but reluctantly he took his ear away.

He crawled onto the bed, positioned Suko's head in his lap, and hefted the drill, which was heavier than he remembered. He hoped he would able to control how far the bit went in. A fraction of an inch too deep into the brain could ruin everything. It was only the frontal lobes he wanted to penetrate, the cradle of free will.

Justin parted the boy's thick black hair and placed the diamond-tipped bit against the centre of the pale, faintly shiny scalp. He took a deep breath, bit his lip, and squeezed the trigger. When he took the drill away, there was a tiny, perfect black hole near the crown of the boy's head.

He picked up the syringe, slid the needle in and forward, toward the forehead. He felt a tiny resistance, as if the needle was passing through a hair-thin elastic membrane. He pushed the plunger and flooded the boy's brain with chlorine bleach.

Three things happened at once.

Suko's eyes fluttered open.

Justin had an explosive orgasm in his pants.

Something heavy thudded against the bathroom door.

Suko saw the blond man's face upside down, the lilac eyes like little slices of moon, the mouth a reverse smile or grimace. A whining buzz filled his skull, seemed to jar the very plates of his skull, as if hornets had built a nest inside his brain. A dull ache spread spiderlike over the top of his head.

He smelled roses, though he had seen none in the room. He smelled wood shavings, the sharp stink of shit, the perfume of ripe oranges. Each of these scents was gone as quickly as it had come. Lingering was a burnt metallic flavour, a little like the taste that had lingered in his mouth the time he'd had a tooth filled in Bangkok.

Shavings. Roses. Cut grass. Sour milk. And underneath it all, the smell of rotting flesh.

Suko's field of vision went solid screaming chartreuse, then danger red. Now Justin was back, a negative of himself, hair green, face inky purple, eyes white circles with pinholes at their centres like tiny imploding suns. And suddenly something else was in the frame as well. Something all black, with holes where no holes should be. A face swollen and torn, a face that could not be alive, but whose jaw was moving.

A hand missing most of its fingers closed on the back of Justin's hair and yanked. A drooling purple mouth closed on Justin's pale throat and tore away a chunk.

Suko managed to sit up. His vision spun and yawed. The reek of rot was dizzying, and overlaying it was a new stinging smell, a chemical smell he could not identify. Something salty ran into his eyes. He touched his face, and his fingers came away slicked with a thin clear substance.

The thing wrapped skeletal arms around Justin and pulled him off the bed. They rolled on the floor together, Justin's blood foutaining out of his throat, the thing grunting and lapping at it. Ragged flesh trailed from its mouth.

Justin wasn't screaming, Suko realised.

He was *smiling*.

It was the boy from the bathtub. Justin couldn't see his face, but he could smell the Clorox, raw and fresh. He had carved a great deal of flesh off of this one, as well as removing the viscera. But he had not yet cut off the head. Now it was snuggled under his chin, tongue burrowing like a worm into his wounded throat. He felt the teeth tearing at him, chunks of his skin and muscle disappearing down the boy's gullet. He felt one of the bones in his neck crack and splinter.

The pain was as shocking as an orgasm, but cleaner. The joy was like nothing he had known before, not when he watched his mother die, not when he tasted the flesh of another person for the first time. It had worked. Not only was the Asian boy still alive, but the others had come back as well. They had never left Justin at all. They had only been waiting.

He got his arms around the hollow body, pulled it closer. He cupped the cold rubbery buttocks, entwined his legs with the thrusting bones of its thighs. When its jaws released his throat, he pressed his face against the voracious swollen one, pushed his tongue between the blackened lips and felt the teeth rip it out. His mouth filled with blood and rot. He swallowed, gagged, swallowed again.

A head rolled out from under the bed, pushing itself by frantic motions of jaw and tongue. The severed ends of the neck muscles twitched, trying to help it along. Its nose and left eyebrow were pierced with silver ringers, its empty eyesockets crusted with blood and greasy black makeup. It reached Justin and bit deep into one of his thighs. He kicked once, in surprise, then bent his leg so that the teeth could more easily get at the soft muscle of his groin. He felt his flesh peeling away.

The upper half of a body was pulling itself out of the closet. Its black-lacquered nails dug into the carpet. Ropes of intestine trailed behind it, coming apart, leaving a trail of shit and ichor on the rug. This one had been, possibly, a Mexican boy. Now its skin was the colour of decaying eggplant, and very few teeth were left in its gaping mouth. Dimly Justin remembered extracting them with a pair of pliers after the rigor mortis had slackened.

It tore Justin's belly open with its hands and sank its face into his guts. He arched his back, felt its fingers plunging deep, its mouth lapping at the very core of him.

The small pleasures of his life — reading, listening to the music of another time, choking the life out of boys and playing with their abandoned shells — were nothing compared to this. He wanted it to go on forever.

But, eventually he died.

The corpse from the bathtub chewed at Justin's throat and chest. Half-chewed pieces of Justin slid down its gullet, into the great scooped-out hollow of its abdomen, out onto the floor.

The corpse from the closet sucked up the liquor and partly digested meat it found in Justin's stomach.

The head bit into Justin's scrotum and gulped the savoury mass of the testicles like a pair of tender oysters.

They seemed to know when to stop feeding, to refrain from pulling him completely apart, to leave enough of him. When he came back, Justin knew exactly what to do.

Suko stumbled out of the bedroom and slammed the door behind him. Something was rolling around and around in the refrigerator, banging against the inside of the door. He almost went over to open it, only caught himself at the last second. He wasn't thinking very clearly. His head felt wrong somehow, his brain caught in a downward spiral. He did not understand what he had just seen. But he knew he had to get out of the apartment.

No problem, a voice yammered in his head. *Stay cool. Chill out. Don't have a cow, man.* He barely knew the meaning of the words. The American voice seemed to be receding down a long black tunnel; already it was so tiny and faint he could hardly hear it. He realised he was thinking in Thai for the first time in years. Even his native language was strange, a flurry of quick sharp syllables like little whirling razor blades slicing into the meat of his brain.

He fumbled with the complicated series of locks, yanked the door open and nearly fell into the hall. How had he entered the building? . . . Up a metal staircase, through a door at the end of the long dark hall. He reached it and let himself out. The hot October night seared his lungs. He could smell every poisonous particle of exhaust blanketing the city, every atom of shit and filth and blood baked onto the streets. Not like the ripe wet kiss of Bangkok, but so arid, so mercilessly dry. He felt his way down the fire escape and around the corner of the building.

The empty street seemed a mile wide. There was no sidewalk, only a steep curb and a long gray boulevard stretching away toward some other part of the city. There were no cars; he could hear no traffic anywhere. Even with his head feeling so strange, Suko knew something was wrong. L.A. streets were often empty of people, but there were always cars.

Far away at the next intersection, he made out a small group of figures straggling in his direction, bathed in a traffic light's red glow. For a long moment he watched them come, trying to be sure they were really there, wondering what he should do. Then he started toward them. The blond man had done something awful to his head; he needed help. Maybe the figures would be able to help him.

But when he got closer, he saw that they were like the things he had seen in the bedroom. One had a long fatty slash wound across its bare torso. One had been gouged in the face with something jagged; its nose was cleaved in half and an eyeball hung out of the socket, leaving yolky fluid. One had no wounds, but looked as if it had starved to death; its nude body was all bone-ends and wasted hollows; its genitals shrivelled into the pelvic cavity, its blue-white skin covered with huge black and blue lesions.

When they saw him, the things opened their mouths and widened their nostrils, catching his scent. It was too late to get away. He couldn't run, didn't think he would even be able to stand up much longer. He stumbled forward and gave himself to them.

The little group closed around Suko, keeping him on his feet, supporting him as best they could. Gouged Eyeball caught him and steadied him. Slash Wound mouthed his shoulder as if in comfort, but did not bite. Lesions nudged him, urged him on. Suko realised they were *herding* him. They recognised him as one of their own, separated from the flock somehow. They were welcoming him back in.

Miserably, Suko wondered what would happen when they met someone alive.

Then the hunger flared in his belly, and he knew.

NICHOLAS ROYLE

QUESTION SEVEN

The ads appeared regularly in several magazines in the personal columns, and it hadn't been that difficult to save up the cash. For several months Priestly forwent luxuries. The salary and commission from his sales job were more spectacular than his lifestyle had ever been, and by cutting down on his expenditure still further, he would eventually increase his investment.

One thousand pounds sat on the coffee table in two piles of 20s earmarked for Andrew. His ad was one of several similar that Priestly had picked out of the personal columns. '£1000 desperately needed by young man. Anything legal considered.' Andrew was due to arrive in half an hour. He would be just the latest in a string of advertisers lured to Priestly's flat. Maybe Priestly should have got used to the waiting by now. But still he was nervous. And excited.

Again he checked the beer supply in the fridge and then went to inspect the bath for the fourth time that day. It had to shine as white as new teeth tonight. As he leaned over the bath he caught sight of a scuttling form out of the corner of his eye.

Priestly froze, fear stirring the acids in his stomach. He had to force his eyes to look directly at the thing he had glimpsed.

And when they did he couldn't look away.

The spider had come to a halt, its body suspended amidst a forest of legs. Priestly shuddered. The creature could do him no harm yet it terrified him. Its very stasis threatened movement in any of eight different directions. He imagined the brown and grey abdomen bursting between his molars like a boiled pea and instantly became nauseous.

He had once been unable to kill them, terrified in case of some dreadful reprisal. And removing a live spider meant scooping it into a receptacle and throwing it away outside. But if he used a piece of card or newspaper as a scoop, he imagined he could feel a throb of intent through the paper. It would climb up and touch him. If he used a cup it would have to be thrown away. No amount of scouring with abrasive powders would make the cup reusable.

Priestly attached the shower hose then ran the hot tap and tried to wash the beast down the plughole. Its legs curled into a protective mesh and the steaming water seemed to effect no injury. It bobbed around the plughole and resurfaced twice before disappearing. He kept the tap running, knowing from experience that it could be clinging on.

He decided not to inspect the bath, shivering at the thought of touching the enamel where the spider had been. He wouldn't be using the bath himself, after all.

The doorbell startled him out of a light slumber twenty minutes later. He sat up suddenly, staring at the coffee table. *What the hell was all that money doing there?* Then, as the bell rang a second time, he remembered. He plumped the cushions and pressed his hair flat with his hands, guessing, in the absence of a mirror, that it looked all right. He glanced into the bathroom, which was the last room before the front door, and shivered as his eyes took in the empty bath.

He opened the door to a young man with a nervous smile and three days' beard growth. Priestly had insisted on him coming unshaven, leaving the young man to assume that that was the client's preference.

Priestly introduced himself as John and invited the young man in. They stood in the living room for a moment, guardedly sizing each other up. Priestly was aware of the money burning a hole in the table-top. He felt nervous himself.

'Nice flat,' said the young man.

'Have a drink,' said Priestly simultaneously. 'What would you like?'

Andrew shrugged, put his hands in his pockets.

'Beer,' Priestly said, answering for him.

Priestly fetched two cold beers and they sat in the big armchairs at either end of the coffee table. They drank and talked about trivial matters: Wimbledon, holidays in southern Africa, West End musicals. Priestly recognised in Andrew a base level of taste which in some way resembled his own cultural vacuum.

Steadily the pile of empty cans grew in the wastebin and Priestly sat on the arm of Andrew's chair. He had been careful to drink much more slowly than the younger man, who now appeared quite drunk. Though it felt unnatural to him, Priestly put his arm around Andrew's shoulder and stroked the back of his neck. Andrew leaned back and smiled. Returning the smile, Priestly ran the back of his hand over Andrew's beard.

'Shave for me,' he wheedled.

'But I thought . . .'

'Yes, I did. But now I want you to shave it off.'

Priestly reckoned Andrew was too drunk to care. And too drunk to shave.

Answering the magazine ads Priestly had sent letters full of detailed personal questions. They were the kind of letters to which one might have sought answers in a less direct way before diving into a relationship. Most of the questions were decoys. Are you an optimist or a pessimist? How possessive are you? Do you go to the cinema once a week, once a month, or once a year? The only one that interested Priestly was question seven: do you have any phobias, what really scares you?

Andrew was the latest in a series of respondents who confessed to particular phobias shared by Priestly. Previously they had been just mind games. Now it was time to get physical. Andrew, like Priestly, had a mortal fear of seeing his own blood.

Priestly filled the bowl with hot water and produced cream and a disposable razor. Andrew leaned on the bowl and the heel of his hand slipped on a bar of soap. He giggled. Dipping his hands into the bowl, Priestly began to lather the cream. A dreadful excitement was coiling in his stomach like a serpent. He lathered Andrew's chin, the young man no doubt taking his eagerness to mean something quite different.

Andrew gripped the razor and stared at the wall.

''s no mirror,' he slurred.

Priestly dug into the back of a wooden cabinet and extracted a small round mirror which he was careful to regard at an oblique angle as he passed it to Andrew. The young man held it up and Priestly side-stepped. The snake of fear in his stomach beat its tail from side to side as he watched Andrew drag the razor down his cheek and nick his chin on the jawbone. A spot of blood appeared and ballooned. Priestly felt light-headed. Andrew carried on shaving. He cut himself again below the ear.

'I want you to shave your legs,' Priestly said. 'Get into the bath.'

Andrew looked unsure. His eyes were bloodshot and glazed; his breath stank of alcohol. Priestly guessed he hadn't yet seen the blood.

'Do it!' Priestly ordered, with the firmness of a lover, or a torturer.

Andrew took another chunk out of his chin, then kicked off his trousers and climbed into the bath.

His legs were difficult to shave, the hair being so thick, and the razor became blunt, meaning he had to press harder. When, through his drunkenness, he saw blood his eyes opened wide in terror but Priestly told him to go on. Andrew shuddered and dropped the razor. Priestly leaned over and picked it up from the bottom of the bath. He switched the tap on and with the shower hose cleaned the blade. Then he took Andrew's hand, now cold as ice, and folded his fingers around the razor. He lifted the hand so that the razor was touching the skin, then pulled it upwards, feeling the keen edge of the shinbone just beneath the skin.

'Shave!' he said as he let go. Andrew looked at him like a little boy punished, fear stretching his pupils. Priestly repeated his command — 'Shave!' — and the boy obeyed. Priestly could see him trying to be careful, but the effect of the drink had not altogether left him and the trembling of his fingers endangered him further. He cut himself more and more deeply and barely winced. Priestly wondered if he was going into shock. Soon blood was spattered all over the bath and spiralled into the plughole like the spider before it.

The effect of the bloodletting was not as strong as he had hoped for. Maybe because Andrew had not been expecting it. The drink and homosexual subterfuge had both misled and protected him. Consequently, Priestly found less fear to feed on in the young man than he hungered for.

For the next time he decided to be more open and straightforward from the beginning. The stooge had to know what was coming and be prepared to undergo the experience for the money offered. That way the fear would taste richer.

'I want you to put this on,' Priestly said to Terry, a thin-lipped man with a wispy ginger moustache and haunted eyes. Terry took the hood and examined the drawstring, looking doubtful.

'I have to put this on, keep it on all night and then you'll give me the money.'

Priestly nodded.

The man was scared. 'Why?' he asked.

'I told you before. I want to confront my fear.'

'Why don't you do it, then?' he demanded, trembling.

'I want to confront it vicariously,' said Priestly. 'Through you.'

'You're a fucking weird bastard,' Terry hissed, momentarily emboldened by anger.

Priestly stared at him and said nothing. Terry held his gaze but his pupils dilated like black mirrors, so that Priestly had to look away. He said: 'That's not your concern.'

Terry studied the hood again and Priestly began to feel the fear coming off him, part odour, part energy. Priestly, too, began to shiver and lose moisture to the thirsty snake in his belly. A cold spider clutched the small of his back and ran up his spine to make quills of the hairs on the back of his neck.

And yet he was safe.

The other man would live the nightmare.

Terry put the hood on but convulsed and had to tear it off again. Priestly drank his panic like an elixir.

'I can't do it,' Terry whispered.

Priestly considered this and walked across to the coffee table. He picked up a wad of banknotes and thumbed it. *How badly do you need the money?* Terry threw his head back, breathing deeply. What was going through his mind? Clearly he was rethinking. How important was it to pay off those gambling debts? Maybe he wanted a forged passport. Or a private abortion for his girlfriend, some smalltown gangster's little lady wife? It seemed unlikely. But Terry needed the money and the morality of the situation was of no concern to Priestly. He would pay the man like he had paid Andrew and the others. In his way he was helping them.

The need conquered the fear and Terry put the hood over his head and pulled the drawstring. He stood there, his cloth face collapsing and swelling in time with his rapid breathing. While he remained relatively calm, Priestly led him out of the living room, across the hall and into the bedroom, where a coffin lay waiting alongside Priestly's bed.

'I'm just going to lay you down,' said Priestly, lifting Terry's feet clear of the sides of the coffin and guiding him down. The padding would make it comfortable, not unlike a bed, giving Priestly the time to grab the ventilated lid and jam it into place.

Terry shouted and lashed out immediately but Priestly sat on the lid and drove the nails home. Terry shrieked questions and pleas but they were rendered unintelligible by the hood and the lid and his rapid descent into total hysteria.

Priestly lay on his bed and was convulsed by fits of shuddering as the terror of premature burial overwhelmed him, and then he went into paroxysms of ecstasy when his mind acknowledged his safe remove.

Terry screamed for almost an hour, then fell silent. Priestly was drenched in sweat. The scratching and snapping of fingernails didn't begin until later.

Priestly wasn't finished.

The living room and kitchen were quiet and in darkness. In the bedroom an electric alarm clock flagged the passing seconds in silence. The digital display threw a red stain onto the quilt cover. Nothing stirred. Yet in the stillness there was a noise, maintained at a level that was almost inaudible. In the hall, the telephone sat mutely on the bookcase. Motes of dust settled without disturbing the air. Still, hovering above the silence the noise continued. A shifting, a sliding. Like static on a radio behind a locked door at the end of a corridor. Random but unbroken. A lifting, a falling. Brushing, scraping, tickling.

In the bathroom Priestly knelt on the floor facing the bath. Here the noise was louder. A scraping, a slithering. Priestly's complexion was pallid, drained of blood. His eyes were open so wide it seemed the skin at the corners might split. But it wouldn't matter because his face was just a sheet of blotting paper on which his pupils were drops of ink. Inside, he was at absolute zero, though his pulse raced.

In the bath were 20,000 house spiders.

The pet shop owner had said he needed at least a week's notice. Priestly had said he could have it. The man had then demanded an exorbitant tip for delivering and unloading them.

They came up almost to the rim. A moment of sheer terror when Priestly had thought they could climb out had given way to mixed revulsion and fascination. They couldn't get it together to climb on top of each other in order to escape the slippy confines of the bath.

Reason suggested that you would do anything at all if you *really* needed the money. Yet Priestly knew he could never submerge himself in the bath of spiders. Not even to save his own life.

The idea revolved around his mind as he sat staring at them. After a time it ran out of energy and died at the base of his skull, leaving his mind empty of all that had gone before.

The doorbell came as a shock, though the caller was on time. He sat without moving for another minute staring at the seething tangle of bristly legs and ripe bodies. Pressing his hands on his knees he rose slowly to his feet, knee joints cracking. He turned from the bath and walked into the hall. Priestly opened the door and instantly his mouth fell open.

The man extended an arm and Priestly recoiled, the snake of fear suddenly awoken and spitting venom in his abdomen, snapping at the walls of his stomach. The man advanced, pushing Priestly in the chest, forcing him backwards into the first opening, the bathroom.

It was no accident.

The man tried to push him over the edge of the bath. Priestly struggled, fighting back with all the strength of panic. But the other man seemed to possess an unstoppable determination. Priestly shrieked as he pitched over the edge and pivoted in mid-air for two seconds before falling into the bath of spiders.

He closed his eyes and mouth but felt them on his face and in his hair. Would his mind snap? It would be a relief. Hands held him down. He became aware of a creeping sensation on his arms and legs. The spiders had crawled up his trousers and sleeves. They reached his armpits and groin where their numbers swelled like traffic at an intersection. Instinct drove them on to investigate every gap and crack. Why should they stop, he thought, when they can go further?

As he thrashed out he caught glimpses of his aggressor's face, and that made the thousands of spiders seem trivial even as they popped and burst.

When he'd opened the door it had been like a mirror falling into the doorway from hell. In it he had seen a replica of himself. But that same person, the mirror reflection he had studiously avoided all his life, was scarred. The face was gouged and scored by razor cuts, streaked with dried blood and scabbed. The hands that pushed him under again were ragged and torn. Several nails had been ripped off; from beneath others poked splinters of wood.

Priestly tried hard not to, but when his will failed and he finally did scream, the spiders tumbled into his mouth.

JOHN BURKE

A GAME OF CONSEQUENCES

The slim, red-headed girl appeared halfway through the party, when
everybody was noisy and putting on a big act of sharing the festive
spirit. The dull routine of other days of the year was suspended.
Enjoyment, itself a routine decreed by senior management, was obligatory. The Deputy Divisional Executive clinked wine glasses with a
computer programmer he had every intention of declaring redundant
early in the New Year. A media man wondered whether a blonde sec-
retary he had been lusting after for weeks had drunk enough to let him
stroke her bare shoulders without accusations of sexual harassment flying around.

Nobody saw the red-haired girl come in. She was simply, all at
once, there. Very calm. Obviously hadn't had even one drink yet.

'Just like last Christmas,' muttered Mr Weybright into his third
double gin.

Henry Charlton looked through the shifting tangle of heads and
glasses and sweaty foreheads, and tried to get those cool yet predatory
features into focus. She looked — there was only one rather odd way
of describing her — quietly eager.

He said: 'Do you know her?'

Weybright shook his silver-grey head. 'Not sure I'd want to.' A
paper streamer sagged into his gin. He pulled it out with a resigned air.

Weybright, thought Henry Charlton, was really getting past it.

Two men steered two giggling secretaries towards the buffet table,
leaving a gap for him to stare straight at the girl. She, at any rate, was
not one of the crowd. She had arrived when it suited her, not as part
of a deferential departmental group. You could see that she would leave
any time she chose.

'Any idea what department she's in?'

'Heaven knows,' said Weybright. 'Heaven — or the other place. Never see her about during the year. All I do remember . . .' He faltered.

'Well?' Henry prompted him.

'Silly, I suppose. But I'm sure she was the girl poor Drummond was talking to last year. You know, just before he fell into the well of the building and was killed. Coincidence, of course. I imagine she's just one of the girls from downstairs. So many of them nowadays. You see them once, and don't ever see them again.'

Never again. Henry Charlton was conscious of a sense of loss, of desolation, of life sliding away from him before he had ever known what it really meant. The same routine, the same timetable day after day, week in, week out: the train to the office each morning, back each evening, the same meaningless conferences and the same petty rivalries in the same drab departments. Through the oppressiveness of the room a chill struck him as if somewhere a window had been opened on to the night air.

Weybright had shuffled away. Henry gripped his glass and walked over to the wall where the girl stood alone.

'Quite a crush,' he said banally.

Her eyes were green and responsive. 'Isn't it?' And then she said: 'Why are you so glum about it all? No Christmas spirit?'

'It's so phoney. So predictable, just a carry-over from the daily grind.'

'There are worse things.'

'Are there? Sometimes I wonder.' He glanced down at her long, slim fingers with their incredibly long nails, and realised there wasn't a glass in her hand. 'Look, let me get you a drink.'

'That's predictable too, isn't it? The usual polite, predictable ploy. All part of the pattern. And you've just about had enough, right?'

'This is my first glass.'

'I didn't mean the wine. I meant the job. And everything that goes with it.'

'I didn't know it showed.'

'But it does. You're restless. And I'm a collector,' she said in a dreamy, purring voice that pulsed into his head like secret music, 'of restless people. It's part of my job.'

'What department are you from?'

'Personal Claims.'

'I don't think I've come in contact with them yet.'

'We make claims on people. We've been doing it for a long time.

166

But we're always bringing our methods up to date and discarding the old ones.'

'Claims *on* people? I don't quite get you.'

Her unwavering, intense eyes seemed to be mocking him.

A group on the far side of the room began a rowdy romp involving banging a lot of chairs about.

The girl said: 'Would you like to play a game? Just between the two of us?'

He held back the obvious, crude answer. But something between the two of them, something to break the monotony, was certainly beginning to itch in the recesses of his head.

'Name it,' he said. 'And look, do let me get you a drink.'

'I like to keep a clear head when I'm playing.' She had thin but vivid lips, the colour of a bruise. And her voice was growing hoarse; almost greedy. 'It's called "Upon My Soul". I ask questions, and you have to answer. You can tell the truth or lie, and I have to guess which is which. But if I say you've got to start your answer with "Upon My Soul", then you've *got* to tell the truth.'

'And if I don't?'

'Oh, you'll see.'

Noise pounded in on them from both sides. Her idea of a parlour game seemed incongruous in the middle of all this.

'How's it supposed to work out in the end?'

'You'll see,' she said again. 'It's rather like a game of consequences. And if you cheat,' — her smile revealed white teeth, tinged with a dark red which must have come from her lipstick but looked more like blood — 'I'll have your soul. Agreed?'

His breathing quickened. It was too early to tell her that some of his soul was already reaching out for her. For the time being, safer just to say: 'Agreed.'

She asked him if he liked his job, and he looked at the silly faces swirling around him and the fattest and most detestable of departmental managers and deputies and all the rest of then swirling around, and said no. She asked him if he ever had dreams of breaking loose and starting all over again, and he said yes. She asked if he were married. After a brief hesitation he admitted that he was. They might as well get things clear right from the start.

She looked pleased rather than disappointed. Then she reeled off a string of questions that were not nearly so personal, and he answered then automatically. The game was a pretty footling one. He wondered why he had bothered to start it. But when she came just a few inches closer, and her breasts enticed him and he got the faint heat from her skin, and looked at her sinuous mouth preparing for the next question, he was impatient for her to go on.

Suddenly she said: 'Upon your soul . . . is your marriage a happy one?'

He was aware of the restlessness surging up in his flesh. It was more powerful than the memory of Marjorie and their two boys and the house they were so fond of and the life that had really been so comfortable. Ordinary, yes; but comfortable. A happy marriage? All their friends thought so, and envied him. And he had always felt pretty complacent about it.

But if he said yes, the girl might shrug and move on to someone else. He didn't want that. His body wanted hers.

'No,' he said.

'Upon your soul?'

'If you insist —'

'I do.'

'Upon my soul,' he said, 'no.'

'Now,' she said quietly, 'I have your soul.'

There was a terrifying satisfaction in her face. He tried to make a joke of it. 'I think you have. What are you going to do with it?'

She took him by the hand. Her fingers were icy cold in spite of the clammy heat of the room and the heat he had felt from her body so few minutes ago. She led him through the crush and out into a corridor with windows on one side that looked down into the central well of the building. On the other side of the corridor were the familiar grey doors, like all the grey doors on each of the twenty floors.

She opened the third door.

He stared down into something that could hardly be part of the office block. No part of any cosy, predictable everyday world. His throat was dry. She was making no sound, yet he felt the passionate vibration of her gloating laugh.

He managed a whisper: 'What the hell is that place down there?'

'Just what you've said. You call it hell, but I' — the laughter was real and exultant now — 'I call it home.'

'But you can't . . . I mean, just because I played a silly game with you, you can't . . .'

'If I'd appeared with horns and a tail, you wouldn't have played, would you? Probably thought I was a nut in fancy dress for the party.'

Trying to speak was like trying to force words out through the choking quagmire of a dream.

'Once upon a time,' she went on, 'we used to appear in that sort of thing. Very melodramatic. Nowadays we use more modern means of communication.'

He wrenched himself away from her. She went on laughing. He could not shut out the sound of it even when he put his hands over his ears and stumbled through the doorway and across the corridor.

Windows in the block were always shut in order not to throw the air conditioning off balance. Yet right in front of him a window was open. As he reached it and saw the drop of ten storeys, the voice behind him became a shriek of ecstasy.

Now it was too late he knew there were worse things — far, far worse things — than predictability and the boredom of routine. And knew upon his soul there was no escape.

STEPHEN GALLAGHER

THE BACK OF HIS HAND

Billy had done a lot of walking and pacing that morning, mainly to keep himself warm. He'd marked out a stretch of the pavement across the road from the tattoo parlour, and by now he knew it like . . . well, like the back of his hand. As long as he kept to this same piece of ground, he'd know the minute that anybody came along and went inside. He'd tried the door several times already.

But it was still early.

There was a greasy spoon café almost opposite the parlour. It opened at eight, and Billy was on the doorstep when the proprietor came down and drew back the bolts. The proprietor was a stocky man, dark-haired and not so tall, and he seemed to be in sole charge with no help. He made no comment as Billy shouldered past him, leading with his well-stuffed kitbag. The café interior didn't look much, but it was clean. The warmth of the place folded itself around him like a blanket. He let himself relax a little, almost as if he'd been wound up tight by the cold.

He picked out a table that was close to the café's paraffin heater but which also was near to the window. The window was already beginning to mist up on the inside. He could still see the tattoo parlour from here.

When the man came over to take his order, Billy kept his gloves on and his hands under the table. The man seemed not to notice. Billy ordered the full breakfast with nothing spared.

Though Billy had his problems, lack of money wasn't one of them.

The man went around into the back, where he had a radio playing, and Billy could hear kitchenware being moved around on a range. It was a reassuring, almost homely combination of sounds. He yawned, and stretched his back. He'd been hitching all through the night, and had landed here in this seaside town at some utterly godforsaken hour of darkness. He'd zigzagged the country, leaving a trail that he was pretty sure would be hard to follow, and he'd kept his gloves on all of the time apart from when he'd needed to pee, and that he'd done only in locked cubicles on motorway service areas. Two gloves weren't necessary, but one glove would have looked odd. It might have attracted attention to him.

And attention was the last thing that Billy needed right now.

He'd never been here before. But the name of the place had stuck in his mind from just a couple of years ago when about a thousand bikers had descended on the place and settled in for a long Bank Holiday weekend. The bikers had been able to protest to the TV cameras about how misunderstood they were, the police had picked up plenty of overtime and had the chance to wear all their spiffy new Darth Vader riot gear, and the local traders had made a mint out of everybody; in fact, just about everyone had gone home happy although not one of them would ever have wanted to admit as much.

The town looked different now. The dawn sea battered at an empty promenade, and the wind howled through the deserted spaces of the new shopping centre. Most of the guest houses had hung out their *No Vacancy* signs and roped off the two-car parking spaces that had once been their front gardens. He might find a place here tonight where he could go to ground for a while, but it might be better to move on. It depended on whether he could face another night in transit. He'd never thought of himself as a soft case, but the last few hours had been the most miserable of his life. He'd waited out the time before daylight in the town's bus station, sitting with his bag and drinking weak piss-flavoured tea from a machine and trying to look like a legitimate traveller between destinations. A soldier on his way home, maybe; he reckoned that he could look the part and he carried a genuine forces kitbag as well, bought from Mac's Army Surplus Store. He'd watched a total of three buses come and go, all almost empty. In the phone booth he'd found a Yellow Pages with most of its yellow pages ripped away (there was no paper in the squalid toilet, and it didn't take a genius to put two and two together) but there had been enough of the directory left to tell him what he wanted to know.

He looked out through the fogging window again. No action across on the far side of the road. According to the listing, the tattoo parlour was the only place of its kind in town. The whole biker scene had led him to expect more but, what the hell, one was all that he'd need as long as it was the right kind of a place.

It looked like the right kind of a place.

There was no shop window. The entire facade apart from the entrance had been boarded up and painted white, and this had become a background for a riot of hand-drawn lettering by someone who clearly had an eye for colour and design, but who equally clearly wasn't a trained signwriter. The style fell somewhere between 'sixties psychedelia and freehand baroque; across the top it read STEVE, 'PROFESSIONAL' TATTOO ARTIST, and the rest of it crowded out the frontage completely. From here, it was almost as if the building itself had been extensively tattooed, as an example of the owner's craft. It was the inverted commas around 'PROFESSIONAL' that had impressed Billy the most. That showed an education.

Breakfast came.

Billy realised almost too late that he'd pulled his gloves off without thinking, and his hands were on the table. He quickly drew them back and slid them underneath as the proprietor set a huge plate before him. 'It's hot,' he said, and the stuff on the plate was still sizzling.

Billy waited until he'd walked away, and then he rearranged the sauce bottle and the cruet set and propped up the plastic menu wallet so that it would screen his hands from the counter.

He kept an eye on the parlour as he ate. It was his first genuine meal in more than twenty-four hours, not counting grabbed snacks and chocolate bars along the way. A couple of transport drivers came into the café shortly after he'd started, but they didn't sit close. On the pavement opposite a few people walked by the parlour, but no-one went in.

He'd finished. He ordered something else. It was starting to feel as if this was an open-ended situation that could last indefinitely. His attention began to wander, so that after a while he only belatedly realised that he was actually watching someone over at the door who had stopped and seemed to be about to enter.

He sat up, and paid attention.

It was a man. A youngish man, tall and skinny, with an unkempt thatch of hair and some kind of a beard. He wore thrift shop clothing and carried a plastic Sainsburys bag. Billy didn't get the chance to see much more because then the man was inside, the darkness of whatever lay beyond swallowing him up as the door swung shut to keep out the rest of the world.

He finished, and went over to the counter to pay. He held the canvas handles of the kitbag with his gloved hand and paid with the other, so that nothing looked suspicious.

Then he crossed the street to the tattoo parlour.

There had been a padlock on the door, now there was none. The hasp and staple, both new-looking, hung open; the hasp had been crookedly fitted and secured, not with screws, but with nails. One of them had been bent over and hammered flat — either the work of an amateur, or the world's least 'PROFESSIONAL' carpenter. As before, there was nothing in the frosted glass of the door to say whether the place was open for business, or what its hours were, or anything. Billy pushed, and it opened. He went inside.

There were no lights on downstairs, but a door stood open to the daylight of a grimy kitchen beyond the main room in which he stood. Billy could hear somebody moving up above.

'Hey,' he called out. 'Anyone around?' and he heard the movement stop. A moment later there was the sound of a hurried tread on an uncarpeted stairway, coming down. As Billy waited, he looked about him in the gloom. The walls showed the signs of bad plaster under too many layers of cheap redecoration, none of them recent. There were signs in the same flamboyant, spidery lettering as the frontage outside (*Strictly over 18s only — proof of age may be required*, and, somewhat less tactfully, *Not having a tattoo? Then Fuck Off*) and then poster after poster showing about a hundred different designs. He saw cats, dragons, jaguars, skulls, women, swords, daggers, scrolls . . .

'What is it?'

The man stood in the kitchen doorway. Seen from closer-to, he had the look of an aged juvenile. His eyes were of a blue so pale that he would probably always seem to stare no matter what he might actually be thinking, and his hair had a coarse, faded texture like curtains left hanging for too long in the sunlight. He seemed a sensitive type.

Unlike Billy.

'Look,' Billy said, 'before anything else, I'm talking five hundred quid and no questions asked. If that interests you, then we'll take it from there. If it doesn't, then I'm walking out now and I don't want to be followed. Is that understood?'

And the man said, 'Five hundred quid? For real?'

'I can show it to you if you don't want to believe me.'

'I'm interested,' the man said.

And Billy, looking at him, thought Yeah, I reckon you are . . . because he knew a Junkie when he saw one, and this starved-looking specimen had to be one of the classic examples. So then he looked around and said, 'Well then, how about some light?' And the Junkie, suddenly spurred into nervous action as if being jerked out of a trance,

turned around and seemed confused for a moment as if he was so over-
come by the idea that he'd forgotten where the switches were.

The overhead tubes flashed once or twice, and then one of them
came on. The other just glowed orange at both ends, as if in resentment
of its brighter neighbour.

The room didn't look any better. Quite the opposite. There were
old grey vinyl tiles on the floor, the self-stick kind that often don't. A
few of these had lifted and shifted, exposing the grimy wood flooring
underneath. There were four straight-backed chairs over against the
wall, and in the middle of the room a single padded chair with a head-
rest that was somewhere between the kind that you'd find in a hair-
dresser's and the kind that you'd find in a dentist's. The dentistry
image was continued in the form of the hanging tattooist's needle on
the end of its balanced and jointed support arm, with a system of long
rubber drivebelts and gearwheels running all the way back to the
motor at its base. On the table alongside the chair were a rack of needles, some dyes, and a bottle of Savlon antiseptic.

Billy said, 'Show me your hands.'

The man frowned, puzzled.

Billy said, 'If I'm going to pay you that kind of money, I want to
see steady hands first.'

'I've got steadier hands than you,' the Junkie said, offended, and
held them out; they weren't exactly rock steady, but they weren't
unusually shaky either.

Billy said, 'You shoot up already this morning?'

And the Junkie said, 'That's none of your damned business. Now
show me the money.'

Billy put the kitbag on the padded chair, and unzipped it a little of
the way. It was enough to show some of the bundles of used notes,
most of them still in cashiers' paper bands, that were inside. The man
stared.

Billy said, 'You haven't even asked me what I want you to do, yet.'

And the man shrugged.

'For five hundred, who gives a shit?'

This was going to work out.

So Billy zipped up the kitbag again and then removed his glove and
rolled back his sleeve and he held out his clenched fist, knuckles
upward to show the dragon tattoo.

'I want this taken off,' he said.

The man looked at it. Billy guessed that he had to be casting a professional eye over the design. It had cost Billy a lot of money, some ten

years before; his friends at the time had told him that the man they were taking him to was the best in Europe. He'd been a big fat slob who hadn't looked like the best anything of anywhere, but Billy had been interested enough in the designs he'd been shown. They made the ones on the walls around here look like fingerpaintings.

The Junkie looked up at him. 'Taken off?' he said.

'Completely off,' Billy said. 'You can do that? I mean, you can do it here and I don't have to go into a hospital or anything?'

'I can do anything you want,' the man said. 'But am I allowed to ask why?'

'No, you aren't,' Billy said. 'Lock the door, and let's get down to it.'

The man looked again, and shook his head in disbelief. And then he made a little shrugging gesture as if to say *Well, it's your tattoo and it's your five hundred, so what does it matter to me?*

And he went to bolt the door from the inside.

Billy looked at the chair. It had a padded arm support at right angles to the seat, and the armrest had worn right away to the dirty-grey foam at its end. He felt his heart sink. Much as he knew he needed this, he hadn't been looking forward to it. Billy hated physical discomfort, not least his own. That ten years before he'd almost fainted when, after much more than an hour with his eyes screwed shut and his teeth gritted and his insides scrunched up tighter than a washleather, he'd finally looked at the new pattern on the back of his inflamed hand and seen the tiny beads of blood that had been welling up from every needle strike. This was why he'd only had the one hand tattooed, instead of the matching pair that he'd intended. Much as he'd wanted the dragon design in the first place, he'd never been able to bring himself to go through the experience again.

And now he was sorry that he'd ever had it done at all . . . now that it was *that* close to landing him in jail.

'Shall I sit here?' Billy said as the Junkie turned from the door.

'Wherever you like,' the Junkie said.

'Will it take long?'

'I shouldn't think so.'

Billy took off his coat and climbed into the chair, and laid his arm on the rest. It was at right angles to his body, and raised as if to fend off a blow. As he was doing this the Junkie was scratching at his beard, looking down at the tattoo needles and other implements on the table.

'Is this going to hurt?' Billy said.

'Oh, definitely,' the Junkie said, nodding absently.

'What about blood?'

'Lots of it,' the Junkie said. 'You don't make an omelette without breaking eggs.'

'Oh, shit,' said Billy, and turned his face away.

The Junkie said, 'If it was me sitting there, I'd take something for it. Painkiller. You know what I mean?'

Billy turned his head back again and looked at him suspiciously. 'You mean smack,' he said.

'Not necessarily. There's other things you've never heard of. You wouldn't feel a thing and, even if you did, you wouldn't much care.'

'These other things. Do they have to go in through a needle?'

'For something like this, yeah.'

'Oh, shit,' said Billy, 'I hate needles.'

'It's okay,' said the Junkie. 'I think I've got a clean one.'

'Oh, shit,' said Billy.

So the Junkie asked for another fifty and Billy offered another ten, and they finally settled on the fifty because Billy hadn't got a clue how much the stuff was really worth and, besides, a hard light seemed to come into the Junkie's eyes which suggested that he'd conducted this kind of negotiation a thousand times before.

And, besides, Billy was getting scared.

'Wait here,' the Junkie said finally, and disappeared upstairs.

Billy slumped back in the chair with a feeling of miserable resignation. He wished that he didn't have to do this. He liked his dragon tattoo, and would be sorry to see it go; he'd had it for so long that it was like a part of him, and he was hardly even conscious of it for most of the time. That, in a way, had been his downfall. When he'd been standing there at the Building Society counter with the replica Luger and the open shopping bag and the ski mask (courtesy of Mac's, once again), the last thing on his mind had been the chance of his tattoo being picked up by the cameras. He'd been wearing his gloves, but the glove had ridden down the back of his hand and uncovered almost all of the design.

And then two nights ago there he'd been, sitting at home with a few cans of Draught Guinness in front of the TV while his mother pottered around upstairs, when up had come one of those *Crimewatch* shows where they asked for help with real-life cases and all the TV people who wished they were working in movies got the chance to ham it up doing crime reconstructions. He'd been watching it all with a sense of professional interest when, in a segment that they called *Rogues' Gallery*, he'd found himself looking at his own last job from an unexpected angle. He hadn't recognised himself straight away, but then he'd felt an inner leap of joy at the realisation that here he was, making the big time at last.

But then the joy had turned to ice as they'd taken a part of the picture and blown it right up and there was his one-of-a-kind tattoo, filling the screen from side to side and clear enough to be recognisable.

He'd packed his kitbag and been out of the house without any explanation that same night, almost within the hour. They were saying that the police had linked him with a string of other jobs. There was even a reward. Some of the people that Billy knew, they'd have sold their own parents for medical experiments if there was a drink in it for them. And the worst of it was that the people whom Billy knew, also knew Billy.

Millions of people watched that show. Those who made it crowed about their successes every week, and Billy sure as hell didn't want to become one of those. Even if his own friends didn't turn him in for the reward money, he'd inadvertently given the police a gift that they couldn't ignore. Small-time though he was they'd stay after him, like a man scratching around in his own behind until he dug out the peanut.

Somewhere upstairs, coming down to him through the ceiling, there was the sound of a floorboard being lifted.

Less than a minute later the Junkie was coming back down the stairs, and when he appeared in the doorway he was holding the same supermarket carrier bag that he'd had in his hand when Billy had first spotted him. In his other hand, he held an ordinary kitchen plate. On the plate lay a hypodermic syringe, an unlit candle, and a soot-marked spoon.

'Oh, shit,' said Billy, and looked away again.

'I told you, it's clean,' the Junkie insisted, setting everything down on the worktop. 'It's a brand-new needle. I take the old ones down to the clinic, and they do me a trade.'

'Wait a minute,' Billy said, and even in his own ears it sounded like the beginnings of a whine. 'I'm not sure this is a good idea. I don't want to get hurt but I don't want to get hooked on anything, either.'

'Nah,' said the Junkie, undoing Billy's cuff button and starting to push back his sleeve. 'That whole thing's just a myth.'

'Really?'

'Really,' said the Junkie. 'I've been using this stuff every day for the past four and a half years. If there was anything to it believe me, I'd know.'

'I'm just going to look over here,' said Billy.

The Junkie seemed amused. 'You really that scared of needles?' he said.

And Billy said, 'I'm not scared of anything, I'm just going to look over here.'

A couple of minutes later, he said, 'Was that it?'

'That was it.'

'You're pretty good at this.'

'Thank you. Just relax and let it start to work on you. I've got to find a few things in the kitchen.'

Billy lay back and closed his eyes. Maybe he could feel something already, he wasn't sure. He thought you were supposed to get a rush all at once like you were coming your brains out, but it wasn't happening that way. He wondered what would be next.

He knew even less about the art of tattoo removal than he did about the art of tattooing. Some people said it simply couldn't be done with any success, others that you had to go to a really expensive clinic and maybe even have skin grafts and everything. But then he'd heard that what they did was to use needles to hammer bleach down into the skin, deeper even than the inks that they were being used to eradicate, and he'd thought; Well, it doesn't sound pleasant but it doesn't sound too complicated, either.

And then he thought, the kitchen?

And he thought; Oh my God, he's going to use ordinary household bleach, and he started to sit up with the intention of getting out of the chair and heading for the door without a single look back; he could maybe just wear a bandage and tell people that he'd been burned and his hand was taking a long time to heal, and then he could settle in a new town and meet new people and he wouldn't have to go through anything like this at all . . .

And then a great sense of warmth and well-being hit him all at once, and it was better than coming his brains out because, to be honest, he'd always had this little problem of self-control that he never liked to talk about and always had to apologise for, and he sank back into the padded seat and, hey, wasn't it just the best and most comfortable chair in the history of mass-produced furniture?

'Getting any effect yet?' the Junkie said as he laid a few things out on the table alongside, and Billy said, 'I dunno. Maybe.'

He let his head fall back. It felt as if it was sinking into the padding about a foot deep or more. He smiled stupidly.

'Last chance to change your mind,' the Junkie said.

And Billy said, 'Do it.'

The Junkie asked him to flex his fingers and he did, and then he had to ask the Junkie if anything was happening because he couldn't feel any feedback at all. The Junkie told him that was fine, and so Billy turned his face to the sweat-scented vinyl in the knowledge that when he sat up again, it would be over. He could move on, start again; and if anyone came looking, he could hold up his hands and say *Who, me?* with total confidence.

Move on. That was about what it entailed, because with or without the tattoo there was no going home. Thought about in the abstract, back when he hadn't actually been obliged to make the break, the notion had even held certain attractions; there was a lot of shit in his life that he'd always reckoned he could happily leave behind, a lot of arguments and all kinds of resentments, but somehow he couldn't see it that way any more. He kept thinking about his video collection. Every Saturday afternoon he liked to hang around street markets and car boot sales, looking for old stuff that the video libraries were selling off. He had all the *Halloweens* except for the first one, every one of the *Friday the 13th* movies, and almost a complete set of the *Police Academies* except for the one that was too new to have made it through the system yet. All lost. His mother would probably give them away or even just throw them out, the way she had with his comics all those years ago. Some of those comics would have been worth real money today. If he'd still had them, he'd never have needed to turn to crime at all.

Obviously, his troubles were all her fault.

He winced. Something hurt.

'Sorry,' the Junkie said. 'This isn't quite as sharp as I would have liked.'

He'd been drifting. That wouldn't do. The last thing he needed would be to fall asleep and then wake up with the job half-done and the Junkie gone and his bagful of money gone with him. Even worse . . . what if the Junkie followed *Crimewatch?* Stranger things had happened. He'd know that the reward was more than the five hundred that Billy had offered, and Billy could wake up surrounded by police.

But if the Junkie had ever owned a TV, Billy reckoned that he'd probably sold or hocked it long ago. Not much danger there. But as far as the security of his kitbag was concerned, he'd already shown the Junkie what was inside.

Better to stay awake.

Concentrating his attention as best he could, Billy searched around for a conversational opener and then said, 'How long have you been doing this?'

'About ten minutes now,' the Junkie said. 'It's not quite as easy as I thought. I'm trying to do it neat and there's all kinds of stuff in the way.'

'I meant, how long have you been doing tattoos?'

'I don't do tattoos,' the Junkie said.

This struck Billy as not a bad joke at all. He said, 'So what's the big sign over the door and all the needles and stuff?'

'Oh, they're Steve's. He's the tattooist. But he doesn't open the shop on Wednesdays.'

Billy frowned in his stupor. 'So, who are you?'

'I'm Kevin. I just rent the upstairs from Steve. The roof leaks and it's a dump, but he lets me have it cheap as long as I pay him cash. I think it's a tax dodge. But I owe him more than a hundred in rent and he was going to throw me out; this means I can pay him off and have some left over.'

Billy let his mind work on this one for a while, to no great effect.

And then he said, 'But if you're not a tattooist, how come you know how to do a tattoo removal?'

There was a long silence.

And then the Junkie, his voice sounding as if it was coming from a long way away, said, 'You wanted someone who could take off the tattoo?'

Billy sat up. He could only manage about halfway.

He looked.

The Junkie was sitting there on one of the hard chairs from by the wall, looking politely puzzled. He was spattered with red from the chin down, as if he'd been mixing up something nasty in a blender and had forgotten to put the lid on. In one hand there was a big, none-too-sharp looking kitchen knife; in the other, a towel that he'd been using to dab his working area clean. On the padded support before him, Billy's wrist had been tied down with a length of bandage that appeared also to be serving as a tourniquet.

But the most curious thing about the entire scene was the clear piece of daylight that was showing between Billy's hand and arm.

The Junkie said, 'Don't judge it by what you see right now. It'll look much better when it's finished.'

Billy gawped at the sight. Couldn't take it in. Still he felt no pain, no sensation at all from the shoulder down. The Junkie was watching his face, trying to guess his mood.

He was lost for words. Except, perhaps, for the phrase *Hanging by a thread*, which dropped into his mind unbidden and wouldn't go away.

He didn't dare move.

Not an inch.

He looked at the Junkie.

And the Junkie said hopefully, 'Do I still get the five hundred?'

FREDA WARRINGTON

MY NAME IS NOT JULIETTE

Philip knew there was something wrong with Jennifer. All the way to the theatre she'd seemed on edge for no reason. Now as the house lights dimmed her smile was fixed, her eyes scared. He felt irritated. If something was up, why couldn't she just come out with it?

He leaned across their small daughter Sarah, who was sitting between them, clutching the programme. *The Ballet Lenoir presents Swan Lake*, said the curling letters.

'I'm told this is going to be something pretty special,' he said. 'It had better be; tickets cost a bloody fortune. Glad the *Mercury* is paying for us.'

Sarah — seven years old, her feet dangling over the edge of the seat — was wide-eyed. Philip envied her innocence. This was an event that would cast its magic through the rest of her life. For him, a theatre critic, it was merely a job.

In the moments before the overture began, the auditorium was filled with rustling darkness, a palpable anticipation. But Jen was smiling too hard, as if she were here under sufferance and trying to be nice about it, as always.

'Just relax and enjoy it, okay?' Philip said brusquely. She winced at his tone, which only annoyed him more.

Blonde, compliant Jen, always putting everyone else before herself. No man could wish for a better wife. But God, her ridiculous moods made him angry sometimes. He'd have it out with her later, but now the curtains were gliding apart, the green and silver world of *Swan Lake* opening up to absorb him.

Jennifer could hide nothing from Philip. She knew she was irritating him and that there'd be a row when they got home. Anxiety formed a hard ball in her chest. She had these few hours, while the swan maidens spun their magic on the stage, before the showdown — but suspending real life was a trick that eluded her.

She envied Philip's ability to detach himself. She envied Sarah, who was oblivious to everything but the unfolding story. The ballet was a classical production with no modern grotesquerie. There was an underwater quality to the dancing, an ivory-tinged slow motion dream seen through rippling light. It was mesmeric. Yet, like a nervous swimmer clinging to the side, Jen could not fully lose herself in it.

She knew her worries were trivial, even pathetic. Only that her mother wanted Jen to stay with her at the weekend and Jen, as usual, couldn't say no and dare not tell Philip. He would be furious. 'Not again!' he'd shouted the last time. 'You're my wife, you can't be at the beck and call of your mother all the time. She'll never get her claws out of you if you keep giving in!'

Easy for him, when he wasn't prey to her parents' subtle emotional blackmail. Jen tried to please them all, ended up being slammed between them like a squash ball. It was her own fault, of course. She could be bright and breezy and cope with anything — until there was a row with Philip. Then his voice raised in anger and his piercing stare were all it took to wake the demons of her childhood. His hostility made her a little girl again, frightened and confused. She couldn't bear it, would do anything to be loved again.

Anything to protect herself from the demoness of her nightmares, the slayer and punisher of bad children: Lilith.

It wasn't rational for a grown woman still to be afraid of a myth, Jen told herself. But she couldn't rake out the poisonous weeds sown in childhood.

It wasn't her parents' fault, even though her father was something of a tyrant, her mother an emotional manipulator. It was her Nan — her father's mother — who'd told her the stories of Lilith.

Jen tried to concentrate on the ballet but the stage seemed as distant as a television. Memories fell like a veil between her and the real world. The dark, high-ceilinged room, Nan bending towards her, the streetlight outlining her thin beaky nose. Nan smelled of mothballs, lavender, and of the damp that pervaded her house; and although she wore bright, cheap crimplene, Jen seemed to picture her in black satin and lace.

Six-year-old Jen had been disobedient. Her father had told her to stop playing with a china figure she'd picked up. She had defied him, and a moment later the figure had slipped out of her hand and shattered. An accident, but her father, incensed, had dragged her along two streets to her grandmother's house. 'I'm not having this child back in the house until she learns to behave like a civilised human being!' he said, and dumped her there.

He never explicitly asked his mother to punish Jen. He didn't have to. Nan had her own ways of dealing with disobedient children.

'D'you know who Lilith was?' Nan had Jewish European ancestry but her accent was from Sunderland, where she'd been brought up. Jen didn't know where Sunderland was, but she thought of it as some strange dark netherworld where witches came from. Sundered Land. 'Adam had a wife before Eve. The first wife's name was Lilith, but she was wicked and disobedient, just like you, pet. She wouldn't do what Adam told her. Instead she ran away into the wilderness and turned into a horrible demon who flies around at night looking for bad children. Lilith married the Devil, see, 'cause she's as wicked as him and she can't ever have real babies, only demon-babies. That's why she takes revenge on women who can. She hates them.' The story was always muddled, senseless, yet unspeakably frightening. Jen felt Lilith's presence in the room, snake-like and shadow-black. 'Hates them. She'd like to take *all* their children away and suck their blood. But God won't let her because it wouldn't be fair, would it? So he did a deal with her. He said, "I'll protect the good children and you can have the bad children, because they need to be punished." So when a child is bad, along comes Lilith and takes them away. D'you understand me, pet?'

Little Jennifer nodded, chewing the hair of her doll in fright.

'If you're bad she'll take you away in the night, bite your throat and suck out all your blood,' Nan said confidently. 'Have you been bad enough for Lilith to come? Wait and see! If you're still here in the morning, it means God's forgiven you. Then you'd better not be a naughty girl, ever again!'

Then Nan had locked her in the bare, damp bedroom and left her there until morning. Left her to watch for movement in the shadows, to transform the bulk of clothes of furniture into threatening figures. Jen had a clear picture of Lilith. A grotesque woman with long black hair, who wound across the floor like a snake, her body clothed in coal-black wings. All night she waited for Lilith to slither from under the bed.

She cried herself to sleep, clutching her doll. When she woke in the morning, the doll was gone. She went half-mad trying to find it, until Nan led her up to the attic, saying, 'Perhaps Lilith came after all.'

There was the doll on the dusty floorboards, its dress torn off, its plastic limbs mutilated, red stuff smeared all round its neck and trickling down its pink torso.

'Ah,' Nan said wisely. 'Lilith didn't take you, but she took your baby. It's a warning, see? You've got to be good all your life, or she'll take your *real* babies away. But be an obedient girl and you'll be safe.'

It was a warning Jen never forgot.

The grown-up Jen felt a white-hot anger at her Nan for terrorising a small child, but the fear had come first and was stronger, more primeval. Nan had been obsessed with the mythology of sin and punishment; perhaps she thought she was doing Jen good, or perhaps she was just plain evil. Whatever, Nan's death, when Jen was fourteen, did not make Lilith go away. On the contrary, it only seemed to unleash Lilith from all restraint to fly free in the darkness. Only now it was not herself Jen feared for, but her daughter.

When Sarah was born, Philip had mocked his wife for putting a Hebrew amulet in the cot to protect the baby against Lilith. 'Since when have you been Jewish?' he said incredulously.

'You don't understand. My grandmother —' She tried to explain, but Philip wouldn't listen.

'I'm not having this superstitious nonsense! I don't know what's got into you! You don't even believe in God!' No, nor in angels or devils or Adam and Eve. Only in Lilith. And she'd had to stand and watch Philip tear up the paper charm and throw it away. Since then she'd learned to hide her true feelings from him with lies.

That was Jen's fault, too, for marrying someone just like her father; a big, dark, self-obsessed man who took her completely for granted. Both loved her conditionally according to how "good" she was. But being perfect for her husband and perfect for her parents were two different things, and the difficulty of balancing them was wearing her thin . . .

Suddenly, in Act III, the ballet's enchantment hooked her at last. The ballroom scene, where the sorcerer sends his daughter Odile to seduce Siegfried away from his true love, Odette. The ballerina spinning across the stage in glittering black was a striking contrast to the dazzling white of the swans. Odile was breathtaking, and she caught Jen's attention as the other dancers had not. Such expressions in her long white limbs, her gracefulness, the way the dark costume moulded itself to her body. She radiated arrogance, yet mimicked Odette's vulnerability to perfection. She seduced Siegfried and the audience with equal ease.

Odile pirouetted, eyes fixed on one spot to keep her balance as she turned — and that spot was Jennifer's face. In lakes of kohl, Odile's eyes were jewel-cold, and they hung on Jen's gaze, scorching her with their coldness.

And they recognised each other.

I know who you are, said the dancer's stare. *I know your disobedient thoughts and all the little lies you tell to keep people quiet, so they won't see you as you really are. But your sins will find you out and you'll be mine.*

And Jennifer thought, *Lilith*.

This was idiocy, of course. This was paranoia. She realised it but she still couldn't stop it. Knowledge impaled itself in her like a thrown knife and quivered there. *This woman is Lilith. This woman wants to hurt me. She is going to steal my husband and kill my daughter.*

Jen glanced at Sarah. Her daughter was spellbound. So was Philip, in a different way. She'd seen that look before, when he saw a stunning woman and thought Jen wasn't watching. He ran his tongue over his lips, twice.

Jen began to feel sick and shaky. There was a sack of sand in her chest. Beginning of a panic attack, no reason for it — but that was the essence of phobia. Irrationality. She clutched the scratchy velvet arms of the seat. *Breathe, damn it. Just remember to breathe.*

'Bloody superb,' Philip muttered. 'There was pure evil radiating from her!'

When *Swan Lake* came to its poignant end, and the company took their rapturous curtain calls, Odile was absent. The audience shouted ecstatically for her; still she did not appear. As the house lights came up, Philip rifled through the programme. 'Strange. Odette and Odile are traditionally danced by the same ballerina. But that Odile wasn't Odette.'

Jen was exhausted with tension. All she wanted was to go home, take a valium, and sleep. Leaning over, she said, 'Look, it says there: Odette/Odile, Marie Darby.'

'I know, but it wasn't the same girl,' Philip said excitedly. 'Was it, Sarah? They looked quite similar, but it was just clever make-up.'

Jen didn't know why he was so worked up about it. She found his excitement distasteful, like inappropriate lust. 'Who is it then?'

'The owner of this company is a woman called Juliette Lenoir. But no-one knows anything about her, no-one ever sees her. I think that was her dancing Odile! Why does she make a mystery of herself? Why dance anonymously? There could be a real story in this, not just a one-column review. Come on.'

'Where?'

'We're going backstage.'

Jennifer's heart sank. 'We should go home. Sarah's tired.'

'No, I'm not, Mum,' Sarah said vehemently, bright-eyed.

'They won't let you in,' Jen said desperately.

He tutted, exasperated. 'Come off it, Jen. I'm known by the theatre staff. It's part of my bloody job, for Chrissakes!'

'Oh go on, Mum, please,' said Sarah, looking up with dark excited eyes. Jen gave in, covering her anxiety with a smile. What the hell did it matter who danced Lilith? Slip of the tongue. Odile.

The painted brick corridor behind the stage stank of dust and damp and musty material, years of sweat and greasepaint. Ropes hung from the shadows and the walls were lined with hampers. A murmur of voices came from the dressing rooms.

'God, I hope she's still here,' said Philip.

Jen, feeling awkward and out of place, prayed she was not.

A swan maiden in costume went past, delicate in snowy tulle. Sarah stared at her in awe. 'Excuse me, mademoiselle,' said Philip, all business-like charm. 'Could you tell me where I might find Juliette Lenoir.'

The dancer looked startled. 'I'm sorry, sir, she's not available.'

Jen was relieved, but Philip persisted. 'That was her dancing Odile, wasn't it?'

From the girl's guarded reaction, he'd obviously guessed right. 'When Madame dances she doesn't advertise the fact. She won't see you. You'd be wasting your time trying.'

'That's a shame. It would mean so much to my little girl.'

The swan maiden smiled and bent down to Sarah. 'Well, she can meet the rest of us. Would you like that? What's your name?'

As they were talking, a woman slipped past in the background, wrapped in a lavender cotton robe. Jen's heart gave a heavy thud of recognition. She said nothing, but Philip had spotted her too. Rudely he rushed in pursuit, calling, 'Madame Lenoir! Could you spare a moment, please?'

The woman stopped and turned. Her face, scrubbed of make-up, was unexpectedly fresh and young, but her eyes again turned Jen to ice. Clear polished agate swirling with shades of silver, violet, blue, captivating and glacial. Her hair was loose over her shoulders, a crinkled mass of black all dishevelled from being compressed under the feather head-dress.

She seemed smaller than she had appeared in costume, but no less stunning. It was an unapproachable, transcendent beauty. Watching Philip with icy appraisal, she stood half-turned away as he spoke to her, denying him, shutting him out.

'You danced tonight, but your name wasn't in the programme.' Philip had — on the surface, at least — an easy manner that usually disarmed stubborn interviewees. 'You're extraordinarily young to be the director of a ballet company. I imagined Juliette Lenoir to be much older. I'm Philip Linley —'

'A journalist?' she interrupted. Despite her name, her accent was English. Her voice, cool and gentle, gave nothing away.

'I'm the theatre critic of the *Evening Mercury* and I'm about to write an ecstatic review of tonight's performance. The problem is, there is very little information available about the Ballet Lenoir. I'd be so grateful if you could spare a few minutes to tell me something about the company.' He smiled. 'I'd assume you'd prefer it if we got our facts straight?'

Juliette Lenoir almost returned the smile. Not quite. 'Journalists are vampires, are they not? They suck out their victims' lives and smear them in black and white over something that's not fit to be used for cat litter.'

It struck Jen that Madame Lenoir was teasing Philip.

'No it's not that sort of paper. We're perfectly respectable.'

'I'm sure you are, but I don't give interviews.' She sounded final. But then she turned, looked straight at Jennifer, and seemed to change her mind.

Again Odile's searchlight stare went into Jen. A beam of hostility. A look that actually could kill. Jen felt a fist clench in her stomach and she glanced around anxiously for Sarah, relieved to see her still with the swan maiden.

'That is, I don't give interviews as a rule. But this time . . .' Lenoir spoke slowly, still gazing at Jen. Then her gaze flicked to Philip and she smiled. *Serpent!* Jen thought. *God, why do I hate her so? I've never hated anyone on sight like this.* 'We'll see. But not now.'

'Over dinner?' Philip said eagerly, subtlety deserting him.

'No. Meet me here . . . on Sunday evening. There's no performance then. But I'll talk to you only on one condition; that you bring your wife and child with you.'

He looked dismayed, but hid it with a laugh. 'I don't normally take them to work.'

'I don't care what you normally do, Mr Linley,' Juliette Lenoir said sweetly. 'If you want the interview, bring them. I would like to know you all.'

Looking at Sarah, she touched her tongue to her upper lip.

Philip was about to leave for the assignation — for once not feeling seen-it-all-before jaded but giddily excited — when Jen started again.

'Don't go, Philip,' she said. She was standing in the hallway, having made no attempt to get ready. He felt like slapping her. All weekend she tied herself in neurotic knots over a simple interview that was actually nothing to do with her.

'Why the hell not?'

'I don't know,' she said helplessly. 'It's late. I don't like her. Just don't!'

'For God's sake, Jen, how can you not like her! You don't even know her! Anyone else would give their right arm to meet an artist like her! What is your problem?'

Jen didn't answer. He felt too preoccupied to get really angry with her. He held her shoulders. 'Look, she insisted I take you and Sarah with me. If you don't come I might not get the damned interview and it'll be your fault. Now get Sarah ready and get your coat!'

It wasn't like Jen to be so stubborn, but she pulled away. 'It's much too late for Sarah to go out! We're not going. Why is it so important, anyway?'

'Shit!' said Philip, losing patience. 'I've had enough. Stuff it, I'm off.'

As he made for the door she followed him, pleading. He grabbed his coat and slammed the front door in her face. I can't handle this cryptic hysteria, he thought savagely. Why the hell does she have to get into such a state about nothing? Anyone would think I was hoping to have an affair with Juliette Lenoir.

As his car slipped though the orange glow of the street lights, Philip worked out how he'd explain his wife's absence to the dancer. Sarah not well. Yes. Why the hell did she want them there, anyway? If it was a chaperon she needed, she could provide her own. He must see her again at all costs, and he didn't care whether he got a story out of it or not. Lovely Juliette. Love, lust, whatever it was, he couldn't get her out of his mind.

When he arrived he found the theatre in complete darkness. Sunday, no performance, everything locked up. His heart dropped with the certainty that there was no-one here, that she'd forgotten or never meant to come in the first place. 'Bloody prima donna,' he muttered.

But he found the stage door unlocked so he went in, feeling for a light switch in the darkness. He found one but the dull click brought no burst of light; power must be off at a master switch. Looked like she hadn't turned up; still, he'd make sure. Holding a copy of Saturday's *Mercury* under his arm, he felt his way along the wall towards the dressing rooms. The stillness had a strange intensity, as if the ropes and curtains and played-out emotions exuded weight into the darkness. The building creaked, ancient pipes gurgled. Suddenly his foot hit something solid and he stumbled forward, barking his shin on a hard edge.

Swearing, Philip remembered the matches in his pocket and lit one. The glow flared white on a "No Smoking" sign and slanted across the short flight of steps into which he'd blundered. They led up to the stage. Might as well check it, nothing to lose.

The flame burned his fingers and died, just as he reached the wings. In blackness, the stage sets were a maze around him. As he fumbled for another match, he heard a disembodied voice.

'You shouldn't play with matches backstage, Mr Linley. Fire regulations. Didn't you see the sign?'

Philip drew a sharp breath. Her voice seemed to come from the centre of the stage. Carefully he eased his way around the painted panels and felt the cool space of the auditorium opening in front of him. She said, 'But you could lend me a match, anyway?'

He managed to light another one. Her hand touched his and he jumped, not realising she was standing so close. He caught a glimpse of her opalescent face as she took the match from him and turned away. She was a fragment of a silhouette; a cobweb of hair and a curved shoulder. She bent down and other small lights began to appear. She was lighting a circle of candles around herself. When she had finished she straightened up, and he saw her at last.

He gasped out loud. She was wearing a black t-shirt, skin-tight black leather trousers, a lace shawl looped messily around her neck, and heavy, buckled boots. He simply hadn't expected her to be dressed like that; he'd imagined her in a classic dancer's style, maybe a pale leotard and wrap-around skirt. But it was very nice. She was unbelievably enticing, with the candles throwing light and shadow from below.

'Is something wrong, Mr Linley?' she asked, sitting cross-legged on the boards in the circle of light. The way she looked at him seemed hostile, mocking. He couldn't work her out at all.

'Good evening, Madame Lenoir,' he said. 'No, I'd just made my mind up there was no-one here. Thank you for coming. I brought last night's *Mercury* so you can read my review.'

He held the paper out to her, but she made no move to take it. He dropped his arm, feeling awkward. He said, 'Rather than scramble around trying to find the master switch, shall we go somewhere more comfortable? There's a very nice wine bar —'

'I'm quite comfortable here,' she said. Then she smiled. 'You think I'm peculiar, don't you?'

He grinned back. 'Well, I have to admit I've never met a director of ballet quite like you.'

Her sweet tone turned to steel. 'I asked you to bring your wife and child. Where are they?'

'I'm sorry, but Sarah was running a temperature. Jen couldn't leave her.'

He saw from the coldness of her eyes that she knew he was lying. 'I asked you to bring them,' she repeated patiently. 'It was important.'

'I'm afraid I don't understand.' He lifted his hands in a *Give me some help here* gesture. 'Madame, I only want to write a feature for my paper, I don't see —'

She stood up and took a step towards him, hands on hips. Candlelight slid over the satiny contours of her legs. 'Why would I think you wanted to do anything else?'

How the hell did you break the ice with this woman? "Peculiar" was an understatement. 'I don't deny I'm attracted to you. The truth is, I think Jen is jealous. She seems threatened by you. I just couldn't persuade her to come. However, I can assure you that I intend to keep this on a purely professional level.'

'Unless,' said Juliette. She moved towards him and put her hands on his shoulders. 'Unless, you thought, something like this happened.' And to his absolute astonishment, she put her arms round him and kissed his neck. Philip was so startled he froze. Juliette didn't know he'd fantasised all day and night about just such a scene — but the reality of it was nothing like the fantasy. It was weird, unsettling, passionless.

'Perhaps, I'd better go,' he said.

'Doesn't Jen do this to you?' She nipped the angle of his jaw between his front teeth. It hurt. He began to feel both frightened and aroused, his groin stirring, aching. 'I asked you to bring her! I don't care about your newspaper or your ego. It's your wife and little girl I want.'

Her words chilled him. He held her arms, torn between pushing her away and kissing her. She was shaking a little. She seemed . . . angry. 'What the hell do you mean, you want . . .'

'I bet Jen doesn't do *this*,' Juliette said tightly. Her teeth closed on his throat. Jesus, she'd leave him with a love bite! Philip began to panic but he couldn't push her off. She bit harder . . . and harder . . . until all the tendons down his neck screamed and then what felt like two little scalpels stabbed through his flesh and he began to fall down into the darkness.

In the darkness, Jen was talking to herself.

'You say, "Do you love me," and they say, "For ever," but what they really mean is, I love you today because I'm in a good mood. The next day you ask again and it's, "Not today, you've been a bad girl." That's how they control me, my father and mother, withholding their love then dispensing it in little parcels as a reward. I'm like a dog begging for the crumbs they drop. Now I do the same with Philip because I don't know any other way. *I don't know any other way. Lilith, so please, for God's sake leave me alone.*'

She lay in bed staring at the ceiling, listening to the slow thick beating of her heart. Waiting for Philip to come home. Once she dropped off to sleep and dreamed that she got up and went into Sarah's room and there was a serpent rearing up over Sarah's bed, its thick black neck glittering like sequins. It had a beak like a swan, and in the beak was the paper charm that was meant to protect Sarah. And on the bed Sarah lay cut and mutilated, only she was a doll with pink plastic flesh and glass eyes . . .

Jennifer twisted violently out of sleep, sweating. Something other than the nightmare had woken her, some sound intruding on her doze. She lay rigid, straining to hear something. She sensed the house lying dark and still around her. Nothing to fear, Sarah safe in bed.

'Shit, I've got to stop this,' she whispered. 'Philip, damn you, why don't you come home?'

She thought she heard the front door open. She sat up and put on the bedside light. Utter silence. Must have been the neighbours. Trembling, she took her valium bottle from the bedside drawer and was fumbling with the cap when the bedroom door burst open.

The handle hit the wall with a bang that made the door shudder in its frame. Philip stood in the doorway, his face the colour of damp newspaper, streaked with sweat. His eyes were terrible. 'Jen,' he said hoarsely.

He surged into the room like a drunk, kneeling on the edge of the bed and crawling towards her on hands and knees. She struggled to evade him but the bedclothes pinned her in and she couldn't move.

'Stop it!' she said, high-pitched. 'For God's sake, what's wrong with you?'

He thrust his face towards hers. 'She's here, Jen. Don't know how. I was in the car and she was on foot but she still got here first. Got to get you out, she . . .' His eyes went blank and he passed out across her, a dead weight.

Then she saw two purple wounds in his neck, streaks of blood running along his collarbone.

Weak with panic, it was all Jen could do to pull herself free of him. 'Philip!' She shook him, bent her head to his heart. It was beating, slow and heavy. He was breathing steadily but she couldn't bring him round.

While she had lain listening for Philip, had Lilith already entered the house, silently, without breaking windows or locks? How long had she been here?

Jennifer felt overpowering terror, but no surprise at all. It was as if she had been waiting for this all her life. She looked at the telephone. What could the police do about Lilith? Could a doctor heal a bite?

No-one could help her. She had to face Lilith alone. Sarah . . .

Suddenly she was no longer timid Jennifer but the feral mother who would fight and and claw to protect her child. She was up and running across the landing to Sarah's room. There was no serpent, no dismembered doll's corpse. There was nothing.

The bed was empty. Jen flicked the light on, as if that could make her reappear. 'Sarah!'

Gently now. Don't panic. Lilith is cunning.

Jen crept downstairs, making as little sound as possible. Through the crackled panel of glass in a hall door she could see lights in the sitting room, strange faint glimmers that came from no lamps she and Philip possessed. Fear strangled her heart. She dare not, could not go in . . .

Think. She slid softly into the kitchen and took the biggest, sharpest knife from the block. She gripped it hard. They were vegetarians so she'd rarely used it, never slipped it into flesh . . .

The lights glittered red through the glass. She paused, staring at two distorted shapes moving through the dappled panes. One belonged to a slim woman and one to a child . . .

Jen flung the door open and cried, 'Sarah!'

Her daughter, in pyjamas, turned to the door, looking startled. Behind her, hands on the child's shoulders, was that woman, Juliette, Odile. Lilith, with her huge cold eyes and fountain of serpent-black hair. They both gazed at Jennifer as if caught in some shameful, intimate act.

For a moment, all Jennifer's anger was directed at her daughter. 'What are you doing, you naughty little —'

Sarah's face fell. 'Juliette was teaching me how to dance. Look, Mum.' And she arranged her feet in first position and curved an arm to the front, side, above.

'We were waiting for you,' Juliette said softly. Her gaze spilled ice-water over Jen's rage. 'Sarah wants to be a dancer. I think she would be very good. Don't you think,' her gaze swept down to the knife in Jen's hand, 'that you had better put that down before you frighten Sarah? You are upsetting her — not me.'

Lowering the knife, Jen tried to sound calm and in control. 'Sarah, go to your room.'

'But Mum, I like Juliette, she was —'

'Don't argue,' Jen stared at the demon, willing her to let Sarah go. 'Go to your room and stay there.'

Juliette lifted her hands from the child's shoulders and Sarah ran out of the room, shutting the door behind her. Jen's relief was momentary. Now she was alone with the creature who'd sucked Philip's blood. And the creature was sitting down on the sofa, composed and malevolent in the light of the five black candles she had lit on the coffee table. Heavy scents drifted from them; sandalwood, jasmine, myrrh, making Jen dizzy.

'Why did you attack my husband?'

Juliette shrugged just a little. 'He made me angry. He offered me a drink. Take your pick. But what makes you so sure it was me?'

'Because I know you!'

'Really? And who do you think I am?'

Jen was holding the knife so hard her hand went numb. She said, 'Lilith.'

Juliette looked genuinely startled. 'How did you know?'

The admission was a kick in Jennifer's breastbone. Until then she had subconsciously hoped Juliette would deny it; as if it would have been easier to deal with a simple vampire or homicidal maniac. Anyone but *Her*. 'You're not in the shape of a serpent, you haven't got wings, but I always knew you'd come for me. I could never be good enough to keep you away. But it's not fair! I've tried so bloody hard!'

Juliette looked hard and quizzically at her. 'I knew I must come to you when I noticed you in the audience. When I see someone like you, I can't leave them alone until it's finished. I have to kill the child.'

'No!' Metallic shivers slid down her shoulders, her spine. 'Take me, not Sarah. I'm the one who's been bad. Please, I'll do anything —'

'That's it. *You'll do anything.*' Juliette stood up and began to walk around the room. Her volatile restlessness filled Jen with fear. 'By pleading with me, you give me this power over you!'

'Give you —'

'God, I hate this,' Juliette murmured. Her face gleamed like nacre and her lips lifted over neat teeth. She looked insane. 'I don't want to do this, I hate it, but you give me no choice! The child is bad. The child makes you unhappy.' Juliette came towards Jen with all the electric energy of Odile, her hair like a cloud of black silk. 'Who is Lilith? Answer! Who do you think she is?'

'A demoness,' said Jennifer, breathing fast. 'The mother of vampires and the enemy of mothers. She comes in the form of a great long-necked serpent with rustling black wings. Seducer of husbands, child-killer.'

'I thought so. You listen to their voices but you ignore your own voice.' The vampire stepped closer, smiling bitterly. Jennifer raised the knife, determined to keep her away from Sarah. Juliette gave her weapon a contemptuous glance. 'You can't stop me. The child is here.'

'No.'

'Here in the room, Jennifer. Inside.'

Then Juliette came forward in a rush and she was Lilith; dark, corrupted beauty, rage and pain. Her mouth was open, her neat canine teeth lengthening as Jen stared, sliding down their sockets and locking into place with a faint crunch. Sharp white fangs. The weird familiarity, the near-ludicrousness of the image from film, only heightened Jen's horror. The reality was . . . hideous.

Jen made a lunge with the knife, missed. It fell from her fingers as Lilith caught her arms and pinned her against the door. Her fangs drove into Jen's neck like nails. Pain throbbed through her from head to foot.

She felt the blood leaving her veins. Vile sensation, a diffuse tingling all through her body, a swimming sickness. The whole room was falling on her like a billowing brown tent . . .

She was lying back in the armchair. She must have blacked out for a moment because now Lilith was a few feet away in the middle of the room. She did not look sated or content. Instead her lungs filled and emptied as if they would burst her slender ribcage apart. The look on her face was one of such terror that Jennifer forgot herself in an instinctive burst of concern.

'Juliette? Oh God . . .'

The vampire lurched back and caught herself on an arm of the sofa, seeming to brace herself against some internal pressure. Then her mouth opened and she began to breathe out what looked like a wobbling bubble of blood. The blood did not fall but hung in the air above the carpet, like a mass of liquid in space, undulating.

It began to drift towards Jennifer. It took on a shape. A girl-child.

Jennifer let out a cry. The child was rippling, dark, featureless. And it was still attached by a maroon strand, like a hideous umbilical cord, to Lilith's mouth. Her lips were a stretched O around the viscid string and her eyes bulged as if they would fall from her skull.

Jen put up her hands to keep the child away, but it kept coming, impaled itself on her fingers and broke, like a soft-walled sac of fluid. Blood gushed and formed a gleaming pool on the carpet. No child. Just the dark lake on the floor. Lilith spat out the end of the cord and slumped back, gasping, like a woman delivering up an afterbirth.

The silence roared like machinery in Jen's ears. She hung over the side of her chair, dry-retching.

Hands on her head, gentle. A glass of water at her lips, cold liquid as compelling as wine. She looked up into Lilith's face and saw that the vampire was calm again; cloud-white unhuman beauty, eyes of amethyst and lapis, her hair the long black wings of a fallen angel.

Jennifer realised she wasn't frightened any more.

'I am sorry, Jennifer,' Lilith said quietly. 'It almost kills me to do that. Sometimes I wish it would. When I see a child I have to kill it.'

'I don't understand,' said Jen.

'Let me tell you who Lilith really is, though you will soon come to know it for yourself. You said she was evil; but men have only called her evil because they fear her. They split women in half; good and bad, virgin and whore, submissive and disobedient, Eve and Lilith, Odette and Odile. But we are all one. Lilith's crime was her refusal to be dominated. She is rage and freedom and sexuality, all the things that women are not meant to be, even today, because men so fear them. Yes, she is dark, but darkness is only the essential complement of light. It is mystery; not evil. How people fear mystery!'

'And love it,' said Jen.

'Yes.' The vampire tenderly stroked her arm. 'To deny Lilith brings disaster, but that's what men and women have done for centuries. The child I kill is the child inside the adult, Jen. The infant that makes you crave love and approval, keeps you helpless and dependent on others for your sense of worth. Lilith despises that need. She strangles it so you can grow and be yourself.'

'Did you do this to Philip as well?'

A sour half-smile. 'It is not so easy with men. Sometimes they do not . . . survive. But sometimes . . .'

Jennifer wasn't concerned about Philip. She realised that her anxiety had gone. It was the first time she had been free of it for years. In sheer relief she put her arms round the vampire's neck. 'Juliette,' she said.

But the vampire took Jen's wrists in her thin cool hands and disengaged herself. 'My name is not Juliette. Juliette Lenoir does not exist. Stop this. You never need to cling to anyone again.'

And Jen knew it was true. The child was dead, her true self rising from the ruins. 'But how did this happen to you? Were you ever human?'

The dancer moved away, avoiding her eyes. 'I don't speak of it, dear. Let us just say that it is the price I pay to go on dancing.'

The air was narcotic with incense. Jennifer looked at the dancer's slim form moving against the smoky light and thought how beautiful she was. I would like to stay here and look at her for ever . . .

She heard the cry coming from far away but rushing in fast; a throaty yell of despair, a battle cry. Philip burst into the room, his face wild. He saw the knife lying where Jen had dropped it, seized it and lunged towards Juliette.

'No!' screamed Jennifer. She flung herself between them, thrusting out her hands. She did not feel the blade enter her flesh. She fell back onto the carpet, found herself staring at the black handle of the knife sticking up from her palm, her fingers curling up around it from a swamp of blood. But Juliette — Lilith — had vanished.

They sat together in the firelight, Philip gently holding Jen's bandaged hand. She looked at him affectionately but remotely, seeing now that he wasn't like her father, not some monstrous patriarch whose word was law. He was just like her. Too stupid not to play the roles they thought were expected of them. The same went for her parents, for that matter.

They sat without speaking of what had happened. Jennifer was not sure Philip understood or even remembered too clearly. But he had changed. And Jennifer would never forget.

Sarah was sitting on the floor, looking at a book about the history of ballet. One of Philip's reference books that he'd owned for years. She loved the pictures. Watching her, Jennifer thought, am I repeating the same mistakes my parents made with me, brain-washing her in a thousand tiny ways that only the smiling doormat is worthy of love — while the Lilith part of her is feared and shunned until it rises in a rage and bites back?

Over Sarah's shoulder Jen saw a photograph of Margot Fonteyn in mouthwatering red net, languishing in the arms of Rudolf Nureyev. *Marguerite and Armand*. But the child pressed her finger to the portrait below it. 'Look, Mummy.'

Jennifer leaned down and recognised a scene from *Swan Lake*; poised in grainy monochrome, the sorceress in black, Odile. The photograph had the ashen charm of an older time, and the caption read, 'Violette Lenoir, a world-renowned ballerina of the 1920s and '30s; still considered one of the greatest dancers of all time.'

The dancer was unmistakably Juliette. Her elegance, her cold compelling eyes, everything about her shone through the veil of distance and time. Unchanged in sixty years. Unchanged in eternity.

While Sarah, too serious and reflective for her seven years, with her long dark hair and grey eyes, seemed to take on an eerie resemblance to Juliette — Violette, Odile, Lilith. Jen shivered, seeing that her daughter was not an extension of her but something apart.

Someone who would never need a visit from Lilith.

GAVIN WILLIAMS

THE SPECIAL FAVOUR

The girl who lives next door to me is screaming again. I can hear her through the walls. I can hear her almost all of the time now. It is worst at nights when she can't sleep, and so — more often than not — neither can I. I lie on my bed in the clammy dimness of a summer suburb's night and I think about her. I consider whether there is any way in which I might help ease her pain? I wonder, briefly, if I could do the Special Favour for her, then decide, of course, that it would be too risky. Not next door. No.

In a vain stab at respite I catch a late night bus to the edge of town and trudge up to the top of Beacon Hill. It is no good, though, because the city just howls at me. The sleeping houses scream.

I put my head between my legs to block out the sound, seal over myself with arms and fingers as masking tape. Naturally, it does no good. The noise is on the *inside*. After some time of more of this, and then some time after that of gazing up at the stars, I decide to go home. Luckily, when I get back indoors I am tired enough to sleep.

The next day — before the girl's early morning morphine has had time to wear down — I go out cycling. I wear shorts and a top of skin-hugging lycra, arm pads and knee pads with a contoured helmet; an all black outfit streaked with stripes and slashes of luminous colour. I guess I must look a bit like a courier.

I don't mind. I'm off, I'm flying. The air glides round me like spray and I feel as though I'm aqua-planing through life, frictionless, impervious. Muscles and carbon fibre click, slip and lock, flow and flex together as one machine. I gurn and I grin, yell on through the wind as the black road unspools behind me all the way down to the city.

This is the time I like best. For a few gorgeous minutes, maybe quarter, sometimes even half an hour, it frees me from space and time and worry. They all just splash away in an oily trail back to the sub-urbs. My spine and brain are filled with momentum, the music of motion, and so there is no room for anything else.

Most importantly it mutes the screams. It's like they scrawl their nails along my back but the delirious speed means they can't ever get a proper grip. They are present as a gentle skirl, out on the periphery, like spirit voices whispering.

It never lasts, though. Today life is brought rudely back to me while I idle at traffic lights on the outskirts of the city centre. Sitting next to me is a smart-looking woman in a mini metro with the win-dow rolled down. Her exhaust gouts smog but it is the news fumes from her radio which smother me more thickly. Uninvited, the 'Today' programme tunes into my concentration. It says:

'Yet another victim this morning, in what police are describing as the most persistent and brutal trail of murders they have had to follow in more than twenty years.'

I frown and spur on, kicking back hard against the peddles. But it is too late, my fugue has already been broken.

With my rhapsody gone the shrieks surge up and swallow me, reduce my thoughts to red scribbles with their din. I don't know why I do this, it is the same every morning. And yet the purity of the ride always lulls me to forget, to think it will be easier than it is. But it never is. I should learn better, and yet I never do.

I only come into the city to see my friends, otherwise I couldn't stand it. I have very many friends here. I couldn't desert them all. I go first to see Hattie in the park. She has had a bad night and someone stole her shoes while she slept. I go to Dolcis and buy her some more, bring back some sandwiches and a can of Seven Up as well. We feed the ducks together and chat.

After I've made sure she is all right I visit the old boys down by the recycling bins and under the railway bridge, plus swap a few words with the bus drivers coming off the night shift. On my way over to the Special Needs school where I help out for a few hours every morning, I banter with some construction workers and help folks set out their stalls in the market.

When I get to school the screeching between my ears is so painful that it tempts me to scowl. But I can't, not for the children. Instead, I persevere and smile. Smiling always makes me feel better.

This is how the rest of my morning is spent, looking in on all of my friends, helping out here and there, trying to stay happy and per-suade others to feel that way if I can.

After lunch I will do the rounds of the retirement homes but first I need a rest, so I head far out into the country. Gradually the hurly-burly recedes and I relax. The absence is like cool, still water.

My curse, you see, is that I can actually *hear* other people's insanity. Not their thoughts, mind, just the open mad storm of their head's bad blood. Wordless apocalypse vibrating through the tectonic plates of my skull, chasing flickers and jags of white noise along the dark contours of bone, rattling static against my teeth. Roiling and rolling, raging over and over again with obsidian pain; a screaming black void just screaming.

Often I see colours. Mainly I see red. But sometimes it is blue or caramel or lavender. And scents, too, that's what I get. Most people's lunacy smells of jasmine. The girl from next door gives off cinnamon.

Perhaps this is why I try to salve the lives of others, to keep their pain away in order to stop its echo from bothering me? So, therefore, it's all just selfishness on my part? I hope not.

I love the country, it makes me serene. I meander along shady, leafy lanes, puff my way up steep inclines then free-wheel down the subsequent slopes. The sun winks down at me through the trees, dapples and smiles, banishing the city's stench of dementia.

The sound of healthy minds is like the gentle sea washing by, but I can't even hear that by now. There aren't enough people here to think up a collective noise. Still waters.

I pause next to a lake and regard the birds nesting peacefully in trees on the opposite shore. I should come back here to live, in amongst all this green. It is where I used to stay. Before. I worked on a farm then, way up north, nestled down in the peace. The quiet. I never felt impelled to do the Special Favour for anybody there.

The winters would be hell, though. So lonely. In the cold I would miss all my friends, and them me. The city may wail but at least it is warm with people, even in winter. There is never ice on the ocean.

Maybe I could work out some time-share scheme? Rent out a rural place for the summer? For in the summer my burden is twice as ponderous. The summer seems to drive people mad, pressure cooks them, steaming hysteria into every crevice and cranny. Mania sweats out of them in a cloud and I choke, cough up on all that agony. The green mind rescues me from these ruminations and I relax once more, stare out across the placid water.

When I eventually weave my way back from the rest homes I decide to brave town again, so as to stock up on essentials. Outside W H Smith's, though, I find myself suddenly transfixed.

I stand very still and gaze through the plate glass at the serried ranks of newspaper stands. Every front page clamours the same headline, records the same death. It is the story that was on the radio this morning, except lit up in livid, tasteless Technicolor.

I stroke my chin. This is bad, very bad. Yet I feel so distanced from it all, as if it can't quite get at me. Like I'm sealed in emotional cellophane.

More than anything it forces me to think again of that poor girl's plight next door, of how I could help her if only I had the courage. Of how I *must* do the Special Favour for her. But the *danger*. . . On impulse I buy some blood red lipstick. The woman at the counter lends me a slightly askance look. I quickly tell her it is for my girlfriend then hurry out.

When I get back to my street I dawdle on the corner which has the best vantage of her house. I think there is the suggestion of movement in the lounge but it is difficult to tell through the net curtains. During the day both her parents work so mainly she is left alone.

There is a bus-stop just by where I am standing and a couple of neighbourhood women are waiting there. I smile and greet them both even though I don't know either well. They assume, I suppose, that I'm there for a bus too and turn back into their own conversation. Surreptitiously, I eavesdrop. I just about manage to cloak my surprise when it transpires that they have been scrutinising the house as well.

'Apparently, she hears voices,' Neighbour Number One says. The other returns her a puzzled look.

'Voices how?'

'It's why she had to come back from that place, the what-ever-it-was, the *hostel*. They couldn't do anything for her there. And that's why she only goes to hospital when she's so sick they have to feed her through a tube. It's not an eating disorder, she isn't bulimic. She's mad. I told you, she hears voices.'

'Voices? You mean like she's schizophrenic? The *voices* tell her not to eat?'

'Not really. Apparently she thinks they are ghosts inside of her. The voices of the dead whispering to her, and she wants to get them out. So she binges and purges. Late at night she crams herself full of food then makes herself sick. Apparently. I guess she hopes that the voices will just get flushed out with the vomit. Maybe she's trying to kill herself to be free. Maybe she wants to die and join them.'

'Wouldn't suicide be quicker, in that case?'

'Maybe,' says Neighbour One stiffly, bristling suddenly. 'But I wouldn't really know. That's what other people say. I'm just telling you what other people have said.'

Afterwards their conversation becomes clipped and brittle and they don't talk about anything else interesting before the bus arrives. They both look at me a little oddly when I don't get on.

That was foolish. I shouldn't have let myself be seen outside her house, looking in at it and with no pretext either. But, equally, the women had information that I need if I am to go ahead with my plan. I retreat indoors.

In the evening the murders are on the television again, which leaves me frowning. They top the bill on every bulletin, the grisly details recounted shamelessly time and again. I catch that the police have no immediate suspects and that they are combing the neighbourhood for leads, before I flick it off in annoyance.

Roughly half an hour later, across the way, I see a pair of policemen apparently conducting door to door enquiries. By the time they reach my house I have turned off all the lights and electricals so as to pretend I'm not in. Thankfully they swallow the ruse and carry on along the row.

I crouch in the dark 'til I'm sure they've gone, interrogating my indecision all the while. Should I do it? Should I? I go and take out my hunting knives, sharpen them half-heartedly, uncoil the large rubber sheet. Roll it up again. I just can't, it *is* too hazardous.

Some time after eight, as it begins to dim outside, I hear noises through the walls. They are arguing next door, or something. Voices needle the captured air. I spread-eagle myself flat against the wall, tuck my ear in tight against the plaster to listen.

It is difficult to tell exactly — single phrases are discrete but the rest is mud — however, I gather that they are attempting to calm her, not arguing as I first suspected. I hear her say, 'I am full of voices,' and repeat it. Then, 'They press up against my skin, whispering for release.' To my horror she suddenly begins to sing; an icy, high ululation, wordless and terrifying.

Her madness surges. She makes me see blue, squalls of boiling amethyst purpling against the back of my eyes. Shrieking babbling blue, louder and louder until it feels as though my forehead will rip. I keel over onto my side.

The next moment I presume they must have sedated her as the singing stops and the static in my head contracts to a dull groan. Gasping, I can only lie there. For hours that's all I do.

She wakes again near three, after the others have retired, and goes about her secret purge. I hear her retching into the toilet bowl, hacking up what she has gorged. Afterwards she too sleeps. Her dreams continue to hurt me, but finally I have the strength to stand and go to the bathroom, fumble on the light. The minutes crawl by, but I feel better

I paint my face all scarlet with the gory lipstick I bought and daub my teeth black with boot polish. I stare into the mirror for a long time, and wonder, do I dare?

I sigh. I smile. So be it. If I *must* do good then there it is. I am doing what is best for her, for her family. I have to keep on reminding myself of that. Best for everyone. This time when I sharpen my knives I do so like I have a purpose. I buff them up to a fiery lustre then retire to bed. Tonight I sleep much better.

I am woken in the morning by the monotonous tweet-tweet of the dawn chorus. It sounds like a mob of digital watches chiming all at once. I rise like a ghost, pale shadow on the mirror across the room, and go for my morning ride.

There is a chill on the wind that buffets me, the summer has gone cold in one night. But it doesn't matter, I am one with my bike — the metal, my purpose — we hiss along the asphalt like the whisper of spirit voices. I will not have time to call in on any of my friends today, I have other plans.

When I return — once I have showered and cleaned my teeth — I begin my preparations. I brush my teeth ten more times that day, four of those in the last fifteen minutes before I go to see her. In the early afternoon I go out to stand by their low garden gate and peer in. She is standing by the rose bushes, swaying slightly as if in a strong breeze, her face upturned to the sun, eyes closed.

She is a woman, really, I suppose — nineteen next birthday — but the size she is at the moment she only looks like a girl; diminished, desiccated. Her flesh appears gossamer fine this close up. I worry that if I startle her and she swings around too quickly her jaw line will slice straight through the skin and her head will simply topple off. My paper girl will shred herself merely by walking into my arms, disintegrate in a snow of origami diamonds under the cut of bone scissors. I cough, she looks over.

'Hello.'

'Hi. You live next door, don't you?' her voice creaks out like a nib on parchment, her lips and throat are papery dry.

'Yes.' I gather she is going through one of her lucid periods. Earlier, I glimpsed her through the window dancing all alone, tracing invisible arcs in the air with her spoke-like elbows. She regards me expectantly then tells me her name and invites me in. I tell her mine and we shake hands. I am very careful not to hurt her with my grip. There is an uncomfortable pause. I stare away at the flowers then suddenly say:

'It has occurred to me that I might be able to do you a favour.'

Instantly, her eyes go misty and she starts to giggle. I have lost her. 'You can hear them can you? Can you hear them, too?' she demands quietly. 'Well, *can you*?'

'Look, would you like to come through to my house and we can discuss it there?' I ask, a little desperately. To my surprise she accedes, albeit in a lilting, sing-song tone. But once we get inside she rushes from room to room pressing her palms and cheek against each wall, as if she is listening. A thin noise issues behind her as she hurries upstairs to my living room. As I follow I strain to catch what it is . . . She is singing. I mumble something about coffee and stumble to the kitchen. When I return she has planted herself in one of the easy chairs.

All of a sudden she is lucid again, active eyes tracking me closely. Her sanity fades in and out like a poorly tuned television. I step right up to the window and thus out of her range of sight. I notice her head twitch as she tries to locate me. Is she nervous? It didn't seem so before. I certainly am. She's twitching after me all the while so I go and stand directly behind her chair.

'So what's this favour?' She asks, turning slightly. She still can't quite see me.

'Well,' I say. 'It's like this.' And then I take her head in my hands very suddenly, one palm clamped across her mouth in order to tame the frightened yelp that comes.

She is so flimsy that it isn't even necessary to break her flesh in order to kill her. I simply wrench her neck forward and feel the pebbles of her spine go pop beneath my fingers. It is a great relief. Her body doesn't deem it necessary to let slip any demeaning reflex spasms either, or futile dead kicks. Her screaming in my head — which had fanned to an almost intolerable level in this close confinement — abruptly ceases. I breath out slowly, ghost tickles on my lower lip.

This part of my task has proved much less arduous than it often does. In an ideal world, though, I probably should have used poison. Then I wouldn't have had to risk ripping free or losing any part of her flesh, which is always possible. Unfortunately, now the most distasteful part of the bodily work is upon me. Tenderly, I remove her clothing, fold and pile it neatly on the bed. Then I hoist her up — she weighs less than a large dog might — and bear the body to the bath to dismember it.

I have already arranged my tools there and draped the rubber sheet carefully into the tub, ensured that it droops over the lip so that no blood or other matter can escape. A fresh human corpse is obviously a mind-bogglingly difficult object to dismantle but balanced against this I know that my knives are absolutely razor sharp and that I myself am very, *very* strong. First, however, it is important to flay her.

The sheath of her skin comes off easily, in even sized pieces, rather like a two-piece swimsuit in fact, slipping off the red underneath, leaving her naked and alone. I duck my eyes at this intimacy.

Effectively I dice her up, to make the segments easier to swallow. Criss-cross, I mesh her in a net of incisions, divide and counter divide until I am done. Even so it still takes an age — hours upon dreadful hours — to devour her entirely. The foulest part is when I have to lap up fugitive blood which has jellied in the creases at the bottom of the sheet.

But then — drenched in crimson dew and belly obscenely distended — I am finally able to go collapse in my favourite chair. I actually believe I manage to doze for a few minutes before awaking with a start to the realisation that I must go and scour the house for any stray fragments of her I have missed or dropped. No, my meal has been intact. It is done.

Of course, a human being would not have been able to achieve what I have achieved. Not been able to cleave so cleanly through bone and gristle, muscle and sinew. Never have been able to tooth down such a lush, raw, *vast* feast. It is lucky then that I am not particularly human. Not human at all.

At this point I go and lie on my bed to begin the digestion. It is a long and involved process which eclipses the whole of my concentration, requiring the absolute zero of distraction. Even that, though, is nothing when set against the regurgitation.

Not out of mouth or anus does she return. No, she uses my entire surface area. I condense together the disparate wisps of her flesh deep down inside of me, and then they are ejected at their own speed. They force their way up through the soft strata of my derma ever so gradually, slipping, sliding carefully through the internal films and folds until they bloom through the velvet topsoil. Still they are caught beneath that supple frosting and I have to tug the wedge shapes through the final muffle of my own epidermis. I actually need to use my fingers to peel them free, like sticky toffee coming off silver paper on a hot summer's day. Even then they are difficult to fully detach, trailing a gauze of membranous strands, that I must delicately roll in like I'm making bloody flesh candy-floss.

Of course, each cubed segment does not come out in sequence. I have to assemble her like a huge, slick jigsaw before I can dress her in skin again.

I know it is finished, and that I have missed no part of her in the reassembly, when flim-flams of furtive lightening begin to jigger between the pieces. The whole jigsaw visibly starts to shake. Then her skin goes back on.

It will take some time to complete. Humming to myself I go to the kitchen to cook some proper food. Every now and then I look in on her to see how she is getting on. Once I am sure everything is going to plan I afford myself the luxury of a shower. Also, I go and burn my clothes in a metal bin well away from the house.

Eventually, I take her garments with me and push a comfortable chair up to beside the body. I sit and examine the finish of her perfect skin, how the lamplight glides over it, dances, glitters, flares into translucency. When I notice her eyes flit beneath their lids I gently ease her into the clothes and fasten everything down.

Not a moment too soon. She snaps awake and jack-knives into a sitting position, intact once more. Exactly as she was before we began. Well, not quite. She says:

'God. I'm so hungry I think I could cry.'

'Here, I did this for you,' I smile and pass her over a plate of bacon and eggs. Just before taking it, though, she flinches away.

'Hey, where am I?' she snaps, a little afraid.

I give her a puzzled look. 'Er, next door. Don't you remember? You locked yourself out. I was making us some coffee and when I came back you were fast asleep on my floor! I would have moved you to the sofa only I hear you've been ill and I didn't want to wake you. You seemed to be sleeping so peacefully. Mind, you've been out for hours so the coffee's cold.' I smile again. Phantom recognition dawns across her face.

'Oh, right. Yes. We don't know each other that well do we?'

'No. But I only live next door so, if I may say, I think we might well become friends.'

We both grin together that time.

I have ingested her madness. I have taken all of her inside of me and silted her, *purified* the very stuff she is made of, unthreaded, removed the madness, re-threaded; purged the voices after my own fashion. Radical surgery indeed. I have done her this favour. Yes, I am *impelled* to do good.

Just after she leaves a livid scarlet hue invades my skin like dye, while at the same time my teeth gradually stain up black. It is dangerous to hold her insanity inside of me for too long. Already it is straining at the warp and weft of my flesh, feathering me inside, itching to change my skin, burning. The weight of its bolus rests up against my breast bone. I have to get it out of me quickly.

Out into the night I go. The whizz of my tyres splits the silence of the unlit street. I have begun to blister, scab up, my surface is literally bubbling with the canker. It is melting my flesh with its black heat. My face hurts, shifts, spills.

It doesn't take very long to find him, though. His colour is very deepest violet, almost the hue of night, and his stench is that of deadly nightshade. He is very hot for it and has already killed once tonight, has gone roving the gloomiest corners of the town afterwards. Perhaps he is fantasising of tomorrow's headlines? I catch up with him under an unlit bridge in the park.

By this point my teeth have been forced to spike out in many sharp directions at the shrink-wrap of my skin, almost threatening to burst its elastic. I must appear very fearsome.

He half screams, stifles it, turns to run. Of course I catch him, though — within a matter of paces as it happens — and hug him tightly to me. So tight that I am in danger of buckling his bones within their precious skin packet. He sobs.

I put an extra vicious twist into my grip and he screams on reflex. The passover only takes a heartbeat — for me giving has always been much easier than taking away. I kiss his open mouth and her madness goes into him. The impact of it stuns and when I open my arms he rolls slackly to the ground, cracks his head against the curb.

While his eyelids flutter I take the time to have a closer look at him. He is a big man, strong man, heavy with meat. It would take a long time for *him* to dwindle down to five stone, and many months after that before he finally succumbed to death. I smile in the darkness.

When he wakes he is disorientated and tries to stand but I knock him down again.

'Who *are* you?' he whinges in awe.

'I've just done you a favour. Done everyone a favour, in fact.' I say, ignoring him.

A look of comprehension and fear dashes across his face.

'What are those voices?' he cries. 'Who's talking? *Where are you?*' His head lashes around wildly, mane of hair flailing left and right on the air, searching for the source of the sounds. I can't hear a thing.

'Those are the spirit voices. I believe if you don't stop them soon you'll end up mad. They'll whisper away to you all the time, you see. Perhaps they live in your body, your stomach even. You could drown them with drink, or food maybe. Or get them out in some other way. You'll figure it out though, I have faith in you . . . The voices of the dead,' I say and I smile at him. 'I think I can hear them cheering.'

JAMES LOVEGROVE

DEAD LETTERS

Bert was a big man who looked like he could have been a rugby forward or a professional wrestler or a nightclub bouncer but was too gentle of nature to have been successful in any of those violent occupations. In fact, Bert worked for the Post Office. He possessed a slow, methodical brain, which made him ideal for sorting, and for thirty-seven years Bert did just that, sorted, until the machines came along that read and separated in a fraction of the time it took Bert — conscientious, reliable old Bert — to perform the same function.

When the machines came along, it seemed to Bert that that was that. He was near retirement, and they were taking on a lot of younger men and women now, people who actually understood how the machines worked and could operate them. It was time for Bert to bow out nobly, the last of the old guard, take his pension and his fishing-rod and move to a bungalow in Worthing to watch telly and read novels and the newspaper.

His bosses had other plans for him. In the extending, expanding, full-speed-ahead-rocketing industry of mail delivery there was still a need for slow, methodical workers to do the jobs that required efficiency without urgency. Bert's bosses sent him a letter. They enjoyed sending letters; it made them feel they were getting their hands dirty, actually touching the greasy cogs of the engine.

The letter, when it finally arrived, described Bert in glowing terms (he was "a valuable, if not indispensable, asset") and went on to enquire if he would be willing to accept a transfer to a different department where he would be "in charge of and/or solely responsible for the distribution and/or disposal of undelivered and/or undeliverable correspondence."

Bert's brain churned this one over for a while and came up with the translation: dead letter office.

Dead letter office? He'd rather retire!

But then he thought about his friends who had retired. He thought of how they measured their hours with pint glasses and hip flasks; how they faded day by day; how boredom sucked the essence out of them, leaving them wrinkled husks of men. He thought about their rheumy, dreamy eyes that begged a question: Where did it all go? Theirs was the shock and surprise of a punter who sees all the horses past the finish post and his isn't among them, hasn't even left the starting gate. Eh? What happened?

Bert thought about this the way he usually thought about things, long and hard, and gradually his mind changed, turning over like one of those snowstorm-globe novelties that tourists like to buy, slow-swirling confusion settling again to clarity. He composed a reply to his bosses and started at the dead letter office the following Monday.

The job banished him to the lower basement of the depot, where every morning he was greeted with canvas sacks full of undelivered correspondence. For the most part this consisted of circulars, shrink-wrapped catalogues and all the other junk mail that accumulated inside the front doors of abandoned shops and the homes of the recent-ly deceased. Bert thought it was a shame, what with the trees being whisked off the face of the planet at a rate of knots, that so much paper should be wasted selling products which people could go out and find for themselves if they really wanted them, and wearily he marked it all to be consigned to the incinerators.

Business letters he opened and read and gauged as to their impor-tance. Usually they were junk mail thinly disguised, further pieces of sales pitch dressed up in formal brown envelopes with the name and address of their victims framed in their little cellophane windows. Bit of a nasty trick that, he thought.

Private correspondence, on the other hand, was sacred. It deserved respect for the effort that had been put into it, the care taken, the time spared. Bert regarded opening and reading private correspondence as very much a last resort, when every attempt to decipher the hand-writing on the envelope or make sense of an insane address had failed. Even then, Bert looked only at the name and address of the sender (if there was one) at the top of the letter inside, then copied this onto the envelope, folded the letter back into the envelope and taped the flap shut. He would never had pried into another person's words. In fact, Bert wished he could write on the envelope, *I haven't read this — hon-est.* But who would believe that? Besides, it amounted to a confession that the temptation had been there.

The letters which he did read, and was delighted to read, and read because no one else would read them, were those addressed to *Santa Claus, The North Pole*. He loved the lists, painstakingly detailed in case Santa should go to the wrong shop or buy the wrong make or model. He chuckled over the requests for trips to the moon and wishes no parent could fulfil ("Please could you send my little brother to Timbuctoo and make sure he never comes back?"). He smiled at the protestations of goodness that bordered on saintliness and the apologies for crimes committed over the past year, wishing that his greatest worry was that he had knocked over a vase and blamed it on the cat. He delighted in the spiky cacography, the way the lines of writing veered more and more from the horizontal the further down the page they went. Although December was Bert's busiest month, it was also his favourite. He took all the Santa Claus letters home with him and placed them in a folder. Each year he bought a new folder to fill.

Cynics might scoff, but Bert — the big, timid man, hidden away from daylight in a chamber in a lower basement in a depot in a city — was perhaps the closest the world would come to a real Father Christmas.

Three years almost to the day that Bert was shunted off to the dead letter office, it arrived.

It was compact, lighter than an aerogramme wafer, with no stamp, and was addressed simply:

> Dearest
> There

That was all, two words on two lines. Bert tutted as he slid his finger under the flap. Honestly, there were some odd sorts around.

The sender's name and address at the top of the page turned out to be even less illuminating than the recipient's. It said:

> From Your Darling
> Here

Bert scratched his head and was preparing to crumple the letter up when he found himself reading the first line. Well, it was only one line . . . But once his eye had begun to wander, he could not call it back.

My Dearest,

My heart grows sick while we are apart. It aches as it beats and with each shuddering throb seems ready to burst. When will you reply? When will this winter absence turn to spring? While you are there and I am here, snow surrounds me, the landscape is stripped of its beauty and I am cut off from everything that makes living bearable. A word from you, a single syllable, would be more welcome to me than the first bud on a branch, the first song of a returning bird, the first blade of grass. When will I see you again? When?

All my love,
Darling

Smiling, Bert read the letter again. Someone, he decided, had been buried too long in books of poetry. Perhaps a lovelorn student had hunted through pages of verse for these pearls of love-wisdom; perhaps an ageing spouse, hoping to rekindle love's first fading flame. Bert couldn't tell. The sentiments were immature, but their expression was adult. Or was it the other way round?

He held the letter up to the unshaded lightbulb that hung from the ceiling on a length of plaited flex. You know, he hadn't seen the paper of this quality in . . . oh, ages. It captured the light. The light suffused it from corner to corner, from edge to edge, so that the lines of writing stood out like black bars against the sun. It fluttered drily yet felt as smooth as cream, and it was thin, so thin it all but disappeared when turned sideways. The nib that wrote on this delicate stuff would have to be flawlessly smooth.

It shouldn't have been sent. It was a mistake. Nothing this precious and delicate should have been surrendered up to the mangling jaws of the Post Office. Nor, by any rights, should it have survived intact the lugging and manhandling that every letter had to endure.

Bert took the frail miracle home with him, keeping it for the same reason he kept the letters to Santa, as a thing of simple faith that flew in the face of common sense.

About a month later, the second letter arrived. Again it was for Dearest, There and again it was written on the same translucent paper. Bert opened the envelope with what he hoped was reverence tainted by forgivable eagerness.

My Dearest,

Time passes, and slowly your face decays in my memory. I can see its outline and know it to be handsome, and I remember the colour of your eyes and know them to sparkle, but I cannot mould the parts together to create a picture of you. I am left with a shape without form, an idea of beauty, and a hint of sadness.

Without you and without your words to inspire it, my memory is a clumsy, blunt instrument, and my heart the poor craftsman who blames the inefficiency of his tools when he ought to blame the failing of his art.

Send me words, send me art, send me love,

As I send you mine,
Your Darling.

Several things about the letter puzzled Bert, most of all whether Darling was a man or a woman. The handwriting, normally a dead giveaway, was rounded italics, a product of learning rather than nature, and therefore not obviously belonging to one sex or the other. And the words "handsome" and "beauty" could be applied equally to a man as to a woman, so that didn't help — assuming in the first place that the letter was being sent by a member of one sex to a member of the opposite sex . . .

Bert showed this letter and its predecessor to his friend Harry (retired, widower, dismal) over a pint of bitter. Harry squinted at both for a while, slipping one behind the other, one behind the other again, while Bert searched his face for a glimmer of enlightenment. Eventually Harry set the letters down in the empty ashtray to keep them from getting soaked by the wet eclipses left behind by their pint glasses, took a swig of bitter and said, 'Pretty.'

'Pretty?'

'The paper. Must've cost a bob or two.'

'But what about the words? What do you think? Do you think someone's playing a joke?'

'On you?'

'On me, on the Post Office, I don't know.'

'Don't make much sense as a joke, does it? Looks more like a head-case to me. I mean the words are pretty too, but a bit . . .' Harry tapped his temple. 'If you catch my drift.'

'That makes sense to me,' said Bert. 'He, she, whoever it is, is in

217

love. Really, truly in love.'

'My point exactly, Bert, my point exactly,' Harry said with a grin, and waved his froth-streaked glass at Bert with significance.

Bert sighed. 'Same again?' he said, reaching into his pocket.

The letters from Darling started arriving regularly, one a month, usually towards the end of the second week, at the latest by the beginning of the third. They traced Darling's mounting desperation, the increasing urgency with which he or she longed for an answer from Dearest. Dearest's reticence was "like the Arctic wind that cuts to the bone with innocent malice". Dearest was "the kindest and cruellest creature that ever lived". Dearest was by turns "beautiful" and "beastly", "exquisite" and "evil", "ravishing" and "ruinous", "tender" and tormenting", sometimes both in the space of a single sentence.

When Harry cast his expert eye over each instalment, he would look sly, tap his temple as before, and say, 'Now, what did I tell you? Nutty, and getting nuttier by the month.'

And Bert would wonder (but never aloud) who was the biggest nutcase here: Darling, for writing to an imaginary lover letters that would never reach anywhere; Harry, for dismissing love as a madness; or himself, for being captivated, swept up, swallowed whole by the letters. Was there something wrong with him because he looked forward to Darling's next missive with schoolboy anticipation, counting down the days? No, he decided. Not when the letters made a dull job a little brighter, his confinement to the bowels of the depot that little bit more bearable.

Then one morning Bert received a letter from his bosses similar to the one which had informed him of his transfer to the dead letter office. This one informed him that his services would no longer be required as of next Friday. (The letter gave him the statutory month's notice, or at least it would have, had it arrived when it was supposed to.) The bosses added that they very much appreciated the decades of hard work and unstinting loyalty Bert had given the Post Office, but owing to circumstances and/or situations beyond their control the dead letter office was to be closed down. He would receive his full pension, of course, and would he accept their deepest sympathy and/or sincerest hopes for the future?

Bert bent his head, gritted his teeth, and lodged a protest. What about the children's letters? What about the private correspondence? What about the arrows of love that never reached their intended targets? (He cribbed the metaphor from Darling's most recent outpouring.)

The smooth running of the mail delivery industry, replied his bosses, was their greatest concern, and they were gratified to see that it was his too. The sorting machines, they told him, could now be programmed to spot such mistakes and/or anomalies and direct them straight to the incinerators, thereby making immense savings all round in effort and/or time and/or care. They appreciated his drawing their attention to the problem and/or were moved by his display of company spirit right to the very end. Might they again offer their deepest sympathy and/or sincerest hopes.

Bert's final days at the dead letter office drifted by. The flow of letters dried up. The machines were already hard at work tossing away the unwanted catalogues and the lists for Santa and the private correspondence without a second glance, with barely a blink of an electronic eye. It pained Bert to think that Darling's future letters would, once sealed, never be read, that the strange, delicate paper would be lumped in with the rest and burned to ashes. When it pained him too much to think about it, he went to the pub with Harry, drinking for the sake of drinking, even though drinking didn't do much except get him drunk.

Bert's last day arrived, and there was going to be a party that afternoon when the whole depot would turn out to present him with a gift they had all chipped in for; then they would wheel in a cake that said, in letter of piped icing, To Bert, Best Wishes On Your Retirement; and when everyone had eaten a slice they would stand in a circle, shuffling with embarrassment, and sing "Auld Lang Syne" — all of which filled Bert with dread. These rituals, these last rites which Bert himself had helped administer to the old men and the old women before him, feeling vaguely sorry for them as everyone was no doubt feeling vaguely sorry for him today — this really was the end, wasn't it? Now he had nothing to look forward to except beer and oblivion. He nearly called in sick, but decided that he had to attend. It would have been rude not to.

There was a letter waiting for him in the dead letter office, a small envelope, that extraordinary paper.

Bert snatched it from the table and tried to drive his trembling finger under the flap. Then he felt a peculiar twinge at the back of his mind, as though his thoughts had snagged on a thorn. He looked around. Had a piece of furniture been moved or something? No. Then he looked down at the envelope in his hands. He turned it over.

The handwriting on the front was not Darling's. The letter was addressed:

> Darling
> There

Bert had to restrain himself from tearing the envelope apart. He fumbled out its contents and began to read, his eyes gaping wide to drain every last drop of prose from the page:

> From Your Dearest
> Here
>
> My Darling
> What can I say? I must reply. Your sweet words have moved me and my love cannot stay silent forever.
> I have abused you as no lover has abused a love before. I have ignored you when I should have cherished you. If my face has grown faint in your memory, it is because the real me is wan with shame and pale with remorse. Would that I had vanished from your memory altogether, for I deserve to be forgotten, never forgiven!
> But I beg you now, and will if necessary beg you to the day I die . . .
> Forgive me. Forgive me. Forgive me.
>
> All my love,
> Your Dearest

BEN LEECH

THE HARROWING STONE

'*I will always love you,*' Davies remembered, were the last words he said to her before the end began. '*I will always love you, more than life itself* . . .'

It sounded melodramatic now, the kind of thing that someone says in a badly-scripted movie. But then, those were the films that Pamela enjoyed; what he called "sloppy films". He'd rarely watched them with her, preferring to take himself off to the study to work on a forthcoming lecture, or potter with the book he'd been slowly cooking in his head for the past five years. Pamela, meanwhile, made the lounge her own, turning out the top light in favour of the glow of the coal fire, settling herself with chocolates and some wine and a box of tissues within easy reach. Davies left her to it, not bothering to come downstairs until well after the movie had reached its predictable conclusion. For it embarrassed him to see her openly weeping at such nonsense: and whether the ending had been happy or sad, she still wept the same way. Davies often said to her, smiling awkwardly or sometimes with a little frown of puzzlement, 'Well, you got your money's worth with that one . . .'

Strange thing, but their loving was always better, more profound, more passionate, after one of Pamela's sloppy films. Maybe it had reminded her of something that the slow mundane drudgery of life had tended to make fade. Or perhaps it was just wishful thinking on Pamela's part, the creation of a brief illusion of romance in a marriage it had never truly touched. Whatever, Davies never troubled to question it, and certainly not to disdain these peaks in his wife's sexuality, that somehow seemed to tear aside a curtain of possibility in his own perception, before weariness or fifty years of implicit cowardice in himself allowed it to swirl back, making everything as it had been;

rather dully adult, rather drearily civilised. Until the next time.

Except that now, there would be no next time. Professor Michaelides had been confident in his diagnosis of acute myelocitic leukaemia, when Pamela had submitted herself to the regime of tests, which were the outcome of her initial visit to Doctor Barratt, over six months ago. Barratt had known enough to know that something was seriously wrong, and had referred her to Michaelides at the City General with an alacrity that had alarmed Davies immediately, although Pamela, being her usual self, had told him it would be better to wait and see.

Well, they'd waited, Davies now reflected, and they'd seen. From an unknown starting point — some random radioactive particle or a quirk in the terrifyingly complex labyrinth of the genes — the cancer had ignited from a spark to a firestorm that was burning through Pamela's blood, and would consume her life entirely before the autumn was out. The radiotherapy had taken away her hair, the chemotherapy had drained her to a pale ninety-pound invalid with the glossy sunken eyes of one who sees death drawing close. Davies found, to his intense shame and self-loathing, that he could hardly bear to look upon her any more. And when he'd said that he would always love her, he recognised that he'd been speaking to the Pamela he had known before this horror, the one who had completed his life by joining it, twelve years earlier. *That* Pamela, he realised as something dark ripped itself free in his chest, was already dead.

Or so he had imagined, until ten days ago, when he had been working late at his tiny book-filled room at the university. Davies had always dwelt in the world of academe, finding refuge and comfort in ideas and abstractions, rather than in the mundaneness and ultimately narrow parameters of real life. In recent years he had given up reading newspapers, and rarely watched the news broadcasts on TV, conferring upon world-shattering events the same importance and interest in his mind as vacuous back-fence gossip. He did this, he knew clearly, because reality frightened him. Its bleakness, its disappointments, and perhaps most poignantly its ephemeral nature, drove him to turn his back on it — to explore instead the endless universe of the imagination, of legend and folklore, mystery and myth. As a by-product of his fear, he had earned his doctorate by studying Jungian archetypal iconography as manifested in middle-eastern religious texts, and moreover had become a successful and well-respected lecturer and researcher, with several technical papers to his name. Davies had thought his life well-established and secure, if predictable, until the dreadful certainty that Pamela would die exploded in his brain.

He came across the existence of the stone quite by chance, during what he termed one of his "north sea trawls" through the literature — a week's time-out, netting all that he could for possible assimilation into his teaching syllabus; or perhaps a new thread he could develop for the book. It was a reference, nothing more than that, a snippet among the thousands of fragments of ancient lore that was the raw material with which Davies worked . . . The story of a stone that possessed the power to heal, if faith and courage enough were invested in the phenomenon.

His immediate impulse was to dismiss it outright, or at the very most to note it down as a potential item for further research. That's what common sense told Davies to do, and under any other circumstances he might have listened to the voice of his reason. But the situation was unique in his experience, and desperate: and beyond the fear he felt on Pamela's behalf, and the dark anticipation of the loss he was imminently to suffer, Davies raged at his own helplessness in the face of this crisis. That nothing could be done to save his wife's life, or even prolong it, was final confirmation of the insufficiencies of modern technology and the twisted path the societies of the west had taken . . .

But what if the power of machines and drugs and reductionist knowledge was meagre in comparison to the greater forces that moved in the earth and through the cosmos? The landscape of mythology was rich with evidence of subtle but pervasive energies that accomplished for the ancient peoples what modern engines and silicon chips attempted feebly to do by artificial means. And what if these energies, personified in the archaic gods, still surged and rippled through the universe, reduced by millennial man to scraps of local legend, embodied in the ludicrous antics of esoteric fringe cults, or a motif in a directory of folklore?

Davies chuckled and flipped over the page of the huge volume . . . Paused, and turned back. Even as he tutted at his own superstitious folly, he noted down the motif categorisation, glanced at Pamela's picture in its silver frame on his desk, then left his office to make the short walk down to the university library.

Within the hour he'd found nine specific cross-references to that particular stone, plus hundreds of others that would draw him into the more extensive but probably less pertinent field of places of pilgrimage, holy wells and sites of angelic manifestation. Perversely perhaps, Davies gave no credence to these other sources, but found himself growing excited, growing *eager*, to learn that an academic colleague at the University of Leicester had made a study of the stone that was the object of Davies's interest. There would be no harm in speaking to Dr Calvert, at least, and there might be a great deal to be gained from it.

Davies returned to his room and asked the switchboard operative to put through the call, remembering a conversation he'd once had with Ronnie Chapman, his Head of Faculty, on the very subject of superstition.

'We are the product of all the generations of humans that have ever been,' Chapman had said. 'Right back to the time when some four-foot-tall hominid looked up from the veldt at the stars, and saw our destinies there. So, if people ask me whether I'm superstitious, I say no — touch wood. . .'

Fate and synchronicity had been mere abstractions to Davies, and he was still inclined to treat them as such despite the fact that Jenny Calvert was completing a sabbatical at Oakhills, and was renting rooms not two miles from Davies's own home. It turned out, when eventually he spoke to her, that she'd visited the university on several occasions, and had read his unpublished thesis in the very library where he'd chanced across her name . . . Except that "chanced" was perhaps the wrong word to use, Calvert teased him gently, as they arranged to meet.

Three days later, at Calvert's first floor apartment in one of the leafy avenues characteristic of the city's southern suburb, Davies found himself disconcerted, almost gauche, in the woman's presence. Doctor Jennifer Calvert looked to be in her early thirties, with shoulder length copper-coloured hair, lucent green eyes and a vivacity in her every word and gesture. Davies felt like a gawky little schoolboy before her, though she did nothing to exploit her advantage, nor even seemed to notice the effect she was having upon him.

He sat at her invitation, and while she went to the kitchen to make coffee, Davies glanced down at his mid-grey pinstripe suit, crumpled and uncomfortable at the end of the day, and the faded stain on his sober blue tie, the remnant of some hastily-eaten meal he'd never bothered to have washed out. He stood and looked at himself in the mirror above the mantel, acutely aware of his six o'clock shadow, receding hairline, the broken veins in his nose that he tried not to think were the result of chronic over-drinking, and the gradually-swelling paunch across which he now planed his hands, making a half-hearted effort to draw his stomach in . . .

The reflection of Jenny's reappearance from the kitchen startled him. Davies flushed, his mind stumbling over a dozen excuses, all immediately discarded, as to why he should be studying himself so intently.

'I've been sitting all day,' he mumbled, grinning stupidly. 'Needed to stretch my legs . . .'

She smiled — devastatingly — and placed the tray of coffee things on the table between them.

Their conversation took an hour to reach the point of Davies's visit, moving slowly from abstruse academic discussion to the dread of loss that lay at the heart of the man's motivation. But even as he told Calvert about Pamela's illness, he felt the anger and foolishness rise in him and surge through. Tears prickled in Davies's eyes; not of release or hope, but of self-contempt that he should have allowed his own weakness to bring him here tonight.

'You must think I'm stupid,' he said, having done with the burden of shame in his outburst, 'just a stupid old crank who's made a complete fool of himself coming to see you like this! I'm not here for information — I don't want to include the stone in my work . . . I want —'

'You want,' Calvert said, calmly cutting through his revelation, 'to use the power of the stone to heal your life.'

'Not mine. My wife's.' He told her of Pamela, and of the prognosis of her leukaemia which would see her dead by Christmas.

'And you feel angry and bitter, perhaps, and helpless in the face of this tragedy.'

Davies nodded, startled at the woman's perceptiveness.

'So did I,' she added, 'when it happened to me.'

'You?' Davies was stunned. 'Someone you know . . .'

'No, not someone I know, Jeff. I was diagnosed with carcinoma in my left leg. The tumour was malignant, and although they operated, some fragments must have remained. The tumour came back, then metastased to my stomach and other leg. It happened with frightening speed — weeks, Jeff. There was no time to do anything, except perhaps pray.'

Her smile this time was a little ironic, twisted almost into a grimace.

'Your husband must have been a great support to you.' Davies had quickly noticed the plain gold wedding ring, at the outset with something that might have been envy.

'He was.' Calvert poured more coffee, the smile vanishing.

'I'd like to meet him some day.'

'He's no longer around.'

'Oh, I'm s —'

The woman stood up and moved to the window, speaking half to herself as she stared out over the skyline.

'Brian was like you; a disbeliever. I had come across the existence of the stone years before: part of my postgraduate work was to help survey standing stones and mark stones in Scotland — in the south-west, to be exact, the Dumfries and Galloway region. And there are thousands of them!'

Calvert chuckled at this. 'Many of the stones we found weren't even on the maps. Previous surveys had either not been thorough enough, or time or money had run out before the work was completed . . . Or perhaps some monoliths were not regarded as being of great enough archaeological importance to count. Whatever . . .

'We worked in teams, transecting gridsquares we'd plotted from O.S. Land Ranger maps. It was bad procedure to've done it, but we split up from time to time, to get the job finished more quickly. I daresay,' Calvert said wryly, 'that if we'd gone by the book, I would never have come across the stone.'

Davies noted the slight emphasis Calvert placed on the definite article.

'So, how did you — I mean —'

'I slipped and broke my ankle. I was maybe a mile away from my nearest team mate, and in those days we had no mobile phones, you know. I resigned myself to a long and tedious wait for someone to come looking. Never in a million years did I imagine I'd be walking out of the valley myself, less than an hour later.'

Calvert turned to face Davies, her eyes grimly alight. 'There's a power in that glen, centred on the stone,' she said, quietly but with absolute conviction. 'And I'm sure it's but one of many such points, scattered over the Earth. People have been using them for thousands of years — the knowledge goes way back, beyond the dawn of human consciousness; a way of tapping into the deep wellsprings of life . . .'

She could easily have sounded unbalanced, glamorised by the illusion of miracles. But even while Davies found himself caught in the suave mesmerism of her words, he knew that Calvert was too clear-headed to have been beguiled, and too honest, he judged, to peddle such a cruel deceit.

'How —' He felt his voice catching in a dry throat, sipped coffee and asked her, committing himself now to the path: 'How does it work . . . I mean, how do I go about using —'

'There's no sorcery involved. You take your wife there and lay her on the stone — You'll see that close to the megalith is a cairn, the entrance to which is protected by a capstone. Don't go into the cairn, Jeff,' Calvert added, breaking the contact of his gaze. 'Just make your wife comfortable on the capstone, and wait.'

'And then?'

The note of impatience caused the woman to look up sharply. 'And then the universe turns strangely and shows you its guts!' Calvert laughed brittly. 'There's a lot I can't tell you.' She sounded angry in turn and, Davies noted with a shadow of unease, almost guilty.

'You mean, there's danger?'

'Do you love your wife?'

'Completely,' he answered at once.

'Where there's love, there's no danger.'

'I don't understand you, Doctor Calvert.'

She smiled at Davies's retreat into formality, the smile growing ghastly as she explained. 'The rules of science and the rules of reality sometimes coincide. You get nothing for nothing, Jeff, whether it's the second law of thermodynamics, or the more fundamental precepts you'll encounter at the stone . . . The first time, as I lay there in agony, an eagle flew over. It was looking for nourishment . . . Then, there was a mist, a mist that came out of the cairn — and — something — inside the mist . . .'

'My God,' Davies whispered. Calvert shook her head.

'I doubt that. The mist came over and touched me — *breathed me* — and I was healed. But shortly after, as I walked away to try to find the others, I found the body of the eagle in the grass.'

Outside, it had started to rain. Drops speckled the windows and Davies was momentarily distracted.

Calvert stood up and brusquely began clearing away the cups and spoons.

'But afterwards —'

'I've said too much already.'

'I have to know!' Davies yelled, moderating his voice with a great effort. 'I have to know that you aren't just making all of this up . . .'

Unexpectedly, Calvert dropped the crockery back on the table with a clatter. One cup shattered. She took a step towards Davies and, to his surprise and discomfiture, hiked up her skirt. Both legs were disfigured, the left one more badly. A long scoop of flesh was missing, from just above the knee to a little below the thigh. The muscles of the upper right leg were twisted like ropes. Davies found himself gawping. Calvert thrust her hand under his chin and forced him to look at her.

'My husband loved me dearly. But events have tears, Doctor Davies . . . I hope I never see or hear of you again!'

The nurse had gone home and Pamela lay in narcotic sleep, snoring gently, in the bedroom. Her face, her grotesque cadaver's face, was lit only by the moon-pale streetlight through the window.

Davies entered quietly, stumbling a little in the doorway. The whisky-high had been brief, and now the long downslope had generated in him a mood of trepidation and self-pity, and a depthless rage that the fabric of life should be so callously woven.

He stood for a few moments, swaying gently, listening to the fluttering exhalations from the bed. Pamela's mouth sagged open slightly, a dark pit; and her closed eyes, sunken in the final stages of her illness, mirrored that blackness.

A ragged sob tore itself free of the tightness in his chest. Davies swallowed back a grief and controlled himself. He shuffled over to the bed and knelt beside Pamela. Her once-familiar features, so white, so transformed, held a child's innocence.

'I will always love you,' Davies whispered to her, choking on the rush of emotion. 'I will always love you, more than life itself.'

He settled down beside her, drifting quickly into sleep, wondering with his final conscious thought how far he was able to trust the truth of his promise.

When Davies announced he was taking Pamela for a holiday, no-one argued otherwise. His colleagues at work, acquaintances and friends, Professor Michaelides, even Pamela herself, all understood that she was going away to die. Her condition had deteriorated rapidly over the past ten days, and there was nothing else — no medical procedures to be undertaken, no words to be spoken, that could alter the inevitable outcome of the illness.

Davies made his plans with the cool efficiency that characterised his work at the university. He tidied his desk, left detailed instructions for his stand-in, and copious notes for his students; booked a room in a hotel ten miles from the glen, whose location Doctor Calvert had described to him in detail; and rented an Isuzu Trooper for the journey, that being what he considered a sensible choice of vehicle.

They set out at ten a.m. next day, crossing the border by six and turning north from Dumfries two hours later. The weather had been good throughout the journey, but now vivid streaks of charcoal cloud layered themselves along the western horizon, underlit as the sunset advanced like a fire left untended.

'Looks like rain,' Davies said, making idle conversation with himself. He and Pamela had spoken little on the way up, she dozing in the main, except once to explain to him that she had never wanted to change her life — that she was happy, even with the end of things so close. Now, nearing their destination, all the undefined fears and unadmitted doubts clarified in Davies's mind to a blinding terror at what he knew he had to face — coupled with the equally powerful certainty that he would be unable to do so.

He slammed down the gears roughly and turned off the main highway, using the inadequate signposting to verify Calvert's directions. Suddenly there was no other traffic on the road, and the hills rose around them. Davies gunned the four-track's engine, dropped into second and accelerated up a rise, slowing and then stopping to absorb the panorama of the night. He turned off the engine, wound down the window, and listened to the subliminally soft buffeting of the wind the whole while, feeling the force of long centuries taint the air like the cloying scent of the soil. Davies knew with a factless understanding that Jennifer Calvert had not lied to him. Here in this place of hills and loneliness, power older than thought or conscience lay quiescent, but sensitive to the ephemeral flickering lives of men. Holy wells, sacred waters, dragon paths, stones that echoed the sky and the stars; these were just a few of the manifestations of the power which came from behind the shadow, from the moment after the moment past. Davies felt it in his blood and bones, and was mortally afraid.

He stretched to twist the key in the ignition, pausing as a new sound pierced the air like a needle through cloth. A voice, calling. A voice, coming closer.

Davies turned on the engine and reached down under the seat for the wrench he habitually kept handy, in the event of being threatened. Pamela had lapsed again into sleep, and Davies chuckled shakily to be here, essentially alone, with a stranger approaching.

The headlight beams, uptilted on full, showed nothing. Davies depressed the clutch and gear-shifted into reverse, and by the bright reversing lamp saw a figure hurrying to catch up with the vehicle.

It was a young man, a student type, his long hair tied in a ponytail — a fashion Davies had long thought ludicrous — his arms waving madly to attract the driver's attention. He was hampered both by his backpack and bulky parka, his shouts becoming increasingly frantic with the fear of being left stranded.

Davies stepped from the Trooper, keeping the wrench out of sight in the folds of his coat. He smiled amiably. The look of relief on the young man's face was pathetic to witness.

'Oh . . . oh, man, I thought you were going to . . . I need . . .'

'You need a lift?' Davies said. 'No problem.'

The man's words were coming between thirsty gulps of air. He nodded, grinning, bending forward to prop his hands on his knees, the better to catch his breath.

'I thought I could make Glenbarra by nightfall . . . Hitched up to the Thornhill turn . . . Didn't realise it was quite this far . . . Stupid, really . . .'

'Yes, stupid.' Davies still sounded friendly, and when the man looked up he saw his rescuer was smiling. Davies allowed his dislike of the hitcher's ponytail and neat goatee beard to bloom fully, loathing the man's gullibility, hating the easy-going warmth in his eyes.

'Very stupid,' he added, lifting his arm and bringing the wrench down with a sharp crack on the young man's skull.

The hitch-hiker dropped soundlessly at Davies's feet. Davies flopped him over on to his back and rummaged through the parka's many pockets until he found a wallet, which he placed under a near-by stone, not wishing to know the name of the man who would die so Pamela might live; wanting it all to be cleanly anonymous. Then, using a handful of grass, he wiped away the blood and checked the damage he'd inflicted. The scalp bore a three-inch split, and when Davies pressed his finger against the skull, he thought he felt the bone give a little spongily. His blow with the wrench had not been very finely judged, but although the man's face was paper-white and his breathing shallow, he was alive . . .

Which was all he needed to be for Davies's purposes.

Davies bundled the hitcher into the back seat of the Trooper, positioning him so the scalp wound bled into the parka and not over the seats. Then he used his mobile to ring through to the hotel, explaining that there'd been an unavoidable delay at home, so he and his wife would now be arriving in the early hours. The hotel proprietor wished Davies a safe journey, his voice congenial and lilting with its soft lowland burr. Pamela roused to semi-consciousness but failed to notice the passenger. Muffled up in her coat and headscarf, like a Russian peasant, she looked a lot worse than the young man, quite grotesque. Davies soothed her and told her they were nearly there, and she should rest. He poured out a measure of the liquid morphine Michaelides had provided to ease Pamela's pain, and tipped the cup to her lips. She drank, smiled weakly, and ebbed again into sleep.

Davies strapped himself in and gunned the Isuzu's engine, flicking on the wipers as the rain he had been expecting began, the first outrider droplets speckling the windscreen glass.

He felt strangely calm.

Another hour of steady driving brought Davies close to where he thought his destination should be. He had come to a junction. A single-track road cut to left and right, from nowhere to nowhere, in the darkness. During the last fifteen minutes, the landscape had changed around him, the hills moving in more claustrophobicly, their slopes littered with tailings, which were the remnants of the galena mining that had brought the area its only prosperity, over a century ago. The world beyond the reach of the Trooper's beams was utterly lightless. Not even a farmhouse out there, Davies thought, as a subtle apprehension drifted through him.

He checked Calvert's written directions, took the left turn, then a right about a half mile farther on. He was off the road entirely by now, his way marked only by the phantom of a trail, a suggestion of a track beneath the wiry moorgrass.

For the first time, the vehicle struggled on the upslope, the wheels slipping once on the rain-slick surface. Davies eased off the accelerator and let the four-track take itself to the crest of the rise. The powerful headlamps twin-beamed towards the heavens, then dropped down and spilled light into the little glacial valley.

He saw the monolith at once, a square-topped roughly-hewn column of rock, leaning maybe ten degrees with the slow shift of soil over the millennia. It stood at the northernmost point of the capstone, as Calvert had mentioned, that rested on three more supporting stones amidst a scattering of other boulders. There was nothing else to be seen: the small secluded glen was quite featureless apart from the cairn:

no more than a grassy crater in the wilderness, the turf here and there interrupted by protruding knucklebones of rock.

Davies exhaled slowly, glancing briefly at Pamela before trickling the four-track down into the valley.

He brought the vehicle to a halt twenty yards from the cairn, allowing an even spread of light, yet keeping the Trooper close enough at hand. No preamble was needed — as Calvert had told him, there was no sorcery involved. Davies had simply to lay Pamela on the capstone, place the anonymous victim nearby —

'And catch a bus to China,' Davies muttered, chuckling to himself. That's what his father used to say at Guy Fawks' night as he read the instructions on the fireworks . . . 'Place on a firm surface, light the blue touch paper, and catch a bus to China . . .'

Davies's smiled faltered and vanished. Those safe times seemed very far away now. Everything seemed very far away.

He set to work, easing Pamela free of her seatstraps and carrying her to the cairn. She was as light as a child, like a poorly constructed caricature of a woman, made of canvas and sticks. She mumbled something as Davies set her down, her face to the sky. He adjusted her headscarf and looked at her for a few seconds, at the raindrops falling on her parchment-yellow eyelids, before returning to the Trooper to drag out the body of the victim.

The young man's breathing had worsened. It was sawing in and out, in and out, swiftly and shallowly, and his skin was waxy and sweating. The back of his head had become a mass of congealing blood, which had soaked through the parka's hood and spread into the padding of the seat. As Davies hauled him by his feet on to the grass, the hood ripped softly free of the upholstery, and the black matted hair ripped softly free of the hood. The wound, opened again, oozed profusely.

Davies's expression was anguished as he dragged the man towards the monolith. Calvert had said that "the giver" should sit against it, out of sight of the recipient of the healing force. He arranged the young man thus, his head lolling — then lifting of its own accord as Davies looked on, aghast. One eye gazed like a fractured opal in Davies's direction; the other showed only white, where the eyeball had rolled upwards. There was little co-ordination in his facial muscles, which rippled and spasmed as the brain's electrical circuitry went haywire. He managed a few guttural sounds, which were totally meaningless, then seemed to acquiesce to some hidden imperative . . .

Blood ran suddenly from both nostrils, and the young man's

mouth was unexpectedly clogged with dark, jellylike matter. His head sagged sideways and the opal eye emptied of light.

'Oh God . . .' Davies whispered it as though to damp down the onrush of dread. 'Oh God . . . Oh God . . .'

For a few instants his thoughts flew apart in all directions. Pierced on the point of his panic, he had no idea what to do next.

Then, like a drenching of icy water, the tension in the air around him started to change. It became palpable, like a thickening, *an imminence*.

Davies's back was turned to the wind-borne rain; numb and stiffened with stooping. He straightened with a grunt of pain, half stood — then cried out shrilly at what he saw.

Spiralling streamers of mist were reaching out from under the capstone, welling up from the blackness of the cairn. The first of the delicate tendrils were already curling with a feminine elegance around the lip of the granite slab, as though feeling their way tentatively towards Pamela. One thin filament reached her chin, her lips, and slid between them into her just-open mouth.

Now Davies began to shudder, not at the appearance of something beyond the realms of the known — his adult life had after all been dedicated to the exploration of such forces — but at the way the situation seemed now to be slipping beyond his control. He turned his attention quickly and briefly back to the young hitch-hiker, pressing his index and middle fingers into the soft flesh beneath the boy's chin, to confirm what he already knew; then in a blaze of futile rage pushed the corpse roughly away.

On impulse Davies whirled and for the merest second considered dragging Pamela off the capstone and back to the Trooper. Better that her death should be conventional — and sane — than that she should suffer this, and he be witness to the terror.

But the process of conjuration was already too far advanced for action. The opalescent mist, gathering and shot through with a lustrous glow like abalone shell, had now risen up from beneath the capstone on every side. Contrary to reason and the ways of the natural world, the haze was poised above her, and with a silent and seductive grace was generating shadows . . .

They formed out of nothing, seeming not even to be a thickening of the smoke, nor any mysterious coagulation of the night. Simply shadows, making sense now in Davies's mind; becoming a form, revoltingly lean, of impossibly angled limbs and a head somehow swept back with bizarre severity. It was nothing sent from heaven.

The revenant hunkered down, straddling Pamela, its mouth moving closer and closer to her face.

'No!'

Davies's howl of distress was taken by the wind and spirited away. The phantasm paused and tilted its face to stare at him, transforming the nature of the man's raw fear by the agony held in its glittering eyes.

It hissed like a reptile under threat, swung back and kissed the woman in a gesture of tenderness, its malnourished fingers gently stroking the woman's hair in the moment of her ruin. Something rare and fleeting passed between them. Pamela's flesh settled back on the brink of its long dissolution.

Davies had backstepped a few paces, wracked with a terrible bright guilt, a powerful shame, that he had allowed this to come about. Two deaths, utterly avoidable, if only he had followed Calvert's guidance and prepared himself to play this by the rules.

You get nothing for nothing, and once the creature was called, feeding must inevitably follow.

Now it slid fluidly from the capstone and with an ease and buoyancy quite unnatural, moved quickly in Davies's direction.

Davies shrieked in despair, fear rather than courage driving him to tear his eyes free of the apparition and run along the blinding beams of the headlights to the four-track parked nearby.

He stumbled around the side, wrenched open the driver's door and twisted the key in the ignition. The powerful engine bellowed into the night.

Ten yards away, the shade writhed closer, all the world's suffering implicit in its smile. One long emaciated forelimb lifted, the hand turning palm upward for the delivery of Davies's soul.

He screamed hysterically, dropped the handbrake and jammed his foot on the accelerator.

The Trooper's wheels whined, spinning on the grass momentarily, then gripped as the vehicle shot forward. Davies retained the presence of mind to keep his hands on the wheel, but averted his eyes in the final split-second, anticipating impact.

A cool draught blew through him, through the honeycomb and marrow of his bones. Every cell in his body was touched, seeming to shrink back like flesh peeled raw of skin.

Then there was a second of confusion, until Davies made sense of the rain-glimmering darkness and recognised the edges and bulk of the cairn just ahead.

The Trooper smashed into it at speed, hurling him through the windshield and out onto the capstone.

He rolled, ripped and bleeding, against Pamela's corpse, as the Harvester of pain swept out of the valley and moved south.

One of the Trooper's headlights still glared at a crazy angle into the darkness. By its illumination, Davies saw the sudden excrescences on his skin just a moment before the indescribable pain surged through him: the torture of age, cancer, smallpox, polio, pneumonia, plague, septicaemia, typhoid . . .

The four-tack's single headlight flickered as circuitry burned inside; guttered and faded a few seconds later. But not before Jeffrey Davies had died, of everything.

Sunt lacrimae rerum. Events have tears.

JOAN AIKEN

QUANDO TU VAS

The mountains stand up all around. Snow-covered in winter, grey or yellow or blue in summer. They are not so close — ten miles of flat land lies between, almond orchards, cornfields, and the gullies of the great river that seam the country in all directions, like veins in a hand. It's beautiful. I could never consider living anywhere else. It's my home. In May the fields are blue-green, like deep water; in August, baked, parched, the colour of maize bread. 'I don't know how you can endure it, year after year,' Edward said. 'Don't you *ever* think of moving away?' 'Never,' I said. That was when we were friends, when I used to call him Eduardo. Before I had taken his wife.

'Looking over there, over this town wall,' I said, 'every day I can see changes. A tree grows, a shadow moves. The river runs in winter, dries in summer. I shall love it in just the same way until I die. I want nothing better.' 'I can't understand that at all,' said Eduardo. 'It's beautiful, of course — or why would I be living here? — but I want comparisons. I want the sea, islands, lakes, big cities, cold northern countries, fens, forests. That's why I live the way I do.'

Edward is an air pilot. He had chosen the right profession for his roving nature.

For the first few years after he came to live in Duron — I will not say "settled", that word would never describe Eduardo — he flew for a big international company, Interworld, flew everywhere, all over the globe. But then, after MaryAnn had her miscarriage and they were told "No more children" she begged him to take a job that would not whirl him away for such long periods of time. 'Please, please, Edward dear — just in Spain,' she begged. 'So that I shall be sure I can expect you home at least one or two days a week.'

Not that MaryAnn was one of those clinging, dependant girls. She had a beautiful voice, she taught singing, gave music lessons, played the guitar, and spent hours listening to her records, of which she had a huge collection. She was passionately fond of music. But, also, she soon had friends all over our little town. She learned Spanish very fast and, in the end, spoke it better than Eduardo.

We had met on the coast in Ribadesella. He had a week's leave, they were spending it with English friends who owned a Timeshare apartment, and they had decided to search for something similar. 'Why not look farther inland?' I suggested, meeting them in a bar, taking an immediate liking, as everybody did, except those who hated him on sight, to Edward's lively intelligence, his warmth, his fun, his fondness for banter and wisecrack. And MaryAnn was so pretty; quiet, but very, very pretty, with a pale skin, a delicate mouth, and clear, understanding eyes that would light up wonderfully if somebody said a thing that caught her fancy.

I was visiting my aunt Fortunata, who had fallen ill and wanted a nephew to keep her company until she had expressed her last wishes.

'Why don't you come back with me when I go to Duron?' I said to Eduardo and MaryAnn, when my aunt's affairs were settled. 'Property is much cheaper inland, you could find a beautiful house to suit your taste for a tenth of the price you would have to pay on the sea-coast. Many of the little inland towns are becoming depopulated, it is very sad. And Duron is a beautiful place. I would not lie to you! I shall be glad to give you the benefit of my help and advice, knowing everyone there as I do.'

At first they were doubtful. Would MaryAnn be lonely? On the coast side she had English company; at Duron they would know nobody, not a soul.

From the beginning, though, I could see that Edward liked the idea. He was one of those men — they are not so rare — who have two standards of behaviour for themselves and for their wives. 'After we are married I shall be unfaithful to you as often as I choose,' he told MaryAnn when she first accepted him (imagine it! But I know this to be true, for they both told me the story at different times). 'I shall sleep with other women as often as I please, because that is my nature. You I shall love best always, but others I must have. You, however must never, never betray me! A woman must not do so! That would be another matter entirely.'

And MaryAnn accepted the bargain! Of course she was very young at the time, only twenty. Also, of course, she did not then truly believe him, she thought she would be the last woman in his life, the one who could cure him of his promiscuity. But she did say, 'Make sure, then, that I know nothing of what you do, Edward. So long as I know nothing I shall be happy.'

In this way, she was able to believe in his fidelity.

He kept all his activities from her. But he told me; over the bar in Esteban's little tavern. He told me of girls in New York, Paris, New Delhi, Athens, Lima; and then, when, after the miscarriage, his range was reduced, he told me of ladies in Madrid, Barcelona, Leon, Malaga, Seville, Cordoba.

I never criticised him. It was not my place to do so. Had he been my brother, or any relation . . . But he was not. We were simply friends. He enjoyed being candid about his affairs with me. And I greatly enjoyed his company — his wit, his humour, his wide interest, his knowledge of the world — all these were something quite outside my experience.

Who am I, after all? The baker of Duron. So was my father before me, and my grandfather. And my great-grandfather. The same great cavernous oven has been in use, here, for more than a hundred years. When a fine new batch of bread comes out (and I bake good bread) you can smell it all over the town.

MaryAnn did not eat a great deal of bread, but just the same she used to come in almost every morning: 'Just to breathe the air,' she used to say, laughing.

When I am not baking I write; I write stories. I used to think that some day I might send them to an editor in Madrid or Barcelona and then, all of a sudden, my name would become famous all over Spain, like Cervantes or Galdos.

But that was before the thing happened with MaryAnn.

One day — I still do not know how it came about — she somehow learned what Edward and I had been keeping from her all this time. She found a handkerchief, a letter, something. She discovered. And what pierced her most deeply was that, to him, it did not seem at all a serious matter; indeed he told her he was quite astonished that she had not suspected sooner. After all, he had honestly warned her! 'And there was Carmen!' he said. 'And Milagros! And Rosie! And Louise! Do you really mean to tell me that you never realised? How can you have been so simple, so green?'

In her distress she came to me. I was her oldest friend in the town.

'What I mind worst of all,' she said with tears rolling down her cheeks, 'is that now we are enemies. If I go into the kitchen and he is standing at the table, he does not look round, to see what I am doing, to see if I need something. He just stands with his back to me, as if I were not there. And, out of doors, if we walk together, he never notices whether I am at his side or have fallen behind; he walks as if he were alone. This I cannot endure. For I still love him, Jaime!'

'Well,' I said, 'you must wait. Have patience. All may come right still. I am sure he loves you. Wait a while.'

I talked to Eduardo. 'She is very young still,' I said. 'She has had a bad shock. She is lonely. Be kind to her.'

'Oh!' he exclaimed impatiently. 'She is being such a martyr about it! I can't stand the reproachful way she stares at me with her big sad eyes.'

A year passed. Every day I wrote MaryAnn a letter: somehow I felt that it might help, if she knew she had a friend who was continually thinking about her. I poured my soul into those letters, writing them at odd times in the bakery between batches of bread; and then at night I tucked them under her door. They had taken a big house in one of the two streets, the other street, in our town. What did I write? About life, about the town, about the country around it, the cornfields, the almond orchards, the nightingales, the fish in the river, the poplar trees, the orchids growing on the roadsides, the neighbours, the sky, the mountains. The whole world, I told her, was waiting to comfort her, it would be a sad waste of her spirit if she were to fall into despair just because of one man's shortcomings.

At the end of the year she came to me in the bakery one evening when I was pounding the dough. And she said:

'You are right, Jaime. I will not despair anymore. But I shall not stay with Edward, because I no longer love him. I love you, Jaime. Will you have me? Can I come and live with you? — I will learn to make good bread,' she said.

And so that is what she did. It caused a great scandal in the town at first, but we have such scandals from time to time, and then they die down. All the neighbours were fond of MaryAnn; and of course they are accustomed to me, we have known each other since we were all born; and I am the only baker in Duron; so they went on coming to me for their bread, and many of them went on taking music lessons from MaryAnn.

Eduardo was another matter.

I have never seen a man so angry.

'You have betrayed me!' he said, raging. 'You were my friend! I confided in you, and this is how you reward me! With my own wife!'

He called me vile names, he would have liked to fight, wound, injure, castrate, kill me; but, being a person of sense and sobriety, I took care to keep friends around me until his first passion had died down.

He begged to see MaryAnn, he begged and besought her to come back to him, but she shut herself up in my house and refused to see him. Despite what she had said, I think she still did love him and was afraid she might relent; that was why she would not see him.

She brought no possessions to me save her boxes of gramophone records and the thick bundle of my letters; she wanted, she said, to leave all the rest of her life behind. And she repeated her promise to work hard for me.

She did work hard; and we were happy together. Until she became pregnant.

Edward had quitted the town. When he found that by no means could he get to see MaryAnn, I think he was so greatly wounded in his pride that he could no longer remain in a place where all knew that his wife had left him for another man; he packed a bag and drove off, leaving his house empty.

MaryAnn had our baby, but it was born dead. And it killed her; our doctor told me that she was never going to recover from it.

'She had only a few weeks to live,' he told me. 'She best make her peace with God.'

'I *am* at peace with God,' said MaryAnn when she heard this. 'He and I have no secrets from one another. But I would, very much, like to see Edward just once more, so that he and I can make our peace together. Would you mind doing that for me, Jaime? Would you mind finding him?'

I did mind, but naturally I could not refuse. So I drove (having by telephone discovered his whereabouts) to Bilbao airport, at a time when he would be there, in order to wait for him and tell him the news and bring him back.

When you are in the throe of a bitter sorrow, trifles often have the power to print themselves very strongly on your brain. That season in Spain we had an advertising campaign, signs that you could see erected on hillsides all over the country: "QUANDO TU VAS, VA VOLVO."

As I sat waiting for Eduardo, that sentence kept beating, kept repeating in my mind. "Quando tu vas, va Volvo."

When at last I saw Edward I was quite shocked, for he seemed to have aged by twenty years in the last twelve months, his dark hair was grizzled with grey, and there were deep furrows from his nostrils to the corners of his lips.

'MaryAnn is dying,' I told him. 'She wishes to see you. Will you come back with me to Duron?'

He could hardly bear the sight of me. I could see that. But at last he said, 'Very well. I had better come in my own car, which is here. I will follow you.' And so he did. I was quite glad not to have his company in the car. And so we drove one behind the other all the way, past the signs telling us *Quando tu vas, va Volvo*.

At my house, I went into the room, and said, 'I have brought him.'

Then I walked into the bakery and started preparing the dough.

He did not stay with her long: perhaps ten minutes. And I did not see him go; I was putting the first batch of dough into the great oven.

After that, feeling the house very quiet, I went into the bedroom and found that she had fainted. Filled with terror, I sent a neighbour running for the doctor, who, when he came, said, 'She will not now last more than a few hours.'

Before the doctor's arrival I had noticed the room disordered. A box had been pulled out from a closet: the one containing my year's letters to MaryAnn. With fury I realised that Edward — my enemy, my bitter enemy — had taken those letters away with him.

MaryAnn returned very slowly to consciousness. She knew very well that she was dying.

'I am so sorry to leave you, Jaime,' she said to me. 'You have been the best husband a woman could wish for. I have brought you little good, whereas you have done me nothing but kindness. And now will you do me one more?'

'Of course,' I said.

'Play some of my favourite records for me as I go. The Mysterious Barricades, and the Pachelbel canon, and, especially, Bist du bei Mir. They are there, in the case. I would so much like to hear Bist du bei Mir just once more.'

I looked in the case, found the first two, and put them on, one after the other. MaryAnn lay quietly listening.

But the third record, Bist du bei Mir, was not where it should be. It was her great favourite; it had been there the day before. It was nowhere. That rat, that snake, had taken it, because he knew she loved it best. He had taken it, along with my letters.

And so MaryAnn had to die without that comfort, the Bach song: 'Be thou with me and I go joyful, to death which is my rest.'

After she was buried I made my plan to be avenged on Edward. I planned exactly what to do.

He has a horror of rats. I remember an evening when he was sitting in the bakery, watching me work, and one ran across the floor; he went white and sick with shock, he nearly fainted.

'I can't stand them,' he said, laughing shamefacedly when I brought him a glass of cognac. 'They are the only things that turn my bones to jelly.'

I have reserved a seat on one of his flights, and I have brought five rats with me hidden in a bag of hay. At present they are quiet, tranquillised, and will not attract notice, but by the time we are all on board and the plane has taken off, they will begin to wake up and grow lively. As I sit here, in the airport lounge, nursing the bag on my lap, I think of all those signs, striding across the country on their thin legs, carrying their message: QUANDO TU VAS, VA VOLVO.

The flight is to Seville, where Eduardo had, or still has, a girl called Pepita. There will be plenty of time on the journey for the rats to wake up. My seat is well at the rear, where he will not see me, but I shall stand up, after a while, and walk forward towards his cockpit.

Then we shall see . . .

Stealing that record, which he knew she loved best, was heartless. How could he do such a thing to a dying woman?

But it is the loss of my letters — a whole year of work, of passion, of my soul's outpouring — that I find utterly impossible to forgive.

CLEO CORDELL

THE WITCH MARK

The sound of raised voices and nailed boots on the baked earth was distant at first, but growing louder by the second. Cecily climbed up onto the broad wooden window ledge and peered through the lacy branches of the trees that bordered the house. Out beyond the blindseed fields, where the ripe crop rustled and undulated, she could see the flare of rushlights.

The men were coming for her mother. No one told her this, but she sensed it somehow. And she was afraid. Her mother sat on a stool by the fire, rocking back and forth, weeping and wringing her hands. At the sight of the strained white face, pinched by fear, Cecily felt icy shivers running down her back.

She was ten years old. In her short life she had known only the love and comfort meted out by the two women in her life — Grandmother Phillipa, tall, stately and wise, and her mother, strong, beautiful, a little distant. Her father, taken up with the work of raising the difficult crop of blindseed was absent from the house for long hours. It was the women who set the rhythm of her days, who taught her and sang to her, and spoke of the mysteries of growing things.

But this night her world rocked on an axis. Her beloved mother was in danger and she did not know why.

'Do something, Alverd,' Grandmother Phillipa said to Cecily's father. 'Go out and reason with them. They'll listen to you. Tell them if you can bear the burden of it, they must.'

'Things have gone too far for talking,' Alverd said. 'Your daughter's brought this on herself with her whoring!'

Phillipa's face twisted with disgust. 'Whoring? Is that what you call it? You fool! You don't understand, do you? You should get down on your knees and thank Meara. Without her there would be no Harvest

Home. You men — with your petty jealousies! Had it been another one's wife you'd have taken your turn with the rest.'

Alverd rounded on her. 'Don't you accuse me, you damned old harridan! This is all your doing. Like mother, like daughter, eh? The legacy is handed down they say. Well she's been found out. You too. Now you'll both reap your reward!'

'Reap you say. Oh, that's rich. You'll not reap a crop again if you let them take her!'

'What's the use of this arguing?' Meara sobbed. 'They'll take me anyway. I cannot stop them. Men want only to destroy what they fear. Alverd, look to Cecily for me, I beg you. You would not turn against our daughter, would you?'

Cecily cringed under her father's scrutiny. He looked as if he hated her.

'She's stays because she's not like you, wife. And that's the only reason,' he said.

With a muffled cry Cecily stumbled from the room. She did not understand, but somehow she had offended her father. Half blinded by tears, she dragged open the door to the tiny cupboard under the stairs and crammed her small body inside. In the stuffy darkness that smelt of dried apples, gourd fruit, and wicker baskets she felt safe.

The voices from the sitting room were muffled, but she heard Grandmother Phillipa say, 'I'll deal with this, daughter. There is one way to save you, but you must be brave. And you, Alverd. If you ever loved Meara, don't dare say a word. I'll do all the talking.'

Cecily was amazed that her grandmother dared to give her father orders. She was in awe of him herself. He was a shadowy figure, but when in the house, his word was law. There was the sound of the iron poker being pushed into the fire. Then a long moment of silence. Cecily could almost feel the tension. She imagined her father and her grandmother glaring at each other, like two yard dogs fighting over a bone. As there came a banging on the door, her mother gave a sudden cry of fright. 'Oh, Goddess! They will take me!'

'Whist now, Meara. Things will go right. You'll see,' Phillipa said. 'Mind you do as I bid.'

The house seemed to ring with men's voices, all of them raised in anger. Cecily wanted to press her hands to her ears to shut out the voices, but something made her open the cupboard door a crack and listen.

'Give her up, man,' one called. 'She was seen to be the one. There's no doubt about the mark. Our wives won't stand for it a moment longer.'

'Aye. It's for the best,' called another. 'It will be difficult. We all know how much . . .'

'Aye,' Alverd called, his voice breaking with distress and bitterness. 'You do know. That's what I cannot stomach. What she's given you, ought to have been mine alone.'

Just then Grandmother Phillipa's voice rang out, piercing the night with the clarity of a bell. 'No need for all this fuss. Come inside, but quietly now. You'll frighten the child. And don't you stamp mud into the matting. You may watch and see the task done, then get home to your wives and let us be. There's no need for a killing.'

Cecily strained to hear, to gain an impression of what was happening. As if by a miracle the angry voices faded and the men came silently into the house, the only sound that of their nailed boots striking the stone floor. The steps stopped abruptly and she heard murmurs of surprise or horror.

'This is not seemly,' someone said. 'Cover her.'

'Nay, it must be done. You have the right of it, old woman,' said another. 'If you do this, no more will be said. And she may keep her life.'

There was a collective gasp and then the sound of sizzling, the hiss as of steam rising. Meara screamed and screamed. A sound of high echoing agony that chilled Cecily's blood. She caught the acrid smell of something burning — something bitter like fur or blood.

'God. Oh, God,' her father sobbed. 'Forgive me, Meara. I never meant this to happen.'

Then came her mother's voice, gentle but halting and rough-edged with pain. 'It's done now, Alverd. Let it be. It's over. Please, leave now. All of you.'

Soon after, the men went quietly away. Cecily felt her fear draining away with their going. They were not going to take her mother. But what had been done to her? She had not heard anyone scream like that since she helped her grandmother with a birthing.

From the sitting room there were low murmurs, no more voices raised in anger or accusation. After a time, Cecily crept out of the cupboard. Her grandmother was alone in the room. She was on her knees pushing a tangle of bloody rags into the heart of the fire. The room smelt strongly of the clean, pungent scent of woundbane.

'Where's mother?' Cecily said. 'What happened to her?'

Phillipa turned and smiled reassuringly. There were lines of strain on her face. 'She's gone to bed. And your father with her. She'll be safe

247

now. Let's speak no more of it. It's late for you to be abroad. Come, off to bed with you too.'

Cecily wanted to ask what had happened, but something in her grandmother's tone stopped her. She did not protest when Phillipa unlaced her gown and removed her shift and knitted stockings, as she had used to do when Cecily was much younger. She sensed that Phillipa gained comfort from coddling her. But she was puzzled when Phillipa ran a practised eye over her nakedness, turning her this way and that as if looking for something.

'Is it bathing night?' she said shivering, for it was cold in the loft she shared with her grandmother, the chill of leaf fall already in the air. The single oil lamp gave out hardly any heat and little light.

'No, love. It's not,' Phillipa said, giving her a hug before pulling a bedgown of blindweave over her head. 'And you have no need to worry. Your mother's fate will not be yours. Now, it's time you were asleep.'

The downy fabric slipped over Cecily's skin bringing instant warmth. The smell of the material, like honey and dried bark, was redolent with memories of long hot days. 'Grandmother,' she began. 'What did father mean about the legacy being handed down?'

'I'll explain if the time comes,' Phillipa said, stroking a fold of the shimmering blindweave. Her face was pensive as she said under her breath, 'Though I pray to the Goddess that it never does. Two times has it befallen my bloodline. Like lightning, the burden ought not to strike in the same place twice. It may just as well befall another.'

Extinguishing the light, Phillipa undressed and climbed into her own bed. In a few minutes Cecily was asleep, the events of the night lingering only in her dreams.

The next day Cecily went to work in the fields with everyone else. The haulm of the old crop had to be raked up and burned and the land prepared for seeding.

Cecily's mother worked beside her, a flat basket at her feet for collecting the few pods that clung to dried up stalks. Blindseed was too valuable to waste even the lowest grade pods. Cecily saw the sidelong glances darted at her mother, the expressions of distrust mixed with pity. Her mother ignored the other women, working steadily through the day, although she moved stiffly and was hunched over as if she had an ache in her belly.

'What's the matter, mother?' Cecily asked, when they sat down at midday to eat their bread and cheese.

'It's nothing that can be helped,' her mother said, smiling painfully and reaching out to stroke Cecily's dark plaits. 'Don't you worry about me. The trouble will pass.'

Another of the women, sitting close by said, 'Oh Meara. If only you had kept it secret. People can cope with things if they're not thrown in their faces.'

Cecily's mother did not answer, but tears welled up in her eyes. She packed away their food and went back to work.

During the next few weeks, the fields were sewn. The villagers watered their field-shares and kept away animals and birds from the seed beds. It was Summer before the first green shoots broke the soil's surface. Everyone breathed a sigh of relief and a party was thrown to celebrate the birth of a new crop.

Tension in the village relaxed somewhat. Cecily's mother was more relaxed too. The other women spoke to her in hushed voices and even smiled occasionally. It was as if they had forgiven her. But Cecily felt that something was different about her mother. Meara was more withdrawn now. She no longer went out for long walks alone in the moonlight. It was as if she was somehow diminished. Cecily could not exactly explain the difference, but she sensed it.

And her father was different too. He came home earlier, the fields needing less attention while the blindseed crop was young. It would be some years before the adult vines needed constant guarding, and more yet before the valuable seed ripened enough for harvesting. More often than not, her father would walk straight into the kitchen, his muddied boots leaving tracks on the rush matting, and nod curtly in the direction of the stairs. Meara would drop whatever she was doing and hurry up to the bedroom, her head bowed and her cheeks burning with shame.

The sounds that floated down the stairs disturbed Cecily. Many times she had heard the rustlings, the loving whispers in the night. Those were comforting sounds. But in the daylight, the creaking of the bed, the hushed whimpers and moans, her father's tortured cries were different, upsetting somehow. Her mother's voice, low and tearful, sounded pained and lost.

When she spoke of this to her grandmother, Phillipa said tight-lipped, 'It is his way of punishing her and himself. You'll understand when you're older.'

The blindseed grew slowly, clothing the fields with its lush blue-grey leaves and brittle stems. Cecily grew too, becoming taller and lean of limb, keeping pace with the valuable crop. When the blindseed had been four years in the growing, Cecily along with the other village girls went out into the fields to see to the tying-in of the new shoots to the network of supporting canes.

They day was hot and sweat ran down the inside of Cecily's leather basque. Despite having tucked her skirt up between her legs and securing it to her belt, she felt unbearably hot and sticky. It was backbreaking work and she decided to go to the stream to fetch a drink and cool off. It was shady amongst the black Alders that grew on humps of moss-covered soil. Cecily dangled her bare feet in the stream and soaked a kerchief in the cold water. After she had drunk, she lay back, covering her forehead with the soaked cloth.

She must have dozed, because she was suddenly wakened by a sharp pain in her neck. She felt the place on her skin, where there was a lump, but no sign of whatever insect had stung or bitten her. Almost instantly she began to feel dizzy. Rising unsteadily to her feet, she hurried home. Bursting into the kitchen where Phillipa was baking bread, she managed to sit down just before she collapsed. The side of her neck was swollen now and tender. Her head ached abominably, the pain of it stabbing behind her eyes.

'Did you see what stung you?' her grandmother asked as she sponged her neck with dilute woundbane. When Cecily shook her head, she went on, 'Hold still a moment. Ah, there's a sting in there. I must get it out.'

While Cecily gritted her teeth and tried not to draw away, Phillipa probed the tender flesh with a pair of bone tweezers. The pain made Cecily's eyes water.

'It's in deep. Never seen the like. Ah, I have it,' she said triumphantly, holding a barbed sting aloft. Attached to the sting was a tiny sac of venom, still pulsing gently.

'Ugh. Is that it?' Cecily said. 'It looks small for all the pain it's caused me.'

Phillipa looked closely at the wound. It was more a cut than a little hole. The tiny edges of flesh were inflamed, raw looking. A thin yellowish fluid leaked from the cut. 'Hmm. It's an oddly placed wound,' she said thoughtfully.

'What?' Cecily said, sensing that her grandmother was more perturbed than she cared to disclose.

'I think this hurt needs some special attention,' Phillipa said, making up her mind. She went to the wooden chest where medicaments were kept and returned with a phial of some kind of white carved stone.

Phillipa poured a few drops from the phial and rubbed them into Cecily's neck. Cecily caught the scent of honey and dried bark and knew that, whatever else the salve was made of, it contained blindseed oil.

'There,' Phillipa said, binding a strip of cloth over the wound. 'That'll heal cleanly now.'

Cecily went back to her work in the fields the next day. The insect bite on her neck wept into the wound-cloth for a while, then a crust appeared on top of the red lump. By the end of the week the wound had healed, but it left behind a slightly raised mark, roughly circular in colour and of a purplish-red. Cecily, conscious of the scar, took to winding gauzy scarves around her neck. The other young girls took Cecily's actions for vanity and copied her. Soon everyone forgot that there was a reason why Cecily wore her scarves.

Two years passed and small green pods appeared on the blindseed vines. A watch was set up, so that the crop was protected from theft and extremes of temperature by both night and day. And now the village began preparing for the night when the pods would be ripe and the harvest might be gathered.

Late Summer spread a net of hazy days and jewel-bright moonlit nights over the land. Cecily felt an odd restlessness inside her as she looked up at the swollen moon through the loft window. The shadows in the yard below looked purple and as soft as velvet.

'How do we know when the time is right for harvesting?' Cecily asked her grandmother.

Phillipa gave her a strange look. 'There are certain men who can predict the very hour when the pods ripen. It is crucial that the harvest begins just then. A few hours later and the crop starts to spoil.'

'How do these men know the exact time?' Cecily said.

Phillipa did not meet her granddaughter's eyes. 'It is something secret — not meant to be spoken of. There is danger as well as honour involved. For the chosen few, the rite is dark and powerful.'

Cecily was intrigued. She sensed that her grandmother was concealing something from her. 'You can tell me,' she said. 'I'm not a child any longer. I'm almost a woman.'

'Aye,' Phillipa said. 'That you are. You're your mother's daughter right enough. And that's a blessing as well as a curse.' She grasped Cecily's upper arms suddenly. 'Listen to me, beloved. If you need help, come to me. I'll know what must be done. I've done it before. It's an abomination, but it's the only way.'

Although Cecily pressed her grandmother to explain, Phillipa would not be drawn. 'I've said enough already. Perhaps too much. But I'll not have you harmed, child. Not like Meara. I'd kill first! Now, leave me be. I've work to do.'

Three nights later Cecily could not sleep. The scar on her neck felt itchy and sore. When she pressed her fingers to it, it seemed as if it was newly swollen. Getting up quietly, so as not to wake Phillipa, she went into the wash-room and splashed cold water on her neck. The skin felt hot and tight and she wondered whether the old insect bite had become infected.

By the light of a candle, she looked at the scar in her looking-glass. The round mark seemed redder and there was a faint swelling in the centre of the raised area. It looked like a little nodule and was surrounded by paler spots. Cecily was alarmed. How ugly it was. So disfiguring, like a wart. She hated the idea of anyone seeing it and reached for one of her scarves. Wrapping it tightly around her neck and tucking the ends into her bedgown she went back to sleep.

When she woke sometime later it was still dark. She could hear Phillipa's soft snores. The square of window showed her a night sky pricked with points of starlight. She stretched and became aware of a strange feeling inside her. It was as if her bones were made of something that vibrated with a high sweet resonance. Surely light flowed through her veins. There was an odd pulsing in the base of her belly. A feeling like melting butter in her loins.

She stood up and went to the window. The pull of the big-bellied white moon was strong. Beyond the trees that bordered the house, she could see the blindseed fields, the lush growth more than head-high. The blueish leaves swayed gently in a wave-like motion as breezes rippled through the fecund vines. A scent wafted towards her of honey and rusty dried-bark, and underlying it a warm and tantalising musk.

Silently she descended the loft ladder. In the barn below the cows breathed hay-scented breath on her and the hens clucked contentedly as she passed. Outside the night air was warm and soft as a caress against her skin. The blindweave of her bedgown pressed against her bare limbs, the fabric rippled and flattened to her body by the gentle breeze. With no clearly formed idea of where she was going, Cecily moved towards the wood which gave onto the fields. There was a sense of unreality about everything as if it was too bright. The monochrome of moonlight seemed too dazzling in its contrasts.

She reached the fields and walked along the edge, the grass tickling the soles of her bare feet. The blindseed vines rustled, their felted leaves whispering to her as they cast shadows to dog her steps. She saw the lookout sitting under a tree, his arms folded on his chest. Even at that distance she could smell his youth and strength. He looked up and saw her, his eyes widening as he took in the tumble of her glossy dark hair, the thin bedgown that seemed pasted to her slender form.

He did not speak as she sank down beside him and reached out her hand. She recognised him as Jaloon, the son of the blacksmith. Without a word she drew his face to hers, kissing him deeply. Her hands moved of their own volition, fingers seeking out his muscles and taut expanses of his skin. His hands in turn moved over her body, claiming and possessing what had never been touched before. Despite her willingness, her need, his touch alarmed her senses and set her nerves thrumming like the notes of a lyre.

Jaloon pushed her onto her back, trembling in his eagerness as she spread herself before him. As his hands tore at his breeches, Cecily fumbled with the scarf at her neck, frantic suddenly for a new, and as yet unheeded, fulfilment. As Jaloon's erect penis sprang free, pressing against her inner thigh, she grasped the back of his head and drew his mouth towards her neck. Jaloon groaned and thrust his cock into her.

A red spear of sensation pierced her loins, but the pain of it was lost in a potent wave of ecstasy as Jaloon closed his mouth over the raised scar on her neck and began to suckle. Trickles of pleasure seeped downwards as the sweetly pulling sensation gathered pace. Jaloon teased the nodule with his tongue, bit at it with the edges of his teeth, and moaned softly as the sweet-sour liquid seeped out and began to flow down his throat.

Cecily cried out as he moved within her, the slippery maiden blood easing the path for his engorged organ. She clawed at Jaloon's buttocks with one hand while holding him clamped to her neck with the other. As he suckled she felt the drawing-out of her energy, even while she drew energy from him. A few moments later, Jaloon tensed and spilt himself inside her. Cecily unfulfilled, arched her back as his mouth still moved against her neck. His tongue snaked out to probe the nodule. Cecily shuddered, her body exploding in a climax as he nuzzled her and took a final deep pull of nourishment.

When it was over, she stood up and left him without a word. Her task was done. There was no need for words. Jaloon sank back against the tree, asleep almost before he had refastened his breeches. Other men appeared silently from amongst the field of vines. They had seen. All of them were eager for her. She accepted each of them in turn. As they thrust within her, bathing her womb with their seed, so they suckled and took life from her. All was done in silence. When it was over, the men melted back into the fields.

Back in her bed in the loft, Cecily curled up and slept as if drugged. She did not feel Phillipa gently remove her stained bedgown, clean away the blood and semen from her thighs, and dress her in a clean gown. Nor did she feel the gentle hands on her neck as they smoothed back her dark hair and examined the newly formed nipple. Phillipa smiled, with pride and tenderness. She took the nipple between thumb and forefinger and squeezed gently. A trickle of whitish liquid trickled down Cecily's neck. Phillipa sucked her fingers clean. Her head seemed to burst with the power of light and life.

'Good night, daughter of my daughter,' she whispered and left Cecily to sleep.

The next morning Cecily had only a vague recollection of walking in the moonlight and a residual soreness between her legs. The itching and tingling of the scar on her neck had gone and the raised area seemed flatter, the little nodule less prominent. She went about her work with her usual enthusiasm and gave no more thought to the unsightly wart on her neck — covered at all times by her scarf.

The next night, and for six nights after that, Cecily went out into the moonlight. There were look-outs posted at intervals around the blindseed fields and Cecily visited each of them in turn. Old or young she took each man as her lover, always urging them to suckle from the scar on her neck. And every night the witch mark gave up its thin milk, which tasted of honey and sour dried bark. Cecily writhed in her lovers' arms, while they plundered her soft white body, but her pleasure came only from the hot mouth fastened leech-like to her neck. As she shuddered and cried out in the throes of orgasm, the nipple pulsed and swelled, rippling on the tongue of her lover.

Then one night, Cecily awoke to find Phillipa sitting on her bed. She rubbed her eyes, confused by this change in her new routine. Her body hungered, and the mark on her neck itched and burned in its eagerness to be drained. As she put up her fingers and touched the strongly erect nodule, a warm trickle dripped down her neck and soaked into her bedgown. She felt a surge of irritation. Why was her grandmother awake? She was eager to be outside.

'It is over,' Phillipa said. 'Your task is done. Can you not hear the bell tolling? That's the signal for the harvest to begin. The men you empowered with your touch and your blessed witch-milk have predicted the hour with accuracy. The pods are swollen and purple, almost bursting with high yield. The harvest will be the heaviest for many years. All the village will become rich. Without you there would have been no blindseed crop, but they will soon forget and come looking for the woman who lured them into carnality. You made them forget themselves. They rutted like joyous animals. In the old days you would have been revered, but these are ignorant and dark times. Now, love, I have to help you. It will not be pleasant, but it must be done.'

'What do you mean?' Cecily said. 'What must be done?'

Her eyes widened as Phillipa unlaced the front of her gown and allowed it to fall open to her waist. On her ribcage, there were two ugly puckered scars, about two inches under each of her sagging breasts. 'You see, love. I had two marks.' She laughed huskily, remembering for a moment. 'Oh what pleasure the men had from me! And I from them. Enough to last a lifetime.' She recovered herself quickly. 'Your mother only had the one in her armpit. Some of us are born with them. Others, like you, develop them at the right time. When they have served their purpose they are best removed. For believe me, the men — aye and their jealous wives too — will come looking for the woman who bears the witch mark. In their ignorance they think it's simply the mark of a whore.'

Cecily's hands began to tremble as her grandmother moved around the loft. She saw now what she had missed earlier. There was a charcoal brazier at the back of the room. Placed deep within the glowing coals was an iron poker. It seemed to her that the years peeled away and she was once again ten years old and hiding in the cupboard under the stairs. She remembered the dreadful sounds of her mother's agonised screams and she knew what had been done to her. She knew also why her father had punished her mother for her supposed whoring.

Slowly she turned her neck to the side, exposing the nipple to the light. It was swollen and purplish. She felt the throb of it echo in her belly and craved the touch of hard fingers on her, inside her. A drop of witch-milk gathered at the slitted eye. Cecily knew then that the hunger would be with her for as long as the nipple produced its milk. But the blindseed no longer needed a sacred vessel to harness and hone the power of its tenders.

The glowing end of the hot poker was like a firefly in the darkness. 'I am ready grandma,' she said and her voice shook only a little.

JOEL LANE

THE PLANS THEY MADE

These days when I think about Kieran, it's like he's always been dead. He'd have liked that. I knew him for nearly eight years. The first job I had after leaving school was in a video shop. He and I were assistants, and mostly our shifts didn't overlap; but sometimes I'd be unwrapping and cataloguing stuff while he was checking it for defects, or vice versa. We'd chat about new films or the shit everyone was renting. Sometimes, we'd compare muttered notes on what a patronising cunt the manager was. Same as any job. You never think about where the people you work with might end up. From working in a video store, Tarantino went on to become a famous director. Kieran went on to become a statistic.

We stayed in touch after I went to college. A few years later I got a job that required me to be near the South Birmingham train line. So I moved to Olton, the district where Kieran had always lived. He was still in the same rented flat as before, though he was working as a garage technician now. It was piecework, so his income was sort of uneven. He made up the deficit by copying and selling pirate videos. Mostly bootleg copies of films not yet available, plus some Dutch porn that seemed pretty mild to me. It's sad when minor copyright infringements are legislated into some kind of moral abomination. Kieran loved films. I tended to go for particular kinds of film — horror, crime, brooding European stuff — but Kieran would lock directly onto particular characters and scenarios that meant something to him, wherever they came from.

Back in the video shop days, he got me to watch *Running On Empty*. If you don't know, it's a film about a family on the run from the FBI for a crime the parents committed in protest against the Vietnam war. The children inherit everything: the guilt, the anger, the loss of freedom. The eldest son, played by River Phoenix, has to decide between his parents and his own needs. It was that conflict of loyalties that really moved Kieran, I think. His parents were divorced, and he'd never been able to distance himself from the feud between them. Later, we both saw *My Own Private Idaho* in a bootlegged copy of the cinema print. River Phoenix stood out in that film, because he was the only good thing in it. A similar role, in some ways. Not rebellious youth, but youth in pain — unable to reconcile his origins with his life, trying desperately to make sense of a damaged world.

I think Kieran was envious of that intensity. He might have felt it inside, but he didn't live it. He bought an electric guitar, but could only play strictly R&B stuff: pub music. He lacked the confidence to travel. Alcohol and films loaned him the gift of freedom; he didn't possess it. Mind you, he wasn't bad-looking in a solid, Brummie kind of way. Women either mothered him or played games with him, depending on their own past history. He'd been going steady with some girl for a while, I knew; but by the time I moved to Olton, he was alone.

One of the things that damaged Kieran — that stopped him moving on from a rather destructive background — was his involvement in fandom. There's like a hardcore of *Dr. Who* and *Star Trek* fandom in the West Midlands. I'm not sure why. Kieran used to say it was like the Bible Belt in America. The fan belt, sort of thing. He was capable of getting very wrapped up in TV series like *Twin Peaks*; but it was the idea of an alternative worldview that appealed to him. The fandom thing of taking something intrinsically trivial and using it to replace the world wasn't really what Kieran was after. But he found the people in the fan subculture attractive. What he didn't realise, at first, was that they applied the same fucked-up rules to their own lives as to their viewing habits.

'They're just like children,' he said to me. 'You're either their best friend or their worst enemy. They'll fall madly in love with someone and then forget them a week later. All they can see is some image of themselves. Fucking roles.'

One particular episode, when Kieran was about twenty, had left a mark on him. A young woman known for her imperial manner (her background was middle-class, but devoutly Catholic) had started going out with him. After a couple of months, she'd invited him to stay at their parent's house in Leeds for the weekend. When they got there, with no warning or apparent reason, she ditched him. He spent two days in a state of shock, feeling unable to leave. No-one spoke to him. On the Sunday, he went home alone on the train. She phoned all of their mutual friends and told vicious lies about him — Kieran never told me what exactly. The entire group froze him out. According to Kieran, 'they needed someone to reject.' One of them told me Kieran was immature. I thought he was naive, but not frozen into childhood like they were.

That wasn't his longest or deepest relationship, of course. But it damaged the more important ones that followed. His series of bad jobs hurt him just as deeply. But then, the nineties are the first postwar decade in which working hard doesn't mean making a living. Changes in the employment laws now mean that unless you've got the right background, the right voice, the right friends, then poverty is just a fact of life. Class has come back with a vengeance. The people hit by that generally blame themselves, of course. But round Olton everyone was blaming Europe, or blaming immigrants. Poor fucking Brummies — the poverty of the North combined with the prejudices of the South. It's not all like that; but there are some districts — Acocks Green, Olton, Northfield — where the hatred of life is branded into the air like a skid-mark on a pale sheet of tissue paper. At least there's a kind of truth about inner-city violence. Suburban misery is something else again. It's unreal. The smallness of it.

We used to meet up on Friday nights, go to the Westley Arms or the cinema in town. Sometimes Kieran's friend Steve, who played bass guitar on the pub circuit, would drive us out to one of the little villages strung on the main road to Warwick. There were usually a few of us, crammed into the car and singing along to one of Steve's compilation tapes. Too often , there was some bad news — a friend losing his job or getting robbed, a couple breaking up, a death — to be talked over and dissolved in alcohol. I used to feel it would be unlucky to miss one of these sessions, as if being there guaranteed the continuity of other things. It was a ritual, obviously. A communion of pints and talking and late-night Baltis and music and more talk. But if I had to say what it was about, I wouldn't say it was male bonding or machismo or any of that stuff. I'd say it was a fear of dying. Or of never having been alive.

Sometimes in mid-week, Kieran would phone me up to say he had a new video. We'd drop into the off-license and then go back to his flat to watch it. I'll always remember him in that room, lit only by the flickering screen. His intent, stubbled face, the slanted fringe of black hair. The posters on his walls, constantly working free of the Blu-tack. The little statues: aliens and religious icons. The dark crucifix. The battered electric guitar, rarely plugged in those days. But the video was the chief occupant of the flat. Brand new films in blurred, pirated copies. Crackly old prints of *film noir* of German Expressionist classics. Inexplicable one-offs like *Eraserhead* or *The Tenant* or *Kanal*. Nothing was too disturbing for Kieran's taste. But increasingly, his real passion was for American road movies. *Easy Rider, Badlands, Thelma and Louise, Wild At Heart.* It was odd. For someone who didn't like travelling. He used to say everywhere was the same. But he adored these films. It made sense in a way.

Money was always the great worry for him. As a tenant, he'd never paid rates; so the poll tax and council tax fell dead on top of the rent. He kept hoping that sooner or later, the pieces of his income would all fit into place and he'd be out of debt. When the National Lottery started, he tried to conjure up winning lines out of the serial numbers or ISBN codes on videos. By then, the repair work was drying up. Whenever he had any spare cash, it went on films or music or cheap brandy. He ate next to nothing and always wore the same few clothes; black sweaters or T-shirts, black jeans. When he started going out with a local girl called Theresa, in the spring of 1995, I used that as an excuse to see less of him. He was bringing me down. It sounds bad in retrospect, but you try being there. I assumed he'd get his act together with Theresa's help. Whatever.

A typical incident from that phase of Kieran's life was the evening I went round to give back a Nirvana bootleg tape he'd lent me. Nobody answered the bell, though I could see the light was on. I rang three times. Then Kieran opened the door. He was a bit shaky and very pale. The flat smelt of alcohol.

'Sorry Dave,' he said. 'Been up late.'

His voice was slow, childlike. His glasses were missing; I assumed he'd been asleep. Then I saw the empty frames on the table, and the pieces of shattered glass. 'What happened? Are you OK?' He nodded, looking confused. 'It's all right,' he said. 'I don't want better eyesight, Dave. I want vision.' Then he sat down on the couch and gazed at the TV, which was off. Something on the floor caught my eye: a glint of metal. I stepped towards it. Kieran didn't react. By the wall, in shadow, a few coiled lengths of steel wire. They seemed to flicker, like embers in burnt coal. I looked beyond them to where Kieran's guitar hung on the wall. Its neck was twisted, the face smashed open. 'Did someone break in?' I asked. Stupidly.

Another time, Theresa phoned me to ask if I knew where Kieran was. He wasn't at home or at the garage. She was worried. 'He's been really strange lately. Like he's seen a ghost. Or *not* seen a ghost when he was expecting one.' He came back late the same night. Later, I found out where he'd been. He took me there.

From Olton to Acocks Green is a very brief train journey; but there aren't many trains these days. The Acocks Green station is on a long road lined with old trees. It was November. Rain had printed the outlines of leaves on the pavement. Branches waved their tatters of skin in the fragile light. Torn pages from a girlie magazine were scattered outside the wire fence of a primary school. A stray dog, or possibly a fox, emerged from behind the railway bridge and ran down a side-road. Kieran walked in silence, glancing around as if trying to photograph the view in his head. I'd seen him like this before. In a group, it didn't stand out so much. Suddenly he turned and said to me, 'You're the only person who could understand what I'm about to show you.'

On the edge of Yardley, we came to a bridge over a canal. Kieran stopped and looked down through the trees to the black water. Dead leaves, bottles and cans floated on the surface. There was a steep slope down to the canal towpath on either side. From the trees lining the roadway to the cutting was not so much a slope as a drop. Just beyond the cutting, a derelict house stood in a narrow strip of wasteland. Years of exposure had stripped all the paint from the woodwork. The windows were boarded over. The door was open on a nest of darkness. There was no roof, only a few rotting beams framing the skyline. Kieran walked on. The next building was the local Methodist church, where a footpath led through to the cemetery. We stopped there, in a roughly circular clearing marked by several fir trees, with headstones and monuments all around. I noticed inscriptions dated as far back as the 1890s, and some stones that might have been older but were eroded to blankness.

Kieran wrapped his arms over his chest and stared at a white angel on a marble block. Its wings were beginning to flake away. He glanced suddenly through the forest of headstones, as if looking for someone who wasn't there. Then he turned to me. 'I've been coming here since I was a kid,' he said. 'Ten, fifteen years. Nothing's changed. That house has been empty, just the same. The canal, the derelict house, the graveyard. Don't you get it? First you're born . . .' His eyes glinted. I touched his arm. He smiled emptily at me. 'Do you know what it's like being in a house with two people who don't talk to each other? Who use you as an emissary, so they can go on moving apart? Until you're stretched between them, like a road that goes on forever? Why doesn't that fucking house fall down? Nothing ever changes.' He walked away, rubbing his eyes viciously with the sleeve of his coat. I followed him. I couldn't think of anything to say. We passed the empty house to the line of bare trees above the cutting. Kieran stopped. Then, without looking back, he pushed his way through the trees and kept going.

He didn't reach the water. Part way down, he bounced off a hidden bit of rock and flew sideways into a tree stump. He lay still, curled on his side like a baby. From the road he seemed impossibly small. His mouth darkened with blood. I screamed helplessly. There didn't seem to be any safe way down. The road was empty. I ran to the nearest house that had a light on, knocked and asked to use their phone. Within a few minutes three paramedics had got him down onto the towpath. It took much longer to get him back on the street. Night fell as we drove to the hospital. It was very quiet in the small ambulance. Kieran was unconscious. I went to phone Steve, asked him to contact Kieran's parents or Theresa. When I came back, he was dead.

The next few days were a confused blur. I felt hopelessly tired and slow-witted. Quite a few of Kieran's friends were at the funeral. Nobody felt like organising a wake. There's something wrong about funerals. Watching a coffin go into a hole in the ground, like a dentist filling a cavity. And Kieran's parents trying to be polite to each other. That was the worst aspect of the whole business. I kept imagining some noisy, drunken funeral going on just out of earshot. Kieran's real friends welcoming him into their underworld. A few days later, the images started.

Always in poor light, like silhouettes folded into depth. And only when I was on my own. On street corners, in alleys, coming down staircases. A boy smashing a train window with his head, leaning out and laughing. Two silent women in a car, going over the edge of a ravine. A man with a flute, walking blindly around the same backstreets. What I *actually* saw, with my eyes, I couldn't tell you. They were only outlines, twisted like scraps of burnt celluloid. Black tinged with red. Cheekbones but no eyes. Gone before I could focus or reach out.

There were others that seemed more real. One night, I was passing by a city-centre nightclub on my way to the bus. The street was empty. I saw a boy stagger through the doorway, take a few steps and collapse onto the pavement in a pool of light. His pale hands twitched violently. His mouth opened. The darkness of it spread across his face until there was nothing there. A few days later, I went back to the Acocks Green cemetery. The derelict house was unchanged, its door still half open. I pushed the rain-soaked wood, felt it shift. Inside, a man was crouched on the floor, pointing a shotgun into his own mouth. A broken syringe lay by his feet. The room had been in darkness before I opened the door.

There was more. A lot more. But I tried not to remember. It would have been easy for me to cross-reference these ghosts. At Theresa's suggestion, most of Kieran's videos and tapes had been passed on to me. I'd hidden them away in the attic of the house where I was lodging. The one time I'd gone up there, I'd seen a young man with staring eyes slowly taking a rope down from a clothes rack. There was no-one I could talk to. When the grief subsided, the images would surely go away. But it wasn't so easy. I began to lose my nerve: hiding in the flat at weekends, panicking whenever a car passed me in the street or a dog barked.

Early in the New Year, I decided it had to end. The attic was unoccupied when I took down all of Kieran's stuff. Not all — his family had kept the TV series and some of the commercial films — but I had the stuff that mattered. The offbeat stuff, the bootlegs. I packed it all into suitcases, and borrowed my dad's car to take them across town to the Sandwell Valley. I drove carefully, hoping the police wouldn't stop me for any reason. Kieran's collection was enough to get me jailed for possession alone.

It was getting dark as I stopped the car on the gravel track, just before the ground became too uneven for driving. Behind me was something that looked like a wartime shelter. In front, the trees thickened into a forest. Youngsters came here to fuck or take drugs. There was nobody in sight, though I could hear a dog barking some distance away. I decided to go into the trees, for cover. The ground was damp; the smell of decaying leaves was like unwashed human flesh. I dropped two suitcases in a small clearing, emptied them and went back for the rest.

When I returned to the clearing, he was there. Crouching by the pile of videos, hands outstretched. Blue denim jeans, short hair just a shade darker than blond. Intense eyes that fixed me through the still air. *I love you, and you don't pay me.* I spilt the remaining boxes onto the pile. He didn't move; he just flickered like a trapped frame on a video. 'Fuck off,' I said. 'Where were you when he needed you? It's too late.' Now it was over, these fragments of myth still hung around, like stale food at the back of the fridge. I poured a can of lighter fluid over the boxes and lit a match. His face dissolved into the column of smoke.

This wasn't an act of censorship, I told myself. It wasn't the films themselves I was destroying, only Kieran's copies of them. Bootleg tapes. And bootleg ghosts. The heat exploded the plastic boxes, spreading ribbons of film like dried blood. Huge complex ashes drifted in the heat, breaking where they touched the branches of trees. The smell of burning plastic made me feel giddy. I thought my mind was about to dry out and tear in half. Soon, there was only a blackened crust welded to the scorched ground. The leaf-mould was too damp to catch fire. I wiped my hands on a tree trunk and went back to the car. I must have inhaled some fumes, because the chill took hours to leave me.

Kieran's not a legend. He doesn't live on in my dreams. But I miss him. Sometimes, these days, I see him in silhouette, staring at the video screen from somewhere behind the wall. And it seems like the dead and the living are on opposite sides of a great pane of glass, trying to look through but only able to see their own reflections. Early this year, the house by the Methodist graveyard was demolished. The space had been boarded over. But anyone who wanted to could still jump through the trees into the cutting, into the cut.

CONRAD WILLIAMS

FAILURE

Patrick stepped from the bus into a Cologne morning filled with pigeons and rain. The Rhein moped away to his left, flat and grey, listless as he himself had felt this past month or so. Sigi had grown impatient with his lethargy and bombarded him with insults when she returned from the museum to find him staring out at the lowering sky or lounging in the bath, his skin pruning like that of an old man. 'I can't carry the both of us,' she'd say, fretting waspishly at a cigarette. 'You must find work. Your studies don't eat up that much time that you couldn't wait on tables a few hours each week. You must find work.'

Come midnight, when they were shivering beneath blankets in her bed, she would parry his advances and sometimes weep into her pillow. Patrick's argument that his research would suffer should he have to find employment no longer made an impact on Sigi. 'What if we were to split up? What then? You would have no choice.'

She was right, of course. Patrick had proved something of a parasite these past few months as what had begun as a very casual relationship turned into something more intimate without any discussion or analysis forthcoming from either party. An irony existed in that he had had a job before he met Sigi; basic administrative duties in an accountancy firm just off Konrad Adenauer Ufer. Dull, but it paid for the essentials. And then Sigi, followed by infatuation, love and a complete loss of responsibility. Instead of turning up to work he would spend hours grazing the dips and swells of her body. They would sneak off to walk the banks of the river for hours on end, feed each other apfel strudel driving a borrowed car on the autobahn with the windows down and Nirvana's *About A Girl* slinking from the speakers. And then Sigi finished college and landed a job at the Arts and Crafts

Museum just as Herr Schellenberg reached the end of his tether and told Patrick his absenteeism was unacceptable and it would be for the best if he found a job elsewhere.

But it was so much easier to vegetate in Sigi's flat.

Until now of course. 'There are no opportunities, Sigi,' he appealed, a few nights ago. 'For every job there are three people available.' And her riposte: 'You *make* your opportunities!' It was a tiff that had escalated at frightening speed, culminating in Sigi's threat to either kill him or herself. Though he guessed the warning to be hollow, the sheer fury and frustration in her voice had finally shocked him into accepting that measures needed to be taken. He had called Josef as soon as he had a moment alone.

Last night they had made love for the first time in weeks. It had been a cold, textbook affair. Head resting on his chest she'd said: 'Patrick, I'm at my wits' end. There is talk at the museum of laying off some of the staff. The recession is picking people off one by one. If I lose my job, we lose this.' Her gesture took in what their life meant to them at the moment, all of it within arm's reach: a few books, a suitcase of clothes, a photograph album. The flat itself. He made her breakfast and kissed her goodbye, watching the way she moved down the steps to the street, pony tail bobbing.

He followed Josef's directions, angling down a cobbled road beneath an archway off Pfälzerstrasse where blouses and towels hung out to dry whipped about like strange birds trapped in netting. He seated himself outside the café beneath a birch tree filled with copper chimes and let their music relax him, knowing that Josef would doubtless be ten or fifteen minutes late for their meeting.

Patrick had met Sigi at a party thrown by an ex-girlfriend who lived in Koblenz. Patrick guessed he'd been invited just so Heidi could rub his nose in the success she was enjoying these days: she was like that. He went along just for the sour victory of proving this prediction and he was not disappointed; Heidi was swift to show him her new boyfriend (a tanned, flat-stomached astro-physics graduate called Wolf); her new flat; her car; on and on and on. He bumped into Sigi in front of the open fire where surreptitiously they tossed Heidi's business card to the flames at the same time and howled over the coincidence of such an act.

'Oh but wait,' she'd said, stifling her laughter, 'it wouldn't surprise me if this fire was being fuelled with Heidi's precious business cards.

Isn't she just insufferable?'

She didn't apologise when Patrick told her she was a former girl-friend, a matter that impressed him. Within the hour they'd traded telephone numbers and lingered over a goodbye that had left Patrick dry-mouthed and palpitating, remarkable for the fact that their prox-imity had only encompassed a handshake and eye contact. It pained him to think of her, six months on, her eyes less vibrant, her posture collapsing in on itself. He wondered if she had any ambition left; cer-tainly the fiery creature he'd once seen her to be had grown sullen and maudlin. It wasn't all his fault, surely?

'We'll take a drink, I suggest. To celebrate our meeting again. It's been a while, no?' Josef towered above him — he was almost a foot taller — and clapped a huge hand on his shoulder.

Inside the café they ordered bottles of Pils and spent a while split-ting open pistachio nuts, watching the video screens.

'Thank you for coming Josef. I know how busy you are.'

'Remember summer? Three years ago? The last time we spoke.' Josef chewed slowly, fingernails worrying at the hasp of his Filofax. His suit rippled and shone so readily it might have been made from water.

'Of course I do. You know I do.'

'It was not an enjoyable time. For you, that is. Especially for you.'

Patrick shook his head. 'I know. But I'd be interested in something like that again. It would be worth the fear.'

'Things are that bad?'

'Worse. I think Sigi will leave me if I don't find some money soon. I've been such a shit to her.'

Patrick felt the weight of Josef's gaze, and the thickness of the silence that spread between them. Then Josef leant close enough for Patrick to smell the sweetness of his breath, his lavish perfume.

'I have excellent contacts these days. In this city there works a man who can make you rich, if you have the stomach for what he would do with you.'

'This is how you make your money?'

'Christ no! I'm not desperate. I . . . *supply* him with his raw mate-rials. He pays me well, but then, so do many of my business associ-ates.'

'I don't like that. *Raw materials*? This is how you see me?' Patrick took a long swig of his beer. Around them, the bar drew in towards them, as though air were being sucked out of the building, pulling everyone closer together. Patrick could smell aftershaves clashing; a hot volley of cooked sausages; even the tacky, sugary teats depending from the liquor optics. A barmaid wearing luridly coloured hair extensions pulled the hem of her tee-shirt down till the cotton creaked. Patrick watched a single gem of sweat stroke a line from the back of her ear to a gold choker where it sizzled brightly.

Josef, for the first time, was betraying his impatience with a long suck on his teeth and a crinkling in the soft folds at the corner of his eyes. 'Why are you here? In Köln? Do you remember your reasons for coming here?'

'Of course I do,' said Patrick flatly. 'To broaden the scope of my research.' The words aired as dispassionately as those of a child regurgitating rote-learned multiplication.

'This is untrue. You came here to make money. You came here for the butchers, you said. Medical experiments were limited in Britain; their wages weren't enough to pay for the drugs you needed in order to put your belly right after filling them with chemicals week after week. *You said.*' Josef stressed the last words with a poke of his finger into the limp shield of Patrick's shoulder blade.

'So what if my feelings are different now?' Patrick argued, all the while thinking: *He's right, the bastard's right.* There'd been that time when the 8th and 15th of each month meant a trek to and from Leeds so that he could swallow half a pint of an untested lemon and lime flavoured drink called FYBOGEL which was being hailed for its potential cholesterol reducing properties. Was it worth £1000, travel included? Hardly. There'd been the 3Cs too; Common Cold Centres he haunted during the late 80s till research funds became so piddling that they closed down. It had felt like he was being made redundant — only without the severance pay. He'd talked to a few friends about the dismal situation, one of which had suggested getting in touch with Josef. Josef with his Technicolor labcoat promises of injections and induced muscle spasm and sleep trials and mild Electro Convulsive Therapy. All designed to line his ruptured pockets with marks and pfennigs. He'd come across the water, helpless as a Bisto kid, floating on the anaesthesia which poured from Josef's lips. In the foetus crease of sleep he'd danced with molecules that whispered their drowsy names into the very gristle between his ears: thiopentane, helothane, enflurane. He spent soporific breakfasts popping "jellies", his body gradually becoming conversant with the torpid heat of temazepam and omnopon. In the University library where he was to land his doomed job, amputated chunks of sunlight scattering the dust and people, scalpels grinned at him from the pages of the *British Journal of Surgery*.

'Who is it you know? What can he offer me?'

Josef's presence seemed to diminish, a salesman who has hooked into a big fish and can finally relax. As he softened, he slid into the chair next to Patrick and blinked for what must have been the first time. Now he was at eye level with Patrick, his clout retreating, Patrick could only wonder at the chameleon nature of his character, the way he had piled on so much unspoken pressure, his bullyboy charm.

'You can make £12,000.'

Patrick scoffed and turned to look into his friend's concave face, at the wide spaced eyes that seem almost to be turned in towards each other. A smile played in there, like a candle in a bowl, tinting the edges of his face with light. *Fuck*, Patrick thought, *he really means it*.

'Yeah,' he humoured, 'and what would I have to do for twelve grand?'

Josef's smile faded. He wore the countenance of one searching a set of features for steel, for inner grit.

'Die a little,' he said.

Sigi was asleep under the yucca, headphones on. The only light in the room came from the dancing equaliser on their stereo and the violet neon from the snooker hall across the street. He left it that way.

She came to bed hours later and he watched her undress from the half mask of their blanket. Sigi rubbed her neck where the cold had stiffened it and applied a little night cream to her cheekbones and fore-head. She brushed her hair. She lahhed a fragment from whatever song was looping in her mind; something that sounded like *I got so high, I scratched till I bled* before killing the light and smothering his chest with her heartbeat. Her mouth and cunt made gummy demands on his skin but it was too much like being dabbed with open wounds. He pushed her away and felt her dampness on his thigh tighten and dry. When her hand scooted under his leg to gently mash his balls, peel the skin back from a reluctant hard-on, he tried to relax. Her thumb capped his tip, smeared a tear of fluid over his glans and: 'Fuck me, Pat. Come on.'

The flesh across his chest tightened so swiftly he almost heard his skin tearing. In there, bloated within its cell of ribs, he convulsed and spat; a leathery knot tiring all the while. His fear travelled quick as his blood; he dwindled in her fingers.

'What's wrong?' her voice was thick with sex. She sat up. He saw the spike of a nipple against the window; a curtain of hair sweep the wedge of her brow; cilia eyelashes flutter in uncertainty. He imagined the purple net of veins stutter on his retina. Ear-drums concussing with the pressure of his blood as if it wanted to be away from the body which contained it.

Again, her question, voice see-sawing on a fulcrum of confusion, not yet knowing whether to lend weight to the cynical end or its charitable opposite.

'I'm tired.'

'What have you got to be tired for?' The sudden injection of outrage, for the first time, was unable to find its way through to him. He lay there, numbed as she ranted, to her credit finding new ways to express old, old things. But it didn't matter how much she dressed the words up; they could make no impact on him any more. He wondered if that was because their content was stale or the person delivering them was no longer so vital to him. And, consequently, was that feeling merely forced by his reluctance to tell Sigi where he had been, what might be in store for him? Was he trying to hate her in order to spare her?

He listened to the music of her body when finally she slept. All of it seemed circular, reproductive: the wet mechanics of her breathing; the dull knell of her heart; occasional glottal murmurs. It all sounded too insular and stale. He knew that trawling his memories for something soothing was likely only to fret him more but he couldn't prevent a regression; insomnia seemed to be its perfect bedfellow.

Meat. Sunday afternoons hanging round the kitchen with the cats waiting for Mum to finish roasting the hunk of dead stuff in the oven. Patrick liked lamb best; the fat blistering and loose on the rich, dark meat. He was never able to finish his serving, mainly because Mum always dished out too many slabs of the stuff but also because he didn't want Gatsby and Mac to go without a few scraps from his plate. And one time, everyone was rushing around for some reason or other: Dad had a meeting to attend; his sister Mo was helping a friend with her display at an art gallery. And Mum was gearing up to go to a yoga session — she wasn't eating till later. Only Patrick was free of obligations: he tooled around with Gatsby, a ping-pong ball and Dad's shoe while Mum clattered her timpani orchestra on the old Belling cooker.

Tucking in while Mum stuffed a duffel bag with leggings and leotard. The first cut of Patrick's knife brought a dribble of blood from the spongy pink cross section of meat; it spread in a watery pool to infect his mashed potato. Dad and Mo were mopping up spillages, scraping and slurping: pulpy noises at the centre of his world. He imagined blood forming a thin wash on their gums, swilling hotly in bellies packed like haggis. Then a whitening as the kitchen faded and his chair didn't feel as though it could support him properly.

Dad leaning over him: vermilion lips peeled back. Clotted, meaty breath.

Patrick had steered clear of red meat ever since.

Hours later he slid from the sheets feeling misshapen, as though, during the night, he'd been eclipsed and gently crushed by a giant fist. He scrimped breakfast from a curl of bread in the larder, a rind of tired cheese. Coffee was in abundance but he could hardly brew up without rousing Sigi. He didn't want her questioning him; he didn't want to let on as to the nature of his insomnia.

Josef's BMW was a lozenge of black assuming form out of the soupy half-light beneath the railway bridge. Inside (against the fetor of leather upholstery), was a fleeting whiff of freesias, money — a stale waft of fanned banknotes — and doublemint. Patrick listened to the whispering engine, the chuckle of an unseen fountain. Water always made Patrick feel cold. His upper arms he pushed against the shivering shanks of his chest, hoping Josef wouldn't notice and misinterpret the gesture as fear but his friend was busy clipping a large cigar.

'Well?' Patrick quailed at the pleading in his voice. He so wanted to prove his mettle, not only to Josef — and Sigi — but to himself. Since his voice broke he'd been cursed with a reedy delivery, lacking any character building inflection, any gravel or, conversely, any silkiness, like the brogues he'd known when relatives visited from Ireland years ago. People like Josef, though no bigger in stature, could pinch out Patrick's light with an articulation only dreamt by the other.

Josef wouldn't allow himself to be hurried. He bolted the cigar between his teeth and torched it with a match which seemed to have extended from his fingers. 'You — *paff* — told — *piff* — her — *poff poff*?'

'Of course I did.'

'The boy lies. He lies well, but not well enough.' For the first time Josef eyeballed him. The buffer of smoke made his face appear unstable; his mouth roiled around the cigar and Patrick found it easier to follow the orange pastille of its coal than the eyes behind it.

'Christ Josef, if I told her, do you think I'd be here? I'd be out on my arse. Better I just do it and come back with the cash. Then I'll tell her.'

'Because then, if she kicked you out, you'd have your own money to take care of you, instead of hers.' He grinned: the cigar grew erect, gleaming on the narrow bridge of Josef's brow.

'Look, it was you. You who encouraged me to go for this. Why do you want to piss me off about it?'

'Because I can. So easy.' He shifted the gear out of Park and into Drive; let the car mosey over the cobbled alley till, hitting the main street, he dipped his foot and Patrick was pressed back into the bucket seat. If he looked out of the passenger window on his right, the houses and hedges — all that was solid and detailed — grew molten.

Sloe-eyed Sigi passing him a dry Martini. 'See?' she said. 'See how you have to make sure the glass is cold? Now rinse it with vermouth and throw the excess away; you just need to coat the glass. Pour your gin from an ice cold shaker. Olive.'

The way she pronounced olive — as Oh-live — made him laugh. Her lips were wet with traces of cocktail; teeth too as she smiled, as though the reaches of her mouth were flush with a layer of cellophane. This image clogged in his mind as they took a series of lefts and rights through an area of the town he was unfamiliar with (gabled roofs and streetlamps like unfinished gallows; block buildings with pastel slivers in frameless windows). A woman in white with a gash of red silk at her throat rode by on a piebald horse. Trees encroached, first dotted between, then concealing and finally replacing the houses on the city's limits. Patrick suddenly realised he was wearing the necklace Sigi had bought him during the summer — the last gift she had proffered before their current impasse. It was a simple claw of metal gripping a blueish enamel swirl which he wore on a leather cord. He liked its weight against his sternum; during lovemaking, it would answer the knock of his heart against his ribs with a dull call of its own. Sometimes, as she peaked, Sigi would draw it into her mouth and suck on it till her bucking waned.

'This is how it shall be.' Josef spat the butt of his cigar out of the window and didn't speak again till the electrics had sealed it once more. 'We go in. I talk to Brandywine and Losh. You do your stuff. We get paid. We go out.'

'*We*? *We* get paid?'

'Yeah, *we*. I'm acting as your agent on this, remember.'

'So what's your cut?'

'Not as painful as your cut, I can assure you.'

'Bastard.' Patrick felt like ordering him to stop so he could get out and walk home. 'Maybe I should become an agent.'

'You don't have the contacts or the cuntishness. And you speak German with all the composure of a tightrope walker with one leg suffering from Parkinson's who is in the midst of morphine withdrawal.'

'What's your cut?' Patrick didn't really want to know any more, but he'd just caught sight of a building through the net of branches up ahead and felt the first slow convulsion of fear in his loins. Hearing his voice — and Josef's smug rejoinders — was helping to nail his panic down.

'Six k.' And then, as if parrying any protest of Patrick's before it was aired: 'Do you know how hard it is, liaising? How perilous? There are butchers in this country, Patrick. I've worked laboriously to get you this and you can be sure you'll be treated well. Proper anaesthetists, sterile conditions that are second to none, excellent post-op and Intensive Care facilities.' He risked a cheeky glance, perhaps gauging the humour of his friend before mugging: 'If you snuffed it here, the quality of your death would be orgasmic.'

Patrick sneered; his hands were greasing up. He couldn't summon the spit he needed to coat his words with venom. 'Not funny,' he wheezed, but Josef was corpsing, ratcheting the car into a space it seemed was designed for a motor half the size.

'Let's be having you, my lad,' he soothed, releasing the child lock so that Patrick could get out.

The air. The air was brittle and rarefied, as though cleansed in a filter made of pure ice. When his foot crunched satisfyingly into the gravel of the car park, he thought his metatarsals had powdered from fear-weakness.

'I can't do this,' he whispered as Josef steered him into the revolving door.

'But you will, all the same.'

They were met by a woman in a starchy, cream suit. She wore her hair in a Thatchered black hive; a silver brooch in the shape of a heart clung to her left nipple area.

'Imogen,' she said, a rising note on the last syllable so it seemed she were addressing Patrick thus. He was about to deny the name before realising what she meant, not that he could have summoned the clout required to send adequate breath past his vocal cords.

An odd gesture busied her hand: it dived down, index finger pointing to the floor, thumb stuck out at 45°. The rest of her digits tried to press themselves against her wrist. Patrick saw, very clearly, a tendon and a vein rise against the skin, like flaccid rubber hosing suddenly made stiff with water. Her other hand fussed at the back of his, making his knuckles hot. 'If you'll just wait here,' she said, 'I'll get Dr Losh to come and see to you.'

There were no paintings or flowers; nothing resting on the desk marked *Reception* bar an open ledger, pages blank. There wasn't even a receptionist. Or any of the bustle Patrick might have associated with a hospital.

'Who said this was a hospital?' countered Josef when Patrick explained his unease.

'What is it then?'

Josef didn't answer. Instead, he led the way forward, down a corridor that was at least as bland and thinly antiseptic as he would expect. At the far end, a trolley came into view, pushed by a tall black man who wore a mask and glasses which filled with white light when he turned his head to look towards them. Patrick saw something small and dark fall from under the crumpled blankets. They didn't appear to be getting any closer to him, despite Josef's devouring stride. The trolley, and its guardian, disappeared into the white perfection of the opposite wall; Patrick could hear a dodgy caster protesting in diminuendo.

'Know the tools of your torture,' said Josef, but his mouth was shut. Somehow, without his knowing, Patrick's hand had been subsumed by his friend's. At last, they reached the end of the corridor and Patrick could see the splash of red that had fallen from beneath the blanket. This, at the same time as a man dipped through a doorway, hand extended, beard shifting to display a greenish scythe of teeth. Patrick leaned over, not to accept his salutation, but to catch the gloops of flesh which were sagging from his cheeks before they hit the floor. He couldn't stop the left side of his face from melting.

Patrick splayed both hands — a kind of *Whoa, let's just calm everything down and be rational* gesture. 'This is an unorthodox procedure,' he meant to say, but his lips kept stumbling on the fourth word. His knuckles itched where she had been fussing at them.

'I'm Reuben Losh,' the beard said, slipping a business card into Patrick's shirt pocket. 'What's that? Unearth a what? An ox?' Josef and the doctor laughed; Patrick watched their faces mingle, mouths folding together like something monstrous and Picasso-like, tilting on different planes.

He found that he could move much more freely now that Josef had let go of his hand, but it was probably because he was lying on a trolley, fading fast, losing all sense of what was ceiling and what was floor.

Brilliant light. So bright it was almost liquid; so liquid he could see the splinters of colour refracting, some of which he could give no name to because of their immediacy and freshness.

'Patrick . . .' Losh swam into view, his head causing an eclipse of the operating spotlights. His beard was like the copper wire graveyard of an electrician's dustbin. 'I want you to meet Dr Olivia Brandywine. She'll be monitoring you while I still your beating heart, ha ha.'

Patrick didn't see Brandywine, only felt a hand cup his shoulder, and catch a peripheral glimpse of flesh that seemed bleached and smooth to the point of plasticity. 'We'll need to send you deeper, Patrick,' she soothed, with a smoke-scarred voice that was not unpleasant. 'I'll be administering a general anaesthetic and then Dr Losh will puncture your femoral artery. We need to feed a catheter along the vessel to the sinoatrial node in your heart. Once we've found that, we'll send some radio waves to cause an arrest. I want to record your body's reaction —'

Another sting in the dip of his arm. Shouldn't I be given a medical first? He felt heat sweeping up towards his neck.

'– and then we'll have you up and out of here before you know it.'

00.01

black upon me like that zoo time when a murder of crows falls out of the trees a strange sudden autumn full of screaming and mummy scratched from lip to ear and my heart full in my throat dreadfully sorry dreadfully sorry madam shall i call an ambulance here sonny have an ice cream courtesy of the management

00.02

maggie's lips cold and blueish when she kisses me christmas day messing with mistletoe what will you do if i pin some to my fly maggie hey maggie and laughing and the smell of her breath oaten and chocolatey and wild and a lipstick heart on my wrist we run through forest brambles and the welts are still healing on my legs when she tells me it's all over

00.03

sigi (oh sigi i love you) tossing me off for the first time in the back of her beetle as night spreads itself across the industrial estate and i come into the wad of tissues she's stashed up her cardigan sleeve and she's amazed at my quantity and she kisses the tip even as it twitches and weeps like something rent open and left for dead

00.04

I'm feeling cold. And halted, funnily enough. A feeling of stasis —
could be my pumpless blood, settling thanks to a gravity it's never
known before. I'm able to think though there's a godawful storm at the
edge of my awareness, like a piece of paper lit at the edges, eating its
way towards the centre, but no pain, only a tickling sensation deep
inside. No ships sailing towards me for that rubicon moment. No dark
tunnels or horizons of white light. No out of body

00.05

*experiences like the time i burned my hand on the electric ring on
mum's old stove watching the clean red spiral blacken must be cool now
but such a depth of pain that i can't even bring it to mind but mum being
mum always mum pressing her mouth against the hurt and blowing gently as i cry my heart out*

00.06

*in the bowl of my home town the rarity of snow whitens the grimy
avenues and dad readies to take my sister mo and i on a walk to the land
of far beyond where's that i ask him far beyond he replies pulling on my
wellies and we go out i'm humming a song from the beatles film on tv let
it be and the warmth in my fingers and toes retreats and we all make
breath sculptures in the chill down by the canal where they're landscaping
and knocking down old pill boxes and strange roads filled with glass cob-
bles the fallen tree is ash coloured with mould and snow and dad's daft say-
ings the camels are coming hurrah hurrah and even my sister's tiny tears
looks frozen to death in the dusted patch of rhododendrons i spy a red
swatch of cloth brighter than blood we've arrived dad says*

00.07

*morgan and me eating blood oranges on the train to Manchester we've
got seven quid between us all of it going on the new police album and at
birchwood station she gets on board and sits opposite her eyes like smoke
made solid smiling at us at the sticky glaze on mouths agog and before we
reach piccadilly morgan's getting all cheeky with her saying give us a sticky
snog love and shoving his fist up his top thrashing it around to mime a
heart out of control when she blows us a kiss*

00.08

There's a definite kind of brittle coldness suffusing my limbs now
but it's not unpleasant. Not like I can feel Death's fingers giving me a
massage. The voices are calming and sufficiently distant to negate my

understanding their content. I have the image of Dr Brandywine in my head with her tapered fingernails deep inside me, coaxing my heart awake. Sigi. It's a feeling Sigi gives me all the time. I have that achy feeling of missing her, even when she's near. We've been together a long time now, yet still I get excited when I know I'll be meeting her later in the day. I can't remember how tender her mouth feels against my own

00.09

room is a cell as i grow and more stuff accrues softening the corners erasing the concrete structure of the four walls and helping me lose my sense of place and belonging which i think is precipitating this huge unfocused dream i have though less a dream and more a wall of irresolute significance which includes what might be a stairwell for want of something banal to defuse its threat something approaches from the dark gulf larger than my mind's confines will allow more momentous than the most extravagant unfurlings of imagination like viewing a fragment of film at a magnification of x10000 all detail lost but the power of violence and substance and movement inflating in my head it comes back regularly it comes even now

00.10

is it death?

00.11

sigi rubbing the oiled wishbone curve of her cleavage into my face steering her nipples into and out of my mouth cupping her breasts together with her remarkable hands pressing their delicate independent weight upon me till it's hard to breathe and the thud in my head does it belong to me or to her

00.12

o me o my o god

Coming out of it hurt even more. Through the pain, he thought of birth and was almost able to conjure the moment his lungs were shocked into use for the first time. How many of us are born again? he thought, as the trauma of re-animation retreated, having left its fire smouldering in every shred and dribble of his body. His eyes felt poached and tender; the light seemed too much like living matter, crowding his immediate space with swimming motes — he didn't know whether the headache was a side effect or a result of the insufferable thereness of day.

Only when the colour began to leech back into his vision did he realise he had been without it. Shapes acquired depth and mass. The chair. The table. Josef. He was looking down on Patrick with an expression of dismayed fascination.

'What is it?' Patrick asked, through a mouth that felt numb and tight. 'Have I been amputated by mistake?'

'No, you look fine. Just a little pale, that's all.' Josef recovered his joviality, plonking himself at the foot of the bed. He fished a cheque out of his waistcoat pocket. 'This'll keep you in bratwurst for a week or three,' he said, planting the piece of paper on Patrick's bare chest. 'The doctors wanted me to tell you all went swimmingly. They say you can come back in six months for another stint. If you're up to it.'

'I don't think so.'

'Ah, come on. You're strong as a piece of my great aunt's knicker elastic.'

Patrick kicked Josef off the bed. 'You do it, if you're so keen. Please leave me alone now.'

Josef made a performance of pulling on his driving gloves. 'Can't offer you a lift back into town I'm afraid. Meeting a client in Dortmund this afternoon.'

'I can go home?'

'Of course. God, anybody would think you'd undergone major heart surgery.'

After Josef had gone, Patrick lay still for a while, listening for the knock in his chest. It was there, but it sounded hollow and sluggish. He dressed slowly and wandered the corridors till he found the reception where they'd entered, God, just two hours ago. There was nobody to see him off.

Outside, the light was waxy and uncertain, smeared about wads of cumulus like some brilliant resin. He handed over most of his change on the bus back into town, and spent the journey trying not to examine the stagnation within him. It was as if his soul had been taken out and washed of all its interesting impurities and flecks of self. He didn't feel alive, he just felt as though he was living.

He got off in Herzogstrasse and watched the sky spin around the twin towers of the cathedral while he grew accustomed to the flail of traffic and pedestrians. Walking back to the Kunstgewerbe museum, he checked the faces of those streaming around him. All were pinkish and vital; varnished eyes and teeth like tablets of ice. He felt stunted and tired in comparison; catching his reflection in a darkened window he was appalled to see how jaundiced he looked. The dough of his face appeared to lack elasticity. Turned off and switched on he'd been —

like a car or a transistor radio. Drinking coffee in a backstreet bar, Patrick's hunch that he'd been soiled, or abused, took on an ever increasing concretion. Should he have been counselled before leaving? He fed coins into the telephone on the counter and dialled the number of the institute on the back of Dr Losh's card. Nobody answered.

In the museum he watched Sigi arranging a pastel display through the gallery's glass doors. The sunlight had sliced her in half. Even from here, fifty feet away, he could see it playing on the wet curve of her mouth, the loose filaments of hair. In he went. Her smell was upon him; the same sweet odour that rose from the bed when he turned back the blanket in the morning.

'Sigi?'

She twitched her head his way but said nothing, continuing with her task, perhaps a little more starchily now.

'Sigi, I've made a little money today. A lot, really. I want you to have some.' He reached for her but she ducked away before striding backwards, hands planted in her back pockets.

'Is that picture straight?' she asked, so softly it might have been to herself. She hadn't looked at him yet.

'Sigi.'

Now she fastened him with the angry green of her eyes. If she saw anything lacking in his countenance she didn't let on. 'We're through, Patrick. Can't you see that, honey?'

'But I've made some money.'

'Congratulations. Go and spend it. And then wonder where the next lot is going to come from.'

'If it hadn't been for you, I'd still be earning at the accountancy firm,' he regretted the jibe, and the way he'd said it as soon as his mouth was shut.

'Get a life, you sad bastard.'

'But I love you,' he finished lamely.

'I'm tired,' she said. She seemed almost not to notice him, to be looking through him, as though he were made of glass or water. 'I don't want you to be there when I get back tonight. I'm sorry.' She tried a smile; her lips merely thinned. 'I'm sorry.'

Patrick scuffed about the flat for a while, desultorily bagging his things (a piffling amount) and delving into his past for happy moments to feed the sense of loss that must come to him soon. He considered a number of follies: he'd open a vein in her bath tub, burn the cheque in front of her, leave the cheque on her pillow. In the end, he did nothing, simply sat in her rocking chair by the window and watched the boats fart and froth in the Rhein till darkness crept upon the city, flooding it with streetlamps. His body still felt strangely bland and ropy; the squish of meat in his chest was making him ill. He lit a candle and tossed his keys on to her desk. As he went to the door, a book caught his eye. It was lying flat on her shelf whereas the others were erect, a volume he'd given to Sigi early on when gifts and cards were exchanged as gladly as kisses and hugs. A novel she enjoyed, as he recalled. Picking it up, he leafed through, bending to smell the paper's age. His riffling was halted by the card, a simple white affair with a pale heart sketched into a corner. Inside, his hesitant hand, in dark ink:

Always.

ALSO FROM TANJEN

THE PARASITE

Neal L. Asher

Jack is the pilot of a cometary miner. On his final mission, the one which will make him rich, he encounters something in the hold of his ship, something which has been held in the ice of a comet for millennia.
Set in the future of military take overs, rising sea levels, and satellite industries, this is a story of high tech subterfuge and violence, which asks; what is it to be human? And what might the human race become?

ISBN 0952718316 — Price £5.99

"top quality SF from one of genre's hotshot new talents"
Dragon's Breath

"anyone who cares about the future of British literary SF should check it out"
SFX

EYELIDIAD

Rhys H. Hughes

Baron Darktree is a highwayman searching for gold he buried when he was younger. It's bad enough he has to put up with insults from his younger self (now a portrait he carries on his back), and that the map tattooed on his eyelid is no longer visible, but when he gets mistaken for Beer'or, the pagan god of golden beer, he begins to wonder how bad things can get.

Oh, much worse . . .

ISBN 0952718324 — Price £5.99

"Richly and hilariously imaginative, teeming with memorable images, and inimitably Welsh"
Ramsey Campbell

"the jaded fantasy reader will find much to enjoy here"
Flickers 'n' Frames

"imaginative slice of surrealist fantasy"
Samhain

RECLUSE

Derek M. Fox

A letter from a mysterious woman is all it takes to turn
Daniel Lees's world upside-down. He suspects his wife of
having an affair. He believes his children are in danger
from something that stalks the moors. He is haunted by a
past that will not leave him alone.
Finally he has to face up to what he really is and battle
against the nightmare that has threatened to destroy
everything he holds dear.

ISBN 1901530000 — Price £5.99

"*Recluse* is the chilling journey into the heart of a nightmare.
Reader beware – Derek M. Fox is set to be a new Master of
Fear."
Mark Chadbourn

"maintaining a cracking pace and an iron grip on the
reader's attention."
BBR Directory

MESMER

Tim Lebbon

When Rick sees his ex-girlfriend at a motorway service station he knows he must be losing his mind. For Penny had been brutally murdered and left to rot in a ditch eight years earlier. In trying to find answers to insane questions Rick finds himself immersed in a world where the dead can live again, a world controlled by the evil powers of the Mesmer.

ISBN 1901530027 — Price £5.99

"Mesmer is absolutely superb. Lebbon's going to be big one day. Start reading him now."
Simon Clark

SCATTERED REMAINS

Paul Pinn

A collection of short stories to celebrate the 750th anniversary of the Bethlem Mental Hospital, the origin of the word bedlam. Each story is an examination of mental illness within the dark underbelly of human nature. Make sure you read this with the lights on.

ISBN 1901530051 — Price £6.99

"Soul-searing . . . totally bleak, remorseless and nihilistic."
Pam Creais, Dementia 13

"Black, claustrophobic, full of dirt and death . . . I like it."
Dave Logan, Grotesque Magazine

PRISONERS OF LIMBO

David Ratcliffe

When the Carter family move to the new estate they hope it will mean the end of their troubles. Tommy Carter is never *out* of trouble, and Lucy Carter has a weakness for bad men. These hopes are soon dashed when they discover they are the only residents and the estate is half-finished. It soon becomes clear that somehow they have passed through a barrier of normality. In this world the dead are alive, the past is the present, and everything is in monochrome.
The problem is how to escape and return to the *real* world before it's too late.

ISBN 1901530043 — Price £5.99

"A dark, dirty tale — horror noir at its finest."
Night Dreams

All titles are available from good bookshops or direct from Tanjen Ltd, 52 Denman Lane, Huncote, Leicester, LE9 3BS (post and packing free)